WASH**ED**

by

Eugenie Laverne Mitchell

To: Kuudiena

Love! E. Laverne Mitchell

Darkness is dispelled by light so stay in the light.

i

"Special thanks firstly to God for inspiration, vision and amazing grace, who gave me my daughter Donna Marie and the rest of my family who encouraged me and provided the backbone on which I rested, which kept me strong and helped me to keep on pursuing the dream; those of my family and dear friends who provided much needed and invaluable critiques; my colleagues who believed and helped to keep the dream alive; those who helped to breathe life into my baby - Alan and those at Cooper Johnson and Damonza and lastly those who have supported me since the release of "WASHED": Anne-Marie; Elaine; Lorraine; Sat; Sam; Mimi to name but a few. Thank you and may God bless you all".

PROLOGUE

Hi, my name is Cherie Johnson and you will encounter me in the story you are about to read.

Let me welcome you on board for the ride, on a journey which begins in the late 1970s – I am not certain of the exact date because it was before I was born.

Come, please make yourself comfortable - you can sit right here next to me if you like. There is plenty of room on board so you can invite anyone else you want to come along.

Mine is an unusual story, though you may recognise some everyday occurrences in the mix. It can be likened to a tasty dish, perfectly seasoned - let me whet your appetite by giving you a taster of what is in store. Key ingredients include a good measure of wit to make you smile or laugh out loud, whichever takes your fancy; there is some thought provocation to keep you intrigued; then there is just a pinch of sadness – some irony too; but the main ingredient is love – elusive love, untrue love, unrequited love, undeserved love, mutual love, forgiving love, unconditional love - pure love, true love. And I almost forgot – there is just a sprinkling of mystery too.

You will read about my dreams, my aspirations and my achievements (so far) as I share the stage with another star and many other interesting characters that give added flavour to the dish and provide entertainment during the journey, helping to create the highs and lows as the story dips and crescendos on its way to a beautiful finale. Get ready for the adventure and don't forget to fasten your seat belt.

Oh well, I must go now and leave you to sample the dish for yourself - hope it's seasoned to your taste. See you later.

CON

GW01260551

Prologue

CHAPTER 1

The Beginning

The letter from Tyrone arrived on 16 May 1984 and Jean's world was turned upside down. Up until she received that letter, she was under the impression that she would join him in America soon and that they would get married. She loved him so much and dreamed of the day when she would bear his name – Mrs Jean Syrenson – she often repeated as she stared at her smiling reflection in the mirror, lost in daydream land. She had counted herself blessed to have met such a wonderful and considerate gentleman like Tyrone, one who loved her and took care of his responsibilities, she had thought with a smile each month when she received much needed money from him to support their daughter. But upon receiving that letter, in a blind and confused rage, Jean had written back to say she didn't need his money, that she would bring her daughter up by herself. She closed the bank account into which he made the transfers and later ripped up all his letters, including the cheques he began to send without even opening the envelopes. "Hell hath no fury like a woman scorned," and Jean had been truly wronged - cast aside, discarded like a piece of rubbish by a man she had given over four years of her youth to. And she rued the day that she met Tyrone Syrenson, and allowed him into her life, and she hated the memory that she had given a deaf ear to the protestations of her parents that he was not right for her.

An only child from a staunchly Christian background, Jean was brought up in a strict fashion by parents who were members of the Mount Zion Miracle Pentecostal Church. Her mother Esther and father Jesse ensured that moral values and standards were regimentally instilled into their daughter from an early age.And they were more than a little concerned when she started to date Tyrone Syrenson - they believed she was too young, at 16, to be romantically involved. Their disapproval was verbalised strongly, not only were they concerned as to Tyrone's true intentions, but they were also less than impressed by his background. His family visited church only occasionally, and were by no means what could be termed "blood washed" Christians. Tyrone did not fit the profile of a potential good husband for their only daughter. However, their protestations fell on deaf ears, and Jean who was usually of a docile character, began to demonstrate signs of rebellion, so they backed down. But although forced into accepting the courtship, Esther and Jesse watched the couple like hawks and chaperoned them wherever they went.

Most of the brethren that attended Mount Zion supported Jean's choice - they knew Tyrone to be a decent young man, committed to the church and to God. He rose further in their estimation when he got baptized and began to play a significant role in the church as a talented musician and singer. And as time passed Jesse and Esther too were won over by Tyrone. They came to accept that he was the gentleman husband that they had prayed for, for their only daughter, not just because of his apparent commitment to Christ and to the church, but also because he conducted himself in the best possible manner. Charming and charismatic, he always said and did the right things, treating Jean like a royal lady. He took her to the best places and often bought flowers and chocolates for her and occasionally for Esther, who in turn became his most loyal fan. So the relationship was allowed to continue without further objection.

Just over two years after they begun dating Tyrone's family immigrated to America. He remained in London because he was in the middle of his college education. His parents asked their next-door neighbours, Mary and Wilf Hendry, an elderly English couple with the aggregate age of 150 years between them who were more like family than neighbours, to keep an eye on him. The Hendrys had known Tyrone since he was born and had also known his father when he was a boy. They had happily accepted the obligation, and Tyrone was left in their trusted care, as though he were a young child, although he had by then turned 22.

After his family's departure, Tyrone spent much of his time in church and also with Jean and her family. Concerned, the Hendrys visited the church to find out where he was spending so much of his time. And upon meeting Jean's parents and exchanging telephone numbers, they were satisfied that they need not worry. Tyrone called over to see them most days and the Hendrys played the role of surrogate family perfectly, extending to him an ever-open door in the same way that they did to their own two children and their families.

As time passed Jesse and Esther grew to trust Tyrone to be alone with their daughter. They received further affirmation that they were right about him when he left college and got a good job working with computers, with excellent future prospects. Soon they began to allow the couple to go out together unsupervised. Tyrone exhibited the most mature and responsible behaviour and always got Jean home before her 9.30pm curfew, convincing Jesse and Esther that their trust was not misguided. All in all he made such an impression on Jean's parents that they could be forgiven for thinking he was God's perfect gift to their only daughter.

However, Tyrone was not the angel that he made himself out to be and not long after being allowed to take Jean out alone he started to pester her to compromise her virtues. Although she had been denied formal sex education by her strict Christian parents, Jean knew from whisperings amongst her peers that sex was taboo for unmarried people, so she defended her chastity vehemently. But Tyrone finally wore down her resolve. He did so by continuously hinting that if she didn't give it up he would be forced to go elsewhere; that if she truly loved him, she would give herself to him; that he would never leave her anyway and that it was only a matter of time before they got married. He tempted her with the suggestion that no-one ever had to know and finally succeeded in leading her to commit the sin of fornication.

At first it happened occasionally, but then Tyrone became more insistent and Jean was forced to compromise more frequently. On the pretence of going to the movies, Tyrone would take her back to his home. They deceived not only her parents, but also the Hendrys. Jean would obediently wait at the mouth of the alleyway leading to the rear entrance of Tyrone's home whilst he entered through the front door and let her in at the back. The Hendrys had no idea what was going on and on the rare occasions that they called by, Tyrone would get Jean to *hide until they had gone.*

Initially their intimacy troubled Jean, causing her to lose countless hours of sleep fretting about the deception. However, as time passed, her heart became desensitized and she worried less, sitting through many a sermon on the subject of fornication, where the speaker spoke directly to her. Sometimes her conscience was pricked and she repented in her heart, but she allowed the intimacy to continue because when she tried to change the nature of their relationship, Tyrone would counter that they were young, that God understood and that His grace would cover their sins. He supported this argument by reference to David and Uriah's wife and how God had forgiven him. He said that every other young person was doing the same thing and insinuated that if Jean didn't, he would consider her backward, and of course Tyrone didn't like old-fashioned girls. He told her that it hurt him not to go all the way - both mentally as well as physically, because he loved her so very much, and of course Jean could not stand the thought of anything hurting Tyrone. When it was required of him, Tyrone "pulled out all the stops" and he always got his way when he hinted that he would end their relationship. "It would be just too hard for me to continue without touching you", he'd say and Jean never failed to give in then, as she had convinced herself that she could not live without Tyrone. As time passed, she became unaffected by the sermons, closing her mind and spirit to the Word.

When Jean became pregnant she did not realise for nearly four months. She knew she was missing her monthly issue, but did not realise why. She wanted to go to the doctor to find out if anything was wrong with her, as she also felt ill most of the time and linked the two occurrences in her mind, but she was too embarrassed to talk about her period to Mr Marshall, their family doctor. Although she mentioned to her mother that she sometimes felt ill she did not tell her about the missed periods - she was afraid to talk to her mother about such matters because when her first period came, her mother had behaved as though it was something to be ashamed of, and had never discussed its true significance with her. And on occasions, when the bedclothes became soiled during her menstrual cycle, Esther would speak to her in whispers, as though some vile crime had been committed, telling her to wash everything, ensuring no traces of blood remained and that her father did not see any of it. And if a stubborn stain refused to shift, Esther would discard the tarnished bed linen furtively. So Jean could not bring herself to raise this obviously sensitive subject with her mother or seek her advice.

When in the third month of pregnancy her stomach began to swell (a sure sign of malady), Jean became convinced that she was going to die and made an emergency appointment to see Dr Marshall. He confirmed that she was almost four months pregnant, but she didn't tell her parents, keeping the secret until five months had passed. Esther noticed that Jean was gaining weight, that she was always nauseous in the mornings, that she was eating like a horse and sleeping every minute that she could, and confronted her. And Jean's tearful admission caused her mother to faint with shock.

When news got out about Jean's pregnancy out of wedlock, the whole church erupted. Telephones rang non-stop and conversations stretched into the early hours throughout her pregnancy and well into the first year after the birth. An official church meeting was held and she was stripped of her positions in the church choir and as a Sunday School teacher, which saddened her greatly. Quite naively she assumed that, as she had now repented she could just carry on as before. However, her position changed drastically - where she was once one of the main youth leaders, she was overlooked completely. Where she had been highly respected by all, some people now displayed what amounted to near contempt for her – talking loudly about her, but not to her and ignoring her when she greeted them. But Jean continued to attend church where she sat at the back and endured the constant stares and whispers. She missed her friends, most of whom now avoided her.

Bishop Stuart privately discussed her mistake with her, explaining that the church could not be seen to condone such. Jean apologised to him and begged for forgiveness. Having admonished her using Biblical references, Bishop Stuart prayed for Jean and tried to console her, displaying obvious sympathy at her circumstances. However, other elder members refused to forgive her, branding her a "Jezebel". But Jean did not blame those who treated her in that way, fully aware of the enormity of her sinfulness.

Apart from Bishop Stuart who greeted her each Sunday, the only other person that kept on speaking to Jean at church was Eve, her best friend. Eve would smile sweetly at her, defying all others. She also continued to telephone her on a daily basis to see that she was okay.

When they passed her in the street some elder sisters looked pointedly at Jean's protruding belly then straight into her eyes, others stared right through her, some slaughtered her with a glance, and if looks could kill she would have died a thousand times over.

But many kindly brethren displayed sympathy towards Jean's predicament, and spoke kindly to her when they met her away from church. However, those same individuals did not speak to her at church, but avoided eye contact, although appearing sad to treat her in that manner.

Most of those nearer her own age displayed a superior attitude towards Jean, turning their noses high in the air as they passed her by, obviously deriving pleasure from treating her that way.

When Jean was in the third trimester of her pregnancy, the treatment got worse. She sat through whole services as the main attraction, eyes diverting from the speaker as heads turned unashamedly to stare at her protrusion. Whispers were audible and ostracism of her was the norm. Not even Eve spoke to her at church now, being forbidden by her parents to have anything to do with Jean. On occasions when their paths crossed, Eve would defy her parents' command and smile timidly at her friend if she thought no-one was looking, but more often than not she would cast her eyes downwards in embarrassment. But although Eve acquiesced with the wishes of her parents not to speak to Jean in church, she continued to call her clandestinely most days. And at least once every week they met in secret in libraries, cafes or parks.

Even the toddlers were warned by their parents and older children to keep away from Jean. This hurt her most - she loved the little ones she had taught in Sunday School, which love had previously been reciprocated. But now mothers ran to grasp the hands of errant tots who approached – if only to smile or say hello, as if for fear that she would corrupt or contaminate them with some deadly disease – as though she were a pariah.

Having endured all that she could take, Jean stopped attending church altogether. She also stopped going to college and did not go out at all. This reclusion caused her to fall into a mild depression - she cried herself to sleep at night, and awake in the mornings. She even stopped going for weekly meetings with Eve, spending her days in bed, getting up only to eat, drink and relieve herself. Consequently she piled on pounds of excess fat. Tyrone soon voiced his dissatisfaction with her appearance, and curtailed his visits – in any case he was not best welcomed by her parents.

Jesse and Esther endured their daughter's sentence with her, for some of the brethren began to avoid them, blaming them for their daughter's error. Yet they never considered the option of turning their backs on Jean or asking her to leave their home – no - they bore the embarrassment with dignity, holding their heads high. Soon after finding out about the pregnancy Esther had spoken to Jean about her behaviour and the shame she had brought on their family and Jean had almost sobbed her heart out, blubbering pleas for forgiveness. And seeing the obvious distress that broaching the subject had caused their daughter, neither of her parents ever brought it up again, satisfied that she was fully aware of her mistake. And, aware of the degree of pain that Jean was suffering as a result of her error, they became silently supportive of her, prayerfully, as well as financially and emotionally. In turn Jean demonstrated her gratitude by showing humility, speaking to her parents in hushed and respectful tones whenever they were near, and revering them with downcast eyes. And not a day went past that she did not thank God for her beloved parents.

There was a marked contrast in people's reaction towards Tyrone, however. He continued to attend church and play in the church band. Having apologised to Bishop Stuart, who had prayed publicly that he be forgiven and stressed how repentant he was, everyone accepted that he had made a mistake. No-one avoided him, but in the main treated him as before, with respect and dignity. The consensus appeared to be that he had been led astray by Jean in the same way that Eve had deluded Adam. All that was meted out to him for his part was a slap on the hand, and a "don't do it again", and he was exonerated by all.

Tyrone consciously added fuel to the fire as he began to behave strangely towards Jean. He insinuated to some that she had inveigled him to commit the sin, and to others, that she had been weak - had she been stronger, she would not have ended up pregnant. And instead of taking his fair share of the blame Tyrone became complicit with those who placed the burden of liability squarely on Jean's shoulders.

He selectively forgot that it was he who had insisted on having sex in the first place and particularly without any protection. And Tyrone's cavalier behaviour added to Jean's misery.

On 14 February 1982 Jean gave birth to her daughter and they called her Cherie. After she had given birth, Jean encountered further pain brought on by the fact that although she still saw Tyrone almost every day, his visits were fleeting and he never took her out anymore. His interest in her had waned and he only had eyes for the baby, whom he called his Princess, and showered with all love and affection.

Not giving ears to the rumours floating around about Tyrone that he was seeing another woman and some remote rumours that he had a two year old son, Jean lived in hope and prayed that Tyrone would set the wedding date and end her misery. Although he no longer kissed or showed any affection towards her, she put that down to the fact that he was just respecting her wishes not to get intimate – although she did feel that he was taking the matter a little too far the other way.

On occasions Tyrone would take Cherie out to spend whole days with him, but would not ask Jean to accompany them. When she offered to go along, he became almost angry, accusing her of not allowing him to spend quality time with his daughter. But unbeknown to Jean, on the occasions when Tyrone took their daughter out, he met with the other woman, the subject matter of the airborne rumours she was turning a deaf ear to.

When Cherie was nearly a year old, the rumours about Tyrone and another woman intensified. Jean now had a name - Evangeline. Eve told Jean that someone who worked with Tyrone had told her that the two were having a relationship - and planning to get married. Apparently they had been seeing each other for nearly two years. Jean almost laughed in Eve's face. She told her she did not believe her and refused to listen any more. When Eve insisted that the rumours were from a trusted source, and that she believed they were true, Jean retorted that whoever was spreading those rumours must be jealous of her and Tyrone's relationship and was trying to break them up.

In light of Jean's reaction, Eve dropped the subject, and even though she obtained further updates, did not relay them to her friend. She felt sorry for Jean, but had tried and failed to make her see reason. It was patently obvious to Eve and almost everyone except Jean and her parents that Tyrone's interest in Jean had died.

The decline in Tyrone's interest started soon after Jean became pregnant. That was when he started to date Evangeline. Soon thereafter he knew that it was over between him and Jean, but just did not know how to tell her. He was glad when she informed him that they would no longer be intimate, because he just couldn't go on pretending - Evangeline had stolen his heart. Tyrone knew then that he could never fulfil Jean's dreams of marriage to him. He was glad that her parents had initially banned him from visiting their home, thereby allowing him the space he craved. However, after the initial kafuffle when the pregnancy came to light, Jesse and Esther had backtracked realising that it was best to accept him as part of the family, and rather annoyingly they had begun to encourage him towards an early marriage insteaqd of ostracising him.

Embracing Tyrone as part of the family, Esther and Jesse started calling him "Son". As far as they were concerned it was just a matter of time before he married their only daughter – and they hoped this would happen soon. Tyrone appeared to go with their plan. However, he quite worryingly began to come up with one excuse after the other to push the wedding date further into the future.

Just before Cherie's first birthday, Jesse spoke to Tyrone about the reason for the delay in fixing the wedding date. Tyrone's main excuse was the same as he had given for not marrying Jean prior to Cherie's birth and just after, that he was saving up for the wedding as he wanted to have a very big affair and had a lot of family and friends. And when Jesse had offered, yet again, to bear the full cost of the wedding, Tyrone had once more refused, exhibiting some anger when he stated that he wanted to do it for himself. Noting his annoyed reaction, Jesse had suggested that he didn't want to do it at all, at which suggestion Tyrone had become fully irate, and stormed out of the Johnson home. Jesse surmised that he had hit the nail on the head, and from then on began to treat Tyrone differently, reverting to calling him by his name rather than "Son". Esther followed suit and the relationship between them and Tyrone became decidedly frosty, although they did not stop him from coming to see their grand-daughter. They began to warn their daughter about Tyrone's true intentions, but instead of taking heed, Jean defended Tyrone vehemently, being blinded by a haze of love.

Tyrone began to plan his escape the day that Jean's father had spoken to him about fixing the wedding date. And when he visited his family in America a few weeks later, he had finalised plans to emigrate, and had sought and found a job there. Three months after his return, he announced that he would be taking up employment in America a month later.

Jean was devastated by the revelation that Tyrone was going away, but remained optimistic. He gave her false hope that their separation would not be for long. So it came as a total shock when she received that letter to say that he had met someone else. That news had broken her heart. "Not Tyrone, not my Tyrone – he couldn't do this to me – no, there must be some mistake," Jean had repeated over and over before collapsing into floods of tears. But there was no mistake – Tyrone had betrayed her.

Following that revelation Jean relapsed into a deeper state of depression and had it not been for God given strength and the love and support of her parents, she would never have pulled through, out of that dark place. She did not at first realise that the woman Tyrone had "met" was Evangeline, with whom he used to work in London. That he had in fact sent for her, having already proposed to her before he left. That he had married Evangeline less than six months after he left. When she found that out from Eve some time later, she became a totally broken woman all over again, falling into a complete depression. Once again, it had taken the love of God and the care and support of her parents and a lot of time to pull her through.

It was possible for Tyrone to hurt her so deeply because she trusted and loved him so much - with every last bone in her body. It had been a peculiar kind of love, the kind that threatened to stop her breath every time she saw his face - that blinded the eyes and rendered the mind powerless, the kind of love that was so, so sweet that it could overwhelm the soul. The kind of love that if betrayed provided perpetual fuel to feed the pain of a broken heart.

When Cherie turned four years old, Gran' pa announced that he had found a job in Brighton, to where he and Gran' ma intended to relocate. They asked Jean to move with them and she was only too glad to pack up and go, leaving behind the harrowing memories - the hurt and pain of unrequited love.

And so they sold up and left London for Brighton. Jesse and Esther did this for their daughter who needed to have a fresh start, turn a new page. Jean was relieved to get away to a place where Tyrone would never be able to find her - to hurt her again. With a new start in Brighton she threw herself into the demanding role of an employed single parent, concentrating on her career as a nurse and raising her daughter.

And although Jean had gained strength through her experiences, her soul had been indelibly seared by an inability to forgive Tyrone's betrayal. She acquired an unhealthy mistrust of men which she carried for most of her life, well into Cherie's late teenage years. That resulted for many years in her never dating any man past the third date.

CHAPTER 2

Looking Backward to Drive Forward

Cherie sat up in bed quickly like a spring just released after being forcibly held down. Seconds later she jumped out of bed and began to stretch her limbs in a series of staccato movements as she yawned simultaneously, tears welling up in the corners of her eyes. Her movements gradually became more fluid as she stretched, yawned, and cried several times more. Then suddenly she shook her entire body vigorously, smiled sweetly and soliloquised – announcing her motto for the day "Cherie Johnson is about to hit the big time – yes I am", she proclaimed, her smile spreading across her face. And her morning ritual completed, she headed towards the bathroom.

Each morning without exception ever since learning to talk, Cherie said a positive motto to motivate her to meet the challenges of the day ahead. Even on mornings when gloom threatened to overwhelm, she would force herself to say something optimistic with as much gusto as she could muster. And when she was in company, she would wait for an opportunity when they left the room to say her motto softly to herself but with just as much enthusiasm. Those who got close knew that Cherie talked to herself in the mornings, but after the initial inevitable questions as to what she was saying and why, most pretended not to hear her. Although some made it apparent that they thought her a little odd, it didn't bother Cherie - she liked herself.

Cherie Johnson at 28 years old is single-minded and strong, her beautiful face composed of high cheekbones, a snub nose, big golden brown eyes like twinkling pools and a complexion reminiscent of warm cinnamon, setting her apart as among the most beautiful of women. Standing 5'8" tall she resembles a super model hot off the cat walk of any of the world's major cities, her shapely limbs and slim hour-glass figure attracting more than her own fair share of attention from the male specie (mostly unwanted), and causing many, if not most, women to involuntarily seethe with envy. Due to such reaction towards her, Cherie became aware of her beauty from her early teenage years, yet she managed to retain her modesty.

A natural beauty, her hair is likewise simply beautiful, and she wears it either in a short curly afro, or corkscrew curls – accentuating her innocent loveliness.

Often described by some as afro-centric (a term which she didn't quite understand), Cherie was in truth proud of her African heritage and demonstrated that pride in the way that she liked to dress on occasions. For some of her favourite outfits were created from West African kente cloth designs and other fabrics and prints that originated in some or other part of the "Mother Land". But as one who appreciated balance in every aspect of her life, her wardrobe was a testament to that fact, African outfits vying for pride of place with the most contemporary designer creations and some rather more casual day-to-day wear.

Her mother, Jean, is Cherie's role model, best friend and super heroine rolled into one. She brought Cherie up by herself, but with more than a little help from her Grandparents, Jesse, ("Gran' pa"), who doubled as a father figure, and Esther ("Gran' ma"). People often commented that mother and daughter were more like sisters because Jean looked so young, a fact which made Cherie very proud and prompted Jean to continuously renew her gym membership and maintain regular visits to beauty establishments. Cherie adores her mother, esteeming her the most beautiful woman alive – and the strongest.

Jean is an attractive woman in her own right, with smooth ebony coloured skin, pretty deep set eyes, an unobtrusive nose and full well shaped lips, but it is not immediately apparent from looking at her that she and Cherie are from the same gene pool. However, Jean did not like being told that her daughter did not look like her, although she had heard that many times over the years. She always reacted to such comments by fiercely denying that that was a fact, and would go on to draw attention to Cherie's cheeks and eyes, which mildly resembled her own. Jean's blind intransigence in insisting that she looked like the beautiful Cherie was borne out of love for her offspring and not narcissism. But deep within her heart, she knew that her daughter didn't favour her much – it had been obvious from the day she was born. All Jean's hopes that the baby would grow more like her had never been realised. Cherie's mannerisms and her personality are different too – for while her mother is something of an introvert, she is naturally friendly and outgoing – just like her father. This Jean knew full well, and the constant nagging reminder of Cherie's father as she watched her daughter develop into adulthood secretly troubled her. But, Cherie remains oblivious to the fact of her resemblance to a father she could not remember because no-one had ever told her.

****

One of her favourite mottos, which she thought up by herself one morning, was "Look backwards to move forward", and Cherie made a point of doing just that at least once a week. And on 14 February 2010, having returned from her birthday celebrations with her family and closed friends, Cherie began to reflect. A birthday always caused her to think about the fact that she was getting older and remained unmarried. And each birthday she said the same brief prayer, "God please provide me with a good man to become my husband", Cherie pleaded. But this year she added a condition which she had never done before, "Lord, by faith I declare that by this time next year I will meet my husband", she affirmed. Then she turned her thoughts to family.

Apart from her mother and grandparents, the only other family that Cherie had ever known were her mother's cousin, Stella, (Gran' ma's brother's daughter), her husband Ronny and their two children, Tia and Annette. There had been frequent alternating visits between the two households when Cherie was growing up. And fond memories of long lazy Summer days, secret pranks and trickery, and crazy pillow fights before bedtime on nights spent with her cousins, remained vivid in Cherie's mind. But especially vivid were memories of the Christmases of her youth.

For back then each Christmas Stella and her family used to visit, staying from Christmas Eve night through to Boxing Day evening and they brought with them much laughter and festive cheer. Their house in the quiet Brighton neighbourhood would be transformed into a boisterous place of unbridled merriment as the three children played, bonded and fooled around, while Gran 'pa regaled Ronny with stories of his adventurous youth (mis) spent in Jamaica, and Ronny countered with much talk of football, the three women in the meantime engaged with small talk and cooking, giggly effortlessly at nothing in particular as the smell of heaven wafted from the kitchen. The main culinary delights were Gran' ma's luxurious slow roasted Turkey with trimmings, Jean's Jamaican Curried Goat and Rice and Peas and Stella's Ackee and salted fish with bacon. And each Christmas Stella would bring from home her special recipe Christmas cake. Unbeknown to the others who were unwaveringly teetotal the secret ingredients included a lacing of potent Jamaican rum and red wine. The last Christmas spent together when Cherie was 12 years old, Stella had surpassed herself in culinary genius and had also put more than the usual measure of rum into the cake. True to form Gran 'pa had devoured more than his fair share of the culinary masterpiece before beginning to joke around, as he usually did on Christmas day evening. The butt of his jokes as always rested on Gran 'ma who proceeded to ignore him. So becoming bored with being ignored, Gran pa turned his attention to other subjects and continued to spew out a non-stop stream of nonsense, causing the children to giggle with amusement, Gran 'ma to perfect further her ability to ignore, Jean to emulate as best as possible her mother, Ronny's pale English rose cheeks to blush the deepest shade of fuchsia (whether with anger or embarrassment one could not tell), and Stella to rebuke, scold and tell off Gran 'pa in increasingly vehement tones. But Gran' pa just kept going back for more cake, which seemed to cause him to lose further control of his mind and his tongue - then he went a little too far. He started to deride Stella on the passion that she had demonstrated when chewing the turkey drumstick and neck bone, laughing loudly to himself at the parody being replayed in his inebriated mind. But Stella did not find it funny. "I'm not in the mood for your silly jokes," she'd warned, eyes flashing, but Gran 'pa took no notice and continued his humorous off-take of Stella's penchant for the turkey's scrag. "So Stella, tell me where you studied to chew turkey bone so –

which school or university did you attend for that, eeeh – what exam did you pass, because you look like a professional to me," Gran' pa had continued undeterred, laughing out loud at his own jokes. Then Stella had flown into a rage. "Okay, that's it, I've had enough of this", she'd announced. "I didn't come here to be insulted," she had proclaimed, and with that had gathered up her husband and children and left that very night, never to return, severing the once tight connection. Cherie had suffered most as a result of the severance and sorely missed her cousins. Although she had many childhood friends, she could never find the affinity with them that she had with her cousins. Christmases and Summer breaks were never the same when they stopped visiting, leaving an empty place in Cherie's heart that remained vacant throughout her teenage years. And despite her mother and grandparents buying her the most expensive and sought after presents, they could never compensate for the lost kinship.

Having enjoyed a very happy childhood growing up in Brighton, Cherie was not best pleased when, at the age of 16, Gran' pa retired and expressed the desire to return to live in London. However, neither she nor Jean was surprised by this announcement because over the years Jesse and Esther always spoke of North East London fondly as their real home. Although they liked living in Brighton, they longed to return to the church community at Mount Zion Miracle Pentecostal Church – to be and grow old amongst their friends.

After much soul-searching Jean decided to give up her job and return to live in London with her parents. She did not relish doing so, the hurtful memories still fresh in her mind. Her best friend Eve had married and moved away from the area too so there was not much to entice her to go back. But she did not want to split up the family and appreciated her parents' needs.

But Cherie remained unhappy with her family's plans to return to London - she wanted to stay in Brighton. She loved its familiar surroundings - her school friends. This was all she had ever known and she worried about the unknown. Many unanswered questions bombarded her mind. Would she be lonely? Would she make new friends? Would she fit in, in the big bad city? What were Londoners really like? Would they be friendly or unapproachable? Would she be robbed or raped or worst? Cherie lost many a night's sleep as images of crimes and shenanigans in London that she had either read, watched on TV or heard through the grapevine pervaded her thoughts. Not even Lester, her mother's boyfriend, who lived in London and commuted to pursue his love affair with Jean, could reassurance her that she had nothing to worry about. For having left London as a toddler Cherie was unable to recollect anything of significance about the City. She did not recall the beautiful semi detached home along the quiet tree-lined avenue where she had cut her first tooth and taken baby steps, where she had uttered her first words, and played happily with neighbourhood children in the nearby park. She could not recall the caring neighbours who often gathered for barbecues in the park or picnicked by the meandering stream on sun drenched days, where she fed ducks and swans with her mother or Grandparents.

However, it began to occur to her that she could perhaps reconnect with her cousins Tia and Annette and as she mulled that thought over and over day after day, she developed a desire to live in London and gradually becoming excited about the prospect. Then she took the lead in "operation return to live in London", which culminated in an uprooting from Brighton and replanting in London on 28 August 1998.

Falling in love with London was easy – Cherie did so soon after arrival and wondered why her family had ever left in the first place. She was excited by the fact that she didn't see the same faces on the bus every morning; she also had a choice of places to shop at - it was so much larger than Brighton and there was so much more to explore.

Having found a telephone number for Stella in Gram ma's scrapbook, Cherie had telephoned her cousins, seeking to rekindle the family flame. However, although she met up with them on a couple of occasions, the spark would never re-ignite, not for want of trying on Cherie's part, but Annette constantly put a dampener on such efforts and those of her more amenable sibling, leaving Cherie feeling more kinless than ever.

Cherie longed to know her other blood relations too. For she was made aware by Gran' ma that there were many maternal second cousins perhaps of a similar age to herself scattered across the globe, though she had never met any of them - like her mother, not even knowing of their whereabouts. It also occurred to Cherie, with some sadness, that she may have paternal relations of whom she was not aware. She knew nothing about her father except that his name was Tyrone, because her mother never talked about him. All Cherie knew was that for some unexplained reason her mother was real mad at her father. She gathered this from Jean's reaction when as a small girl, curious as to why other children had daddies and she did not, Cherie had asked her mother about her "daddy". "Mummy, when is my daddy going to come," she'd asked innocently. "Which daddy – you don't need to know your father Cherie". "He was not a very nice man". "Uuh – he deserted you and me when you were just a baby - ran away to America – you don't need him," was Jean's bitter response. And she had refused to discuss the matter further.

But the romantic image of her father etched into Cherie's mind by her endless fantasies about him caused her to reject her mother's account – her father would not simply leave her and go away like that. So her childhood reveries gathered momentum becoming more vivid. In them he would return to get her some day – and rescue her from the big bad world. Each day she'd replay the vision in her mind, and before falling asleep at nights she would imagine that he would come tomorrow, and when tomorrow came - the next day, and so on, day after day - but after many days, months, years and countless daydreams Cherie became tired and all dreamed out.

Then during her early teens, after digesting into her psyche over many years the information that her father was a deadbeat, Cherie became angry and angrier, which rage grew until seething, the dam burst and she began to take her anger out on other children, becoming a bully in school. No-one could work out why she had changed so drastically from the sweet angelic child she was in her junior years into a veritable monster. She did not discuss the reason for her unruly behaviour, and no-one really knew why she

18

had become rebellious. She kept her emotions bottled up inside – after all, it was nobody's business how she felt – she was entitled to hurt in private.

Thankfully, that spell of bad behaviour lasted for no more than a few short months. One day the stark realisation that her father was never coming to get her because he probably could care less about her and that he was probably having a wonderful life somewhere, rose up and slapped Cherie in the face and her anger quickly dissipated into indifference. From then on as far as she was concerned, what she had never known she didn't need to know - and her dismissal of her father was absolute. And for many years she harboured no longing, as many children who do not know their fathers do, to find or get to know him. She stopped thinking about him, stopped dreaming - pushing him into a closet at the back of her mind and firmly locking the door.

This turning point led to a complete change in behaviour. Where she had become unruly, she reverted to being the most well-behaved, well-mannered girl in her school. Jean, her grand-parents, her teachers and fellow pupils were relieved, to say the least, at this transformation. No-one knew what was happening inside her mind to cause the drastic change in behaviour - perhaps not even Cherie herself, but all she knew was that she started to look upon Gran' pa as her "daddy".

But as she grew and matured into womanhood, the closet door was becoming more ajar with the passing years and Cherie found that she would increasingly more often wonder about her father - whether he was still alive – if so where he was - whether she got her personality from him - whether she had any brothers and sisters or other family. But what intrigued Cherie by far the most was what her father might look like - whether she favoured him. And she would stare into the mirror for long hours studying her features. For over the years any resemblance to her mother had become less obvious, and Cherie realised that she must have taken more of her looks from her father. And this curiosity to know for a fact whether she looked like him had gradually turned into a longing to meet him.

Cherie was thankful that the revelation that her father had

abandoned her had had no lasting adverse effect on her. She had never despised herself as unwanted, due to the fact that her mother constantly demonstrated how much she truly loved her - so much – enough for two.

Having enjoyed a near perfect upbringing, lacking nothing, she harboured no bitterness usually spawned by lack or missed opportunities. Consequently Cherie bore her father no ill will, in spite of the fact that he'd supposedly abandoned her - she just wanted to meet him, for her life could be likened to an almost complete jig-saw puzzle with just one missing piece that needed to be found. She did not envisage that upon meeting him he would become a dad to her after not having been there all her life, she wanted only to put the missing piece to the puzzle. She did however er entertain the thought that they might become friends – but no more. Her heart was fully prepared for mutual rejection or dislike. All she wanted was a chance to see what her father looked like, so that she could bury the nagging curiosity for good.

It wasn't that Cherie was lonely exactly, she had lots of friends and her mother was ever close. And she now had a Step-father, her mother having married her long-term boyfriend Lester Jones. He was as solid as a brick, and was also the tower of strength that had helped them to cope with the excruciating pain of bereavement after Gran pa's death and when Gran ma died two years later.

Lester fitted perfectly into Gran pa's shoes as the father she'd never had and Cherie was extremely fond of his kind, even tempered and caring ways. In truth Lester was not unlike a tower in stature. He bore the monotonous features of any guy next door, but his heart was that of a wise and good king – crafted of the purest gold, but still Cherie was dogged by a longing to know her father.

CHAPTER 3

Promising View

Undergoing a season of reflection, on 15 March 2010, Cherie's motto is "The light from the past shines brightly upon the path of the future", and as she recites it loudly, she considers how wise she is for having thought it up by herself, then scratches her head as she suddenly realises that she may have heard something similar somewhere before, although she couldn't say where. Cherie then proceeds to contemplate her progress in life, also praying and giving thanks to God for where He has brought her from and where he is taking her to.

Graduating from school with three A levels – an A* in Performing Arts, one in English, and a B in Mathematics, apart from the fact that she wanted to be a major star, Cherie had no idea what type of career she wished to pursue. She did not want to go to university, much to her mother's disappointment. Jean had always dreamt that her only daughter would pursue a professional career – preferably as a Doctor or a Lawyer. Cherie certainly had the ability if she had applied herself - and when she informed her mother that she would be going to college to study performing arts, Jean proceeded to do everything in her power to dissuade the proverbial apple of the eye from what she viewed as an unrewarding, potentially treacherous, life path. But all to no avail, Cherie had made up her mind and there was no dissuading her.

Being born gifted with veritably the voice of an angel, Cherie had no qualms about the fact that she could sing. She was constantly made aware of her gift because family members, friends and acquaintances kept on reminding her with requests that she sang to them. And if she was not a humble natured girl, their praises showered upon her after each church rendition would have surely gone to her head and brought out the diva in her. Indeed often such accolade left her struggling to retain her modesty. Many people likened her to a young Aretha, others to Celine but Cherie knew she had her own unique style - although she admitted to sounding similar to Mariah.

In her early teens Cherie discovered that she also had a flare for song-writing, and being assured of her gifting by her family's lavish admiration and encouragement upon hearing her first simple efforts, she developed quickly, honing her skill to that of a prolific crafter. As her ability developed so too did her confidence - she knew she had something special. She dreamt of making a demo and getting a recording contract, of the day she would be "discovered" – and gradually the dream became more consuming.

At 18, each time she looked into the mirror a young, beautiful and talented, hungry young lady stared back at her – she had all that was required to make it as a big time recording artiste and in her mind failing to "make it" would be harder than succeeding. To acquire vast riches and fame was her aim and Cherie was ready to embrace both. She pondered the publicity that went hand in hand with such fame and longed for it – but there was an agenda hidden deep within her heart – she wanted her father to see her on television and in the newspapers – for surely then he would want to know her.

So with the intention of becoming a renowned celebrity, Cherie got a job as a receptionist in the head office of a large recording company, MPV Records, in Central London when she graduated from college. A strategic career move she hoped would put her in the right circles to meet the right people who would propel her into the limelight.

Things seemed to be going to plan when three months later a very attractive young man came in to use the studio. Cherie recognised him instantly – Dijon – the young rap artiste whose last three singles had commandeered the top of the world's music charts. The American star was in London for two weeks, making personal appearances - promoting his current single and album. Whilst here, he was also continuing to work on his follow-up album. Cherie's knees almost buckled when Dijon winked at her on arriving at the studio that first day, and for the rest of the day she was a jittery bag of nerves. Shyness got the better of her and she avoided eye contact with Dijon when he left that afternoon, kicking herself later for having missed the opportunity – perhaps her chance of a lifetime.

The next day Dijon returned to the studio and Cherie took a deep breath, mustered up enough courage and gave him a winning smile. Smiling reservedly he winked in reply but said nothing, leaving her feeling a little foolish for having demonstrated such obvious enthusiasm. But much to her surprise, that afternoon before leaving the studio Dijon approached her desk and stared directly into her face, forcing her to acknowledge his presence. Then obviously revelling in the effect he was having on her he asked her whether she would agree to go out with him that evening. Silence pervaded the atmosphere as Cherie's breath caught in her throat, stifling her reply, prompting an annoyingly assured of himself Dijon to make her mind up for her, "Okay, Cherie, I would have to guess that your reply is yes – so I'll send a driver to collect you out front at 6.00 pm", he said. And then he was gone, leaving Cherie in a "tizz", wondering how he came to know her name. With fleeting irritation she wondered who he thought he was, taking it for granted that she would say "yes". Then she smiled to herself as it dawned on her that good fortune had embraced her and she almost pinched herself to make sure she wasn't dreaming.

Then various thoughts rushed her mind, so many, so fast as though they would almost trip over each other causing a slight headache to develop, but still more questions than answers pervaded her mind. After composing herself the headache subsided, the thoughts filed themselves orderly in her mind and she contemplated each one. What would she wear? Would she go dressed like this? What would she tell her mother? What would she say to Dijon? How would she behave? What if he tried to kiss her? What if….. how ….. when …. Why. Where?

Cherie breathed deeply to keep calm and then the answers came to her. She would ask her boss if she could leave work at 4 pm. Then she would go to her favourite boutique which was only 5 minutes away, and buy something to wear. She would then return to the office and get dressed in the women's cloakroom. She would tell her mother that she was going out with friends after work – after all that wouldn't be a lie, she thought, conveniently overlooking the fact that she did not know Dijon as a friend or

23

at all. And as for the way she would behave, she decided that she would just smile sweetly.

Word got around fast of Dijon's interest in Cherie and their imminent date, and soon even her boss became aware. So, being under strict orders from the parent company to keep the star happy, he was only too pleased to allow Cherie to leave early without asking her for any explanation whatsoever.

So Cherie purchased her outfit, a pretty baby pink chiffon blouse with mid length sleeves which hugged her waist and a black rough silk calf length skirt with ruche detail to one side. Stylish black ankle boots completed the outfit. Cherie applied make up – more than usual – in the ladies room – adding 5 years to herself. She no longer looked like a fresh faced teenager when she stood in the foyer of the building waiting for her carriage to arrive, but every inch the sophisticated young woman.

Dijon's driver arrived early – at 5.55 pm – he referred to Cherie as "maam" and held the door open for her, ensuring that she was comfortable before setting off. Cherie wondered where he was taking her to but did not verbalise her curiosity.

After a ten minute drive he pulled up in front of a large imposing building tucked away in a corner of Mayfair that looked as though it belonged in the 1920s. The driver got out and held the door open for Cherie as she admired the magnificent architecture of the building. He took her hand and guided her from the car and then walked her to the entrance where a concierge approached her, "You're looking very beautiful tonight, Miss Cherie," the tuxedoed middle aged attendant said, once again referring to her by name. "Please come with me," he continued, guiding her by the hand towards the lift as she smiled sweetly. They alighted on the sixth floor – the penthouse – where the attendant walked to the door, tapped lightly and waited. Checking his watch, he then fished a key from the pocket of his jacket and opened the door, gesturing to Cherie to enter.

Upon entering the apartment, Cherie was overawed by the opulence that she beheld. Her feet sunk into the thickest carpet pile as the most beautiful piano music she had ever heard wafted through the air, rendering her transfixed. She looked around drinking in the dreamlike richness of her surroundings – the silk curtains dramatically draping the large windows – the high ceiling and its ornate décor - the baby grand piano – the expensive hand carved furniture, etched in gold – the smell of expensive perfume. "Come on in beautiful," Cherie could not tell at first where the voice was coming from so she stood still as though rooted to the spot. Then she saw him as the music stopped and he arose from behind the piano and walked towards her.

"I'm so glad you came and you look beautiful," Dijon said. "I did not realise that that was you playing," was all that she could think to say, but that seemed to be all she needed to. Then she smiled sweetly.

"Love your accent - you like that?" Dijon asked obviously pleased that she had noticed. Cherie nodded her smile fixed. He came closer to her and took her hand, guiding her towards the piano. "Come on over," he said. He sat down again and gestured to Cherie to sit beside him but she declined, preferring to stand. As he began to tinker the piano keys, Cherie could feel the music deep in her soul and begun to hum. She hummed a song that she had penned when she left Brighton and her childhood sweetheart behind, and Dijon followed, his fingers expertly finding the right keys. "I wish that I could lose myself in your arms," she sung, timidly at first and then more confidently, "But we're so far apart and all I can do is miss you," Dijon stared at her as she sang, his mouth wide open. When she reached the end of the song he applauded lightly then spoke words that she could only have dreamt, "Girl, you can sure sing". He then asked her if he could tape her singing and play it to his manager – Cherie didn't object. She loved to sing, wanted to do it for a living – how could she possibly refuse. So Dijon switched on the recorder and they ran through the song again – this time more proficiently.

Later dinner was served on the terrace and Cherie found herself relaxing in Dijon's company as a cool "end of Summer" breeze wafted lightly and as they ate lobster, and he drank champagne, she pure orange juice, Cherie was prompted to ask Dijon if he was expecting others for dinner, as there was so much food laid out – enough to feed at least 5 other people. However, she could not find the words - all her efforts were employed in continuing to smile sweetly. She remained expectant but no-one else arrived.

Dijon drank Champagne by the bottle and talked incessantly about himself throughout the meal, his career; his ambitions to do a blockbuster movie – to become a billionaire. Then suddenly he spoke music to Cherie's ears, "I might be looking for a female singer to accompany me on two tracks on my next album", he said, the glint in his eye hinting that she might be what he was looking for. Cherie was dumbstruck and became hot and flustered – she did, however, manage to stutter that she had written the song, *Missing You*, provoking further admiration and praise from Dijon.

Cherie tried to eat as much as she possibly could as thoughts of those who might be starving in some small corner of the world bombarded her mind. Dijon on the other hand merely picked at almost everything on the table, eating like a bird with no evidence of conscience. That did not impress Cherie, but otherwise the date was going well.

When he had finished picking at the food Dijon excused hisself and left Cherie alone – he was gone for ten minutes and Cherie began to fidget with unease when he returned. As he walked towards her he appeared to be unsteady on his feet, and his eyes were glazed over. Then he spoke incoherent, "So boo, wha you into then?" He asked several times. This sudden and obvious change in his disposition caused Cherie to surmise that she knew exactly what he was into – substance abuse - and she became withdrawn from Dijon who did not seem to notice.

After dinner Dijon dismissed the butler and they went to sit in the lounge. Cherie was thinking of making an early escape when to her surprise, without request or apology, the star flicked the channel to play an erotic movie. Cherie looked away, embarrassed. However, Dijon did not seem to notice, perhaps as a result of having imbibed way too much champagne and taken heavens knows what else. He proceeded to try and cosy up to her as she visibly shrunk away from him. Then in a scene which seemed to Cherie to be playing in slow motion, he cornered her on the sofa and tried to engage her in an intimate embrace searching to kiss her on the mouth. She resisted, but he forced his mouth down upon hers, robbing a kiss. At the same time Cherie felt his hand on her left breast, pressing hard, intimately, demandingly. She struggled as his hand moved to other parts of her body, but the more she struggled the more aroused Dijon appeared to become. He whispered her name, sounding in her ears like a lunatic – couldn't he see that she didn't want this?

Then Cherie whispered a prayer and soon found hidden strength. She managed to struggle free, grabbed her bag and bolted for the door. Instead of waiting for the lift she raced down the stairs in blinding tears, all the way to the bottom and out of the hotel. She did not stop running until she'd reached the bus stop.

Next day she rang in sick and was off for the rest of that week, and did not return until the following Monday when she knew Dijon was safely back in the USA. On returning to work her colleagues initially bombarded her with questions about her date with the famous star but she refused to discuss it, and getting the message that all did not go well they backed off.

That morning she found a sealed envelope waiting for her on her desk. In his letter Dijon apologised profusely for the way he had behaved and begged her to give him a chance to make it up to her. He invited her to meet him in his home city of New York where he would begin to make amends, but she never responded. He sent her flowers, expensive perfumes and several letters, pleading for forgiveness. Months went by and the letters kept on coming. Then in one letter he asked Cherie if she would sing with him on the album he was working on. He informed her that all she had to do was say the word and he would catch the next plane to be in London with her. He also tried to call her on numerous occasions but she refused all his advances. Cherie was not able to allow Dijon in again - he had gone too far. He gradually got the message and the letters and calls ceased.

Several months later Cherie was surprised to receive a letter from Dijon, once again apologising but going on to say that he understood her decision not to give him another chance. He continued that he only wanted to know that she had forgiven him. Believing him to be sincere Cherie wrote back and offered him the hand of clemency. Thereafter she followed Dijon's movements in the Press and saw he was getting around with several beautiful women. She was pleased to note that he had moved on.

Nearly a year later, Cherie received yet a further letter – a package - from Dijon. In his letter he asked her whether she would consent to his using her song on his next album. He had sent her a recording of the song using a gifted young female R & B singer on lead vocals. It was one of the women to whom he was romantically linked in the two months previously. She couldn't wait to get home and listen to the recording. It was absolutely perfect and when she wrote the song she could never have imagined that it would be so beautifully performed. Cherie listened to the track over and over before telephoning Dijon that very night to give her consent for him to her song. She instinctively trusted him to do right by her, and her instincts were spot on. He sent the necessary papers to sign and a few months after that she praised God for his manifold blessings when she received her first royalty cheque.

Her encounter with Dijon had led Cherie to question whether she did in fact wish to become a superstar. She had sensed a great sadness, such loneliness and confusion in him and a profound emptiness. And the ugliness of materiality and excess veiled his true character. She could tell that he was a nice person deep down but had been influenced negatively by his fame and easily gotten wealth. Cherie did not want that for herself. So she began to consider other career options. She was prepared to work hard for a living. And she took great joy in singing at church, where she received fulfilment from doing something positive and worthwhile with her God-given talent – no amount of fame and wealth could compare with that.

Remaining at MPV, Cherie worked her way up through the ranks until she became an A & R manager. In her limited spare time she also turned her hand to song-writing and produced a demo, but had yet to enjoy the same degree of success that she had with *"Missing You"*. One goal was in her mind as she continued to work for MPV - one day she intended to set up her own artiste management outfit – and in her view her future was promising.

Obscured View

"Nurture your Roots so you can grow", Cherie proclaims on waking up on 22 March 2010, and she muses that she would do just that if she knew where to begin. She has always longed to know more about her family. For although Gran' ma used to speak about the many maternal second cousins perhaps of a similar age to herself scattered across the globe when she was alive, Cherie has never met any of them, and, like her mother, did not even know of their whereabouts.

But the worse thing of all was that she knew nothing about her father - her mother refused to discuss him. And the longing to know her father was growing stronger every day, causing Cherie to become more and more frustrated with the situation.

Before her grandparents passed away, Cherie attended church with them at the Mount Zion Miracle Pentecostal Church, where she sang in the choir. And once, when she'd sung a solo, her grand-mother later commented that she could sing just like her father, causing untold joy to fill Cherie's heart. But when she later pressed Esther for more information about her father, all she found out was that his name was Tyrone, but then her grandmother had clammed up, refusing to divulge anything else.

"Just ask your mother", Gran 'ma had said, repeating the now common citation. But Cherie knew better than to do that, because her mother always went into a bad mood which lasted for days whenever she broached the subject of her father.

Having acquired some information from the elder brethren at the church, who told her that Tyrone was a member of Mount Zion when she was born Cherie had pressed them for further information. However, none of them had any contact details for him or knew of his whereabouts. One of the elderly brothers, Brother Deeks, told her that some years back, he had a chance meeting with her father in Finsbury Park. However, he had mislaid his details and Tyrone had never contacted him.

In the year following the receipt of that information from Brother Deeks, Cherie had frequented Finsbury Park every opportunity she got. Trawling the streets, she looked around for someone whom she thought resembled her, having no idea what her father might really look like. On a couple of occasions, she had even approached total strangers to say that she thought she knew them, but had been disappointed to find that none of them was called Tyrone.

Some of the brethren at Mount Zion told Cherie that her father attended the church for a few months back in 1987. They said that he had asked about her then, but no-one had known where to locate her and her family in Brighton, where they were living at that time.

The only photograph Cherie had ever seen of her father was an old crumpled and faded one that her Gran' ma used to keep in the back of the photograph album and when she was a little girl, Cherie used to sneak a look at it every opportunity she got. She had vaguely made out that he had a similar complexion to her own, and was of a tall and slim stature. He wore drainpipe jeans and a small afro, and that image of her father was vividly preserved in Cherie's mind. Up until the period of her rebellion as a teenager, she would spend hours just looking at that faded snapshot, willing the picture to become clearer so that she could see what this stranger - supposedly her father - really looked like.

Following Gran ma's death, which left a gaping hole in her heart that desperately needed to be filled, Cherie had once again tried to talk to her mother about her father, but she had retorted angrily, *"Don't ask me about that good for nothing creep – you don't need him – you have never needed him before, and you certainly don't need him now,"* before going into a foul mood and spending the afternoon locked away in her bedroom with a *"headache"*. Cherie could hear her sobbing late that night and her puffy eyes the next morning betrayed that Jean had been crying for a long time.

After that, Cherie tried her utmost to stuff Tyrone back into the closet at the rear of her psyche, but try as she may, the interest would not diminish. In order to dull the longing, she threw herself into her work and kept an equally busy social life, leaving little time for anything else. Yet in those brief moments that she had to herself Cherie would think about her father. She would mull over and over in her mind the little that she knew of him, longing to find him but with no idea where to begin her search. No-one seemed to know very much about him except perhaps her mother, the only person that might be able to assist her in the quest to find him, but Jean was apparently incapable of co-operating, leaving Cherie to stumble in the dark. In one season of madness – she resolved to herself to travel to American and find her father, and had begun to make plans to do so – but reality had invoked reason, causing her to face the fact that since she had no idea who Tyrone really was, or what he might look like, finding him would be impossible.

But unbeknown to Cherie, in recent months while she struggled to deal with her predicament, her mother has been wrestling her own demons. Needing a confidante, Jean had opened up to Lester about Cherie's dad. Lester had responded by showing her the love and care of a good and understanding husband, which helped Jean to overcome the bitterness which was at the root of her attitude in denying Cherie the right to know her father.

The past wounds were healing fast and the long harboured malice was dissipating rapidly, but taking its place was an equally negative emotion, a growing guilty conscience, for Jean found that she could no longer justify her position in having denied her daughter the right to know her father all those years. Lately she had begun to see herself as a selfish ogre who lied to her daughter, having allowed herself to be controlled by negative emotions. And she was also becoming more and more afraid, fearing Cherie's reaction when she admitted to her that she had omitted to tell her the full story. Jean feared she would be unable to make her daughter appreciate that she concealed the whole truth from her because she had been so cruelly betrayed – so deeply wronged. She certainly could not reason this through to herself now, and wondered how she could have remained in that dark place of acrimony and denial for so many years. And Jean knew she would have to come clean to Cherie one day very soon, in order to find personal peace. Lately she had been replaying over in her mind the true and complete facts, preparing herself for the early day of revelation when she would have to come clean with the truth. She would have to tell her daughter that Tyrone had left to go and work in America when she was just a year old in 1983, that he had written the following year to say that he had met someone else with whom he had become involved and was intending to marry. She would have to go on and tell Cherie the part she had omitted - the part about her father begging for forgiveness and requesting that he continue to have contact with his daughter, of his desire to support her financial until she was grown up, and his expression of regret and of love for his *"Princess"*.

Facing the truth, Jean had begun to cry daily, sorry for her actions in denying her daughter the love of her father who truly loved her, and leading her into believing that she had been abandoned by a cruel and uncaring dad.

CHAPTER 5

Interchanges and Connections

"Show me your friends and I will show you who you are" Cherie had recited with conviction on the morning of 24 March 2010 - and as she drove to work she was in a reflective mood, a fixed smile gracing her face.

Jean had been over-protective with her only daughter while she was growing up, almost to the point of smothering her, but this apparently had no ill effects on Cherie, who was out-going and friendly. She had an engaging personality, and qualities that instinctively drew people to her. This stood her in good stead when she moved back to London and she had fitted easily into her new environment. Joining the local secondary school sixth form, her personality shone and she quickly became popular. Soon she found herself a member of the elite group – among those who everybody wanted to hang around and be seen with. However, that status had its downside for she also collected a few enemies, completely without her fault or knowledge.

To her surprise Cherie soon realised that she was being gossiped about, even by people she did not know. Some of the rumours being spread were so far fetched that she was amazed at the imagination of those who had concocted them. Some were petty, such as the one that she bought clothes from charity shops - those did not bother her. But others were more vicious and potentially damaging, like the one spread around that she was dating two of the most popular guys in the school at the same time. But those rumours did not apparently harm her reputation. Instead they had the effect of adding to her popularity and soon all the most handsome and well-liked boys in school wanted to date her.

Back then Cherie was careful never to go out with any boy alone but always in a group to avoid any new unsubstantiated rumours developing. The group went out and had lots of fun together. Curtis, a six foot tall hunk, whom she thought of as no more than a friend was part of the group. Then there was Sean, a male model look-a-like who was far too pretty for her to ever fancy and whom she also viewed as just a friend. But Cherie could not make others believe that that was the true nature of their friendships. She maintained all her associations with the opposite sex candidly, being extra careful, not wishing to give fuel to fire the rumours. And although both Curtis and Sean declared their interest in dating her one-to-one, Cherie continuously stressed to them both that all she had to offer was pure friendship, a position that they had reluctantly accepted. At 17 Cherie was not interested in dating anyone - her mother had instilled into her the need to get a good education and all she wanted to do was make her family proud.

After leaving school, Cherie kept in touch with both Curtis and Sean for a few years. And even when they began to date other girls, they continued to look out for her, like elder brothers do their junior sister. However, she lost touch first with Sean and later with Curtis when they embarked on serious relationships.

****

Over the years Cherie had entertained a steady stream of good friends. Her friends were a well-balanced mix drawn from all races - not consciously or deliberately selected – but randomly chosen for varying character traits, no doubt contributed to by the diversity of their cultures and creeds. She was often surprised by her own popularity as people seemed instinctively to gravitate towards her - she never had to try very hard to impress. She was always invited to all the best parties and functions and even those who were mere acquaintances sent her invitations. Some individuals were interested in her popularity and hoped that being around her would reflect on them favourably. Others hoped that they could tag along with her to some social event or other, while others still admired and tried to emulate her.

She had the same effect on both sexes, having both female and male friends and acquaintances - even a couple who could be categorised as "other". She had young, not so young and old friends - black, white, brown, yellow and "other" friends - petite, slim, and fat friends - tall friends and short friends - happy friends and melancholy friends - simple friends and clever friends - deep friends and shallow friends - attractive friends and plain friends - physically beautiful friends and soulfully beautiful friends. But Cherie refused to have any soulfully ugly friends. She did not like hateful, false, spiteful, petty people, people who liked to gossip, or self-important people.

Although Cherie detested show offs or snobs, she liked individuals who took pride in themselves - to an extent. People who took pride in their appearance, in their homes, people who took pride in their jobs and achievements. She liked individuals who had ambition and drive, and she considered the most important quality in a person to be integrity.

That is not to say that she had perfect friends, but if she liked an individual enough in some way, she could overlook less attractive traits of that individual's personality. Most of her friends worked out quite early on what Cherie did not like about them as she was forthright in letting them know what she really thought of them, even if it meant she often had to apologise later for something said out of turn. Any lesser mortal would not get away with some of the things that Cherie would say, but her companions did not seem able to hold anything against her for long. She would apologise if she felt she needed to, buying flowers or gifts for those she had potentially offended, while at the same time stressing that she meant every word, without meaning to hurt their feelings. She would somehow talk them into believing that as a friend she had the privilege of saying almost anything to them but that she still loved them "warts and all". They would quickly get the message that Cherie didn't wish to see the warts quite so much or so often. But she would always stress her own shortcomings, encouraging her friends to criticise her at any time they felt necessary.

****

If Cherie did not like a person enough, she would not bother to admonish them. She would simply avoid them, without providing any reasons why - not returning their calls or attending any functions to which they had invited her. After receiving this treatment for some time most usually got the message - although some did not. Those who persisted in being ignored, by continuing to telephone her, sending her invitations, or even turning up unannounced at her door, would eventually be told, in no uncertain terms, that there was something about them that Cherie detested and that she could not be friends with them.

Tricia Syrenson was one such individual. Cherie attended the same dance group with Tricia when she was 17 – Tricia was a year younger but behaved more like a 25 year old. At first they got along well and on the face of it had many things in common. They were both "only daughters", and could relate to each other in ways that "only children" could. They both liked the same kinds of music and they both liked to dance. And they had a striking resemblance to one another - the same complexion and similar features and statures. Many people - even their teachers - mistook them for sisters.

On the first evening of class, Tricia made a beeline for Cherie, and admittedly Cherie had liked her affable and outgoing nature and found her style of speech endearing. Tricia spoke with a London/New York accent, due to the fact that she was born and spent most of her young life in New York. Cherie also liked her flare for make-up and attire. So when Tricia offered her a lift home on the first evening they met, she had gratefully accepted, wishing to escape the nippy November breeze. Tricia was picked up by her boyfriend and insisted that they drop Cherie at her door to ensure that she was safe, a gesture that impressed Cherie as being most thoughtful.

Within two weeks of their meeting, Cherie had returned the hospitality by inviting Tricia to her home, where she introduced her new friend to her family. The following week Tricia returned the gesture and invited Cherie to meet her parents, who Cherie found to be lovely people - a beautiful couple who were obviously very much in love. Cherie marvelled at the marked difference between Tricia and her parents, for while she was loud and gregarious they were quiet and respectful folk. She liked Tricia's dad best – imagining that her own father must be much like him and he did bear an uncanny resemblance to the image of her father in the faded sepia photo that Gran' ma kept at the back of her album.

The same night that she met Donald, Cherie dreamt that he was her long last father, and it occurred to her that he might well be, although one small detail could disprove that theory - his name was not Tyrone. But the fact of Donald Syrenson's facial features strongly resembled hers, his cinnamon complexion, compounded by the fact of his having lived in America provided much food for contemplation, which thoughts continued to nibble at the fringes of her mind and she intended to broach the subject with her mother, when the time was right. The thought did occur to her that she could ask Donald, but the fear of embarrassment should her suspicions prove unfounded deterred her from doing so.

Not long after their exchange visits, Cherie began to regret that she had allowed Tricia to get so close so soon, for she began to notice an unpleasant side to her. Tricia gossiped maliciously about other people a fact that Cherie hated and asked her to stop. But Tricia totally disregarded her request and soon Cherie began to see other traits of Tricia's personality that she disliked, not only was she cruel in the way that she spoke about others, but by far the thing that jarred most on Cherie's nerves, was the fact that Tricia was apparently a gold-digger, and evidentally, more than a little loose. She only dated men with lots of cash to flash and not only did she date more than one man at a time, but Cherie gathered, that some of the men she dated were married, and others were of decidedly dubious characters. And most of her male companions were over 25, and a couple were "old" – at least 30. It was also apparent that Tricia did not just date these men, but also slept with several of them – she had made no secret of it, divulging to Cherie all the unwanted sordid details of her liaisons, with the object of inveigling her to do likewise.

So Cherie was not inclined to share with Tricia her suspicions that they might be related, but started to avoid her instead, sticking closely to Debra Stewart, another girl that attended the dance classes. She was aware that Tricia detested Debra, for no apparent reason marking her out as the number one object of her malicious gossiping. And Cherie hoped that her friendship with Debra would signal to Tricia that theirs was at an end. But undeterred, Tricia continued to telephone her on an almost daily basis. Cherie did not take her calls, or respond to any of the messages left or return her calls.

One Saturday Tricia rang Cherie no less than 20 times. Cherie ignored the calls, and so could not believe it when Tricia turned up at her door at 11 o'clock that night. In the usual scheme of things, neither Jean nor her parents would answer their door past 10.00 pm, unless they were expecting company, so they ignored the knock initially. However, as it was apparent that someone was home because the lights were on, Tricia kept on knocking and refused to go away, until Jean was forced to answer the door. Jean initially thought the caller had the wrong address as she did not recognise Tricia immediately. "Hi Jean, I'm here to collect Cherie," Tricia said cheekily, causing Jean to recollect.

Cherie was already in bed at that time and came downstairs when she heard the commotion, which had also awoken her grandparents, who lived in the discrete downstairs garden apartment within the same house.

"Collect Cherie to go where at this time of night?" Jean asked, peeved. Just then Cherie came down the stairs, sleepily. Upon seeing Cherie coming down the stairs, Tricia pushed her way past Jean, while speaking directly to Cherie, "Didn't you get my messages – aren't you going to Julie's party tonight. Wayne is waiting outside for you – go and get ready".

Immediately Cherie was no longer sleepy - she was livid "Don't you think I would have returned your calls if I had wanted to go?" Cherie said in a very firm voice. She went on, "You really shouldn't have knocked on my door at this hour, especially without obtaining my permission first, and waking my family up". "Don't you have any manners – don't you have any respect at all?" Cherie gritted her teeth as she spoke, trying to stifle her anger. Tricia glared at her, "cutting daggers", then at Jean and then at Gran' pa, before uttering a string of expletives (an assortment of American and Jamaican ones), whirling herself around and stomping out the door, still mumbling under her breath.

Extremely embarrassed by this episode, Cherie apologised to her mother and grandparents, and vowed within herself never to allow anything like that to happen again. From then on she would subject any potential friend to a vetting period until she was satisfied that they had earned the right to become more than just a mere acquaintance.

Since that incident, Tricia has become a sworn enemy, going out of her way to insult Cherie every time their paths crossed. She would "cut with her eyes (daggers)" at her and then "kiss her teeth" (hiss), before launching into a string of expletives. And if she passed close to her, would walk into her path, deliberately bumping into her while holding her nose. Cherie gave up dance classes to avoid further confrontation with Tricia, not because she was afraid of her, she just wanted to keep the peace. However, over the years their paths would sometimes cross on occasions, as they had a few common associates.

Occasionally the thought occurred to Cherie that she really needed to broach the subject as to the possibility that Donald Syrenson was her father with her mother, so strong was her conviction that he might be, but the time never seemed right.

****

Those who made it past Cherie's protracted vetting stage, of criticisms, apology, gifts, criticism, apology, gifts, affirmation, to the friendship stage, became lifelong pals and defended her fiercely against those who had not been "affirmed". They loved and accepted her for who she was and some benefited from her criticism of them. Like her best friend, Cynthia Payne. Cherie loved Cynthia – warts and all – like the sister she never had. Cynthia was no angel though, and being incredibly beautiful, had always gotten more than her fair share of admirers. She was an outrageous flirt, who had become accustomed to dating and being apparently intimate with more than one man at a time. Cherie disapproved strongly of this conduct, especially after becoming a Christian. She had not minced her words in admonishing her friend, and voiced her disapproval strongly especially as to the revealing clothes that Cynthia wore. Her voluptuous body used to pop out of clothes two sizes too small for her. Cherie, embarrassed by the way that both men and women judged her friend, spoke to Cynthia strongly about the way that she dressed. At first Cynthia accused her of being jealous, but after doing a reality check it had dawned on her that, being completely beautiful, Cherie did not need to be jealous of anybody, and Cynthia had taken on board what Cherie said and changed her behaviour and style of dressing.

Nowadays Cynthia would be the first to agree that she was a better person for knowing Cherie. She now dresses like a lady at all times, and behaves accordingly. And she has met a wonderful gentleman named Benza with whom she maintains a good and healthy one-to-one relationship and hopes to marry one day.

Cynthia only wished that her dear friend could also find happiness, and she has tried to set Cherie up, but all attempts have so far failed – her sister was just way too fussy. She tried setting her up on blind dates, introducing her to family members, friends, friends of friends, colleagues, acquaintances – everything. When questioned as to why no one ever caught her interest, Cherie replied that she was waiting for God to send her a husband, which caused Cynthia to wonder as to her friend's mental state. But she has not given up and tried recently to set Cherie up with one of Benza's good friends, someone that both she and Benza thought was just perfect for her, but Cherie refuses to go on any more blind dates. "I know that God will send me a Christian husband in His own time, so let it rest, right," were her last words on the subject. But as far as Cynthia is concerned, Cherie is taking this whole religion thing way too serious.

CHAPTER 1

Running Late

It's Wednesday 8 March 2010 and Gustave Allen is running late again – a common occurrence which has developed over time into a major flaw on his character. Although he fought against this adversarial trend with all his will, his efforts were consistently thwarted - no matter how much time he allowed to reach his destination, something always prevented him from arriving on time.

"On this occasion though it's definitely not my fault," Gustave mumbled, annoyed with himself, as he began to retrace the afternoon's movements in his mind. Leaving home in Islington at 1.00 pm he had stopped off briefly at the estate agents to pick up the keys of his new property – a palatial home in Radleigh, (a better part of suburbia he could only have dreamed of visiting when he was growing up on the inner city estate where he was born, let alone owning one of the better properties there).

Smiling at his good fortune, Gustave's mind took a brief detour as he thought of his humble beginnings and how well he had done for himself. His smile relaxed as his mind snapped back to the present - arriving at the des res at 3.00 pm, he had stayed briefly to satisfy himself that all was in order, had then secured the house and set off for the sports stadium at 4.30 pm – in good time to arrive at the stadium by 5.30 pm. But he had not reckoned on what seemed like every single car in London converging on the same route, resulting in the gridlock of traffic that now snarled up the North Circular. "Just my luck," Gustave mouthed his thoughts and then glared disgruntled at the dashboard clock like a depressed dog. The cars inched along bumper to bumper, as his thoughts drifted away again, his full attention returning just in time to brake, averting a collision with the car in front. Shuffling uneasily in his seat he resisted the urge to lean on his horn in agitation at fellow road-users whose only fault was being in the wrong place at the wrong time. But as mild insanity threatened to overcome, he took several deep breaths, encouraging his mind to return to normality

The traffic now at a standstill and with nothing better to do, Gustave began to reflect, questioning why he was always late. It seemed he was fated to endure a life of tardiness, because no matter what he did he had so far failed to overcome this nemesis. Frustration began to set in as Gustave recounted some past freak incidences that had resulted in unpunctuality.

There was the time when his somewhat absent-minded friend Marshie, being best man to a mutual friend, had asked him to look after the wedding rings. On the morning of the wedding Gustave had set out bright and early for the church to avoid any possible hitches. Arriving forty minutes early and having taken his seat, he decided to have a peek at the rings, only to realise that he'd forgotten them at home. Frantic, he had rushed home to fetch them, and luckily had just enough time in which to do so. However what then ensued was a catalogue of catastrophes, for after collecting the rings and returning to his car, he realised to his horror that in his haste, he had left both his car and house keys inside his home. So, having alerted Marshie that he was running late he hailed a taxi to take him to the church, but the cab broke down on the way so Gus jumped on a bus, which unfortunately went on diversion. He eventually arrived a highly embarrassing one hour late.

And then there was the occasion when early one Sunday morning, with the roads almost completely empty, and having left plenty of time to arrive at his destination, a freak accident had occurred, involving a solitary lorry which had overturned on the dual carriageway, completely blocking his path and necessitating a detour, causing him to arrive two hours late to collect his girlfriend from the airport.

Gustave's jaw tightened as he pondered and silently vowed never to accept that he was doomed to a life of tardiness. With renewed vigour he resolved that no matter what it took, he would vanquish this arch enemy for good – it irked that he had so far failed to do so.

Becoming bored Gustave involuntarily looked around him at what seemed like a virtual car park. An attractive young woman sat observing him in the car to his right and visibly perked up as he looked towards her. She pushed her protruding appendages upwards in an obviously inviting and almost vulgar fashion while licking her lips suggestively. Gustave looked away quickly not willing to give in to his acknowledged weakness. Looking to his left he observed a well dressed middle-aged man pick his nose with fervour as though savouring every insalubrious moment of the gross act. Unaware that anyone was watching, the otherwise dignified character proceeded surreptitiously to pass the implemented digit across his lips, licking it coyly with his darting tongue. Gustave frowned, becoming nauseous at the sight. He pulled his shoulders upright and sat rigidly, returning his gaze to the car in front.

After a beat, Gustave returned to musing over his inclination towards being late. Most people joked about it as though he actually enjoyed it – but for him it was no laughing matter. He particularly hated arriving late on Wednesday evenings for the training sessions with the youngsters from Young & Strong, a community initiative run by the Born Again Church of God.

Born on 3 October 1979, at 30 years old Gustave Allen was a man with a purpose – to mentor and set a good example to the youth in the community where he had grown up. A true gentleman, Gustave stood 6', 4" tall with a rich complexion evocative of dark brown autumn leafs, and a rippling physique that most men would die for. His unconventionally handsome facial features complemented his stature well - with large almond shaped eyes intricately positioned on his face, his nose straight with slightly flared nostrils – his mouth just wide enough to accommodate his full, smooth, kissable lips. Gustave often sported a small "tash" and "goatee". But sometimes he would be clean shaven, as today - his left cheek betraying a solitary dimple that he knew was an attractive feature – at least people had told him so. His hair was always short and well groomed with light waves, which complimented his features perfectly, making him look years younger. And there was something very special about Gustave – a certain charismatic quality which rendered him highly attractive if not irresistible to most women. He was aware that he had a peculiar effect on the opposite sex, however, although he was conscious of his good look, Gustave could not say why. With his appearance, impeccable dress sense, penchant for smelling good and obvious good fortune, Gus was the ultimate suave, sophisticated, desirable and sought after bachelor.

Those who knew him well called him "Gus" for short - except for his dearly departed mother who had always insisted on calling him by his full Christian name – Gustave. His full name was Gustave David Godfrey Denzil Allen, and he recalled fondly that when he had done something to upset her, his mother would address him by his full name – all five of them, as though doing so was some sort of weird punishment. There was the time when he had stayed out until four in the morning at 16. Although having a perfectly good explanation in that his friend's car had broken down four miles away and they'd had to walk the distance home, he was not given the chance to explain, because as soon as he entered the house he had been ambushed by his mother waiting up for him, "Where you' tink you coming from this time a morning, Gustave David Godfrey Denzil Allen?" "You think you is any man in here?" Alison had twanged loudly, hands akimbo. But that was one of the very few times that his mother had had occasion to recite that tongue twister, for Gus rarely stepped out of line, having been for the best part, a model teenager – a son that any parent would be proud of – almost too good to be true. Now a grown man, he had not changed significantly and he continued to conduct his life with the utmost integrity.

Gus concentrated hard on the road ahead, willing the traffic to move faster, a crease etched into his brow as he frowned. A moment later he got his wish - the scowl disappeared and he smiled revealing exquisite teeth. "At last", he sighed as the traffic began to move - this time significantly, much to the chagrin of Ms lady in the red car to his right who had hoped to catch his eye again, pout at him, flick her hair some more and maybe get hooked up.

Driving quickly and expertly dodging the speed cameras along the route, Gus soon arrived at his destination. He turned into the stadium car park at its rear and, swinging into the space reserved for him, brought his car to an abrupt stop with a slight screech of the brakes, belying the fact that he had been driving way too fast.

Without hesitation, Gus opened the door and exited his car, bumping his head as he did so. "Ouch!" he exclaimed, rubbing his forehead. This was a common occurrence because his car was way too small for him, and each time he bumped his head getting out of it - which was almost daily - he was reminded that, instead of driving this sports edition MXLX, a man of his stature should be driving a much bigger car - one with more head and leg room. He could easily afford to buy another car and still keep the small sports number to indulge himself when the whim took him. But Gus did not wish to own more than one car - he did not subscribe to such extravagances. *"After all how many cars can I drive at once?* he thought. "It's not as though I have a family or anything," he mumbled without realising he was now verbalising his thoughts. He loathed to see well off people flaunt their wealth by purchasing unnecessary items such as numerous flashy cars, and considered that they were just showing off. It had never crossed his mind that they might have a weakness, in the same way that he had a penchant for exclusive well-designed suits, beautiful shoes, and expensive aftershave.

The truth was that Gus liked the MXLX sport way too much to trade it in for another car. The car's performance was impressive, and he also liked the fact that he was one of the few people with this limited edition model. But mostly he enjoyed the look of respect it commanded from his young impressionable protégés. The car screeched *"Bling"*, and Gus liked that just fine, not because he wanted to show off his wealth, but because he knew that it was important that the youths he mentored (especially the young men), saw just how successful he really was, and understood that he was *legit* – and he never missed the chance to stress that he had acquired all his assets through sheer hard work and shrewd investments.

Yes, Gus was a wealthy man (certainly by Wash House standards), although he was more property wealthy than cash rich. And everything he had, had been acquired by legitimate means - sheer hard work, determination, some natural intelligence, acquired wisdom, God-given natural talent, and more than a few blessings along the way – one such blessing being an Angel sent to guide him – his father Cyrus. He thanked his lucky stars everyday for Cyrus' influence in his life and hoped to have a similar effect on one or other of the young people that he helped to train at the after-school sports club.

This zeal to influence the youngsters positively had become more and more forceful over recent months. And he was not just concerned with whether they decided to pursue athletics - he hoped to influence their overall thinking in order to help them to succeed in whatever career path they chose to follow. He hoped, by passing on some of his acquired knowledge and experience to better their lot.

Much thought went into Gus' preparation for the training sessions. It was important to him, as a mentor, to ensure he looked smart and clean - he made an extra special effort on Wednesdays, even though his personal appearance was always high on the agenda. He had a weak spot for looking good. He wore only the very best that money could buy, although his attire was never overstated. Over many years he had honed his skill and perfected looking good almost to a flaw. Those who didn't know him well thought he was something of a braggart, but his close friends and family knew that he wasn't – he was just being Gus. He was not a fashion victim, for he was not concerned with keeping up with the latest trends, he purchased whatever he liked, whether considered fashionable to others or not. And money was no object to Gus where looking good was concerned. He had a particular weakness for top designer creations such as Oswald Silvercut suits, and spent a huge amount of money indulging his Achilles heel.

Looking and smelling good made him feel good about himself, however Gus sometimes felt guilty for spending so much on clothes and aftershave, because he would think about those less fortunate than himself to whom the money spent on just one designer outfit may represent a whole year's salary. Gus reasoned that he worked hard and was entitled to enjoy the fruits of his labour. And if that argument failed to appease, he would silence the nagging voice of his conscience by making substantial donations to one charity or another, or to a friend or family less fortunate than himself, and by so doing the weight of guilt would be lifted.

Today he was attired in a stylist "Sean J" olive green jogging suit and khaki coloured designer trainers with olive green trim and he knew he looked "criss".

Confidently, Gus strutted purposefully across the car park, just a little rhythm in his step, towards the white van bearing the legend "Born Again Church of God", parked near the entrance of the stadium. He walked pass a group of four boys with whom he slapped palms in synchronized "hi fives", and continued towards a well-built older gentleman. "Hi dad, sorry I'm a bit late," he said on approach. Cyrus was leant against the driver's door of the van as though he had just alighted from it – he smiled broadly. Gus smiled back, showing unbelievably white teeth as his face lit up. His smile accentuated his cheekbones and his eyes appeared to twinkle. "I got caught up in the traffic along the North Circular," he continued.

With a look of "I've heard it all before" on his face, Cyrus stared directly into Gus' eyes as he grabbed him by the arm and pulled the younger man toward him, engaging him in a manly hug. "You sure you didn't just leave late - you forget that is me you talking to?" Cyrus lilted in his pronounced Jamaican accent, as he gave Gus a manly pat on the back, oblivious to the fact that his words had hit a sore point.

"Good to see you, son" he continued.

"Yeah – good to see you too, dad - I haven't seen you all week, Gus reciprocated as he smiled in spite of the way he was feeling.

Then they both stood back staring fondly at each other for a beat as any favoured father and son would - there was no mistaking that they were glad to see each other.

Most of the kids that they coached together were from the Young and Strong Youth Club run by the Born Again Church of God, although a few of them were friends of the members of that Project. Every Wednesday Cyrus collected the youngsters at the church and brought them to the stadium in the church van. He was always on time which to Gus seemed like a miracle in itself. And today was no exception - Gus knew that although he appeared to have just arrived, Cyrus would have been waiting for him for at least 45 minutes as they were scheduled to begin at 5.30 pm, and it was now 6.15 pm.

Gus started to strut in the direction of the stadium entrance and Cyrus followed, lagging a little way behind. "Okay, let's get this show on the road," Gus announced enthusiastically as some youths who had stood outside the stadium quickened their pace to keep up with him.

When Gus entered the gym, the other youngsters were already kitted out and had begun to warm up in a haphazard fashion. They stopped to acknowledge him as he walked into the gym. Hi Gus, a short stocky smiling teenage boy called out to him, followed by a chorus of "hi Gus" as the others – a group of about 10 youngsters also acknowledged his arrival. They all came toward him as he approached nearer to them, thronging him as though he were some sort of superstar.

And Gus responded, "Hi, Marlon, Keshia, Jay, Paul, Michael, aah, Derek, Ray, Judah, Leon, Sandra, Donna, aah ... Sorry, sorry, what's your name again – don't tell me – Gaye... ahm, Shaun – is Shaun here?" Gus paused his roll call. "No, he didn't come today," replied a tall fresh faced boy of around 14. Oh, hi Martin - Hi all", Gus said ending his roll call. "Haven't you forgotten something", a loud voice shouted from his right.

"Oh, of course Melissa, sorry, I didn't forget you, I didn't see you over there - hi". Melissa was not best pleased to have been overlooked by Gus on whom she had a huge crush and she began to sulk, pushing out her bottom lip in a babyish fashion. It had not escaped Gus' notice that Melissa had a crush on him, but this did not stir him in any way despite her evident beauty for he viewed Melissa and all teenagers as children to be protected and not exploited.

Ignoring Melissa's vexation, Gus proceeded to remove his jacket, called the youngsters together and began the warm-up proper. As he started the group jogging on the spot, he noticed that Melissa was not joining in. "Can everyone please join in – it's very important that you are properly warmed up before you begin to train as you don't want to get sore or torn muscles," he stressed.

Melissa hung her head and proceeded to *"cut her eyes (daggers)"* at everyone and no-one in particular, ignoring Gus. Gus continued with the exercises, warming up the arms and legs and then going on to the stretching exercises. He glanced over to where Melissa had been, only to see that she had gone to sit on the floor in a corner with her thumb in her mouth, looking like a disturbed teenager behaving like a baby. She continued to ignore Gus and the rest of the group, seemingly disinterested in what was taking place around her.

After a few moments Gus glanced over his right shoulder again, and decided he'd better find out what was troubling Melissa. "Go back to jogging on the spot," he directed the others, and went over to her. "Melissa, why aren't you joining in the warm-up? Did you come here just to sit there?"

Melissa scowled, hissed with her teeth shook her body and turned her back to him.

Just then Cyrus entered the gym, having returned to the van to fetch his stop watch. "Why you kissing you teet at Gus like that Melissa?" "What's wrong with you?" he asked in a gentle but firm tone. Melissa proceeded to hang her head down and then promptly burst into tears. Gus asked her what the matter was but this only caused her to sob even louder, get to her feet and walk out of the gym.

"You carry on with the warm-up I'll go an' talk to her," volunteered Cyrus.

Gus shook his head from side to side and turned his attention back to the rest of the group to complete the warming up.

Following the warm-up Gus took the team outside. It was a bright Spring evening, but a bitingly cold breeze was blowing. He directed them to jog one lap of the track, or as much as their abilities would allow them.

Gus then returned to the gym where Cyrus was now helping Melissa to warm up. He didn't know what Cyrus had said to her, but Melissa came over and apologised to him and then went straight back to warming up with enthusiasm.

Gus and Cyrus turned aside for a moment to discuss the evening's game plan, "I'm going to concentrate on Martin and Donna for the first part of tonight," Gus said, pausing for any response from Cyrus, but on receiving none, he continued. "I want them to develop their 100 metres sprint - I think they have shown real potential". "You can perhaps concentrate on Melissa and Jay in the triple jump. Later, we can concentrate on Michael, Marlon and Judah on the high jump and Paul on the long jump, time permitting. What do you think?" Cyrus nodded his approval, "Yeah, yeah, sounds good to me".

"The others can just practice what they want to tonight and we can check on them to see how they're getting on from time to time, Okay?" Cyrus nodded. "See you outside," Gus said as he started to exit the gym.

Gus was very excited about both Martin and Donna, who had shown real potential in the 100 metres. He wanted to push them a little to help them to develop. He had plans to work towards entering them for the junior trials coming up in August and hopefully they could go on to acquire semi-professional status with the Leighton Green Athletics Club. Gus even thought of managing them himself, if they developed as he hoped.

Jay, Michael, Marlon, Judah and Paul also showed promise in the field events. Melissa didn't show any real potential but she was extremely attention seeking and demanding, and would not have been happy to be left to train on her own, so Gus had included her in the "elite" group purely for the sake of a quiet life. Of all the youngsters Melissa was the one that Gus disliked working with the most. He didn't dislike her it was just that her antics were sometimes extremely disruptive for the group as a whole.

One other youngster, Shaun, was the most talented of all – a gifted natural all round athlete, but with little or no enthusiasm for the sport. Gus had initially been very excited about him. However, he didn't show up very often for training - usually no more than once a month, and had a bad attitude, acting for the most part as though the world was indebted to him big time. Both Gus and Cyrus had tried to encourage him, but to no avail and they did not have the luxury of time or the resources to spoon-feed one individual who could care less, when there were others who were hungry to succeed, and willing to put in the necessary effort to ensure that they did so.

A few of the youngsters showed no flare at all for athletics and Gus hoped they didn't feel left out, but both he and Cyrus knew it was important to concentrate more on those with real potential, who could realistically have a future in sports, although the door was left open for all the kids attending the Young and Strong Youth Club to come along to the training sessions. Most of the youths seemed to enjoy attending the sessions and those who were less talented seemed to look forward to them just as much as the others. It was an opportunity for them to hang out – to interact with their friends. And Gus and Cyrus wanted to encourage their continued attendance, because it meant that they were off the streets and in a safe environment. On cold evenings such as this one, those less serious athletes invariably drifted back into the gym, where they chatted or played badminton or table tennis – others brought playing cards and dominoes. Gus had had occasion to talk to them some weeks earlier when he found out that they were playing for small sums of money. And both he and Cyrus kept an eye open to ensure that this did not happen again. Gus didn't really worry too much about this as the sums involved were de minis, but Cyrus felt strongly that the youngsters shouldn't be gambling even for insignificant sums of money, and he often stressed this to them, without any further proof that they were in fact doing so. On the whole though they tried to demonstrate trust in those who wished to stay indoors and appreciated that they were mostly good kids, Sandra and Derek who were 14 and 15 respectively being very responsible overseers.

It was difficult to create the correct balance between concentrating on those with potential and not making those less gifted develop any sort of inferiority complex. Both Gus and Cyrus knew how important it was to encourage the youngsters to explore their strengths and develop them, and acknowledge their weaknesses without conceding failure. Gus was aware that Cyrus had gone some way towards achieving this by having weekly discussions with the group, where he tried to address their insecurities and to instil into them a positive mental attitude and more self worth. Such verbal mentoring was given by Cyrus before Gus arrived at each session as he was invariably at least 10 minutes late. Cyrus had informed Gus that it was at the Friday Club meetings, held at the church each week, where such values were properly taught and he had been trying to get Gus to attend for some time. Cyrus had also intimated to Gus in passing that he would be obliged if he could arrange for some of his contacts (high profile personalities), to come along occasionally and mentor the youngsters at special events that he intended to organise in future.

It took longer than usual for Gus to call the team together at the end of the session, a good sign that the youngsters were enjoying what they were doing. He was positive that something had really been accomplished tonight. Both Martin and Donna had improved on their personal best times – Martin shaved half a second off his personal best while Donna was 0.10 of a second faster than ever before - an excellent outcome.

"Well done everyone. You worked really hard tonight we are proud of you", Gus said wiping his brow.

"Ummhum", Cyrus grunted his approval as he nodded heartily.

Gus then led the group into a series of cool down exercises, before asking, "Before we call it a day, does anyone have any comments to make about tonight or generally?" Gus said, throwing the floor open.

Martin, a lanky 14 year old, put up his hand as though he was reluctant to do so, and asked "Can I speak to you before you go Gus – it's a bit personal really".

As no-one else indicated a desire to speak, Gus said "Okay, please all go and change. Then he walked towards Martin, but then he paused, "Oh, wait a minute," Gus said, lifting his outstretched hand with his palm open towards Martin as he spoke. Looking across the gym Gus called out to another youngster, "Donna, can I have a quick word with you as well, please". He had been meaning to speak to both Donna and Martin for some weeks. Donna walked quickly over to them.

"I've been meaning to speak to both of you," Gus announced

as Martin and Donna stared expectantly. "I think you both realise that you've shown real potential, and if you are to develop further, you will need to put in some more time and effort. I am willing to put in a bit of extra time with you two if you are serious about developing," Gus stressed before continuing. "We could meet either on a Saturday or Sunday, or some early evenings - Monday evenings might be good for me". "How do you feel about that," Gus paused for a beat then continued without receiving an answer, "maybe you want to think about it, discuss it with your parents – whatever - and let me know as soon as possible – next week – okay?". Both Donna and Martin nodded, "K".

As Donna headed towards the changing rooms, Martin beckoned Gus to an isolated corner of the gym, away from the other boys who were changing back into their clothes in the gym. Gus followed and listened, curious to know what it might be all about, "I know I did good today al'ight, but I know I can do better - much better - if only I had better sports shoes," Martin paused before continuing, "Don't think I'm trying to distress you or anything al'ight, but … I…I…I… wonder whether you have any old sports shoes that you don't want anymore, or something, instead of throwing them away, you could give them to me, Gus". "The one I have isn't very good and won't last much longer, al'ight, and I am serious about getting to be better at my running and so I know I will need good shoes for that - you know that". "I would ask my mother but she can't afford it". "I know she can't". "It's only her alone", Martin leant his head sideways in a "bad bwoy" stance as he spoke. However, Gus knew this kid was not a "bad bwoy" – just fronting. There was something about him that told Gus that this young man would do something with his life, given the right chance. Yes, he had potential and some talent, but Martin had more – much more than that. He exhibited a "can do" attitude which propelled him to achieve far more than others with much more natural ability than himself and there was something else about Martin that Gus could not analyse – but he knew it was a very special quality.

Gus could see it was difficult for Martin to have this conversation. He did not wish to prolong his discomfort and so he responded without hesitation. "Okay, what size do you take?"

"Size eleven," Martin replied.

"I take a size 13 so my shoes won't fit your feet," Gus said smiling. Martin appeared to breathe out heavily, as though relieved by Gus' congenial response. He was thoughtful for a beat, then responded, "Size 13 is okay, even if I have to stuff them, man, it doesn't matter, man, I will make them fit – anyway my feet are growing more every day," Martin gesticulated mildly with his right hand, as he spoke, as though he was moving to music.

Martin reminded Gus so much of himself at that age and this moved Gus somewhere deep inside. "Where do you live?" Gus asked.

"Wash House Estate in Hackney," Martin shrugged in his bad bwoy style. He wanted to ask Gus why but didn't wish to sound rude and so said nothing further.

"Really - I used to live there – what house?" Gus answered incredulously.

"Meeson House," Martin replied equally amazed. He couldn't believe that his idol used to live on the same Council estate as him.

"I used to live at number 20 Leeson House, just around the corner, you know the block facing the park on Havers Street," Gus had the feeling that he and Martin had something in common and now he knew why, he was talking to his homeboy. "What number Meeson House do you live at," his smile remained fixed.

"Number 7," Martin smiled back, but not too widely – he didn't want to cramp his cool or to betray that he was almost wetting himself with excitement. This was his hero and he used to live on Wash House Estate, he thought, excitement threatening to gush out of him.

"My mate Brian used to live at number 9," Gus reminisced, "I used to be always over his house". "He moved away about 9-10 years ago". "I might know your family, what's your surname again", Gus babbled in an excited way.

"Selhurst – my mum is Dionne Brown," Martin replied, warming to the older male.

"Dionne, Dionne, Dionne Brown," Gus searched his mind to remember. "I don't recall the name, but I may know her by sight –

small world, ain't, it?" Gus decided he would give the name further thought later.

"But we just moved there in 2003 - February 2003," Martin continued. "We used to live at number 2 Sinclair House before," he added.

"Yes, I know Sinclair House, at the top of Havers Street, ain't it", Gus cast his mind back in time. "I can drop you off on my way home if you like," Gus said, almost instantly regretting having made the offer. As soon as the words left his mouth he remembered that he hated going to those areas at night as some of the worst characters came out to roam the streets after dark. "Yeah, al'ight," was the inevitable reply from Martin.

"Okay, go and change and let's go and say goodbye to the others," Gus said, biting the bullet. He walked across the gym to talk to Cyrus and Martin headed back to his jeans and sweater that were piled in a corner of the gym. In two minutes he had changed.

After informing Cyrus he was giving Martin a lift home and saying goodbye to the team, Gus beckoned to Martin that he was ready to leave. Gus could hear Melissa complaining to Keshia as he walked away, "It's not fair, why does Martin get to go with Gus - I want to go with Gus". Gus thought it best to ignore her and walked on. Martin followed struggling to walk in his jeans which swagged down towards his knees. And as often as he pulled up the offending garment it quickly swagged downwards again. Gus glanced back, tempted to ask the youngster to hold up his pants but resisting the urge.

Cyrus shouted after Gus that he had forgotten to talk to him about something important but that he would telephone him later, and added, "Martin, pull up you pants no? A wry smile crossed Gus' face as he wondered why he was never so bold.

On the way home Gus stopped off at a late night shopping city in Bywater Hill. He took Martin inside and purchased a pair of top of the range training shoes for him in size 12, much to the youngster's disbelief. Martin thanked Gus profusely as his benefactor played down the benevolent gesture, assuring him that it was no big deal. Gus also purchased some jeans for himself and when he saw Martin eyeing a pair of designers he asked him whether he would like a pair. "You think I'm a charity case, don't you?" Martin retorted unexpectedly.

Gus had taken a liking to Martin and his generous nature had gotten the better of him. He was taken aback by Martin's response, but with hindsight it suddenly dawned on him that he should have realised that Martin was a proud young man who would react in that way since he hardly knew him.

Gus apologised, and hastily tried to reassure Martin that he didn't mean anything at all by his offer. "No, not at all – I just..... I'm sorry, I didn't mean to insult you".

But Martin cut in before he could finish speaking, "Look, I'm really grateful for the trainers al'ight, but don't gwane like I was begging you for no jeans", Martin said, heading towards the exit in a huff, his undergarments exposed to all behind him. Gus followed quickly after him, "Look, I'm sorry - really, I didn't mean to offend you, okay," he said sincerely. "I'll take you home now". They reached the car and Gus got in on the driver's side.

When Martin was seated Gus started the engine and set the car in motion. Silence pervaded the atmosphere inside the vehicle for the first few minutes, Martin did not speak and Gus did not know what might be the right thing to say. As Gus turned on the music player on low volume, Martin mumbled under his breath. "Sorry, al'ight, I know you didn't mean nofink, I just kinda overreacted, you nuh." He looked down at his hands as he spoke, hoping he hadn't hurt Gus' feelings.

"Oh, don't worry about it," Gus responded, detecting the sincerity in the youngster's voice. "I just thought you needed a pair of jeans that fit your waist, that's all," Gus said smiling again, injecting some humour into the situation.

"How d'you mean," Martin smiled back, warming to Gus.

"Oh, the one you wearing appears to be falling down to you knees," Gus' smile widened.

"Oh no that's dark man," Martin said feigning embarrassment by placing his hands over his eyes. "That's style, bruv – don't you know style?" he continued with a synchronised move of his right hand and his head.

"You sure it's style?" Gus teased in a dubious Jamaica accent.

"A little birdie told me it's not really your style, you kno," Gus continued, his smile broadening to almost a grin.

"How you mean not my style – it's everybody's style," said Martin, as he stared at Gus curiously.

"Not everybody's style - it's not my style," Gus became more serious.

"Yeah, that's cause you is a ol' man ain't it?" Martin replied cheekily - now it was his turn to smile. Suddenly Gus' smile turned into the widest grin and he chuckled, enjoying this game they were playing, "I'm not old – I'm only 31 – that's not old".

"31 – that's old, man – that's oooolldd – real old. You're older than I thought. I thought you were only 25," Martin was now more relaxed with Gus.

"How old are you?" Gus asked.

"Fourteen. I'm going to be fifteen in September," Martin replied proudly.

"Well, even if I was your age, I wouldn't wear my pants like that, and you know why, because that is prison style. In prison that's how they wear their trousers down to the knees because their belts are confiscated to prevent them using them as weapons or self-harming. But you youngsters tek it mek fashion", Gus' speech alternated between a London accent and a slightly "iffy" Jamaican twang.

The fact was that Gus did not like to see the kids who wore their trousers hung down almost to their knees, in ignorance of its true significance. He hoped that this conversation would at least get Martin thinking, and was prepared for him to fire the usual questions – how did he know that – who told him so – how did he know it was true. But Martin just became pensive for a beat then quickly changed the subject to talk about the "Shaggy" track that was throbbing through the speakers on a low volume. Gus wondered what Martin was really thinking as he turned up the volume.

Gus finally arrived at the Wash House Estate at 9.50 pm. "Okay, young man, I'll see you next week", Gus said goodbye to Martin as he got out of the car, all the while keeping a watchful eye. Martin leaned back into the car and touched fists with Gus – "See you al'ight and thanks again".

"Don't forget to tell you mother about the extra training," Gus reminded him, "and take my number in case she wants to talk to me about that and to confirm that I bought the trainers for you", he said passing a card to the youngster. "Oh, and I forgot to give my number to Donna - if you see her would you please give it to her", Gus said as Martin placed the card into his back pocket.

"Okay – I'll give it to her tomorrow, I usually see her on the way to school". "We get the same bus," Martin said then he swaggered off into Meeson House and Gus was pleased to note that he was holding up his jeans from falling down.

Martin climbed the stairs to the second floor in record time, and waved goodbye to Gus over the balcony. Gus waited a little while to see that he got inside his front door safely. As he heard the barely audible sound of the door slamming - his cue, he put his car into gear, reversed hurriedly and turned around. As he drove through the neighbourhood, realisation dawned that it had gotten even worse than last time he was there at night. The stench of drugs permeated the open air and the usual dubious looking characters hung about in dark corners. Gus drove out of the estate as quickly as possible. Soon his mind would be on other things - a long hot bath for one thing, and putting his feet up for another. But right at this moment, Gus thought only of flooring the accelerator and creating some distance between himself and Wash House Estate.

CHAPTER 2

Father Takes the Wheel

Gus' love for his father, Cyrus, was resolute and strong and conversely Cyrus loved Gus with all his heart and some more. Such love was evident to observers when they met, hugged and smiled at one another and those around them immediately knew that they were an affectionate father and son.

A 6' 2" bear of a man with a well structured frame, Cyrus had appeared something of a giant to Gus when he was a boy, but he now towered above the older man by a full two inches. At 51 Cyrus retained his handsome features despite the jowls that should distort them. He remained the proud owner of a full head of hair, and although his crowning glory was now fully sprinkled with grey, he still managed to look 10 years younger. Only his salt and pepper hair, greying temples and slightly rounded belly belied the extent of his seniority.

Cyrus was to be credited with much, if not most of Gus' success. It was Cyrus who had encouraged his initial interest in football, identifying his potential at the age of 11; had given him the grounding and grooming necessary to become a top player; had pushed him to train hard, even when he did not want to and would have preferred to hang out with his mates; had set up trials for him with some of the smaller Clubs, in the hope that they would take him on as part of their junior team; had persevered even when most of them had shown little or no interest; had been as relentless as a rottweiler, setting up trial after trial after trial, until finally Walmouth Town Football Club had signed Gus up as an apprentice.

It was Cyrus who had brokered that very first deal – a 1-year apprenticeship at 17, followed by a 3-year contract which paid Gus £200 a week, but with the team's success, having renegotiated his contract, his salary rose to over £800 per week when his contract came to an end.

Gus gained invaluable experience at Walmouth Town, going

on to become their top striker and goal scorer and contributing significantly towards their rise to the top of the third division league table, their subsequent promotion to the second division, and the team's rapid rise to the top of that league table also.

And when the 4-year stint had ended, Cyrus had wisely advised Gus not to sign the new deal put on the table by Walmouth Town, in spite of the fact that they were offering to more than double his salary. Cyrus felt that Gus' abilities had outgrown Walmouth Town, that it would be better for him to move to one of the bigger Premiership Clubs who had shown an interest in him, although Gus had been perfectly happy to remain where he was. It was Cyrus that had drummed up interest and courted the Premier leagues' appropriate personnel, later ensuring that Gus received the proper professional and legal advice.

Cyrus's hunch had paid off, and to Gus' amazement (but not to his father's surprise), he was snapped up by Dowchester City Football Club, following fierce competition from another rival Premiership side. Dowchester were at the bottom of the first division and had given Gus a 3-year deal at a starting salary that was more than double what Walmouth Town had offered and plenty of promotion prospects and perks. Of course Gus was sad to leave Walmouth Town as he had made many friends there and at first felt as though he was letting the club down, but Cyrus had reassured him that it was the right thing to do as a footballer's career was relatively short. Cyrus had also pointed out to Gus that he had neglected his education in order to pursue football, and had to look ahead with a view to securing his future. Grimly he'd stressed that Gus' career could even end early due to injury, and that it was prudent to earn as much as possible while he was able.

Those had turned out to be prophetic words, when Gus was forced to retire at 26 due to injury. He was at his peak and felt he could have gone on to play top level football for at least another 10 years or so.

However, Gus had been shrewd, under the watchful eyes of his father, and had invested his earnings from football and sponsorship deals well. And on his forced retirement his future loss of earnings had not caused much concern. But Gus' loss of status as a professional player had almost devastated him. With Cyrus' encouragement Gus had signed up with an agent, who had secured bookings for him as a guest commentator for television coverage of matches. This had boosted his moral and those earnings had provided further security for his future.

When the bookings had gradually dwindled away, Gus found himself wondering how he would be able to fill the huge void that was left. So his father had suggested that he go back to studying, and following a 2-year course, completed favourably, Gus had gone on to secure his current position training athletes at the Leighton Green Stadium. Some of the athletes were professionals while others were semi-pro. He took training sessions twice a week – Tuesdays and Thursdays – more often before major competitions.

Cyrus had always been there for Gus when he needed him, to guide him in making difficult decisions and had been the font of wisdom and knowledge that Gus could always tap into. Gus knew that he owed the life he now enjoyed largely to his father, but try as he did on many occasions to demonstrate his gratitude, Cyrus would have none of it. He refused to accept even a penny from Gus and also declined to accept any extravagant gifts – save for at birthdays or Christmas. Gus learned from Cyrus' that his contentment was derived from living a simple and uncomplicated life - happy with a roof over his head, food on his table, decent clothes on his back and a decent car that got him from "A" to "B". He valued the love of good friends, good health and most importantly, his faith, more than monetary wealth or possessions.

Faith meant more than anything to Cyrus, who would often testify to Gus of his trust in God's grace. He fully maintained that God's favour was the source of the serenity of mind and stability in his life. And Gus had come to accept that Cyrus was indeed "over-shadowed by the grace and favour of the Almighty", for many years previously his father's building business had gone into liquidation, due to a lack of contracts. With the collapse of the business Cyrus had found himself on the verge of bankruptcy, yet he had always kept a smiling countenance. And Cyrus maintained that it was God's hand that had upheld his goings and guided him away from the precipice of personal insolvency. Gus recalled that

Cyrus had secured a job as a railway station attendant, a lowly position, but one which he had accepted gratefully. And instead of wallowing in self-pity over the lost of his business as most men would have done, Cyrus had kept his joy.

Sports had always been his father's first love and soon after losing his business, Cyrus had followed his own earlier advice to his son and taken up a part-time study course, going on to obtain several diplomas. And when he was made redundant from the railways, it was such qualifications that had impressed the stadium bosses, upon Gus' recommendation, to offer Cyrus his current job as a part-time physiotherapist/trainer at Leighton Green - a job which he loved a lot. But what had been most impressive to the stadium bosses when they interviewed Cyrus, were not his qualifications, but his evident life experience, both in terms of the fact that he'd been training all his life (going to the gym at least 4 or 5 times a week since his teens), and his adeptness in dealing with people. The stadium bosses had never regretted their choice, for Cyrus had proved to be an invaluable member of staff, demonstrating a wealth of wisdom and a way of interacting with the young athletes that seemed to motivate them beyond their abilities or expectations.

The one thing that had made Gus unhappy about his father though was the fact that he continually refused his offer of financial assistance. Gus had sought every opportunity to give Cyrus money, having intensified his efforts when the elder gentleman lost his job at the railways, but Cyrus flatly refused all offered donations, saying that he had all that he needed. It was upsetting to Gus at first that he was unable to give to the one person that meant the world to him, but he had now reluctantly accepted the situation. He had given up offering Cyrus money, yet he watched keenly for any sign that his dad was in any way impoverished. Through such observations Gus became aware of Cyrus' miraculous financial blessings, resulting in his having paid off his mortgage. Cyrus now lived a debt-free and comfortable life, having received a few unexpected windfalls – firstly an unprecedented generous redundancy payout from the railway company and secondly an unexpected bequest from an unlikely source. In addition, Cyrus had received a payout from a pension scheme into which he had paid from his early twenties, had ceased paying in his 30s and forgotten about, which had become payable shortly after his 50th birthday. So Gus no longer worried about Cyrus' financial wellbeing, but tried to splash out on gifts at birthdays and Christmases. The only money that Cyrus would accept from Gus was donations towards his various church funds.

It appeared to Gus that Cyrus' philosophy, "what you give comes back to you", and his life pattern of giving generously to those less fortunate than himself - supporting charities and local community projects, did in fact pay dividends. Cyrus gave not only in financial terms but also of himself – of his time and energy and Gus had come to emulate his father. Over the years he had subconsciously (and lately knowingly) adopted his mentor's attitude, giving generously to worthy causes without reservation. And seeing his own success Gus considered that Cyrus' philosophy was true, the measure in which you gave was measured back to you.

Cyrus' altruistic nature had led him to begin a youth club for the young people in his community at his church and six months ago he had also began a training session at the stadium and had brought Gus on board with that project, getting him involved with coaching the young people from the Youth Club at the stadium. They did this together each Wednesday evening and Gus paid the stadium hire fee, which was at a special reduced employee rate. He felt good about this - it was his way of making a positive contribution to the community and he hoped to improve the future prospects of the young club members in some similar way as Cyrus had influenced his development.

All in all Cyrus was a fine father figure, the best example for Gus to have fashioned his own life after. And Gus was aware that Cyrus had pride of place in the hearts of many others who had also grown to love him dearly, because of his generous and affable nature - but no one loved his father more than Gus.

CHAPTER 3

Diversions and Bad Pennies

Although Gus had met thousands of the world's most beautiful women, he had yet to meet that special one to share his life with and he longed for the day when he could finally settle down and start a family of his own. What hampered him most in his quest was his shyness. He had struggled with that handicap throughout his adolescent years and his early twenties, when all the women he dated were the ones bold enough to make all the moves. Unfortunately for Gus, such feisty ones invariably turned out to be just out for a good time and were not interested in sticking around for the long haul, not that they were his type anyway.

For the main part his love life had so far been beleaguered with failure and loss. However, such losses had so far been largely inconsequential and could be likened to bad pennies falling through a large hole in one's trouser pocket. None had such endearing qualities that were missed for very long.

And on 22 March 2010 as he sat deep in thought, his cup of coffee growing lukewarm, he wondered when his day would come. Philandering did not come naturally to him and he was finding it increasingly unfulfilling maintaining merely physical relationships. Although he was not particularly religious, he found that his soul was becoming more burdened by guilt with each illicit liaison. Lately his mother's face had begun appearing in his mind's eye, and thoughts of his Sunday School days and the voice of old Pastor Wright would ring resoundingly in his ear. "Thou shall not commit adultery or fornication .....". Gus recalled how the Pastor would stress the commandment before proceeding to reel off a daunting list of consequences for default, the worse of which was the dreaded wrath of God. He could not understand how other guys enjoyed casual relationships, often juggling several women at a time. Gus found such arrangements unfulfilling and endured them as it was apparently the norm these days, believing he must be seen to behave like other unmarried guys his age. He did not wish to look out of place while he waited and longed for that special lady to come along.

There had been some ladies that Gus didn't fancy at all who had proclaimed undying love for him and overstayed their welcome in his life. But so far the women he liked had either been unable or unwilling to share his enthusiasm at becoming more serious.

Gus and Maureen Strong had been somewhat an item for the past three years. His relationship with her was one which, at the start, Gus had wanted to take to the next level, and had even contemplated marriage. However, Maureen had not shared his vision and consequently the liaison that was hugely promising at its inception had depreciated to a few dates per year which ran overnight or for a day or two or three, depending on how much time Maureen could spare.

A successful Supermodel, Maureen was a strikingly beautiful 6'1" tall (without heels) statuesque woman, with razor sharp cheek bones that cut along her profile in a straight line from an inch above full luscious lips, into her hairline, just above exquisitely delicate customarily bejewelled ear lobes. Her cheeks were partly symmetrical to her unbelievably beautiful slanted eyes. Her nose resembled a perfectly shaped button. The composition of her face could be likened to that of an ancient Ashanti/Egyptian goddess, but far more exotic and rare. Her body easily resembled a work of art of perfect proportions with smooth even luminescent skin the colour of burnt sugar covering her form from head to toe.

Maureen's amazing features and form provoked far more interest than could possibly be appreciated, from those who on seeing her for the first time stared, spellbound, as though trying to analyse the molecular formation of her genes. And many of the male specie, when in her presence, could often be observed gaping, transfixed by the beauty of her well sculpted face and body.

When she was a small girl, Maureen learned that her Great Grandmother on her mother's side was of mixed heritage - her Great Great Grandfather was pure African from the Ashanti tribe, and her Great Great Grandmother an Arawak (one of the indigenous peoples of Jamaica). Her father also relayed to her stories told to him by his own parents, of his Great Great Grandmother, Bole, who had been an Ibo princess stolen from Nigeria - so incredibly beautiful was she that on arrival from Africa she had been bought by a wealthy and prominent Portuguese gentleman, a widower, for a handsome price, who instead of treating her like a slave, had installed her into his own house as his mother's maid. And tongues began to wag in the small mid-American town where Mr Mendoza lived with his mother and their house maid, when Bole had given birth to a bright coloured baby. Speculation and rumours that Mr Mendoza had fathered Bole's baby became unbearable and when the townsfolk ostracised the family, they had sold up lock, stock and barrel and sailed off to Jamaica, taking Bole and her baby with them. There they became Mr and Mrs Mendoza and they had lived happily together, Bole having given birth to a further four children.

Maureen was unable to account for the other constituents of her genes, but she was aware that the combination added up to incredible beauty – in herself as well as her siblings, beauty that had paved her path through life – opening all the right doors in her career. And not only was she beautiful but she was highly intelligent too, having attained a first class degree in law, in which she intended to practise when her supermodel days were at an end.

Gus was smitten from the first day they met at a media party, and from the start of their friendship made it a priority to spend time with Maureen, making sacrifices where necessary. So awe struck was he that, for the first time in his life, he conceded that he was in love. However it was not long before such amour was dampened by Maureen's obvious message that her career was paramount, and everything else a poor second. Initially reluctant to accept that rule, Gus had tried to change Maureen but over time he came to accept her relentless terms, slotting into her life as and when she could fit him in, which added up to not very often.

When they first met Gus would travel abroad to meet up with Maureen on location wherever she was working. He had done so six times in the first year. However, he found that Maureen was always too busy working, leaving not much time to spend with him, resulting in his being left alone to amuse himself. So in the second year he was less inclined to travel out to visit Maureen, such escapades reserved for only twice in that year. And in the past year they had only met up 4 times, once when he had travelled to meet Maureen in New York and the other occasions when Maureen was travelling through London. In the early days, they would speak on the telephone about 4 times a week but this had become less necessary, dwindling down to 4 times a month or so.

As he made a fresh cup of coffee Gus continued to contemplate the history of his relationship with Maureen.

Resentment began to take a grip as it became more and more apparent that Maureen obviously craved his company less than he did hers. He desired quiet intimate dinners and the like when they could spend quality time together while she invariably preferred to attend industry parties where she could be seen - maintaining contacts was all important to Maureen. Initially offended by such nonchalance, Gus had become conditioned by the loose arrangement and as his interest dwindled, had come to appreciate it. The ever-increasing distance between them caused him to realise that he'd never really been in love but merely infatuated. Admittedly he was still very fond of her - which sane red-blooded male wouldn't be, but marriage was out of the question now. There was no doubt that Maureen was as sweet as honey and just as beautiful, but Gus could never settle down with her for he would never be able to trust her. He was certain that he wasn't her only arrangement – and he himself had not excluded other romantic liaisons. Gus was under no delusions - he imagined that Maureen could have almost any man she wanted and, like himself, must need some tender loving care when he wasn't around.

Apart from Maureen, Gus had been seeing two other females in recent months, the first being Kelly Braithwaite – a 31 year old Amazon woman. Though not classically beautiful, Kelly was very attractive with large lash fringed eyes and evenly proportioned lips. Her complexion was that of golden autumn leafs. Weighing over 17 stone, Kelly stood 5' 10" with an immaculate hour glass figure of gigantic proportions. So striking was her form that she caused heads to turn wherever she went. Whenever she passed by men's mouths would involuntarily drop open. And Kelly had a most peculiar effect on men in the company of their wives or girlfriends, who more often than not became noticeably hot and flustered. She was used to wives or girlfriends steering their men away from her, quickly out of danger. The feature that caused the most commotion was Kelly's "10-ton bottom", as sung about by an up-and-coming Jamaican rapper – an ex-boyfriend of hers. Kelly's rear was famous in its own right - surprisingly high and well-defined, telling of her African ancestry, it curved in all the right places and danced to an invisible tune of its own will as she walked. Kelly's clever rear was talked about by many a man far and wide, and she was notably referred to in another of her ex-boyfriend's lyrics as the original "body beautiful". And Gus, like any other red blooded male was smitten by Kelly's assets.

Born in London of Dominican parentage, Kelly, like Gus had grown up on the Wash House Estate, both attending the same secondary school - St Peter's, and had met up again by chance 9 months ago while out shopping. On meeting up, they recognised each other straight away and even though they had not been close friends at school, exchanged numbers and kept in touch, meeting up on a number of occasions to reminisce.

On their first date Gus was not only smitten by Kelly's ample charms, but he also found that he was drawn to her magnetic personality, for she was as bubbly and charismatic as she was large and curvaceous.

After that first date, they had met up a few more times, always as friends and always getting closer and it had become obvious to them both that there was chemistry coming into play. Deciding he would like to take their friendship to another level, Gus had bared his soul about Maureen and his romantic status, intending to break up with Maureen and ask Kelly to become his girlfriend. Kelly too had bared her soul, confessing that she was "ever so slightly" married with two children, although she assured Gus that she didn't wish to be and was in the process of separating from her husband.

"Well that's alright then", a little voice in Gus' mind had quipped sarcastically as he stared at Kelly in disbelief.

When Gus returned to his senses, he decided it was time to apply the brakes. However, Kelly refused to slow down, and nudged the lever up a gear, simultaneously hitting the accelerator pedal. And Gus had to use all the strength he could muster to slow down Kelly's advances.

They met up just once more after that – just as friends – Gus made that very clear although Kelly appeared to have other ideas. For Gus, the purpose of their meeting was to say goodbye. On that last occasion he encouraged Kelly to talk about her husband, whom he learned was called Kwaku, in the hope of encouraging her to give her marriage another try. He learned that Kwaku was an old-fashioned African man who insisted that Kelly stay home and mind the children while he go out and "club the bacon". Gus surmised that Kelly was a reluctant housewife with twin daughters who was simply bored with the routine of marriage. So he tried to encourage her to spice it up. However, Kelly wasn't listening – she remonstrated and demonstrated, by tactile means, her willingness to forsake her connubial status for good. Gus, being too long without female companionship, was momentarily distracted by Kelly's forthrightness, but on cue old Pastor Wright's voice from the past had resounded in his mind's ear, "For the lips of a strange woman drop as an honeycomb, and her mouth is smoother than oil", just as Kelly made a revelation that Kwaku was the jealous type who had once almost maimed another man with his Kung fu skills for just looking in her direction, saving Gus from certain downfall. So, bringing a swift end to their last date Gus had spelt out to Kelly that their brief friendship had to come to an end. He reinvented Maureen as a jealous girlfriend who suspected him of cheating and who would likely seriously damage Kelly if she found out that they had been dating. Then he had quickly left the scene of the crime, promising to keep in touch with Kelly by telephone from time to time. That was over 7 months ago, but he had never been inclined to call her – conversely he had never received a call from Kelly either.

Two weeks after his last date with Kelly, Gus met Tricia Syrenson, a 25 year old hottie. Tricia was 5' 7" tall with a slim, if regular figure and an ordinarily pretty face. Tricia did not possess the beauty of Maureen or the charisma of Kelly, but she did have something though – oodles of sex appeal and an animal magnetism that Gus and apparently other men found irresistible.

They had met at a party held by one of Gus' colleagues from the stadium. Brian, Gus' colleague and the party host, had introduced them, and at first Gus thought Tricia might be a really nice person. What Brian didn't tell Gus was that he and Tricia had once been an item, but that she had played around on him, finally leaving him for someone richer.

Tricia stuck close to Gus that first evening and they exchanged numbers at the end of the night. To his surprise, Tricia rang him the next day then every day for a week until he succumbed and agreed to take her out on a date. He took her to one of his favourite Caribbean restaurants. Fairly early on during the date, Gus realised that he did not want to see Tricia again because she was not his type – she was coming on too strong for one and Gus found pushiness grossly unattractive. But being a red blooded male, Gus was enticed nonetheless and was powerless to resist Tricia. She oozed sexuality BIG TIME, so much so that he almost broke his "no sex on the first date" rule. Even Pastor Wright's admonitions were drowned out by her siren antics – pouting, suggestively touching and other enticing invitations to treat.

So tempted was he by Tricia that at the end of the evening he promised to call her and take her out again, even though he had had no intention of doing so earlier on. But by the following day Gus had forgotten about Tricia and did not call her, finding no inclination to do so. He was also disinclined to return any of her numerous calls. But Tricia kept on calling on a daily basis, leaving message after message which Gus ignored, hoping she would get the message.

One day a week later Gus decided to answer Tricia's call. He asked her not to call him again and told her that he already had a girlfriend that he had been dating for the past 3 years. However, that did not deter Tricia, who kept on calling anyway.

Two weeks after their date a friend invited Gus to a wedding in Paris and he needed a female companion to go along with him. Most of the guys in Gus' concentric circle had girlfriends and he didn't want to be the odd one out. Although some of his mates feigned envy of his independence, Gus knew that they secretly felt sorry for him not having found that special someone. They would each be in attendance with their various wives or serious significant others and Gus did not wish to play gooseberry to any of them. Maureen couldn't make it, and of course he had no intention of asking Kelly along, and so, to save face, he decided to ask Tricia to go with him. He wrestled with his conscience which suggested that he would merely be using her, but his conscience lost out to the suggestion that she would get a free all expenses paid weekend in Paris in a 5-star hotel out of it and some other expensive gift as well.

So, when Tricia telephoned him later that day Gus answered, speaking to her for a little while before broaching the subject of the trip to Paris. Without hesitation Tricia accepted Gus' half-hearted invitation and so they ended up spending the weekend in Paris and due to Tricia forcing herself on him, they ended up sleeping together on the first night. Gus immediately regretted succumbing to his weakness - but reasoned that Paris has that sort of effect on people.

"BIG MISTAKE", Gus realised when the weekend drew to a close. He was annoyed with himself that he had ever thought of inviting Tricia in the first place - let alone sleep with her. It wasn't long before he (and all his friends) began to realise that Tricia was sooooo not the kind of girl he wanted to spend any time with at all. He learned that she was very shallow, someone he couldn't have a conversation with on anything more than a superficial level. She was nauseatingly pretentious and he could not bear her constant gossiping and "hating" on people - even those she did not know – and she gave a new meaning to the word materialistic. Not at all as clever as she obviously thought she was – he could read her like an open book and she annoyed even his least sensitive nerve endings.

Gus was tempted to cut the weekend short but decided he couldn't let his friend down and so tolerated Tricia that weekend but made up his mind that he would cut ties on returning to London. So on arrival at the airport he put Tricia into a taxi, asked her where she wanted to go, and handed her more than enough money to cover the fare, giving her what he thought would be a last goodbye kiss on her cheek. He lied that he would call, and dutifully waved her out of sight and out of his life – or so he thought. Instead of calling her Gus deleted Tricia's number from his phonebook. However, when he didn't call Tricia that evening, she rang him. Gus answered not realising who it was. He told her that he didn't want to see her again and reminded her that he already had a girlfriend of three years. He then made an excuse to cut the conversation short - after that he re-saved her number and ignored all her calls.

Around two weeks later Gus answered a call from an unknown number, thinking it might be important, only to find that it was Tricia. He spoke to her briefly, "Look Tricia, I can't do this – I told you I've got a girlfriend already – I can't do this – bye". Then he hung up.

Two days later Tricia turned up at the stadium, to see Brian. She was wearing the skimpiest of outfits, and on seeing Gus, began to behave as though they were an item - she was literally all over him. On learning that Brian was not working that day, she hung around anyway – clinging to Gus, overlooking the fact that he was trying to work. She shamelessly sat with her legs wide open, revealing inches of thigh flesh as she spoke suggestively, sending the message that she was available - a happy go lucky sort of girl just out to have a good time. Gus could do with a good time - it had been a long time since he saw Maureen, and Tricia's well-maintained body looked okay to him. With the memory of their Paris liaison still fresh in his mind, Gus struggled against the demon lust, averting his eyes and trying to ignore Tricia as she encroached into his personal space. But he was finally worn down by her sensuality and obvious availability, and allowed his baser instincts to rule his head. And ignoring the screaming of Pastor Wright's voice resonating in his mind's ear, which was drowned out by Tricia's alarming activities, Gus foolishly agreed to give her a lift somewhere when he was ready to leave. That somewhere turned out to be a hotel en route to Tricia's destination, and they ended up spending that night together.

"BAD DECISION" - thereafter Tricia started to behave as though she was his long-standing girlfriend. She would call him and when he did not pick up or return her calls within a week, would turn up at the stadium. Tricia knew how to wear Gus down and he ended up falling back into bed with her on numerous further occasions. Gus began to feel embarrassed for Tricia as well as for himself for being such a dog and unable to say no to something that was so wrong. He gave Tricia more than enough money to get a new outfit and to get her hair done after each liaison. It made him feel better - after all she wasn't getting anything else – not his time, nor his mind and certainly not his heart. Tricia gleefully accepted the money he gave her, but as time went on it became clear to Gus that she took this as a sign that their relationship was more serious than it actually was. In his mind they were not even having a relationship, and certainly didn't want to signal that to Tricia, and so he stopped giving her money.

Thereafter, Tricia began to demand money from him, saying she had to get her hair done or do her nails, or buy some new outfit - all for his pleasure. Gus was caught in a quandary - he felt guilty if he did not give Tricia money – but if he gave her money she got the wrong impression – he had tried ending their friendship on numerous occasions but she didn't seem to get the message and kept on turning up.

Tricia was becoming more and more demanding, asking Gus to spend more time with her. Gus was getting fed up of her demands. Sex was no longer just sex - no longer straight-forward for as soon as the act was over, Tricia would start to make demands on him – softly, softly – but Gus could see what she was trying to do. Tricia was trying to attach some strings, but he had no intention of letting her do that. She constantly told him she wanted to meet his family and had begun insisting that he invite her to his home.

Gus contemplated Tricia's behaviour - she clearly did not want to get the message that he wanted their arrangement to end. She was playing him, playing to win at any cost and she was after more than just his body or his mind. He already had evidence of her materialistic nature by the fact that she became so excited each time he handed her cash. She also talked constantly about money and possessions - there was no doubt that Tricia was one of the biggest gold diggers he had ever met. Yes Gus was well aware of

Tricia's scheming ways – he could read her like a book. He knew she wanted the works – his body, his mind his ring and his money - Tricia wanted his blood. She had picked up his scent like a hungry blood-hound, and was refusing to let it drop - Tricia was hunting for the kill - she was out to secure herself a bag of gold. But Gus was neither willing nor able to let her have even a piece of him.

And so Gus became more determined than ever to stop having anything to do with Tricia. Thankfully, he had never taken her to his home, although it was almost bad enough that she knew where he worked. If she didn't, he would have been able to avoid her months earlier. Gus decided that he had to be firm and control his libido if he wanted Tricia to leave him alone - urgent and drastic action was necessary. It was apparent that ignoring Tricia's calls and not bothering to call her back was not having the desired effect – she was obviously choosing to ignore the message he was sending.

So Gus planned to tell Tricia unequivocally that he did not want to see her, speak to her, give her a lift or sleep with her ever again – really spell out his meaning to her. He was no longer willing to tolerate her bulldozing her way into his bed – into his life. And he was sickened by his own actions, in allowing himself to use Tricia for sex - his conscience had borne all that it could take. The nagging thought that he wouldn't like anyone to use his sister like that, even if she served it up on a plate and refused to get the message was refusing to give his mind a break. There was no doubt that he would miss getting high on Tricia's stuff, but he had to be strong – to go cold turkey.

Thankfully the voice of the long-dead Pastor Wright resounding in his mind's ear when he was alone was threatening to drive him crazy too, so to restore his sanity he had no choice but to end it (whatever "it" was) with Tricia once and for all.

Back in the present, Gus' mind strayed briefly as he realised he needed to make himself another fresh cup of coffee. Then he continued to ponder.

On 14 February Gus rang Tricia to tell her it was over – that he did not wish to speak to her, see her, or have anything to do with her ever again. Tricia was very excited to hear from him and launched into boisterous small talk. Gus listened patiently, gritting his teeth as he psyched himself up to launch into his spiel. Then, deciding that he would wait no longer he cut her off in mid sentence. "I'm calling you because I need to have a serious talk with you". "Please listen to what I have to say - it is important," he stressed pointedly.

"What .....", Tricia tried to cut in but Gus took back control of the conversation. "Please don't say anything before I finish what I have to say - it's important", he repeated. Tricia stifled the urge to interrupt Gus further and fell silent. "I think we are both adults and can't pretend that we don't know what has been going on between us". "Well, I just want to say that, I'm not happy about the situation and it's time to stop it". Once again Tricia tried to cut in... "We're just friends...", she interjected.

"No, Tricia, you and I both know that's not true, we are not just friends, we're not friends at all, in fact". "Friends don't sleep together, Tricia". "You and I sleep together – friends don't sleep together Tricia - I want this to stop". He hadn't meant to sound sanctimonious, as he remembered his ongoing arrangement with Maureen, but Tricia had left him no choice.

"It's not as if we had anything serious going on – I don't know why you're reacting like this", Tricia whined.

"No, we didn't have anything serious, we will never have anything serious, and I don't want to sleep with you any more – I don't want you turning up at the stadium anymore and asking me to give you a lift anywhere". "It's over right – finished," Gus almost shouted before continuing, "I'm sorry, I can't offer you the future you deserve Tricia – okay", Gus softened his voice in an effort to minimise the blow. He finished speaking and then kept quiet to allow Tricia to say what she wanted to, something he had not planned to do previously.

"Who said I wanted any future with you anyway," Tricia tried to control her voice, to sound disinterested but a tremor belied her sadness or anger.

"Well, whatever you want, it doesn't really matter, but I just want you to understand that we aren't going to see each other anymore – this thing is finished, man," Gus was just about to say goodbye when Tricia changed tack.

"Are you seeing someone else - is that it". "What do you mean?" Gus replied, continuing – "Yes, I am seeing someone, as I have always told you – that's it".

Tricia began to shout, "Well, why did you lead me on – take me to Paris and all that – sleeping with me and all that?" she said sounding close to tears. Gus was speechless for a moment then replied, "Because you made it too easy, Tricia", he said, thinking, I'm going to tell it to her like it is. "You were too available, and anyway you said we were both adults and that you were just out for a good time – but it is obvious that you lied – you want what I can't give you, Tricia". "It's best that we end whatsoever it was now". "I can't give you what you want from me, do you understand?" "Don't be bitter - in a few weeks' time, you will see that it is the right thing to do – all good things have to come to an end," Gus' tone was gentle but firm. "You go and find yourself a good man who can give you what I can't – I wish you good luck and goodbye, Tricia", Gus said.

"You dirty ***** creep – how could you use me like that – who do you think you are?" Tricia's voice was now a high-pitched screech as she polluted the air with a single deadly expletive.

"Look, you enjoyed it while it lasted and I enjoyed it while it lasted – we are both adults", Gus said firmly, with uncharacteristic nonchalance. As he spoke he wondered why he had ever gotten caught up in this mess.

"You used me and now you want to just discard me," Tricia whined.

"It was you, Tricia - you allowed yourself to be used – you said no strings attached, remember," Gus repeated, then it occurred to him that he was wasting his time, she would say what she wanted to say and nothing he could say would make any difference, so he fell silent. He was just about to say goodbye when Tricia spoke again.

"If you think you can get away with treating me like this – you better think again," and she hung up.

After a moment it dawned on Gus that it was Valentines Day. "Oh no", he said beating himself up. He felt guilty – he had not intended to do this on the day designated for lovers - he was not

76

that callous. Gus was tempted to ring and apologise to Tricia that he had broken it off on Valentine Days, but the idea was quickly abandoned – "she will think I'm messing around – I best not encourage her", he shook his head from side to side as he spoke his thoughts.

After two minutes Gus' 'phone started to ring again – it was Tricia. He didn't pick up. His 'phone rang and rang and rang at 5-minute intervals all afternoon. And in the weeks that followed, quite bizarrely, Tricia called Gus' mobile several times a day and night. Gus had to switch his 'phone to silent. However as a businessman this was by no means practical. So he purchased a new phone, and informed most of his contacts of his new number, keeping the old phone and number in case any old business contacts tried to get hold of him.

On Wednesday 15 March, four weeks after the break-up Gus arrived at the stadium early for his training session with the youth group and Cyrus. He found surprised to find Tricia waiting for him at the front of the building. This surprised him - he was not aware that Tricia knew that he was at the Stadium on Wednesdays evenings.

"I want to talk you", Tricia seemed breathless as she approached him.

"What do you want to talk about, Tricia?" "I've said all that I wanted to say – there is nothing more to talk about", Gus tried not to become angry, and kept his voice even.

"You think you can just use me and then get rid of me like that – you think you can just dump me like that", as Tricia spoke loudly the blood rose to her face. She grabbed out at Gus as he walked away from her and sucked air through his teeth, making a hissing sound.

Just then Cyrus arrived with the church van and the youths, and Gus walked across the car park to meet them, ignoring Tricia. Tricia followed him, a scowl on her face - fuming. As the youngsters got out of the van, one by one they began to stare at Tricia who was wearing a mini-mini skirt and cropped jacket, rather inappropriate attire for such a chilly Spring evening. Gus walked back towards the stadium in an effort to get out of earshot of Cyrus and the youngsters as he anticipated that Tricia's tirade was unfinished. Oblivious to the many observers, Tricia followed Gus and proceeded to poke him with a well manicured fore finger as she spoke. "I said I wanted to talk to you," she said shamelessly. Now all the youths, Cyrus and Gus turned to stare at Tricia.

Then Melissa commented loudly, "Is that woman a slag or what – look at her skirt – she looks like some big time prostitute", as two of the other girls in the group burst into loud raucous laughter - the others sniggered. The boys just stared and smiled, licking their lips, two boys made lewd gestures, groping and stroking their private parts in a vulgar fashion as they looked on. Cyrus admonished them, "What do you think you are doing – Shaun and Paul, do your parents know that you behave like that in public – Melissa, behave yourself," Cyrus said commandingly, trying to reinstate order, but with limited success. While some of the youths heeded his rebuke, others, notably Shaun and Paul, continued to stare at Tricia while Cyrus was not looking.

At the same time Tricia became aware of the attention she was commanding, which must have affected her because she turned on her 4 inch heels, hissed air through her teeth, cast her eyes towards the sky, flicked her long straight weave and walked off as she said "I hope you know this isn't finished".

****

Tricia marched along Flasco Passage and then turned left into Flasco Road. As she walked she muttered to herself sneering. "***** who does he think he is?" "How dare he think he can just dismiss me as and when he likes – I'll show him". "He doesn't even know (she emphasised the word "know") who he is dealing with". "He really needs to be given a lesson in manners". "Tink 'im can…can just use oman like that an jus dismiss dem as 'im please". "WHOOO does he think he is". "Well, he met the wrong oman this time". "He has never met a woman like me before, 'cause I'm the one to teach him that lesson – ***** ******* cheek, Tricia's language was seasoned with an assortment of expletives, mostly of American and some Jamaican origin, but some were native to Britain, Tricia did not discriminate between expletives.

"Look at me, beautiful, well edicated, classy, girl and cum

78

wan spoil me up – A will teach 'im to mess wid me". "When a finish wid im he will wish sey im neva meet me in im life. I will do everyting in my power to cut him down to size. ********, when a finish wid im, im will wonder wat hit im". "Phew," Tricia exclaimed as she fumed in a curious Cockney/American/Jamaican accent, her cheeks turning dark red under her cream and coffee complexion. The class of swear words peppering her language could be compared with the germs that might inhabit hell's cess pool.

If Gus could have heard Tricia's conversation with herself, he would have been shocked. It had never been his idea to use her - ever since that first date, all he had tried to do was avoid her.

A car approached Tricia as she stood at the bus stop and slowed to a halt. The driver reversed and then lowered his passenger window. "Can I give you a ride, he asked", as he spoke, he looked Tricia up and down as though he was inspecting a very appetising meal. "You ******* *******. You ***** pervert - Wat do you tink me is ....you ***** *****", Tricia burst into a further raucous string of expletives, such as would constitute the dregs of hell's cess pit. The driver became flustered, hurriedly wound up his car window and sped off, just as a couple approached the bus stop and slowed as though to wait for a bus. On hearing the commotion they looked at Tricia as though she was mad. And when she looked back at them, fearing trouble, they averted her eyes and marched on determinedly toward the next stop. Tricia continued to swear under her breath, first at the driver of the car, before directing her fury back at Gus. "The ****** ******". "A gwine teach im a lesson". Tricia kept up this stream of abuse until her bus arrived. As she boarded her bus, she vowed to herself. "I'm going to hurt you Gus, I'm going to hurt you really bad, no matter what it costs me", she concluded. The intention that could be noted from the pronouncement of this final declaration of hers was such that might give the saying "Hell hath no fury like a woman scorned" an entirely new and far more sinister and deadly meaning.

Since that evening Gus was glad that he had heard nothing more from Tricia, but he felt, whether irrationally or not, that she was just biding her time before she once again showed up to cause him grief - just like a bad penny.

CHAPTER 4

Travelling Companions

Where most people have just one best buddy but Gus counted his lucky stars that he was blessed with three. Benza and Raj with whom he had been friends since they were at school together, and "Marshie", whom he met when they were both signed to Walmouth Town Football Club. In Gus' estimation they were equal, and he could not single out any one above the others as a "best" best friend.

Benza still lived at Wash House and Gus visited him from time to time, but was forced to curtail the frequency of his visits due to the "hating" he encountered in that area which had steadily worsened over recent years. He constantly encouraged his friend to move away from Wash House, even offering to pay the deposit on a property in a better neighbourhood for him, but Benza just would not be swayed. "Most of my family and friends still lived in the area….", was his argument. Another excuse was that Wash House was the place of his birth and he wasn't going anywhere. However, he assured Gus that he understood why he no longer liked the area. Benza was fully aware of the dangers and negative elements present at Wash House but, being a creature of habit, he could not bring himself to leave behind the run down estate. However, he did take Gus up on his offer of the deposit, which he used to purchase his flat outright, having been offered it at an incredibly low price by the Local Council due to the fact that his family had been tenants there for over 30 years.

Before his girlfriend Cynthia became pregnant, Benza visited Gus often, but his visits had been curtailed from the day he learned he was a father in waiting. Cynthia was now in the fifth month of pregnancy and he tentatively spent most of his time with her.

Raj had officially moved away from Wash House with his family years ago. But he still worked in the family grocery store on the outskirts of the Estate and quite often stayed over in the flat above the shop,

Marshie was not from Wash House, and did not form part of their "gang of three" (as they were known at school), but he was as good a friend to Gus as the other two nonetheless.

The "gang of three", had never been a gang in the true sense. But they had hung together as a tight knit bunch since schooldays. Back then they had clung together in the face of coercion to join gangs in the true sense, leant on each other and drawn strength and emotional sustenance from one another, whilst sharing, learning from, and watching each other's backs. Their experiences had forged a bond of friendship that most people never encountered in their lives. His bond with Marshie too had been forged from experiences shared, and was firmly grounded on a deep emotional level.

For many years Gus, Benza and Raj enjoyed a boys' night out on a regular basis. Marshie also joined them on a few occasions, but he did not enjoy this escapade in the same way as the "gang of three". He preferred to have Gus all to himself – one to one, and so these days Gus made time for Marshie separately.

Back in the day the gang met up at least twice a month, but this frequency had dwindled down over the years to just once every three months or so. They either went out bowling, or stayed in to watch football, play boys' games, watch movies, reminisce and tell jokes. But by far their favourite thing to do was to go for a meal and clubbing at the "Star Apple" - a restaurant/nightclub just off the Strand. There they ate well, drank well, and danced into the small hours. Gus introduced his friends to the "Star Apple" several years ago, having discovered it himself when taken there for a complimentary lunch during his foot-balling years. He appreciated that at the "Star Apple" only the very best Caribbean cuisine and music were on offer. What he liked most was the fact that at the "Star Apple" the musical content was of a strictly no slackness and no sleaze genre. Violence, profanity or blasphemy and drugs were strongly forbidden in the "Star Apple" zone. This was important to Gus who was careful to listen only to music with moral substance. His friends were like minded - Benza not wishing to absorb garbage into his mind, and Raj not wishing to drink in negativity into his spirit and all were staunchly anti-drugs.

The gang of three were meeting up on, 24 March 2010, for the first time in over three months, and Gus could hardly wait. After tonight he expected their rendezvous to become even less frequent since Raj was planning to get married soon and of course Benza was anticipating the birth of his first child. Marshie too had met someone special, with whom he now spent most of his time.

Gus had to work hard to maintain regular contact with his mates and it looked like his job was just about to get even more difficult than before. He only hoped the get-togethers would not cease completely because they formed a large part of his social life, his family life having splintered with the death of his mother. Cyrus was the only real family that remained close to Gus now. His two siblings had apparently left the family behind. Gus and Cyrus had struggled for years to keep up the lines of communication with Diedre and Marcus. Gus had all but given up on telephoning his sister now. For many years he had done so at least once a week, and being made to endure the cold unenthusiastic reception he received each time. He finally got the message that she was happily married and only had time for her immediate family. As for his brother, Gus did not know where he was living and the telephone number he had for him no longer worked - he only heard from Marcus when his brother could be bothered to contact him. So his friends took the place of his family, making up for his lack of closeness with his own siblings, Gus mused as he checked the time. He had waited on tenterhooks all day, hoping that neither of them would cancel - he knew he wouldn't.

Like a small boy on Christmas Eve night Gus was finding it almost impossible to think of anything but the scheduled shindig. They'd arranged to meet at the "Star Apple" for pre-dinner drinks at 7.30 pm, with dinner at 8.30 pm, later advancing into the small nightclub at the rear of the building where they would enjoy a good old time rave in a tasteful and safe atmosphere.

Gus particularly wanted to interact with his friends at this time – he needed to get his mind off the recent episodes with Tricia. He knew he had done the right thing breaking it off with her. He only regretted that he had not heeded his initial intuition - he would never have gotten involved with her in the first place.

"Brrrr, brrrrr, brrrrr" the telephone interrupted Gus' thoughts

– he was grateful but ignored it. It was 6.00 pm and he was in his office (originally the third bedroom of his town house), trying to wrap up some paperwork before getting ready to go to the Star Apple. Glancing at his watch Gus proceeded to make a renewed effort to plough on with his work, ignoring the telephone. As if getting the message, it stopped ringing. But after a brief pause it began to ring again, interrupting Gus laboured concentration. On seeing it was an unknown number, Gus' initial reaction was to fear that it was Tricia calling him but then he signed with relief as he recalled that the only people who had his landline number were Cyrus, Maureen, Diedre and Marcus. Without thinking further, Curiosity got the better of him and he picked up the receiver.

"Hello", he said then paused to listen.

"Hey, bruv", the familiar voice took Gus by surprise - it wasn't often that he heard from Marcus. The last time was over a year ago, which call had ended acrimoniously when Gus had refused his brother yet another request for a loan.

"I was just thinking about you – yeah, you been running across my mind and I wondered how you was keeping, bruv", Marcus said, trying to sound amenable and concerned all at the same time but failing to disguise the false edge in his voice.

"I'm not too bad", Gus replied warmly and continued, "how are you keeping Marcus – it's good to hear your voice - I haven't seen or heard from you for such a long while". "I have tried to call you many times but the telephone number that I have for you doesn't work anymore." "I have left messages - so many messages for you - but maybe you did not get them." Gus gushed, genuinely glad to hear from his brother.

"So bruv, how's business these days", Marcus said in his own callous style, obviously not having listened to anything Gus had just said to him.

"Yeah, okay," Gus said weakly, his bubble deflated.

"Good, good," Marcus said hurriedly. "So bruv, I was think-ing of passing round you yard to check you," Marcus lilted in his familiar dodgy Jamaican/North London lingo.

"Oh, I was just about to head out," Gus replied - an uncom-fortable yet brief silence followed.

"But you can pass round on Sunday afternoon – it would be great to see you," Gus said trying to appease.

"Yeah, I'll let you know," Marcus replied testily. "I better go now bruv, I'll call you again," he said and hung up leaving Gus doubting that he would, and realising that he did not get Marcus' new number.

After replacing the receiver, Gus felt the beginnings of a slight headache. Encounters with Marcus always had that effect on him – it was such a struggle to understand and connect with his brother. Now he found himself involuntarily worrying about Marcus' welfare, wondering why he had called, knowing that there had to be some reason, "Marcus never just calls to say hi", Gus spoke his thoughts.

To try and shake off the negative feelings Gus put on some music as he directed his mind to getting ready, determined that he would allow nothing to spoil his night. As he showered, the invigorating lukewarm water pepped him up. Stepping out he headed for the bedroom and the wardrobe where he selected a grey dress suit. Removing the trousers, he re-hung the jacket inside the wardrobe. He then chose a casual/dressy light jumper in grey/blue to complement the suit. Then, having applied his favourite scent liberally, he put on the trouser, enjoying the feel of the luxurious fabric against his legs. Fully dressed, he then groomed his well cut hair by applying hair moisturiser - then he added cream to his face, before inspecting the finished look in the full length mirror. Liking what he saw Gus smiled back at his reflection, strutted around the room in time to the music to see that the look remained the same with movement then smiled again, thoughts of Marcus and Tricia briefly exorcised as he turned from side to side appraising his appearance. "You're going to break someone's heart tonight," he thought aloud - something his mother used to say. Suddenly thoughts of Tricia flashed across his memory and Gus vowed aloud, "I am certainly steering well clear of ladies tonight," he said sombrely, "I definitely don't want any complications of that sort in my life for a long while". Then he grabbed his wallet and jacket, took a final glance at his reflection and headed out.

It was 7.40 pm and Gus was running late again. He was driving around in circles, trying to find somewhere to park and becoming more irritable by the minute. Having had no luck finding parking along the road he was heading towards the multi-storey at least 10 minutes away when his luck changed – the lights of a parked vehicle switched on, followed by the flashing light of indicators - someone was moving away just ahead. Gus smiled - the space was tight but he manoeuvred expertly into it with relative ease. As he strutted the short distance back to the restaurant his smile remained in place – luck had shown up tonight.

On entering the restaurant Gus caught sight of Raj right away, sitting by the bar looking debonair and distinguished. "Eh, eh," Raj exclaimed to his approaching friend, suddenly revealing to those around that he was just an ordinary down to earth guy after all. "Look at you," he enthused, rising from his seat. He and Gus demonstrated reciprocal appreciation of each other's appearances by standing back and casting admiring looks each to the other – then they embraced heartily in a masculine hug. Raj, at 5' 8", the shorter of the two men, was dressed fetchingly in similar fashion to Gus. They had always had similar impeccable tastes. His conventional Asian features were offset by his unusually light almond complexioned skin, and with high gloss jet black hair slicked back he reminded Gus of an old Hollywood movie star.

The formalities over, Gus drew up a stool while Raj beckoned toward the bartender. He ordered his friend – a non-alcoholic tropical concoction called "Mango Walk", which Gus drank each time he visited the Star Apple.

"You're late as usual", Raj said jokingly, immediately getting Gus' back up without realising it.

"Where's Benza then," Gus asked disregarding his friend's earlier comment as he sat down.

"Oh, he's on his way. He had to drop Cynthia to her mum's as she didn't want to stay alone tonight". Both men laughed.

"I guess we're lucky that she is letting him out at all, you kno how women funny, funny when dem pregnant and ting". Raj's eyes creased as he spoke. Raj, though born in Kenya, was brought up on the Wash House Estate from the age of 3 years. From his formative years he naturally gravitated towards Caribbean people, and it was no surprise, therefore that he could flow in the lingo just as well as, if not better than, his good friends - his speech and mannerisms indistinguishable from those of Gus or Benza. Gus found himself wondering how Raj would get on with his wife, his parents having arranged his marriage. Although Raj did get some say in the matter his mum and dad had chosen his bride first, and he had then met her only once, while on a holiday in Kenya. And he had accepted their choice without question, relating to his friends that he had fallen in love with his prospective bride on first sight.

As they sat together drinking, Gus' thoughts went back in time to when they were growing up. Raj was a permanent fixture at his house, and enjoyed his rice and peas and curried goat like the most patriarchal of Jamaicans. Gus recalled that Raj preferred Alison's cooking to his own mother's. He also loved reggae – roots, lovers and ragga - with a greater degree of passion than he and Benza, and had amassed a huge catalogue of records, CDS, and DVDs, including some original Studio One pressings, and other rare grooves. His music collection was stored in a whole room all by themselves at the flat above the shop – and he was fast running out of space. In-keeping with his adoptive culture, Raj loved to play his music very loud indeed with a heavy bass line, which he did on a daily basis - and he loved raving.

Raj had also visited Kingston several times so he could experience the culture behind the music, and each time he returned with tons of records and latterly CDs and DVDs, and new slang words and dances which he shared with his friends.

Gus could not recall Raj ever having had an Asian girlfriend, and remembered that his friend had a preference for well built ebony complexioned ladies who shared his lust for life – he had even confessed unquenchable love for a sister on more than one occasion. However, Gus was always aware of Raj's allegiance to his family, and was not surprised that he had agreed to marry someone chosen by his parents - he only hoped his friend was doing the right thing – that he would be happy.

"You must come over and see my new house soon," Raj said excitedly. "I just bought it and I'm doing it up - nearly there – should finish in the next month or so, in good time before the wedding", Raj said proudly. Gus was excited for his friend, in spite of wishing that it was he who was getting married. He almost informed Raj about the new house he had just purchased too, but stopped himself. He didn't want to make little of his friend's achievement. "Yes man - that would be good", he replied.

"By the way, have you bought any other properties lately", Raj asked.

Gus thought briefly and then decided he would tell his friends about the new house – he knew they would be happy for him.

"Well, I wasn't going to say anything", but now you've mentioned it, I just bought a new house too," Gus said quickly, not wanting to make too much of it.

"What another buy-to-let?" Raj asked.

"No, no, I'm going to live in this one," Gus smiled as he spoke.

"Thinking of settling down or something?" Raj said as he looked at Gus quizzically.

"No man," Gus chuckled. "Just needed a bit more space, and wanted somewhere way out of town to chill out – get away from the hustle and bustle sometimes". "Congratulations – yeah sometimes you just need to get away innit?" "Whereabouts is the new place", Raj enquired.

"Radleigh in Hertfordshire," Gus said his tone even, playing down his news.

"Wheeez," Raj whistled. "N-I-C-E one. You've really done well for yourself. I'm proud of you, man," Raj was earnest as he proffered his clenched fist.

As they touched fists Benza walked into the restaurant and headed towards them. Gus and Raj repeated the welcome ritual, rising from their seats and both smiling broadly at Benza, matching his wide grin, they gave reciprocated appreciative all over appraisals.

Most people would say that Benza was the most handsome of the three friends, with dark ebony complexion and music star looks, Benza caused many a female head to turn and look his way. He had pulled back his long locks into a huge chignon that looked far too heavy for one head to carry around. Tonight he wore a dark blue well cut suit - a present that Gus had brought back from

Milan when he had visited that city two years previously. Although Benza had noticeably gained more than a few pounds, the suit still fitted him – but only just. Raj ordered Benza's favourite drink, a double brandy on the rocks as he and Gus sat down.

Benza pulled up a stool and joined his friends. "So, where did you park?" Gus asked, wondering whether Benza had been as lucky as him in finding parking close by.

"I didn't drive tonight, I got the tube. I was going to ask you if I could stay by you as Cynthia is at her mother's and I don't need to rush home," Benza directed his question at Gus.

"Yes, of course you can", Gus replied, relieved – his friend always drank far too much to drive whenever they went clubbing in any case. "It will be just like old times - we can stay up talk about the good old days till 9 am just like we used to - yes man, you are very welcome", Gus enthused.

"I didn't drive either," Raj said.

"What about you Raj, you coming by me as well?" Gus asked excitedly.

"Yeah - course you can count me in". "You gonna take us over to your new place?" Raj asked looking straight at Gus. Benza picked up the scent of news, "You buy another new place?" he said smiling at Gus.

"Yeah, yeah," Gus said, once again wondering how he could play this down. He didn't want his friends, especially Benza who still lived at Wash House, to feel that he had grown too big for them.

"You kept that quiet," Benza said, echoing what Raj had said a few minutes earlier."

"I was meaning to tell you about it tonight. I was waiting for the right time", Gus said apologetically as Benza and Raj both nodded.

"I'll just go and 'phone my dad - he will open up the shop for me in the morning". "I will ask my brother to give him a hand - he won't mind," Raj said, taking out his mobile and walking towards the front of the restaurant.

As he left, Benza and Gus continued the conversation. "I'll invite you and Cynthia over soon, when I have settled in properly".

"I'm going to arrange a dinner party and invite Raj and Marshie as well – just a few close friends…", Gus paused. "And family", he added hesitantly. Gus hoped that Benza did not ask any more questions.

"Yeah, yeah, that would be lovely", Benza smiled warmly, genuinely happy for his friend. "How's Marshie doing these days," he asked, changing the subject, to Gus' delight.

"Oh, he's doing really well," Gus replied, and gave Benza a brief update.

"So Benza – you're going to be a daddy soon". "How much longer is it now," Gus moved the conversation on.

"Just under five months to go now". "I'm really excited, man - I can't wait," Benza replied.

"Do you know what you're having?" Gus said, wondering whether he would be Godfather.

"No, but I hope it's a girl," Benza's eyes lit up as he spoke,

"Girl – why - most men would like to have a boy – a son," Gus looked surprised.

"I know, but I'm not most men – I want a girl - I like girls". "Girls are loyal to their fathers – boys are loyal to their mothers – it's a fact, girls love their fathers more than boys". "I want a little girl, so that I can protect her from the big bad world and be a real good daddy to her," Benza enthused.

"I would like to have a boy first, I guess, if I ever have any kids," Gus looked thoughtful. "Boys are tougher than girls and you can play rough with boys. With girls, you have to be careful in case they break or something". "Yeah, I would like to have a boy first". "I would like to have three children – one boy first and then a girl, maybe, for the missus and I don't mind what the third one is," Gus looked up as Raj returned to his seat.

"Did you get through?" Gus broke off speaking to Benza and addressed Raj.

"Yeah, yeah - sorted. Man, I'm hungry you know - hungry for some good food". "I wonder what's on the menu tonight," Raj said as he stared in the direction of the dining area.

Gus glanced at his watch - 15 minutes to wait – I'm a bit hungry as well you know". Both friends then stared in the direction of Benza, whom they anticipated would join the food debate. Benza was passionate about food and provoked not a little surprise when he did not join in. They soon realised why - Benza was preoccupied. Gus and Raj followed his gaze to the entrance of the restaurant and saw that his attention was drawn to four young women entering the restaurant. The only thing that Benza loved more than food was women - he had always been the womaniser among them. Before he got together with Cynthia, he would go home with a new girl every time they went out clubbing. But that had all changed when Cynthia came on the scene - or so Gus had thought. He was surprised to see that Benza may now be up to his old tricks. Raj looked but then quickly restrained himself. "I'm almost a married man you know bruv, so I ain't going there," he held his hands up in a gesture of surrender. "Well, I'm not married yet," Benza said licking his chops.

"Yes, but you have a baby on the way, remember", Gus was serious as he spoke.

"Yeah, yeah, it's not as if I was going to do anything Bruv – just looking – chill out man. I'm just having some fun". "Just 'cause you want dem all fe you'self." Benza teased and both he and Raj laughed heartily.

"No man, I'm avoiding women at the moment – not tonight". "I'm just out with you boys to have some strictly male fun – just for tonight I want to forget all about women," Gus said as Benza turned his attention back to his friends.

"Look Gus man, it's time you found youself a nice woman and settle down – like me", Benza chuckled. "Look at me, these days I'm like home from work, on with the slippers, dressing gown and newspaper in front of the tele, man". "I don't even go no-where again, man". "I might as well be married". "It's just like I am married already anyway – all but the little piece of paper". "Cynthia wants us to do the whole white wedding thing, big church, white Bentley and all dat, but me no ready yet," Benza said breaking off into a heavy Jamaica twang. "But me happy though - happier than ever before in ma life". "I'm what you would call contented - I found myself a nice woman - she's beautiful, clean, ambitious, she cooks good GOOD, and uummmmhh – say no more – you know what I mean," said Benza, shifting about as he lilted in a mixture of perfect English and Jamaican twang. The three friends all laughed loudly at Benza's expression of domestic and innuendo of sexual bliss.

"Eeh, Cynthia's got this beautiful friend that I think you should meet". "I think she is your kind a woman". "Man - the girl is beautiful". "You know, I'm sure she is your type of woman – I know you would like her, man". "I would love to see you settle with someone like that – beautiful, classy – the girl is nice you know Gus", Benza stressed. "Just let me know and I'll arrange for a nice dinner – just the 4 of us at our place". "It's time you found a nice woman and settle down man," Benza repeated annoyingly.

"Thank you, dad", Gus said sarcastically. He paused before adding, "But are you sure you don't want her for yourself?" "The way you are describing her, it sounds as though you fancy her yourself," and both Raj and Gus laughed loudly at Gus' ridicule of Benza. Benza spoke up in his defence, "No, no man, nothing like that, she's Cynthia's best friend – nothing like that, she's just a nice girl, man and anyway she is a Christian," as Benza finished speaking Gus and Raj burst into another peal of unbridled laughter.

"A Christian – now seriously Benza, what are you thinking – what would me and a Christian girl have in common?" Gus asked.

"The fact that she is a Christian is a good thing, and it shouldn't matter". "The only thing that should matter is the fact that she is a nice girl and you are a nice guy and I want you fixed up with a nice girl," Benza said as Raj nodded his agreement.

"Yeah Gus, you are a nice guy". "You can marry my sister any day, man, serious," Raj chuckled as he spoke, joining the debate. "You know she always had a soft spot for you - you know that Gus". "I would love to have you as my brother-in-law, guy for real", Raj stared pointedly at Gus.

"Yeah, yeah, like your parents would ever agree to that", Gus replied.

"Yes they would - my parents like you, man". "My mum is always asking about you". "She remembers you from when you used to come over to our house years ago". "She still asks about you now – always asking me to bring you around". "She refers to you as "that nice young black boy," Raj said, mimicking his mother's accent.

"Listen, listen, when I'm ready to get married, I will find my own woman right". "Pretty is like my little sister, guy". "I don't deal in that kind of thing, man". "It wouldn't feel right to me – it would be like incest, man". Gus paused as the other friends smiled at his last statement – then he continued, "How is your mother anyway?" "If you arrange it, I would love to drop by for dinner sometime". "I remember she used to make some nice curries and paratas," Gus smiled at his friend as he reminisced.

"Yeah, I'll hold you to that - she would just love to see you – and my dad". Raj held out his fist to Gus who touched it with his own.

"I expect we will all buck up at the wedding anyway," Gus said, continuing, "What date is it again and when are you sending out the invitations?"

"31 July 2010, so note your diaries," Raj said, continuing, "The invitations will come out in the next couple of weeks".

Both Raj and Gus turned their minds to thinking about the wedding plans as Benza once again glanced towards the direction of the four women, who were now loitering in the foyer. "Anyway, women are off the agenda tonight," he said as though endeavouring to convince himself, rising from his stool as he spoke. He glanced at his watch and then exclaimed, "Man, I's hungry - let me go and see if they will serve us 5 minutes earlier," he escaped towards the dining area as he finished speaking.

Dinner was a lavish fare of the very best meats, seafood and desserts. Gus had the lobster, while Raj had the whole roasted fish and the curry goat, and Benza opted for the steak. All the choices were served with a selection of Caribbean vegetables and salads and the non-optional rice and peas – all cooked to perfection. To wash it down Raj had the Irish moss, Gus the Guinness punch, and Benza had carrot juice. They also ordered a bottle of the very best Sauvignon Blanc in the house - Benza drank most of the bottle. Gus picked up the cheque as he liked to do when they ate out - his friends knew better than to argue with him and cause a scene, as he became angry at any suggestion that either of them should dip into their pockets. They had come to appreciate that it made him happy to treat them whenever they went out together, and they liked to make him happy. And anyway at £50 a head they didn't need much persuasion to keep their hands out of their pockets.

After dinner the friends sat and talked for a couple of hours until almost 12 am, when Benza left to order himself a further double brandy on the rocks. On his return he beckoned them into the dance section towards the back of the restaurant.

All three of them and others in the small dance hall stood along the wall as though holding it up and rocked along to the music as it pulsated through the speakers – old school – ragga – R & B – hip-hop – lovers - calypso with some "world" selections. Raj was in his element.

Benza took to the dance floor, convincing one of the four young ladies that he had seen earlier to join him. After some time Raj joined them, followed by Gus. They were later joined by the other three friends who stayed with them on the dance floor, shaking bumping and jiving through number after number. The atmosphere was electric. By 2 am the dance floor was packed as more and more diners entered the dance area. The "Star Apple" was kicking tonight. Gus could not remember the last time he'd had such a good time. Raj became more and more excited as the DJ played some of his favourite records. When each record came on he exclaimed "Tooon", and waved his hands in the air in an over exaggerated, crazy expression of appreciation. He also made various gestures with his head as his body jerked erratically in dance. It was entertaining, if comical to watch Raj dance and Gus nudged Benza as they smiled at their friend affectionately.

Then Benza paired off with one of the girls who Gus later learned was called Diamond and they went off to sit together in the bar. Raj and Gus shook their heads simultaneously indicating that they realised Benza had not changed that much after all. Gus was saddened by this because he did not like Benza's philandering ways and felt that his friend should show more respect for ladies, especially Cynthia who was pregnant with his child.

They continued to dance with the other three ladies, although it was obvious that one of the girls was trying very hard to get

Gus' all to herself. But Gus was not about to allow anything like that to happen. As they danced she shouted above the music, "My name's Shona – what's yours?" "Gus - and you? Gus asked, addressing the question to one of the other girls who replied "Amber". Gus repeated the question to the other young lady who replied "Tracey". He did not wish to be manipulated into a one-to-one corner by Shona so he began to deliberately show more interest in one of the other friends – but not too much interest – he did not want his intentions misinterpreted. This annoyed Shona, who skulked off to sit alone.

After a couple of hours Benza and Diamond rejoined the group. It was obvious that Benza had been drinking heavily and Gus glanced at his watch – it was coming up to 4 am. He whispered over to Benza that it was time they made a move. "Yeah, let's go man," Benza slurred. As he spoke he teetered unsteadily on his feet - it was definitely time to get Benza home. However, Gus had to drag Raj from the dance floor as he petitioned to Gus that the DJ was "killing it with some of the wickedest ragga "tooons"".

They said their goodbyes to the girls. Amber and Tracey responded. Diamond and Shona did not. As they left, Benza spoke to Diamond cockily, "Shame to leave you Diams but I'm a married man - got to go home to the wife". Diamond totally ignored him and continued to sip her drink, making Benza look very silly indeed - he was however sadly too drunk to notice. Gus remembered how stupid Benza could be at times and shook his head from side to side as they left the restaurant.

As they walked to the car Gus lent his shoulder to support Benza as Raj helped to prop him up on the other side. When they got to the car Gus opened the doors and Raj climbed into the small back seat, as he was by far slimmer than Benza who could barely fit into the front passenger seat. In spite of his friend's obvious inebriation Gus was bubbling over at being in the company of them both - he couldn't remember when he had felt so happy. He set the car in motion and headed towards Islington. It started to rain, and the water could be heard swishing against the wheels as the car cut through the night. They drove in silence for a while as the rhythm of the windscreen wipers created a somnolent atmosphere within the little car on its journey through the night. Then the sound of Benza's involuntarily drunken belching spoilt the atmosphere.

Gus cracked the windows as Raj spoke up to maintain enthusiasm, "Man, what a night -. whooo, dem toons man, some a dem I ain't heard since school – wicked, wicked night," Raj enthused. "Yeah, I miss the good times we used to have together". "I couldn't tell the last time I had such a good night out," Gus said. "It's just like the good old days," he continued reminiscing as he directed the car to negotiate the quiet streets.

Arriving home, Gus got out of the car and proceeded to let down the seat to let Raj out of the back. As Benza got out on the other side, he fell to his knees and began to throw up in Gus' front garden, retching violently for a few minutes while Gus and Raj turned to look on at the unsavoury sight. "Benza, I told you to take it easy, man", Raj repeated over and over while Gus said nothing. He felt nauseous at the sight of his friend suffering the shame of over indulgence. He hoped none of his neighbours would be awaken and behold the disgraceful scene.

After they had done their best to clean Benza up, they put him to bed on the recliner sofa. Gus and Raj were too tired and affected to converse anymore so Gus informed Raj that he should sleep in the spare bedroom. Then he went to clean up the garden before retiring to his own room where he lay awake and mused on the vanity of over indulgence - how pointless it all seemed. For Benza's indiscretion had marred what had otherwise been a wonderful evening. Gus decided he would once again have to speak to his friend about curbing his drinking habit. Then he totally relaxed and within a few minutes he too was fast asleep - completely exhausted.

BOOK THREE: TWO WORLDS COLLIDE

CHAPTER 1

Dangerous Bend Ahead

Tricia's mind was churning over as she willed sleep to come without success - a steaming hot mug of cocoa after a hot bath usually did the trick but had failed to put her to sleep tonight. She read through the first two chapters of a particularly boring novel but her mind remained fully alert, her eyes wide open. In desperation she thought about counting sheep, but soon abandoned that idea, recalling from past experiences that she could not visualize sheep. Momentarily Tricia wondered whether anyone else had every succeeded in visualizing sheep. Shaking her head decisively, Tricia reached over and grabbed her mobile from the bedside table - four thirty – almost dawn - she observed, fretting that she would have to get up soon. She pulled the duvet roughly over her head, annoyed, and made one last attempt to drift off. A frown clouded her countenance as she mused that even if she fell asleep now she would only get 2 hours' sleep and she always suffered when she didn't get enough sleep. She would probably have a headache all day - she just knew it – and wouldn't be able to concentrate. "Great" Tricia said as she thought of what her boss' reaction might be.

Insomnia did not come naturally to Tricia who was more accustomed to dropping off at the drop of a hat. She loved to sleep and would nod off in any circumstance - she thought about sleeping during the day when she was at work, and even when she wasn't particularly tired. But for the past week she had not been sleeping at all well. Retiring early had availed nothing – it only meant that she lay awake for longer. And this problem was getting worse each night.

Blinking hard Tricia concentrated, analysing the reason for her sleeplessness. Was it something in her diet - or perhaps she was sub-consciously worrying about her outstanding debts. She shook her head "No – its not that," she concluded. Her credit card debts had never caused her to lose sleep in the past – so why would they now. Perhaps her inability to sleep was due to the problems she had been encountering at work. But yet again she rejected that possibility – Mr Morrells was not important enough to deprive her of sleep.

There was only one plausible cause - Gus Allen – she could not sleep because he was able to sleep – having used her and discarded her – like a piece of dirty rag. "**** Gus Allen," Tricia gritted her teeth as she cursed Gus, muttering a string of swear words under her breath. "I'm going to teach you a lesson you will never forget - you think you can get away with this?" Tricia continued angrily as though posing the question directly to Gus. "I will never rest easy until I've paid you back for disrespecting me, Gus Allen, and payback is well overdue," Tricia vowed as she scowled menacingly. Then, deriving some comfort from having voiced her evil intent, she fell into a fitful sleep.

The alarm broke through Tricia's dream and, half awake she reached over to grab her mobile fumbling to switch off the offensive drone. Then she nestled back deeply into the covers as she thought about what she would do today. There and then she decided she would 'phone into work as sick – she was way too tired and even if she went in, she would not be very productive in any case. "How can I even begin to function on two hours' sleep?" Tricia reasoned. "It's better to throw a sickie than to face the wrath of Grumpy Morrells if I were to go into work tired and unable to concentrate", she said in conclusion.

Ending her unilateral dialogue, Tricia continued to ponder. Friday was the best day for her to be off as the part-time secretary would be in. Anyway, she had to have the day off as there was something more important for her to do – something that couldn't wait a day longer. Yes, what she had to do had to be done today, Friday 7 April 2010. Suddenly she felt extremely sleepy so she re-set the alarm for 9.30 am, two hours' time, and was soon snoring lightly.

"I hate you", Tricia screamed as she awoke from a bad dream. In the dream she was arguing with Gus and chasing him with a big knife when a policeman caught sight of her and began to chase her. He caught her and was proceeding to arrest her when she woke up. Now awake, Tricia pondered how it might feel to deal Gus a fatal blow as a smile spread slowly across her face.

Looking at her mobile Tricia noted that it was just before 9.00 am. Remembering what she had to do today, she excitedly jumped out of bed and proceeded to put on her favourite CD, turning up the volume until the bass pulsated. She moved suggestively to the rhythm and headed for the bathroom. "Oh I'm in charge of my destiny ......destiny...... destiny," Tricia sang along to her favourite track. She continued to mumble the tune as she brushed her teeth.

Allowing the warm shower water to cascade down her body, Tricia luxuriated, loving its comforting feel. In spite of having had very little sleep she felt fresh and alive as she eagerly anticipated the day ahead. Today was important to Tricia because today she intended to get retribution for the humiliation she had suffered at the hands of Gus Allen. Today she would deliver on her promise to make him pay and she would do whatever was necessary – even if it cost her life.

It was 10.05 am when Tricia stepped out of her front door. Her father, Donald, was just returning home from work as a night security guard, a job he had done since his computer business went bust soon after the death of his wife Margaret (who he lovingly called "Mags"). A quiet unassuming man, Donald had very few friends and had led a lonely existence since Mags death. It was five years since she passed away and those years had taken their toll, causing him to look much older than his fifty-two years.

Having inherited an outgoing nature from her mother, Tricia's affability had always been in direct contrast to her father's temperate ways and it made her sick that he had all but given up on life since her mother's passing and was becoming more reclusive each day. As far as Donald was concerned no-one could ever take Mag's place. She was his soul mate in the true sense and he had never been able to find her qualities in any of the women he had reluctantly dated at Tricia's insistence in the past 3 years, so he resolved to remain alone, content with the memories of his dearly departed wife preserved in his heart forever. When he was alone, Donald talked to his wife as if she were present and still alive. Tricia heard him on occasions, callously dismissing him as insane, not caring to take the time to find out whether there was anything that she could do to help her father. But she had not always been so heartless.

Growing up as a young girl and into her early teenage years Tricia had enjoyed a loving relationship with both her parents. But she had changed suddenly and drastically at aged 16, becoming rebellious, erecting barriers and distancing herself from them for no apparently good reason. It was around the time that she was first introduced to and began dabbling with unknown powers.

Later, when her mother passed away she had been sad – but not that unhappy, and it didn't take her long to move on - unlike her father. Tricia had made it clear to Donald that he shouldn't expect her to fill any gap left by her mother's death, "I'm not about to become a crutch for you to lean on", she had informed him cruelly. She viewed him as a weak and gutless man and displayed little or no respect for him and relished ignoring him when he was around, taking pains to keep her distance from him. Conversation with her father was out of the question and when he tried to talk to her, Tricia responded rudely, abruptly or insultingly, whichever took her fancy on any particular day. As a result of such treatment over many months, Donald had backed off and now left her alone. However, he continued to greet her with a "Morning Tricia, how are you," or an "Evening Tricia", without really listening for or expecting a reply. He was becoming more locked into his own world each day, still grieving his loss. Tricia was glad that her father appeared to have gotten the message – if he wanted to waste his life it was up to him but she intended living hers to the full. The door to her heart was firmly shut and bolted.

"Morning Tricia - you late for work?" Donald asked uncharacteristically, looking expectantly at Tricia for a reply. "Great, today he wants to talk, when I'm in a hurry", Tricia mumbled. "Yeah, yeah, you al'right dad – I'm in a hurry now – see you later", she responded gruffly as she hurried away, leaving her father standing by the door – a lonesome figure looking after her. Then she remembered she'd forgotten something, turned on her heels and hurried back towards her father, who smiled in anticipation. But Tricia walked briskly by him and entered the house, mumbling something about a brain and a sieve. Donald, encouraged by the fact that Tricia had at least responded to his greeting, followed her inside but she bounded upstairs quickly, aggressively, leaving him standing alone in the hall. After a while he went into the kitchen and sat quietly alone.

Unlocking the door to her bedroom, which she kept locked at all times, Tricia headed to her dressing table drawer, "There it is," she said having rummaged briefly. She drew out a newspaper cutting which read: *"Prophet Osira – whatever your problems, I can solve them – love life problems – sicknesses – enemies …..".* Tricia nodded as she appreciated the claims of prophet Osira. She then folded the piece of newspaper and put it into her bag.

Hurrying from the house Tricia slammed the door loudly behind her. Hearing the loud bang, Donald emerged from the kitchen, "Tricia, is that you?" he said before realising that Tricia had gone. He went to the window where he watched her walk away, resolving to try and get through to her one more time, to try and rebuild their crumpled father/daughter relationship again. His baby had grown into a woman, a woman he didn't recognise anymore. Donald wondered what had happened to make his daughter so angry all the time. But he didn't blame Tricia - perhaps if he hadn't been so affected by Mags' death, so weak, Tricia would not despise him so. And Donald blamed himself for a situation that had arisen solely as a result of Tricia's inability to love anyone but herself - even her own father.

Momentarily blinded by bright sunshine, Tricia exited the underground train station. It was uncharacteristically bright and sunny for this time of the year – Spring felt more like early Summer today – bringing a feeling of exuberance. The sunlight caused her to squint and she wished she had brought her "darkers". Her first impulse was to look around for a shop where she could purchase a pair of sunglasses, but she quickly deemed it unlikely that she would find anything tasteful to buy in Foxton Green. This area of London was unfamiliar to Tricia and so far she was less than impressed. The more she looked around the more ill at ease she began to feel. Although it was only 11.15 am, there were already several unkempt individuals loitering outside the station. One of them, holding a crumpled brown paper bag, approached her with the request "you got 50p to spare love," which Tricia less than appreciated. She pinched her nose, offended and annoyed by this approach. "What do I look like, the Bank of England?" she mumbled loudly as she hurried away.

After walking for a few minutes, it suddenly dawned on Tricia that she didn't know if she was going the right way. She looked around for someone who appeared decent enough to approach and ask for directions. However no-one in her estimation fitted that bill, so she walked on blindly. Yet another scruffily dressed man approached her - seeing him coming towards her, Tricia held her breath, lifted her head high, looked straight ahead and walked determinedly almost knocking him flying. The man staggered unsteadily as though he'd being drinking. "Uhh, the smell," Tricia said, placing her fore finger beneath her nostrils – she actually felt like retching. Her salvation was the sight of a small shop which she hurried toward and gratefully entered to ask for directions to Fairford Street.

The Asian shopkeeper was friendly and helpful and gave concise and clear directions. Luckily it wasn't too far away – and she was going the right way. After a further 3-minute walk she saw the name plate for Fairford Street and practically ran the rest of the way to her destination. Number 16 turned out to be a shop. Tricia paused outside to get her breath back before entering. On entry, she was immediately engulfed by an overpowering stench of incense and pure perfume that upset her stomach. Feeling like throwing up for the second time this morning she tried to breathe as little as possible until she felt weak from a lack of oxygen. Looking around she appraised her surroundings. There were candles of all shapes and sizes; deities small and large; bottles of potions, oils and concoctions; various dried herbs hanging up, or in packets and bottles of what appeared to be pickles; books large and small with various mystical titles, and a few items that Tricia could not categorise. There did not appear to be anyone in the shop and Tricia continued to look around, wondering what she should do. Suddenly, as if out of nowhere, a tall gentleman appeared behind her. "Can I help you?" he said, causing her to jump and spin around involuntarily. She looked up into the piercing eyes of the tall man dressed from head to toe in white robes. She could not decide what race he was exactly and concluded he was probably a mixture of all races. On his head he wore a white turban type hat. "I, I, ah a ah," Tricia stuttered, finding the tall stranger disconcerting. Taking a deep breath, she composed herself, "I've come to see Prophet Osira", she blurted out. "Yes, come with me, please," the tall stranger said in the Queen's English as he beckoned Tricia towards a door at the rear of the shop which he opened. As he did so a small lady whose ethnicity Tricia could not discern came through the door and into the shop - much to Tricia's relief she was not alone with the odd looking stranger, although the small lady was almost as weird looking. Tricia followed the tall man through the door at the back of the shop from which the little woman had emerged. He went to sit behind a desk and offered her a seat on the opposite side.

And what can I do for you young lady?" the man said looking deep into Tricia's eyes, as he spoke slowly in a very deep voice, as though looking and speaking into her very soul. *"This is like some horror movie,"* Tricia thought and immediately fretted that the man knew what she was thinking. Taking a deep breath she repeated, "I want to see Prophet Osira". "Yes, I am he," said the tall man tartly.

After a pause that was too long Tricia said, "I saw your advert in the paper", and waited for a response.

"And," was the only unhelpful response she received.

"I wondered if you could help me," another long pause.

"Look young lady, I haven't got all day – tell me what you came here for," the tall man replied brusquely. "I can help to guide you, but you have to tell me what you want", he attempted to temper the initial harsh response but unsuccessfully.

Tricia sat rigidly in the chair and took a deep breath before speaking again, "Someone I know – an old boyfriend – has deceived me…..,"

"Are you a lover or a fighter," the prophet cut into the unfinished sentence as he leant forward in his chair. Then quite unexpectedly the man burst into a peal of laughter. "Well?" he said, suddenly serious again – no hint of laughter remaining on his face or in his voice.

"I…I loved him very much but, but he just used me and then threw me away like a piece of dirty rag," Tricia said willing tears to form in her eyes - wanting the prophet to feel sorry for her.

"Are you a lover or a fighter – come on I do not have all day to waste". "Do you want me to help and guide you or not?" the prophet shouted, ignoring Tricia's crocodile tears.

"I have already told you why I am here – I have been wronged by an ex-lover," Tricia said raising her voice then catching herself, she lowered it to almost a whisper as she finished the sentence. She continued, "I want you to do anything you think appropriate to help me".

"I cannot make a decision for you young lady". "You alone must decide if you are a lover or a fighter".

"What is the difference," Tricia asked stupidly. She had come to get revenge on Gus but could not bring herself to say it. The thought that going for the option of a lover might be to her advantage flitted across her mind. Then she was overwhelmed by hatred for Gus and the need for revenge – her emotions seemed to be on a rollercoaster ride.

"It's up to you to decide – are you a fighter or a lover," was the booming response. Another pause as Tricia contemplated. "But if you want I can give you something to help you make up your mind," said the impatient prophet.

"Something like what?" Tricia asked.

"I can give you something to drink that will help to put you in touch with your true self – if you would like that," said the now smiling prophet as he rose from his seat and walked into a small closet adjoining the room. Tricia did not respond.

After a couple of minutes the prophet returned with a small beaker containing a red liquid with flecks of green plants in it, which he passed across the desk to Tricia.

"Drink that if you wish - it will reveal your heart's desire", the prophet said and sniggered. Then he sat down and stared intently at Tricia, unnerving her.

Tricia's hand shook involuntarily as she peered into the beaker at the red liquid. She wanted to ask what it was but held her tongue. She swirled the liquid around in the beaker – looked up questioningly at the prophet who continued to stare at her without blinking – looked into the beaker again and decided that if the liquid would allow her to realise her heart's desire as the prophet said she would have no choice but to drink it. She had come here intent on getting her revenge on Gus, but now she might be having second thoughts and needed to know what was in her heart of hearts. So telling herself that the liquid looked harmless enough, Tricia gingerly tasted the substance. It tasted salty and herby – drinkable. And so she closed her mind, held her breath and drank it, scowling as she did so. Suddenly the prophet burst into raucous laughter.

"I don't feel any different," Tricia thought with relief that she'd not grown another head or something.

"Now, are you a lover or a fighter," the prophet asked intently.

Tricia looked at him as though seeing him for the first time. She no longer found him menacing. Suddenly she knew exactly who she was – a fighter. She began to feel strong - powerful - invincible. "I want him to lose everything," Tricia listened to her own voice as though someone else was speaking. A small part of her regretted what she had just said, but for the main part she meant every word. She wanted Gus to suffer like he had made her suffer. She wanted him to feel loss as she had felt when he ended their relationship – to humiliate him as he had shamed her by dumping her. She had promised to make him pay, and he would – "HE WILL PAY", Tricia shouted.

A growing anger welled up inside of her, which grew until it threatened to overwhelm her soul - Tricia felt as though she would explode. She knew then that the only way she could alleviate this force was to hurt Gus – sort him out good and proper - teach him a lesson. "Uuuuhhh," she said, her face contorted. She felt that her head would burst open from pent up anger and frustration.

"Uuuhhh," she grimaced as she stood up and began to pace around the room. The prophet leaned back in his seat and watched her, "So, you are a fighter uuh," he said before bursting into another peal of manic laughter.

"I just want to teach him a lesson – a real good lesson – he must lose everything, EVERYTHING", Tricia shouted. Then she reduced her voice to little more than a whisper and repeated between gritted teeth while clenching her fist, "Everything – even his life". Then her anger subsided.

"Well I have just the thing for you, young lady," the prophet said as he rose from his seat and went into the closet yet again. He returned with a jar from which he extracted a small sachet which he handed to Tricia. He also gave her a very large indistinctly coloured candle, and commanded. "You must sprinkle the entire contents of this sachet at the door of your enemy. When you sprinkle it, you must call your enemy's name and say what you want to happen to him. When he walks across the powder the curse will begin to work. You must sprinkle it between 3.00am and 5.00am in the morning and then burn the sachet at his doorstep. You have to do this within 10 days. If you keep the powder for any longer a curse will begin to work against the closest person to you. Take heed to my words," the prophet warned then paused. "You must light this candle every morning for at least 15 minutes between 3.00 and 5.00 in the morning until it burns out. The first time you must light it is the day after you sprinkle the powder and every day at the same time". "You must burn it for at least 15 minutes", he repeated. "Here are the words you must chant as the candle burns", he said handing her a card. "If you fail to do this the curse will stop working and reverse". "Take heed to my words," the prophet stressed opening his eyes widely. "He repeated twice more "Take heed to my words," warning her gravely, then he said, "You can go now".

"How much do I owe you?" Tricia said extracting her purse from her handbag.

"You pay me only for the materials – that is £5 for the powder and £5 for the candle - £3 for the liquid". "I have only guided you - you do not need to pay for my direction – it is you who will do the work". "You can go now - I will see you when you return."

Tricia extracted a £20 note from her purse and proffered it to the prophet. He looked at it disdainfully and said "Ask the woman to give you change".

"Thank you very much," Tricia said as she walked towards the door.

"You do not need to thank me - I have done nothing," the prophet replied scornfully.

Tricia left the room and closed the door behind her.

She paid the woman in the shop and then left. As she exited the shop Tricia thought she heard the prophet laughing loudly as he had done during the consultation – but perhaps it was her imagination.

As Tricia left the shop prophet Osira burst into a peal of manic laughter "Silly young woman – you want to control another's destiny". "You pay with your soul to destroy another soul – how convenient" he said and laughed bitterly without humour again and again.

Walking briskly back to the station Tricia contemplated what had just taken place. She was glad it was all over and she would never have to come back to this awful place ever again. She hoped that the spell would teach Gus that he shouldn't mess with other people's lives. Tricia had no doubt in her mind that the spell she would cast on Gus would work. And she had it on good authority that the prophet was very powerful indeed. He had been recommended by a friend of hers – someone who knew about such matters – who told her that he was the best one to consult for dealing with enemies.

****

Gus drove out of the Stadium grounds, followed by the church van. He stopped and waited for Cyrus to lock up before waving goodbye to the youths as Cyrus drove off. Then he followed the van for a quarter of a mile before taking the route leading towards Islington. He did not notice the maroon Fiesta that was parked close to the stadium gates, nor did he notice as it followed them, taking the turn signposted for Islington behind him.

****

Tricia struggled to keep up with Gus as she tailed his car on his way home. She had borrowed her father's car. She did not like driving and was not very good at it – she had rarely driven above 40 miles per hour. However, heart in mouth she pressed on the accelerator - she had to keep up with Gus as it was the only way that she could find out where he lived. Disguised in a large afro wig and large rimmed glasses Tricia fretted that Gus might notice her through his rear view mirror, as several other road users blew their horns at her erratic manner of driving. Luckily for her, tonight he wasn't driving as fast as he usually did.

Gus was feeling drained after the training session and the past two very hectic weekends – one which he'd spent with Benza and Raj, and the last weekend which he'd spent with Marshie. He and Marshie had gone on a nightclub crawl, visiting 3 different clubs in one night and he had yet to recover fully, "I must be getting old", Gus said as he stretched his body. He drove easily through the night traffic, moving his limbs lethargically. Soon he reached home where he intended to have an early night. He didn't notice the car that followed him through and parked at the end of his road.

Tricia ducked down inside the car, just allowing herself sight of Gus as he stepped out of his car. She watched as he walked to his door, opened it and let himself in. "So this is where he lives," she verbalised her thoughts. "Well, not for much longer," she muttered rancorously, feeling excitement well up inside at the prospect of making Gus lose everything. "Why should he have all this while I live in a small room in my father's house," Tricia said completely out of touch with reality as she blamed Gus for her position in life. She had only known him for 6 months and had no idea what he may have sacrificed in order to acquire what he now owned, yet she adjudged that he didn't deserve to have any of it. And as she would not be sharing his life and all the privileges that went with that status, she whispered viciously, "If I can't share it all, then you cannot have it at all", and laughed hysterically at her rhyming rap, as she watched Gus close his front door behind him. She continued her monologue, "You will lose everything", then she fished a little known swear word from the bottom of hell's cess pit and spat it out venomously before driving off - she would be back later.

At 2.30 am on Thursday morning 13 April 2010 Tricia set off to Gus' house. The road was practically empty and driving was easy. It was eerily quiet, since her father's car did not have a music system of any kind. On arrival she parked down the street from Gus's house. She then removed the sachet of powder from her handbag, but clumsily dropped it and had to fumble around to retrieve it without realising that a dusting of the powder had escaped from the sachet. She proceeded to exit the car looked around to see if the coast was clear. Seeing no-one around, she walked towards Gus' house. As she approached the house she slowed her steps, pausing cautiously two doors away. Satisfied that the coast was clear she proceeded. On tip-toes in the deathly silence, Tricia opened the gate carefully so as to avoid it creaking. She entered the front garden then walked to the doorway where she stooped down and took out the sachet that the prophet had given to her. Noting that it was 3.15 am, Tricia set about following the instructions given to her by the prophet.

After burning the sachet as instructed Tricia returned to the car. She paused before entering the car, to take a deep breath and gloat with satisfaction at what she had accomplished - then got in and set off for home. As she drove an involuntary yawn seized upon her and she suddenly felt very tired indeed. "I'm going to sleep well when I get home", Tricia said, feeling satisfied. "Now I will just sit back and watch," she said. "Mission accomplished," she continued and smiled. But had Tricia known about the small trickling of dust that had fell into the car, she might not have been able to sleep at all.

CHAPTER 2

Running on Empty

Following her encounter with Dijon, that glimpse of the negative side of the music business caused Cherie to take the decision that she was not cut out to be an artiste after all. So she became involved behind the scenes, acquiring over eight years' experience. She boasted an enviable degree of versatility, having acquired her experience in various areas of the entertainment industry – mostly in music. And throughout this time she continued to write songs, one of which made it onto an album of a well known R & B singer.

After she left MPV Cherie went to work as a television research assistant, but discontented, after a few months she returned to work in the music industry as a co-ordinator in a large recording studio. She also worked in the capacity of an administrator, later becoming a talent scout for a major label. On leaving that job she took nine months off to contemplate her future, during which time she travelled to many regions of the world, seeking to discover new cultures and her inner self – searching her soul. On her return to London, finding no inclination to continue working for others, she decided to use her acquired knowledge and her own natural talents to guide aspiring artistes towards achieving their musical goal. And so relying on the theoretical knowledge she had acquired on the part-time course she had studied two years previously and her practical experience, Cherie launched into business and Smooth Management was born.

Thousands of hopefuls were auditioned in the quest to find artistes, a humongous task which Cherie could not handle by herself and so had employed the help of her trusted friend George, whom she met while working for MPV. George boasted a wealth of experience gained over 24 years in the business, having begun his career as an artiste in a boy band way back in the 80s.

Masses responded to the advert and were auditioned - they sang and gyrated, they toasted and rapped, they danced and pranced. And Cherie and George agonised for two weeks over their selection, finally choosing Sera Ocel, and Ebony Son, both sing-er-songwriters with superstar potential. When auditions came to a close, several others had come knocking at Smooth Management's doors - Cherie fell in love with the velvet tones of Maxi Black, and George couldn't say "no" to the raunchy, ruckus sing-rap style of Daton Reese. So those two further solo artistes were also signed. Cherie also had a band on her books – "Kingdom Praise", who were "discovered" when they visited her local church and blew the congregation away with their fresh original sound, a combination of jazz, soul and reggae.

Eighteen months on, Smooth Management was running smoothly, with much needed help from Naomi, the part-time PA that Cherie employed soon after she set up. Except for her PA's assistance, 5 hours a day, 3 days a week, and input from George when absolutely necessary, Cherie did everything herself. Smooth Management could be likened to a movie where she played almost every role, including that of general dogsbody. The agency was still in its infancy and Cherie continued to work manically.

A unique outfit, Smooth Management provided a comprehensive service to its artistes - securing bookings for them, dealing with recordings, publishing, distribution and publicity. Every three months or so Cherie organised one-night events where Smooth Management artistes were the only ones featured. She also got personally involved in the production and engineering side of things and sang back-up vocals when necessary. She could never have imagined how much effort and time she would need to put into this venture – now she valued every single second of her day. But her hard work was beginning to pay off.

Under the watchful eye of Cherie, Sera Ocel, Ebony Son and the others have developed into first class recording and performing artistes - a challenging feat to say the least – especially working with Sera Ocel – AKA Serena Orcela. Sera, a Reggae/R & B fusion sing-jay was large on talent but she was also a heavy weight Diva. And as the demand for her and her material increased so did Sera's ego.

With the popularity of Sera Ocel and the other artistes growing and gathering momentum, Cherie was kept busier than ever.

And now she was in the process of arranging her biggest venture yet - a countrywide tour to promote both Sera Ocel's and Ebony Son's new albums and singles, due for release Friday 28 April 2010. Today, Tuesday 18 April, to say that Cherie was running herself into the ground in an effort to ensure that everything was in place would be a gross understatement. The first show would kick off in 10 days' time in Birmingham and there was not enough time left for Cherie to attend to last-minute details.

Today had been the craziest day of all – a major set back had arisen – the designer of the costumes had confirmed that there was a problem with the material for the designs that Sera Ocel would wear on stage. Cherie had to arrange for the design and creation of entirely different outfits at this late stage. On top of that, she had to chase the publicist as the tour was not getting the right amount of favourable exposure.

Sera telephoned Cherie no less than 5 times a day and today she had called a record 10 times so far meaning that Cherie had spent at least 2 precious hours counselling, consoling, cajoling and listening to her harp on about one less than important problem after the other. *"Honestly, the girl is talented but she is also a major pain,"* Cherie thought aloud for the umpteen time today, as she took much needed deep breaths in an effort to keep calm. And as soon as Cherie gathered herself, Sera was on the 'phone again.

"What now", Cherie almost shouted, then calming herself with a deep breath as she picked up.

"Hi, I've been thinking", Sera announced then continued after a short pause, "I don't really think I want to travel up to Birmingham on the bus with the others – I want to arrive in style, so I feel it would be best for me to travel up with you in your car," Sera stated.

"Well, I wasn't thinking of driving up myself", Cherie replied, continuing, "I think it will be best for us all to go on the bus".

"Well, sorry, but I disagree……" Sera argued authoritatively and went on to give a long list of inconsequential reasons to support her argument.

The conversation ended with Sera reminding Cherie, "Don't forget I am paying your wages...", rendering Cherie so livid she almost hyperventilated, but her head dictated that it would not be wise to be rude to Sera for fear she might go into one of her diva strops and not show up for the tour so Cherie bit her tongue and agreed to the Diva's terms.

"Be patient", Cherie kept whispering, encouraging herself, reminding herself that she had so much at stake riding on this tour - too much to lose. But her tongue was becoming sore at being bitten so hard and so often. And not for the first time today she sighed with regret wishing that she had followed first instincts about Sera Ocel, because soon after their first meeting she had gotten a strong inclination that Sera Ocel could be trouble. But she could never have guessed the extent of hard work she would become. Her behaviour was in stark contrast to the politically correct, sober and altruistic messages conveyed by the lyrics of her songs and her diva attitude was driving Cherie to her wit's end, so much so that she now made a personal vow that at the end of this tour she would part company with Sera Ocel for good.

Unbeknown to Sera Ocel, who was basking in the new found glory of her success, she was the proverbial hot potato, ready to be dropped - Cherie could not wait for her one-year/one album contract to end. There was now less than 6 months remaining and Cherie was counting each day.

"Your time is almost up, Ms Ocel", Cherie whispered to herself, then felt a little guilty. However she soon appeased her conscience as she recalled Sera Ocel's most unreasonable antics. As soon as possible she intended to shift her energy and attention to her other artistes, or someone entirely new, who could appreciate success and her efforts instead of taking it all for granted as Sera apparently did.

Exhausted and contemplating the events of the day, Cherie drove through rush hour traffic towards Mount Zion Church, where she taught modern dance at the Project for young people on Tuesday evenings. The Project also ran a vocal workshop at which she taught on Fridays. Cherie was committed to both visions, however, due to the upcoming tour, she had not attended either workshop for the past 2 weeks and making it tonight was the result of a herculean effort.

Pondering deeply as she drove, Cherie contemplated bringing an end to her dealings with secular music altogether. In truth, although her crew were immensely talented and their material tasteful and without crassness, she found no depth of satisfaction flowing from the production and promotion of it. Cherie also acknowledged the strong pull she had been feeling in her spirit lately, away from the secular. As she became more mature in her Christianity, so too grew her desire towards Gospel music. Sera Ocel's behaviour today and the star's general "me, me, me" attitude, reminiscent of Dijon's was hammering home the sheer disillusionment of the secular music business. "This is not what life is all about", Cherie said quietly as a strained expression crossed her face. Further contemplation brought home that in the past year her only true satisfaction had been derived from writing gospel material, some of which she had shared with Kingdom Praise. Most of her Gospel songs were reserved for personal worship and praise. So anointed were the songs that Cherie found herself crying each time she sang them. And the compulsion to write and sing them was growing ever stronger each day. For the first time it dawned on Cherie that she may be receiving divine inspiration - was the Lord "calling" her to do gospel music?

Thoughts of the boys and girls who attended the workshop on Tuesdays jumped to the forefront of Cherie's mind as she neared her destination. In the nine months that she had been teaching them she had grown very fond of each, had missed them terribly these past two weeks, and was longing to see them tonight. She liked each one for differing reasons, but her favourite was Melissa, whom, though very demanding of attention was, beneath the tough exterior, a big softy. Melissa rarely missed a class although she was hopeless at dancing, making up with enthusiasm for what she lacked in ability. However, she was Cherie's star pupil in the vocal workshop, having being gifted with the voice of an angel. Perhaps that was why Cherie liked her so much - she reminded her of herself. She could see real prospects for Melissa - a bright future awaited her, but first Melissa had to be convinced of her own potential, for she was apparently unaware of the great gift that she carried. Cherie was seriously contemplating taking Melissa under her wings and nurturing her. She had even penned a number of deeply spiritual and inspirational songs with Melissa's vocal range in mind. During one of the workshops Melissa had divulged her desire to become "a big time famous gospel singer", evidently without believing that it could be possible. And Cherie promised herself now that as soon as the tour was over she intended to change musical course and begin to concentrate on making Melissa's and other gospel artists dreams become a reality.

By the time Cherie arrived at 7.00 pm she had shed much of the stress of the day. Although she was over half an hour late she was glad she had made the effort, so touched was she by the enthusiasm of the youngsters, who cheered on her arrival, reminding her of just how important the workshops were to them. She only wished she could find competent people to deputise for her when she wasn't available, and had been praying about it without ceasing as she felt near to breaking point. And each day as the tour drew nearer to kick off, Cherie found herself worrying more about the youngsters. She would still try to make the Tuesday evening classes, but she would definitely not be able to make it on Fridays.

It surprised Cherie that she had so much energy to give during the workshop. She strutted, danced and jived the youngsters through their routines effortlessly. Just as she finished the workshop at 8.30 pm, Brother Cyrus came in to remind her that there was a Project meeting tonight, and noting the look of strain as her forehead involuntarily creased, he added "It won't take too long".

Not wanting to let everyone down, Cherie agreed to stay for the meeting - in any case she wanted the chance to raise the question of whether a stand-in vocal coach could be found to cover for her when she was unable to make it.

Cherie brought up the up-coming tour at the Committee meeting, pointing out that she would not be able to make the Friday workshops for the next 4 months. Sister Marriott, the Projects Co-ordinator, informed her that it was impossible to engage a stand-in due to financial constraints.

This was the thought that troubled Cherie on the way home - she reasoned with God that she had no choice because her work was important – she had to make a living after all. The thought that she could ask George to deputise for her at the Friday evening shows was reluctantly dismissed – Cherie knew that she had to be present as only then could she be certain that all would go well. An accusing voice arose in her spirit, that an honest analysis of the situation was that she had made her mind up to do what she pleased regardless, and was not really interested in listening to what God had to say about the matter. This made Cherie feel sad, but she knew that was not true – "was it?" That question hung in her mind. She was exhausted and could hardly think straight but struggled to continue reflecting as she drove slowly along the dual carriageway. She yawned widely every few minutes, while endeavouring to keep her eyes opened and concentrate. Thoughts of Sera flitted through her mind, keeping her mildly infuriated and saving her from dosing off – Sera did have her uses after all.

About half way through her journey, Cherie almost nodded off, but jumped to attention as a black Mini overtook her, cutting sharply in front of her, almost hitting her vehicle before speeding off, horn blaring. Cherie whispered a prayer, "Thank you Lord for waking me up", and wound down her window a little. She would not usually drive when she felt this tired but the need to get home quickly and out early in the morning had compelled her to do so.

Endeavouring to remain alert Cherie encouraged her mind to return to contemplating whether she was in fact putting her work before her ministry. This thought troubled her spirit and in an effort to find alleviation she breathed a prayer, "Lord please forgive me if I am being selfish – don't be angry with me – please remember that I am human and prone to faults," she said as though God was sitting in the passenger seat. And suddenly she heard God speak in her spirit as she did on occasions – he spoke loud and clear – she should move the vocal workshop to Tuesday evenings for the duration of the tour.

Cherie smiled to herself – "That's it", she spoke her thought, then returned to planning silently. Mary-Ann, her deputy and stand-in in the dance group could take the dance class, while she took the vocal class, or they could combine the two workshops as there were some youngsters who took both classes – yes, they could combine the workshops for 3 months, start it at 6 pm instead of

6.30 pm, and finish it at 8.30 pm instead of 8 pm. Mary-Ann could take the dance workshop at 6.00 pm and she could take over on arrival at around 6.30-7 pm and then she could take the vocal workshop from 7.15 to 8.30 pm – perfect. And Cherie thanked God for the wisdom he had imparted to her. She would call Mary-Ann and Sister Marriott tomorrow and ask them to make the necessary arrangements and announcements.

The sign "You are now entering Kesley Park" announced that she was almost home, causing Cherie to become mildly excited at the thought that she would soon step into the warmth and safety of home. She had lived in Kesley Park for the past 2 years, having sold the flat in Walthamstow which she'd purchased with the royalties from "Missing You". She loved Kesley Park, which was a far safer and nicer neighbourhood.

"Wow, eleven o'clock.....already," Cherie said as she glanced at the dashboard clock, yawning mid-sentence. She had left home at 7.00 am and it felt as though she had lived two days in one. "What a day," she groaned, adding a huge sigh.

Cherie turned the corner into her road on the last leg of her journey home. She drew up in front of her house and parked the car in a haphazard fashion, the back wheel wedged against the kerb. Aware but too tired to care Cherie's mind was preoccupied by the thought of food and bed. As she stepped out of her car into the a chilly Spring night a sharp breeze caused her to shiver involuntarily, her jeans, tea shirt and light denim jacket inadequate against the cold. When she had set out that morning, bright sunshine promised a warm Spring day the weather report endorsing that expectation, but it had turned decidedly colder as evening fell. Trembling, Cherie raised the collar of her jacket and walked briskly to her front door. A neighbour putting out his bins for collection the next morning waved hello and she waved back, thinking how lucky she was to live in such a friendly, safe neighbourhood. She enjoyed the contrast between where she lived, here in Enfield, where Jean and Chester lived which was even further into suburbia where she still had her own room, and where her office was situated in the City – in Islington.

Entering her home, Cherie disabled the alarm system before

kicking off her shoes and flopping onto the sofa. After a few minutes she made her way to the other side of the living room where she turned up the thermostat. She stretched her hands upward rotating her body in a circular motion, before flopping onto the sofa again, simultaneously grabbing the remote control from the top of the nearby radiator cabinet and switching on the TV. A pang in her stomach reminded her that she had not eaten and should have picked up something on the way home. "Oh no", Cherie exclaimed, but decided that she was more tired than she was hungry and was not going out again tonight. She thought of fixing herself a snack but found the kitchen cupboards and refrigerator bare and, returning to flop on the sofa, she tried to push all thoughts of food from her mind

Flicking through the channels with the remote control, Cherie was bombarded by adverts and images of delicious food. In an attempt to avoid them, she switched to a 24-hour news channel, breathing a sigh of relief – no delicious and appetising images of food to entice here. And she went some way towards exorcising the demon of hunger by concentrating on the current affairs of the day. Before long she was sound asleep, her head drooped over the arm of the sofa - one leg on the floor - one arm across the back of the sofa, the other clutching the remote control to her body. She was jogged awake when the remote control fell from her grasp with a thud. Moving into a more comfortable foetal position, Cherie fell into deeper sleep.

"What do you mean you're my father, you can't be my father, you're only three years older than me," Cherie shouted to the tall dark handsome stranger.

"I'm the father you never knew and you better show me some respect," replied the stranger.

"Respect, I will never show you any respect, so you better get lost," Cherie retorted.

"Oh yes you will," the stranger shouted angrily. Cherie turned and ran and the stranger began to run after her, but the faster she ran the less ground she seemed to cover. Her legs were so heavy, so heavy, sooo heavy. She was worried that the stranger might be catching up with her – but she looked back to see that he wasn't gaining any ground although he seemed to be running much faster than she was. Then she heard the siren. It was a police siren, they must be coming to help her - but who called them. She kept on running but then noticed that the stranger who said he was her father had disappeared. *"Where did he go,"* she thought. And the sirens got louder and louder until they besieged her thoughts, brrr, brrr; brrr, brrr.

Cherie was awakened from her nightmare by the ring of the telephone. Still half asleep she reached over and grabbed the handset from its cradle. It fell from her grasp and she fumbled to find it on the floor. "Hello," announced the caller. Cherie did not reply but listened, struggling to think clearly - still not fully awake. "Hello," the caller repeated more vehemently, as though compelling her to reply.

"Oh no," if she'd realised it was Curtis she would not have answered – but too late. So she replied, "Hello Curtis".

"Hello, darling," said the slithery voice on the other end, "It's Curtis, how are you doing?" Curtis said, apparently oblivious to the fact that Cherie had already identified him as the caller.

"Oh, Curtis, you just woke me up and I'm really tired," Cherie slurred down the receiver. "Can I call you back tomorrow?"

"Can I come over and tuck you in?" Curtis cooed in his sexiest bedside voice.

"Curtis, I said I will call you back tomorrow," Cherie was annoyed as well as startled by Curtis' advance. How dare he assume that he could telephone her at this hour and speak to her in that manner. Jolted fully awake by Curtis' cheeky suggestion, Cherie decided that she should address the issue. "What do you mean you want to come round and tuck me in anyway?" she said sternly. "How dare you assume that you can speak to me in that way", "Don't forget that we are just friends and we won't be for much longer if you keep up this sort of behaviour". "Have some respect will you and please don't let me have to tell you again," she said sternly.

"Calm down, keep you hair on – I was only joking. Can't you take a joke?" Curtis responded - his tone even. He knew he may have gone too far and decided he'd better be careful what he said.

"I don't like to joke around about such things Curtis – it seems a little bit personal to me," Cherie stood her ground. Curtis did not reply.

Cherie tempered her reaction to his advance and said, "I don't want you to think that the nature of our relationship will change in any way". "You and I are just friends, and that is all that we will ever be". "Is that clear?" Cherie said emphasising the point she had already made but attempting to do so gently.

"Yes mum," Curtis replied patronisingly.

They had known each other from school days, having met when they were both in their final school year. Although they had gone on group dates a few times at school, no romance had developed between them, due largely to the fact that Cherie was not interested in forming any romantic attachment with anyone then – at least that was her excuse. Truth was that she was not in the least bit attracted to Curtis. However, they had become good friends, but had drifted apart when Curtis met Leslie, to whom he later became engaged. They eventually lost contact with each other and in the interim years Curtis had married Leslie and had a son, Davey, now 7 years old. But the marriage had not worked and now Curtis was single again and unfortunately for Cherie, on the prowl.

They had been reacquainted when they had unexpectedly run into each other 18 months ago having attended the same church conference. It was a huge surprise to both and they had resumed their friendship, Curtis making it clear to Cherie that he wanted more than friendship from her, but she in turn making it doubly obvious that she was not interested. Although Curtis' romantic interest in her made it difficult to maintain their friendship, Cherie tried to keep up contact because they had known each other for such a long time, and in truth she did not dislike Curtis. He had a wide knowledge on a multitude of issues, was very interesting to talk to on the right occasions, and she'd learned a lot from him. Lately though Cherie questioned whether the friendship was workable, as Curtis was obviously not getting the clear messages she was sending. He took every opportunity to push the issue of their becoming an item, and she was getting tired or reminding him that they were nothing but friends. And lately he had begun to cross firmly erected boundaries, and she would not tolerate that.

It wasn't that Curtis was unattractive - he was quite handsome in fact and was the most eligible bachelor she knew. Tall with well developed muscles, medium complexioned with conventionally handsome features, he wore his hair cut stylishly low, low as his hairline was receding noticeably. Most women would agree that Curtis was a good catch. Some of the sisters in the church certainly thought so – many no doubt praying that he would approach them. But, although he was very flirtatious, all knew that his true interest lay with Cherie. But there was an absence of chemistry - she loved Curtis as a brother, nothing more and there was absolutely no prospect of that ever changing.

Cherie repented and begged God's forgiveness for continuously informing Curtis that she was not interested in forming a romantic relationship with anyone at present and just wished to concentrate on her relationship with her Lord and on her career, because the truth was that she longed to meet the right man and prayed for God to send him sooner rather than later.

In all honesty she had wondered whether Curtis was God's answer when they had first met up again. And perhaps if Curtis had not been quite so flirtatious with many sisters, Cherie might have given some thought to taking their relationship further, but the trust issues she had meant that she guarded her heart fiercely, had erected firm barriers and Curtis had destroyed any slim chance that he may have had.

The trust issues Cherie had, had arisen many years ago. It was when she and George both worked with MPV Studios, Cherie in administration and George as a sought-after session musician. Their paths crossed when on occasions Cherie helped out as a session singer or in some other capacity around the studio. It started with admiration of his gifts and grew to the point where she practically hero-worshipped George. He knew so much, not just about music but also about life. Cherie learned so much from him and grew to rely on him for solutions. And reliance turned to trust, which before long turned to love. Suddenly Cherie realised that she needed to have George around – to be with him so she sought to be in his company every moment she could. Needing his attention, she endeavoured to attract his admira-

tion and praise when they worked together, and he was enamoured by her talents too. But though Cherie tried to demonstrate to George her true feelings over many months but he seemed to ignore her. She wore make up – new hairstyles – suffered in heels – long false fingernails – figure hugging clothes – all in an effort to attract some reaction from George, but all in vain. So she tried making eyes at him, locking eyes and staring deeply and meaningfully into his. But as soon as George discovered her intentions he averted her eyes. She tried touching him affectionately on his arm to portray her heart but George began to keep a safe distance between them, as though seeking to protect himself. In every way that he could, he demonstrated to Cherie that he did not share her romantic vision. Finally as a last resort, Cherie tried kissing George - they'd attended a dinner party held by a mutual friend, and were among the last to leave. They sat on the patio while their hosts bade others goodbye and, with the single glass of wine that she'd imbibed earlier providing bravado, Cherie got up, walked straight over to George, sat on his lap and kissed him deeply. But instead of responding to her kiss, George had gently pushed her away. "No, don't do that," was all he'd said. Cherie was instantly hurt, for she'd dreamt of the moment that their lips would meet and in her dream, shooting stars flew across the sky and fireworks lit up the night - but not this. "Why not, George, can't you see that I'm crazy about you?" "I just want us to be together – as a couple – we would be so good together," Cherie had babbled, baring her soul. But George did not react as she'd expected, "Please, Cherie, let's not spoil our friendship". "I love you man – but not like that – you're my sister, man", George said looking almost exasperated. Cherie could not believe what was happening and close to tears she grabbed her bag and left.

After that day George tried to keep some distance between them – Cherie could tell and that hurt her even more. And although she wanted to, Cherie found that she couldn't move on and her feelings for George were growing more intense – so strong that it caused her physical pain. She ached to tell him how much she cared and things became more and more awkward between them. George dealt with the situation by curtailing his visits to the studio, until he stopped coming altogether.

For many years after that Cherie carried a flaming torch for

George which burnt a hole through her heart. She had only in the last two years or so managed to dampen down the flames. She'd come to terms with the fact that George was not for her - had swallowed the bitter pill of unrequited love, had survived and recovered - almost completely. And her friendship with George had been restored.

Since then Cherie guarded her heart. She wanted to wait until she knew the other person wanted her before allowing herself to feel anything. But the fact was that even when perspective suitors approached her, professing and demonstrating undying love, Cherie still did not give up any part of her heart to them – and there had been many. With Cherie it was case of "once rejected, a thousand times shy".

"Look, Cherie, I'm sorry, it's just that you are so attractive, you've to cut a guy some slack - you are a beautiful woman". "I'm going to slip up a little sometimes, but I do value our friendship," Cherie listened as Curtis made his insincere spiel. She felt that Curtis was disrespecting her and trying to condone his behaviour by blaming it on the fact that he found her attractive.

"So it's my fault for being attractive then," Cherie said seething.

"No, well, yes - no," Curtis said finally bursting into laugher.

Cherie was not amused, "Look Curtis, I've really got to get some sleep, I've a long day ahead tomorrow," she snapped.

"You're not the only one who is busy, you know," Curtis said still chuckling. "Give and take, that's what friendship is all about," he continued, launching into one of his famous lectures. Cherie did not reply, but just listened, silently questioning whether she was being selfish?

"Okay – I promise I'll behave". "How was your day?" Curtis asked, and without pausing for a reply proceeded to give Cherie every uninteresting detail about his own day.

When he paused Cherie seized a window of opportunity "Oh, my day was the worse day ever, I was so busy – I had so much to do with the tour beginning at the end of next week, and then I had to drop in at the Project as I could not go for all of last week due to work commitments – then there was a meeting when the workshop finished". "I only just got home 45 minutes ago and I am so soo tired," Cherie hoped that Curtis would get the message and leave her to sleep.

"Oh well, never mind, you know if you want success, you have to work hard for it," Curtis ignored her accent on how tired she was. She did not appreciate his words of encouragement – all she could think about was curling up and going to sleep. She did not reply and hoped that he'd take it as a further hint.

"We must meet up for lunch – how about tomorrow", Curtis was undaunted. "Okay, I'll call you tomorrow when I know what I am doing". Cherie tried to grasp a slim chance of finishing the conversation but before she could end her sentence, Curtis cut in.

"Oh, you wouldn't guess who I saw this evening on the way home", Cherie sighed quietly and rolled her eyes.

"Who?" "You remember Kevin from school – big Kev – you remember him –tall mixed race guy who used to live in Hackney. He had a sister named Katie who used to play the double bass in the school orchestra – remember them?" Cherie didn't want to remember Kevin at the moment, she didn't want to think, she didn't want to talk, she wanted to scream, she didn't swear, but if she did, she would definitely want to, she wanted to tell Curtis to leave her alone and never call her again – she was tired and she was becoming more and more irritable. But then Cherie remembered a Bible teaching that admonished patience, and repented of her thoughts in her heart – taking a deep breath she replied. "Yes, I think I have a vague memory of them – didn't you used to fancy Katie", she said wondering and hoping that Katie was still unmarried - perhaps Curtis could direct his amorous attentions toward her.

"That was a long time ago and anyway, she's married now," came the unhelpful response. Cherie sighed.

Curtis went on unperturbed, "He's doing really well now". "He's into stock-broking". "You want to see the car he's driving – top of the range Merc". Then Curtis launched straight on to tell Cherie all about how Big Kev was doing. Cherie started to reply in one syllable sentences – "great"- "really" – "no?" - "lovely," and Curtis went on for another 10 minutes none stop.

"Okay," Cherie thought, I will have to end this conversation.

I will have to be abrupt. She thought of saying, *"Curtis, you have left me no choice, I'm hanging up now – I can't take anymore of this – not tonight – you are driving me up the wall"*. But instead, she said gently but firmly "Anyway, I'm going to have to go now Curtis". "You can tell me all about it tomorrow when I see you". "I'll call you in the morning". "I've got to get to bed now – it's nearly 1.00 am and I haven't slept properly for days and I've got an early start". "So good night and sleep tight – see you Curtis – God bless". And with that Cherie hung up, cutting Curtis off in mid-sentence. Tomorrow was another day and he could bore her some more then. Right now she needed to get some sleep.

Cherie went into the kitchen and grabbed an apple from the fruit dish, obeying the hunger pangs that continued to gnaw at her stomach. She bit a large chunk out of it and chomping loudly headed upstairs. What she needed now was a quick shower - and bed. Finishing the apple she stepped into the shower, lathered up and scrubbed vigorously, as though trying to wash away some of the day's stress. Satisfied she was clean, she then dried herself, cleansed her face and neck in record time and headed for the bedroom where she climbed into bed and nestled deeply into her pillows, allowing her body to become abandoned. She whispered a short prayer, while feeling guilty that she had not knelt down.

Although Cherie expected sleep to engulf her (mind and body in total surrender), it did not, and as the minutes passed she became more and more widely awake. Lying awake her thoughts drifted back to the dream she had earlier. There was always the recurring theme of her father in her dreams of late – she had been having them almost every night for the past year and they were becoming more like nightmares. After waking from such dreams Cherie would wonder about Tyrone's whereabouts and give further thought to tracking him down.

Jumping out of bed Cherie grabbed her laptop and switched it on and then typed her father's name into the search engine. Getting no real tangible results she realised, not for the first time, that she needed more information to help her to trace her father. She had not abandoned the idea of broaching the subject with her mother again but she wanted to wait for the right time. She was unsure how Jean might take this new found interest and Cherie was reluctant to hurt her mother whom she loved dearly. Plumping up her pillow Cherie sat up in bed and browsed for half an hour, mostly the same websites she had browsed before, reaching the same conclusion as umpteen times before. Feeling hopeless, she switched off the laptop and nestled into the duvet and pillows trying to drop off to sleep again. Pulling her legs up into a semi-foetal position, as her breathing relaxed, she felt herself drawing nearer and nearer to the stranger. He waved to her from across a meadow full of daisies, beckoning her to come. She was in the middle of the field when she saw the bull approaching her and she began to run backwards to safety. But the faster she ran, the less ground she appeared to be making. She was running, running, but she appeared not to be moving at all. The bull caught up with her and was just about to maul her when she grabbed hold of its horns and, with super human strength, flung it across the meadow towards the stranger. Then she looked for the stranger but he wasn't there – he had disappeared. She turned to walk back across the meadow, dejected and sad. She had come to like the stranger that waved at her across the meadow but now he was gone. She looked around but he was gone. She walked back to her original position on the other side of the meadow and then, looking up, she saw him again, walking away into the distance. She hurried after him but he his pace quickened. She ran and ran but could not catch up. She began to cry as she could not catch up. He looked back at her and laughed – but it wasn't him - it was the other one the same stranger who had said he was her father. He turned back and began walking towards her, but even though he walked towards her, he was still afar. "My daughter," he said, but she became afraid, turned around and started to run away from him. "You are not my father, I don't know you. Where did you come from? I don't believe that you are my father. If you are my father, how come I don't know you?" Cherie shouted.

The stranger replied, "I am your father and I will prove that I am."

"Okay, go on and prove that you are my father then," Cherie said in her dream.

I will do that," said that stranger and then disappeared again.

Cherie shouted after the stranger "Okay then, prove it – prove you are my father, prove it", so loudly that she was awoken by her own voice - in a cold sweat. She lay awake, tossing and turning for some good time before she dropped off again, into another fitful slumber.

CHAPTER 3

Collision Course

Cherie awoke reluctantly, feeling even more tired than when she had gone to sleep the night before. She stretched her limbs slowly and gradually opened her eyes. After a few seconds she became more conscious and aware of the sun streaming though the crack in the curtains, causing her to blink repeatedly. She pulled the duvet over her head and nestled into her pillow. Then realisation hit her -"*The sun* – oh no, what time is it?" Cherie exclaimed as she jumped out of bed. Grabbing her phone she rushed towards the bathroom, stretching, yawning until tears welled up in her eyes. "Oh no, I'm late," she mumbled as she blinked away tears and stared at the face of her phone for rather longer than necessary as though willing the time to be wrong, stand still, or reverse. It was nearly 9.00 am on Wednesday 19 April and she should have been up and out an hour ago.

Stepping into the shower Cherie tried to think up a suitable motto for the day but uncharacteristically found no inspiration, so settled on one she knew well and had used before, "The early bird catches the worm". Cherie voiced the familiar adage loudly. However, it did not have the desired motivational effects, since she could not fully believe it, as she was in fact running late. A small voice spoke in her spirit that she was being too hard on herself, after all she worked late most evenings and not a week went by without her bringing work home. So Cherie defiantly repeated the motto, adding "I shall accomplish all I set out to do today – yes I will". Then she felt better and proceeded to shower as quickly as she could, dry off, brush her teeth and dress in a clean pair of jeans, a beige tea-shirt, brown sweater and brown leather three quarter jacket.

Before leaving home, Cherie spoke a short prayer, thanking God for the day ahead and requesting His guidance and protection, then she grabbed her gloves and scarf, remembering how chilly it had become the previous night, and headed downstairs where she grabbed her handbag, keys and a CD. She didn't do breakfast, but always had a hot and honey sweetened mug of tea in the mornings. However, this morning she would even forego tea.

Jumping into her car Cherie started the engine and manoeuvred onto the road, at the same time shuffling around to settle into her seat. She turned on the radio and searched for Blue Sky FM, but couldn't pick it up. So she reached over and grabbed the CD from the passenger seat and inserted it. The smooth sound of Laverne Mitchell with Unity's "Nothing can stop you" wafted into the car – immediately lifting her spirit. "Put your shoulders back and head high", Cherie sang along then just listened and meditated on the words of the song as it lifted her spirit to higher heights – and higher still. After a little while she felt strong and focused – ready to meet all the challenges that the day promised. Her mobile began to ring and she reached over and took it from her bag - it was Sera – "Oh no", Cherie exclaimed, then chewed on her bottom lip - Sera would be fuming. She was supposed to meet her at the office at 9.00 am so that they could go for a fitting at the designer's studio, and it was now 9.40 am. Cherie ignored the call - she should be there before 10.00 am and would have to make her apologies then.

Skipping to her favourite track, Cherie breathed deeply to try and compose herself. "I'm under an open heaven, new mercies everyday I see …," the empowering lyrics caressed her ears and soothed her mind. The melody engulfed her in a sea of hope and she became spiritually aware of the great assurance her soul derived from the anointed song.

Then it happened. Creeche" "Bam" "crunch". Cherie was suddenly jolted forward in her seat, "Lord, have mercy - what was that?" She shouted, instinctively jamming on her brakes and applied the hand brake, then she sat still except for her head which turned quickly from side to side, so shocked was she by the impact. Her mind refused to focus properly for a moment or two - then it dawned on her, another car had just hit hers on the rear passenger side. She looked into her rear view mirror and then quickly turned to look back over her shoulder, having gathered her thoughts, intent on getting the other drivers licence number before he drove off. As Cherie fumbled around in the glove compartment for a pen and paper, she kept glancing backwards. She observed that the other driver had parked up a small distance behind her car - then he just sat still and appeared to be rubbing his brow. Armed with pen and pad Cherie opened her door, having the presence of mind to look first to ensure that no other cars were passing close by, before stepping out.

"What do you think you're doing? Look at my car - why didn't you look where you were going?" Cherie said gesticulating with her arms. The driver of the other car did not say anything – he just stared at her. Then he calmly got out of his vehicle and inspected the damage done - first to his own car and then to hers. Cherie was fuming and wanted to tell him so. It made her even angrier that he was obviously taking it so coolly. What angered her most was not so much the damage to her car, which did not look at all serious, but the fact that this accident had delayed her further. "Look at that - this could have been avoided if you had only looked where you were going - as if I wasn't late enough - now this." Cherie nagged, peeved by the fact that the other driver's car did not look to have sustained any obvious damage at all. "I really don't know what you were thinking – didn't you see me?" Cherie droned on. She couldn't stop herself now that she was on a roll. It was not until she said she would call the Police that the other driver spoke up.

"There is no need to do that - I'll give you my details", he said reaching for the pen and paper which she was holding. He proceeded to write his name, address and telephone numbers on it. Then he extracted a card from his wallet and wrote details of his insurance company also.

"Now please can I have your details?" he requested.

"Why should I give you my details? I wasn't at fault," Cherie replied firmly.

"Look, I don't wish to argue about this". "In fact, the damage looks pretty superficial to me". "You can give my mechanic a call and arrange for an inspection," the other driver sounded tired as he spoke. He wrote a further telephone number on the piece of paper and handed it to Cherie.

Cherie had prepared herself for the other driver to be confrontational – drivers always were when a collision took place, and although she found it mildly annoying that he did not say he accepted full responsibility for the accident which was clearly his fault, he was offering to repair the damage. She felt the need to apologise for her over the top reaction. So feeling a little embarrassed she changed her manner of speaking.

"Sorry about my reaction, it's just that I consider that with a little more care this could have been avoided". "I will be contacting your mechanic, and if necessary, your insurance company".

In spite of her apology Cherie's tone remained firm. As she spoke she wrote down his licence plate number – just in case. Then on a different piece of paper, she wrote her own licence plate number, her name and mobile number and handed it to the other driver. As the other driver was behaving so civilised she felt she should do likewise.

As Cherie walked back to her vehicle and inspected the damage more closely, she was pleased to see that it did not look at all serious. She got into her car but before driving away, was prompted to look backwards once more. She was concerned to see that the other driver appeared to be watching her. She noted that he was shaking his head from side as he opened his vehicle door and entered. Cherie felt mildly annoyed by his cheeky gesture - how dare he, after all he should not have been surprised by her reaction, since the incident was entirely his fault. What did he expect? As indignation threatened to bubble over inside, Cherie took a deep breath and she began dialling Sera's number to apologise for being late - at least now she had a genuine excuse.

Gus sat still after Cherie had driven off, trying to figure out what had happened. He did not see the other car coming as he came out of the side road. It was as if he had become completely confused and didn't know what he was doing for a split second. The same thing had happened to him earlier that morning when he stepped outside his home. For a few seconds he didn't know where he was or what he was doing. Gus wondered whether he was losing his mind, quickly dismissing the thought – no, it was just a momentary aberration – nothing more - he felt fine now, he thought reassuringly. However, the doubts as to how the accident had happened nagged at him for the rest of the day and he just couldn't come up with an appeasing explanation.

For the rest of the week Cherie was extremely busy - too busy to think about anything but the up-coming tour. She kept reminding herself that she needed to make time to ring the mechanic to arrange for the repairs to her car, and each time she thought about doing so, she thought about the other driver – he reminded her of someone but she couldn't remember who. His coolness - his cheeky attitude - his failure to verbally admit responsibility for the accident had annoyed Cherie and she now wondered whether she had been duped - whether the mechanic actually existed – she would need to make some time to find out sooner rather than later. On Sunday evening, when her car started to make a strange noise and vibrating, Cherie knew she had to call the other driver's mechanic first thing the next morning.

On Monday 24 April Cherie's motto was "Never put off for tomorrow what can be done today – that's right Cherie, get the car seen to today". So putting aside all other pressingly urgent matters and giving preference to the problem with her car, she dialled the number of the mechanic given to her by the other driver, "Gus" Cherie said, reading the other driver's name and as she spoke his name she involuntarily smiled as she recalled his handsome features. The sound of his name caressed her ears and the feel of the word across her tongue felt good – so she repeated it, before catching herself and wondering what she was doing. Then her attention was drawn to the person on the other end of the line. "Oz Autos," said the deep accented voice.

"Goo good morning … ah, ah," Cherie stuttered, surprised that her suspicions of Gus Allen were proving to be unfounded. "Ah, I had a collision last Wednesday and the other driver gave me your number. He said that you were his mechanic and would carry out the repair works to my car," Cherie paused and waited for a response from the other end of the line.

"Who did you say that was, love?" the voice enquired. "Oh, hold on – Gus - ah, would you believe, I didn't get his full name," Cherie giggled feeling really stupid. I'll call you back". She braced herself and dialled the number given to her by the other driver. There was no reply and the call went through to voice mail. Cherie listened as a voice that she recognised as that of the other driver's declared, "Hi, this is Gus, leave a message and I'll get back to you". She contemplated leaving a message but decided against doing so. She pondered whether the mechanic would recognise the driver by just his first name, where he lived, and a description of his car, and decided it was worth a try.

Calling the mechanic back, Cherie told him the driver's name was Gus – from Islington who drove a black MXLX sports car.

"Oh Gus, yes, I know Gus", came the unhesitant reply. "Would you bring the car along so I can have a look at it love – how about this afternoon – early afternoon as I'm leaving at 4 pm today". Then the mechanic rather abruptly gave her the address. Cherie asked for directions which seemed to upset the mechanic who sighed audibly before asking "Don't you know where we are?" *"Of course I don't know where you are, that's why I'm asking"*, Cherie thought. "No, I don't", she answered, an intellectual edge to her voice. The mechanic sighed again before proceeding to give some rather unhelpful directions.

"Off Mountain Lane, as you come to the petrol station...." (*the petrol station – which petrol station?* Cherie thought but was too apprehensive to ask).

"...you turn right into Severn Road ... drive past the pub and then turn left ... and first right into Peel Street ... then turn right at the church - go straight to the bottom of that road and you will see the garage – you can't miss it". Cherie could not take down all of the directions as the mechanic spoke so quickly, but decided against asking him to repeat it. She would have to look up the directions herself. "What a wasted exercise that was", Cherie surmised as she hung up.

In spite of the fact that she had obtained directions from the mechanic, and looked it up for herself, Cherie got lost as there was a one-way system which completely distorted the information provided in the "Roadrouter", and she had to stop and ask several people for directions. "It's definitely time to invest in a SatNav system" Cherie stated. "Anyway I will need it for the tour", she said as she nodded.

Finally arriving at the mechanics, she was made to wait a further 30 minutes before he could inspect the car. "It's making a strange noise, especially when I brake, and its pulling to one side - I think these problems were caused by the bang that it received when the other driver, Gus, ran into me - my car," Cherie said, stressing that Gus was responsible. The mechanic did not say anything in reply but completed his cursory inspection of the car. When he finished he drove the car outside, handed Cherie the keys and informed her "I think your exhaust has a little hole in it, and the brakes and tracking needs adjusting". "It could be because of the bang it received in the accident". "Bring it in next week Thursday, in the morning and I'll fix it for you," the mechanic said walking back inside the garage.

"But that's too long, I need it fixed by this Thursday - can't you fix it before next week?" Cherie asked.

"No, love, sorry - I can't," the mechanic gestured by shaking his head.

"Please, it's important – it's very important". "I need it fixed this week," Cherie pleaded but to no avail.

"Can't help you love, I just can't do it – I've got too much on - I'm sorry," the mechanic said insincerely. *"Talk about a major attitude problem,"* Cherie thought, realising that it was hopeless to plead with this man - he just wasn't likely to change his mind. So she got into her car rather dejectedly and started the engine.

Driving a little way up the road Cherie parked up, fished out her mobile and dialled Gus' number.

Once again there was no reply and the call was just about to switch to voicemail – she directed her mind to leaving a message when a deep male voice answered, "Hello".

"Hello, hello, I'm the lady whose car you ran into last Wednesday morning," Cherie said and waited for a response.

"How can I help you - have you contacted my mechanic?" Gus asked.

"Yeah, that's really why I'm 'phoning you - you see I went along there today but he said that he couldn't carry out the work until next Thursday, and that's just not soon enough for me - I'm afraid". "I need my car urgently this week as I'm due to go on an important business trip on Friday". "I was wondering whether I could get my own mechanic to carry out the work and bill you for it since it was your fault after all," Cherie stressed again unnecessarily. Then she continued, "And I don't think you are disputing that now, are you?" pausing for a response.

"You say that my mechanic inspected the car?" Gus asked, ignoring her.

"Yes, he did, he had a look at it but said he couldn't fix it until next Thursday," Cherie paused once again.

"Well if he looked at it he will know what work is required". "I'll have a word with him and call you back," then the line went dead – a sure indication that the other caller had hung up. Cherie was taken aback, "Well he could have said good bye," she grumbled.

Later that afternoon Gus returned her call. He said that his mechanic had informed him that he was uncertain whether the work required to the exhaust and the brake were as a result of the collision but that he was prepared to give her the benefit of the doubt. He went on to say that she could get her mechanic to fix the car and send the bill to him, but stressed that the cost had to be reasonable and in line with what his mechanic had estimated. Ozzie had informed him that all the work should cost no more than £350 including repair to the slight scratches caused by the collision. Gus said he would not agree to pay significantly more than that. Cherie accepted the proposition and it was agreed she would get her mechanic to carry out the work. She confirmed Gus' address and said she would send him the bill and they ended their conversation.

"I hope this can be sorted out quickly", Gus thought, *"I don't need all this hassle."* He had so far succeeded in denying to himself that he found the pretty young lady very attractive. The next moment his mind seemed to go off on a tangent of its own, forcing him to admit that there was something about her - something interesting, intriguing even – he could not put his finger on it. This was the first time since their ill fated meeting that Gus had given any real thought to Cherie. But now that he had begun, he indulged

himself, allowing his mind to wander. *"She looks to be perfect girl-friend material - she might fit my bill perfectly"*, Gus thought then dismissed that notion and tried to refocus. But within a minute his thoughts returned to Cherie. *"She certainly has a beautiful face - and something more, she has a beautiful figure too"*, his mind admitted.

Even though Gus had not taken any obvious notice of Cherie during their undesirable meeting, he now realised that the memory of her face, her lips, her eyes, her skin, and even her figure had been indelibly seared into his subconscious mind. And as he allowed his mind a free rein, even the memory of her angry outburst stirred something deep inside of him. It was strange - he had the feeling that he had met her somewhere before - it was such a strong feeling, but Gus just couldn't think where they might have met before. Then a thought occurred to him – he didn't even know her name. Picking up the telephone, he dialled her number and she answered almost immediately. "Oh, oh, I didn't get your name - what is it please," Gus found himself almost stuttering.

"Cherie, Cherie Johnson," was the unhesitant reply.

"Okay, thank you Miss Johnson, bye," Gus wondered what had prompted him to ring back and ask her name. After all he didn't really need to know her name - did he? When the bill came in, he would pay it, and that would be the end of that. "Or perhaps not," Gus said aloud, then catching himself, quickly dismissed any further thought of Miss Johnson.

Cherie thought about the conversation she had just had with Gus. *"He seemed to be so very cool and calm"*, she thought. *"Interesting - yes quite intriguing"*, she found herself wandering what Gus was really like. *"He certainly must think a lot of himself to have referred to himself only by his first name, as if he were a famous star or something"*, Cherie thought as she studied the piece of paper on which Gus had written his details as though seeing it for the first time. Then she looked at his address and noted that it was just around the corner from her office. *"What a coincidence, yet she had never run into him before"*, Cherie thought, smiling at the intended pun.

Pulling herself together, Cherie remembered her priorities. She was far too busy to think about romance. She recalled her love life history, deciding that she was not historically lucky in that area of her life and she did not have the time at present to discover whether her luck had changed. Oh, she'd had her share of past admirers, but they had mostly left something - a lot - to be desired.

As Cherie's mind drifted back to her experience with George she suddenly became uncomfortable with the feelings she was having about this handsome stranger. She did not take rejection well, and had sunken into a mild depression after having to accept that there was never going to be a *"her and George"*. It had taken her four long years to get over that experience, and they had not even been in a relationship. And even though she had moved on from George, the legacy of that experience remained with her – consequently she did not allow anyone close enough to break her heart again. A few moments passed before Cherie found her mind again on Gus and she began to wonder whether now might be the time to take another chance on love.

Bumpy Terrain

Sitting alone in the lounge of his new house on Tuesday 25 April 2010, Gus was deep in contemplation. He was thinking about the strange dreams that terrorised him each night during sleep. And for some unknown reason he no longer felt at ease in his house in town. So he had driven out to Radleigh in the hope that a change in surroundings would help him to relax. Gus could not bring himself to talk to anyone about the recent strange occurrences - he would struggle to explain what was happening to him - he did not understand himself. All he knew was that there was a weird hovering presence that caused him to feel uneasy all the time; that he has been unable to sleep through the night for over a week; and that every morning for nearly two weeks he has been awoken from sleep at 3.05 am exactly. Gus was beginning to wonder whether he might be suffering the onset of some sort of mental disorder - paranoia perhaps or God forbid, schizophrenia, because he felt the presence following him around everywhere he went, although the force was strongest at the house in town.

Luckily the new house was almost fully furnished as the people he bought it from had emigrated to Australia, leaving behind a lot of furniture items that were in excellent condition. Although some work was needed to bring the house into line with his tastes it was comfortable to inhabit. When the renovation works were completed, (scheduled to begin at the end of May, which included installation of a new bathroom and kitchen and remodelling and redecoration of the lounge and bedrooms), Gus intended to purchase brand new furniture, and to move those left behind to one of his up-market furnished rental properties. However, as he now reclined in the beautiful leather sofa, appreciating its top quality design and specification, Gus knew it would be sheer vanity to part with it and decided that he would keep it for himself.

On his way to the house, he had purchased a take away meal, a bottle of his favourite wine and some essential groceries. He went into the kitchen and prepared the meal by spooning it on to a plate, then placing the plate onto a tray. He also opened the bottle of wine and poured himself a glass. With the tray on his lap Gus swivelled his chair round to face the TV and switched it on, flicking through the channels to his favourite news station. He proceeded to eat the takeaway meal whilst watching the news.

Finding the news uneventful and having finished his meal Gus stared blankly at the TV screen, having no inclination to watch any other programme. His thoughts had drifted back to his recent worries. Was he going crazy? Or perhaps he was spending too much time alone. With that thought he reached for his mobile and dialled Benza's number. "Hey man – how you doing – how's Cynthia?" he said, trying to sound cheerful.

"Hi Gus man – I'm good – Cynthia – she's fine. How about you - you okay – you don't sound too cheerful – what's the matter?" Benza replied. Gus could never hide his true feelings from Benza, who could read him like an open book.

"Who me – yeah - I'm okay - I was just wondering whether you and Cynthia fancied a little company tonight", he said, thinking how much he hated Wash House at night.

"Yeah man sure – you know you're always welcome", Benza said warmly,

"Okay, I'll see you around 8.00 o'clock then – can I pick you up a takeaway or something on the way?" Gus asked in his usual thoughtful manner.

No man, it's okay Cynthia already cooked – you're welcome to share corn beef, rice and sweetcorn with us if you like," Benji offered.

"No man, sounds nice but I've already eaten", Gus replied.

"Eight o'clock then" Benza said.

"Okay, I'll see you then," Gus said as he hung up. He felt better already.

As soon as Gus ended his conversation with Benza he set off to drive to Wash House. The MXLX pulled up outside Benza's flat at 7.55 pm and Gus waited for four minutes before getting out of the car and walking to the entrance of the block. He pressed on the buzzer and Benza answered, letting him in. When he got to the first floor where his friends' flat was situated, Benza was waiting to greet him at the front door. "Whaapen? You're early," Benza said, genuine surprise registered on his face. "Bwoy, it's good to see you," he went on and hugged Gus warmly.

"This is the second time in a month, you know," Gus replied as the two friends pulled apart and grinned widely at each other.

Then Cynthia called from the living room, "Hi Gus, long time no see. Benza, let him come in no mek me see how im look".

"Hello Cynthia darling - Bwoy you looking well though". "I can tell Benza taking good care a you," Gus said as he approached Cynthia and bent to kiss her affectionately on her cheek.

"You looking well you' self," Cynthia replied returning the compliment.

"Yes, but not as good as you – you are literally blooming," Gus teased.

"Yes, I am, aren't I," Cynthia agreed as she rubbed her protruding bump.

"What is it, three months or so to go?" Gus enquired.

"Nearly four months – not long now," Cynthia said as she continued to dazzle with her smile.

Benza went over and sat next to her, "Gus, take a seat man, mek you' self at home". He paused then jumped back to his feet and added, "Where are my manners - can I get you a drink," his tone was hospitable.

"Hey ya, I bought a nice bottle of red," Gus said proffering the plastic bag which he held out to Benza. He continued, "Sorry Cynthia, I forgot to bring you something soft – I forgot you can't take alcohol at the moment", he said apologetically.

"Oh, don't worry, I can still have a small glass," Cynthia stated, eyeing Benza as she spoke, who responded "I don't know about that you know, we don't want to get the girl drunk now, do we," Benza smiled broadly as he spoke.

Gus chuckled in spite of himself, enjoying the amorous banter and the company of his friends.

They sat chatting for about an hour before the two men decided to go pay Raj a visit at the shop, having tried to telephone him but unable to get through. As it was only a 5-minute walk away, Benza suggested that they leave the car and walk but Gus was reluctant – he hated walking in Wash House at night, so they drove the short distance. When they arrived, there was nowhere to park outside so Gus parked in the quiet no through road around the corner. He wasn't happy about leaving his car there as it was very dark but they decided to anyway as their visit to Raj would be short.

Raj was just pulling down the shutters to shut up shop when they arrived. They proceeded to greet one another in their usual vibrant fashion before Raj invited them into the shop. "We're not staying too long though Raj," Gus said as he followed Raj and Benza into the shop - then he continued, "I'm parked round the corner in that dark road and I don't want to leave my car there for too long".

"I don't blame you bruv – it's not wise to park there at all," Raj said. He continued, "A number of cars have gone missing from there in the last few weeks – I reckon there is a car theft gang operating in the vicinity". "Really", Benza said, perturbed. "I never heard about that". "Yes, only last night one of my customers parked there for less than five minutes and when he went back his car was gone", Raj said heading back towards the door. The others followed quickly behind him. As they exited the shop, they heard a screech of car tyres, drawing their attention. Suddenly Gus shouted, "It's my car – someone is driving off in my car." Like a shot Benza, followed by Gus, raced in the direction taken by the driver, shouting for someone to follow the thief, but to no avail - the car sped off into the night.

Dejected and out of breath Benza immediately telephoned the Police to report the crime. The incident seemed to be having a worse effect on him than it was having on Gus. He was taking it real bad – even taking the blame and Gus found himself consoling Benza instead of the other way around.

As Benza reported the crime over the 'phone the two friends walked back to Raj's shop where Raj had remained, not wishing to leave it unattended. They stood at the front of the shop discussing the "come down" of the area in recent years and how it was going from bad to worse. They were joined by a few locals who lent their voices to the debate before moving on. Gus said very little. He thought only of the cruel run of bad luck he was having in the past few days.

"It's the youths, man, the youth dem - they don't have the same values that our generation used to have". "They just don't seem to care, they would rob even their mother or father, man," Benza said, sounding like an old man and shaking his head from side to side as he spoke, just like his father used to do. He lowered his voice as he entered the flat, sensing that Cynthia was now asleep. Raj had just dropped them off after Benza won the toss to drive Gus home and they had returned to the flat to collect Benza's car keys. Gus tried one last time to dissuade Benza, "I can get a cab, you kno – Cynthia might need you, you better stay home," he said for the third time tonight, but once again his protestation fell on deaf ears.

Benza looked in on Cynthia, who was sound asleep and they left quietly - it wouldn't do her much good to hear this shocking news about Gus' misfortune tonight – Benza would tell her tomorrow – if at all. He did not want to risk upsetting Cynthia in her delicate state.

They stopped off at the nearest Police station to make an official report of the theft. When they left the station over an hour later Benza drove Gus home.

"Nice place, Ummmh" Benza enthused as he drove into the substantial forecourt. Although the house was impressive, Benza's exclamation was over-exaggerated – he was trying to cheer his friend up.

"You want to come in for a while?" Gus asked smiling as he looked at his watch.

"No – I'll leave it till another time – it's nearly 11.30 and I have to go to work tomorrow," Benza declined.

"Come in for 5 minutes, nah man," Gus urged.

"Okay," Benza said glad that Gus had insisted. He couldn't wait to see this new place. "Wow," Benza exclaimed as he walked into the palatial hallway, "Beautiful place", this time he was not exaggerating.

"You like it?" Gus felt pleased, and momentarily his earlier misfortune slipped to the back of his mind.

"Yeah, I like it, course I like it – it's the biz man," Benza said looking up at the high ceilings wide eyed.

"Come, let me show you around - this is the lounge," Gus said as he ushered Benza into a sprawling room that was perhaps almost the size of the whole of his friend's flat. Gus proceeded into the kitchen, followed by Benza who kept up his expressions of awe. Next he showed him the dining room, and then the study, before leading him up the stairs to the master bedroom - with en suite, and the other two bedrooms. The tour ended in the loft, which had been converted into a huge self-contained living space, complete with shower room and WC.

"You getting married or what," Benza said chuckling.

"Nah – not yet". "I keep telling you and Raj, I need to find the right woman first," as Gus said that he involuntarily thought of Cherie Johnson, but immediately shooed the thought from dominating the forefront of his mind.

"As I mentioned to you before, Cynthia has a really nice friend that I want you to meet, but I don't suppose you will want to talk about anything like that tonight after all you've been through," Benza said backing down.

"I hate to sound rude, Benza, but I am capable of finding my own woman when I am good and ready," Gus snapped uncharacteristically, the events of the night evident in his response.

"Yes, I know that, but this girl is a real diamond, and you're my good friend who deserves a diamond". "I'm not saying that you two will become an item or anything, although that would be nice, but I would just like to introduce you to her," Benza charmed.

"Well, we can arrange that another time, I'll give you a call and we can arrange something", Gus said, his tone apologetic.

The friends hugged and said their goodbyes and Gus watched as Benza walked to his car, got in and backed out of the driveway. He waved his friend off and then closed the door. As soon as he was alone again Gus wished he hadn't allowed Benza to leave so soon. A wave of loneliness and vulnerability suddenly washed over him. At times when he felt this way, he would usually take a drive around which relaxed him, but tonight he couldn't even do that. He went into the lounge and switched on the TV and the CD player, seeking to provide distraction. Sinking into the ample sofa, Gus sighed heavily – it was going to be a very long night.

After a few minutes, his telephone began to ring. It was Cyrus, "Wha 'pen Gus man, how you keeping?" Cyrus enthused

"Oh, not too bad you nuh dad - how are you?" Gus replied, involuntarily mimicking his father's deep Jamaican accent.

"Well, I'm keeping fine, except for a little twinge in me knee now and again – the doctor say is arthritis". "But, I don't know why I been thinking about you all evening - you sure everything is okay?" Cyrus said, suddenly changing the subject and announcing the reason for his call. Gus was not surprised that Cyrus had telephoned him tonight, Cyrus always sensed when all was not well with him. Gus wondered whether he was telepathic or something.

"I'm okay, but someone stole my car," Gus said feeling glad that he had someone to talk to.

"Whaaat – but wha this town coming to? Cyrus exclaimed in a loud high pitched squeal which almost cause Gus to jump.

"You mean someone stole your car," Cyrus said repeating what Gus had told him.

"How...... where it 'appen," Cyrus questioned.

Gus went on to tell Cyrus the circumstances in which the theft had taken place and his father commiserated and consoled him exuberantly - they talked for almost an hour about the theft and other matters.

"You must come over and see the new house", Gus reminded Cyrus.

"Yes, I will have to make time to do that, son." Cyrus promised. Then Cyrus remembered that there was something he had wanted to talk to Gus about for some time.

"Gus, I would like to arrange for you to come along to the youth conference down at the church and give a mentoring talk to the youths, especially the young men," he announced.

"When ,,, when is it?" Gus questioned

"It runs from 1st to the 3rd July, but you only have to come along on one day, although if you could make more than one day that would be wonderful," Cyrus said sounding grateful, although Gus had not yet confirmed he would be able to make it.

"What shall I talk about," Gus enquired, sounding timid.

"Your experiences as a footballer – your career path – your early retirement – your port folio, anything positive just to motivate the young people, anything you say will have the effect of inspiring them to aspire to reach higher," Cyrus affirmed in rhyming style then chuckled.

"Okay – yeah, I guess I can do that". "I would be happy to do that in fact," Gus felt a warm feeling spread throughout his body, the tingle he always got when he did something worthwhile.

"Thank you, son and God bless you". "I will let you know more about the event and we can discuss it more nearer the time," Cyrus said ending their conversation.

The telephone rang again as soon as Cyrus hung up - it was Cyrus again, "I'll come and pick you up for the training session tomorrow if you like," he offered.

"Yeah – if it's not too much trouble, Gus replied. He then gave his new address and directions to Cyrus, and grateful for his thoughtfulness, thanked him. They agreed a pick-up time of 3.00 pm, to allow some catching up before going on to collect the youngsters at the church.

Then Cyrus added, "There is something else that I wanted to talk to you about son – someone in fact". "I would like to introduce you to a lovely young lady that attends my church". "I've been meaning to tell you about her for some time," Cyrus said with a wink in his voice. Gus said nothing, and sensing all was not well, Cyrus added, "Now is probably not an appropriate time to talk about this, Gus, but I've been meaning to introduce you two for sometime". "Tell me to mind my own business if you like, but this young lady is a real gem and, my dear son, you deserve a real gem – they are hard to find these days, mark my word," Cyrus added.

Gus bit his tongue, holding back what he wanted to say to Cyrus. He was sick and tired of people trying to fix him up. This was twice in one night – first Benza and now his father. What did they think he was – desperate?

"Look dad, I hope you won't think me rude if I say that when I am looking for a female companion, I am quite capable of finding one for myself," Gus said in his politest tone. His tone camouflaged the rage he was feeling at what he viewed as an intrusion into his personal life, and counteracted the brusqueness of the words he spoke.

"Anyway, I already have a girlfriend," Gus heard himself saying.

"Oh, have you?" "You don't mean that young woman that is always hanging around at the stadium, what's her name, Tricia - do you?" "I hope not, she is hardly what you would call wife material, is she Gus?" Cyrus said forcefully.

Gus was taken aback by Cyrus' response *"What is this,"* he thought, anger swelling up inside, *"I'm a grown man for goodness sake, but they are treating me like a child."*

"Cyrus, what do you take me for?" Gus' almost shouted, prompting Cyrus to apologise to him.

"Sorry son, I didn't mean to offend you". "It's just that I am concerned about you". "I would like you to meet the right girl and settle down – not just any girl". "It's hard to find the right person to share your life". "Son, I have the wisdom of an older man – I am only seeking to pass on that wisdom to you". "Just look what I have been through because I chose to be with the wrong women". "I don't want you to end up scarred like me, son," Cyrus said ruefully. Gus could detect a deep sadness in Cyrus' voice. He was not fully aware of what his father had in fact gone through in his personal life, he only knew that he had been married more than once, and divorced too and Gus did not understand why his father had been alone for so many years.

Cyrus' first wife had cheated on him with his own brother – *he had found them in bed together after only 6 months of marriage and she later left him and moved in with his brother. After their divorce his first wife married his brother and they were still together after 4 children and over 30 years of marriage. The delinquent couple never apologised to Cyrus for their betrayal, or provided any explanation for their unacceptable behaviour. Unfortunately Cyrus' brother no longer spoke to him and even though Cyrus forgave them and tried several times over the years to make contact with them, the couple never responded to his correspondence.*

"Yeah, just remember that I am not a child and I am not stupid", Gus said, cutting through his father's brief reminiscence.

"I don't need anyone to look for a woman for me, so let it rest nah?" Gus continued hoping his dad would finally get the message. He did not wish to be rude, but he had to let both his father and Benza know where he was coming from.

"Son, I know you is not a child or stupid". "I'm not asking you to date or marry anyone, I just want to introduce you, that's all," Cyrus pleaded – not willing to let go.

"Well, if you put it like that, but we will have to talk about it another time". "I'm certainly not in the mood to meet anyone at the moment," Gus said curtly.

"Well sorry I brought it up tonight". "I realise you are not in that frame of mind at the moment - sorry son, it was a bit insensitive of me – it was just that I've been putting off speaking to you about it for some time now, and well I remembered it tonight – sorry – bad judgment, I guess". "Anyway son, I'll see you tomorrow – 3.00 - and I promise I won't mention anything about this again, until you mention it to me". "So when you feel you are ready, let me know and I will arrange a meeting – okay, son". "Okay, see you then," Cyrus' tone was very gentle.

"Yes, see you tomorrow, dad – and thanks," Gus said hanging up.

After hanging up, Gus thought about the conversation that they had just had. He felt sorry now for the way he had spoken to his father. After all, it was only natural for him to care about his son enough to want to see him associate with the right people.

Before Gus went to sleep he said the prayer that his mother had taught him, the same prayer they recited at Sunday School as a child. He didn't know why he said this prayer on occasions, but it brought him inexplicable peace. He would say the Lord's prayer when he thought about his mother, or when he was sad, and often when he felt lonely. He did not really think about the words of the prayer – it just felt comforting to say them. Perhaps it had something to do with the memories that the prayer evoked, of times when both his parents were alive, of times when his was a true family, of times when Marcus, Denise and he were truly siblings – times he now truly missed.

CHAPTER 5

Tripping Out

Not having used public transport in years, Cherie had forgotten some basic rules, like holding onto something when making your way to the exit. As the driver brake sharply, she was almost thrown to the floor but luckily was caught by strong steadying arms of a fellow passenger. She was on her way to collect her car from the mechanic, having dropped it off earlier that morning. Jean had driven behind her to drop off the car, and gave her a lift to work afterward, but plead as she may, she couldn't get her mother to reschedule her precious afternoon hairdresser's appointment and drive her to collect it. She desperately needed her car for tomorrow 28 April 2010 when the tour kicked off as Sera was refusing to travel with the rest of the crew in the tour van.

As she walked briskly along Cherie mused on what an absolute gem of a mechanic Jeff was – he had agreed to squeeze her in at short notice and put her car to the front of his very busy schedule to ensure that she got it back the same day. Jeff having recently moved to new garage premises in Hackney, Cherie found the new location less accessible than the old. Previously he had been based just around the corner from her office in Islington, but it was worth the sacrifice of her precious time to continue patronizing Jeff.

On arrival, Cherie gathered that Jeff was in a hurry. Without hesitation, he handed her the car keys while explaining to her that he had carried out all the necessary works – replacing the worn brakes (he stressed that the noise from them probably developed because of the collision). He confirmed that the hole in the exhaust would either have been created or exacerbated by the impact. Cherie asked him how much the works had come to and he told her. "Four hundred and ten pounds, that's a bit more than I had anticipated," Cherie said.

Jeff countered, "That is the cost, sorry Cherie - I have already discounted it". He then handed her an itemised list of parts and a breakdown of the costs.

"Okay, no problem, thanks Jeff", Cherie said appreciatively. She continued, "Now you know that the other driver is paying £350 towards this work, right". "I don't know if he can be trusted, but if he doesn't pay up, please let me know and I will pay you". "I'll pay you the extra £60 now," Cherie said reaching into her purse and extracting £60 in notes, while stressing once again, "If the other driver does default to pay the rest, I will pay it myself and try and claim it back from his insurers". Then she asked Jeff to give her the invoice - she would deliver it personally. As she spoke Cherie listened to her own voice, thinking, *"That was not the plan, Jeff was meant to send the invoice. But, well, she had said it now. Anyway, Gus lived just around the corner from her office and she could drop it in later – save on postage."*

The car drove like a dream, "Aah!", Cherie exclaimed. *"Jeff is the best mechanic ever,"* she reaffirmed to herself in thought as she made her way through mild rush hour traffic towards her office. Donny McClurkin's soulful voice rendered "Yes you can...," caressing her ears and soothing her soul as she drove. Later Chevelle Franklin provided further inspiration as Cherie's advance was slowed by heavier traffic. "Joy" pumped through the speakers providing much needed focus and Cherie praised as she droved.

Stuck in yet another traffic jam Cherie found it hard to relax and changed the CD. She played the beautiful personal worship song "I-worship", which soothed her mind and spirit as she drank in the ethereal harmonies and deep meaningful lyrics. Cherie worshiped as she mediated on the words of the song, unwilling to succumb to fretting about the many things she could otherwise be doing. She glanced at the dashboard – it was now 6.05 pm – she anticipated a long night ahead with all the paperwork waiting for her at the office. With the tour scheduled to last 4 months, she faced an awesome task ahead to keep up with paperwork, so she wanted to try and get up to speed before kick off. The collision could not have happened at a more inconvenient time. She had lost hours of valuable time dropping off the car and riding the bus to pick it up, not to mention going along to Mr Allen's mechanic, which had been a complete waste of time. Sera, with her never-ending demands for attention had also wasted too much time. "I sure hope she turns out to be worth the bother," Cherie said verbalising her thoughts yet again.

It was 6.30 pm when Cherie finally arrived at the office and immediately got down to paperwork. As it was quiet she worked quickly and once she got stuck in, the large pile diminished quickly. What she thought would take her up to the early hours to complete she now re-calculated would take her up to around midnight. It was now 8.30 pm and Cherie suddenly realised she had forgotten to drop the receipt through Mr Allen's letterbox. Although there was no real urgency, she decided she would take a break and a short walk to hand-deliver the invoice now. *"I don't want to forget about it and I need a break from the monotony of this figure work – it will take less than 20 minutes there and back,"* she told herself.

And so less than 15 minutes later, Cherie stood in front of Gus' house. *"He's probably out,"* she thought, seeing his car was nowhere in sight. As she approached the front door to drop the invoice through the letterbox, it occurred to her that it was not in an envelope, and so she decided she would knock to see if anyone was in so that she could hand it to them personally. *"It would not be ideal to just drop it through the letter-box as it might be mistaken for junk mail,"* she thought wisely. So Cherie knocked twice and waited expectantly for someone to open the door.

Gus sat alone in the lounge of his house in town – the lights were off – he was thinking. He was trying to make sense of the way he was feeling – low, depressed. It couldn't be just because of the fact that his car had been stolen – oh, he did love the car, but he could always buy a replacement once the insurance issue was sorted out and he received the pay out from the insurance company. And he should get a courtesy car in the meantime. So it wasn't just the fact that his car had been stolen, there was a sense of impending doom – a force that was weighing down on him – a threatening and menacing negative energy. This presence was like a burden pressing down on him, causing him to feel so depressed that he had left work early – at 4.30 pm and taken a cab home. He felt he needed to be alone with his thoughts, but now he was alone he found the feelings of gloom had again new intensity.

The problem with the insurance was daunting but Gus would not usually allow such a hitch to affect him so. Having telephoned them yesterday to report the theft, the insurance company had informed him that the annual premium had not been paid for a month, in which case, he was effectively uninsured. Gus had refuted this and the call handler had promised to make further enquiries and revert. However, she had not done so and he had called them again today. The call handler had promised to make further enquiries and call him back before 8.00 pm – he was still awaiting the call back.

The knock at the door invaded Gus' thoughts – *"Who could that be?"* he wondered. Going to the window he peered through a gap in the curtain and was most surprised to see Miss Johnson standing at the door. Without hesitation or further thought, he hurried to open it for her. As his eyes rested fully upon Cherie, Gus felt something stir deep inside. "Hi, I .....," as Cherie began to speak, Gus' mobile started to ring. "Come in, come in - I just need to get this call," he said flustered. Cherie hesitated – she had not intended to enter this unknown man's home. She opened her mouth to explain that she would not be stopping, but by then Gus was speaking on his 'phone. He motioned to her to come inside once again and she obeyed.

Cherie wondered what was happening to her – she knew she should just hand over the invoice and leave but found herself inexplicably drawn toward Gus. Her head told her she should not be staying but the delectable prospect of getting to know this intriguing stranger better seemed a chance too good to pass up. She felt instinctively felt that she could trust Gustave Allen and if her intuition proved to be wrong, Cherie knew she could always rely upon her karate skills if needs be.

As Gus spoke to the call handler, a worried look clouded his countenance. Cherie observed as she stole sideways glances from the corner of her eye. He arose from his seat and paced around on the other side of the large room opposite to where he had gestured to her to take a seat some 5 minutes earlier. She was growing impatient. She really did not have this time to spare, but felt it would be too rude to just get up and leave now. She hoped he wouldn't be much longer - she would give him a further 2 or 3 minutes or so - she could tell he was having a very important conversation and willed herself to exercise patience.

When 3 minutes had elapsed, Cherie added a further 3 minutes - until it added up to 17 minutes in total that she had been waiting. *"Important telephone conversation or not, I will have to go,"* she thought, and began to rise from her seat. As she did so, Gus raised his hand in a gesture that she should wait. She sunk back into the seat and waited a few more minutes. Soon he ended his conversation and hung up.

"Sorry about that, I just had to try and sort something out". "I don't know if you overheard any of that, but basically, my car was stolen on Tuesday night," Gus said flopping into the armchair next to Cherie.

"Oh, no, I'm sooo sorry – where did that happen - around here?" Cherie asked, looking genuinely concerned.

"No - in the Wash House area in North East London". "Only that's not the worse of my problems". "The main problem is that my insurance company is now denying liability as they are saying that my policy had lapsed," Gus spoke easily to Cherie as though she was an old confidante.

"So, why had the policy lapsed?" Cherie asked inquisitively, yet exhibiting genuine concern.

"Because I had not paid the annual premium which was due over a month ago", Gus said feeling embarrassed. "Basically", he explained, "I closed that bank account about 3 months ago and totally forgot about the direct debit for the annual premium". "Now they are saying that the grace period was 2 weeks and they are seeking to avoid the policy," Gus said turning the palms of his hands upwards in a gesture of hopelessness.

"Oh, you poor thing, and it was quite an expensive car as well as far as I can remember," Cherie felt genuinely sorry for this stranger. "That's very unlucky though, isn't it?" she went on.

"But they should have written to you to advise you that payment was not received," Cherie said wisely.

"Yeah, I feel really stupid – they wrote to me but I foolishly did not even bother to open the letter". "I just filed it away thinking it was the insurance policy". "I usually receive two letters a year from my car insurers - one to tell me of the renewal details and the second sending me the policy. Ordinarily I would check the renewal details but never bother to check the policy. But for some reason I didn't even check the renewal details this time around - I will definitely be opening all my mail in the future", Gus promised himself.

"Yeah, that's a good idea", Cherie said smiling.

"Now I've got to check carefully to see that I haven't overlooked any other direct debits that were set up on that account," Gus said thoughtfully, making a mental note to do that tonight without fail.

"I'm sorry, I was just passing and decided to drop off the invoice for the work to the car – sorry to add to your worries," Cherie said apologetically.

"That's no problem at all," Gus replied.

"It's for £410, but I have already paid the extra £60, so you only need to pay £350 as previously agreed," Cherie said.

"Okay," Gus said taking the invoice from her.

"I should go now," Cherie said rising from her seat.

"Oh, I should have offered you a drink or something – sorry, I've been so pre-occupied with this problem," Gus also rose from his seat - taking the posture of willing Cherie to sit down and allow him to play host.

"Please allow me to offer you something to drink, please," Gus begged and wondered if he was coming on too strong, after all he did not even know this pretty young lady.

Cherie thought of the work that awaited her at the office, decided it couldn't wait any longer but sat down again anyway, "Yes, okay, that's very nice of you", she said.

"What can I get you," Gus asked.

"A cup of coffee would be nice," Cherie said warming to Gus' obviously hospitable nature.

"Coffee coming up", Gus said and headed off to the kitchen. Where he switched the kettle on and returned into the living room to turn on the TV for Cherie. Then he returned to the kitchen and

Cherie could hear him preparing the coffee. The tinkle of a spoon against a cup signalled that coffee was almost ready.

"Do you take sugar?" Gus shouted from the kitchen.

"Yeah, one please," she replied.

Soon Gus returned with a tray bearing two large mugs of coffee. There was also a saucer with an assortment of biscuits on the tray. He tried to pull out one of a nest of tables to place the tray upon a fete that looked to be causing him some difficulty, so Cherie quickly went to his aid. "Thank you, thank you," he said affably.

"Don't mention it," Cherie replied, trying to remember the last time she had been so at ease in the company of a man who was not a platonic friend.

"So, you've heard enough of my problems, tell me a bit about yourself," Gus said, looking intently into her eyes as he sat down almost opposite her.

Cherie was a little unnerved – *was this incredibly handsome and obviously fairly, if not very, wealthy man flirting with her?* Her mind began to race at the possibility. Although she was by no means a materialistic person, when she imagined her ideal life partner, she always imagined that he would be handsome, have a good personality, and be well established. So far first impressions suggested that Gustave Allen ticked all the boxes. But she reminded herself that her priorities were the spirituality followed by the personality and looks of the individual. She needed to get to know not just the superficial person but she must discover the heart. Cherie realised that first impressions could be very deceptive indeed.

Some of her friends, including Cynthia thought that her mark was unrealistically high – and in truth they were probably right for she had deliberately set the bar so high in order to prevent any man from scaling it as she nursed her broken heart following George's rejection of her. But perhaps she was ready to lower the bar now – perhaps just a little – then again if Gus Allen checked out she might not even need to do that.

"What do you want to know?" Cherie asked, deciding she could relax her guard a little and get to know this stranger better.

"Well, I already know your name, I can see that you are obviously beautiful, and you look like a professional person, but I'm not sure – so let's start with what you do for a living," Uncharacteristically, Gus could not seem to stop himself coming on to this lady. The longer he remained in her presence, the bolder he was becoming. There was an urgent desire to know more about Cherie Johnson and it would appear that Benza's training and methodology for dealing with women had taken root – ever so slightly. Benza had taught him to go after what he wanted *"you snooze – you lose,"* which he had explained to Gus meant that if you saw a woman you wanted, you should not let her get away or you might lose your chance. You *"strike while the iron is hot"* - another of Benza's philosophies. Gus hoped these tactics would work for him – they always seemed to work for Benza - that is before he started to date Cynthia and became the family man that he now was.

"I run my own business – Smooth Management – managing a stable of up-and-coming artistes. You may have heard of a few of them – Sera Ocel, if you like R & B Rap/Reggae fusion, or if lover's reggae is your listening pleasure, Ebony Son, the hot new singer/DJ," Cherie spoke of her two main artistes with some pride, confident in their abilities.

"Honestly, I don't really listen to much contemporary music, so I'm afraid I haven't heard of either. But if you were to talk about Marvin Gaye, Teddy, Aretha, Bob Marley, The Twinkle Brothers, Dennis Brown or even Nat King Cole - then you'd be talking my language," Gus said realising he must sound very old-fashioned. However, he was not apologising – he liked what he liked.

"Yeah, I like some of that old stuff too, but I'm more into The Commodores, Earth Wind and Fire, a little John Holt, Gladys Knight and her Pips," Cherie stressed the word "Pips" and they both chuckled.

Gus felt the urge to press Cherie to reveal more about herself, but realised he might appear to be coming on a little too strong – after all he had only just met the lady. So he told Cherie a little about himself - about his job as a coach/trainer and about his football career which ended prematurely due to the injury he'd suffered. He talked about his mother and briefly mentioned his siblings and his father. Cherie did not press him to reveal more than she could see he was comfortable with – after all she had only just met the man.

The two continued to talk as time flew by. As Gus asked Cherie if she would like another drink, she glanced at her watch. "Gosh, is that the time?" she jumped up, seeing that it as now 10.10 pm. "Look, I'm gonna have to go now, I'm afraid, but I had a really lovely time talking to you," Cherie said sincerely.

"The pleasure was all mine," Gus reciprocated.

"My main Artistes, Sera Ocel and Ebony Son's tour kicks off tomorrow and I need to get some very important last-minute things sorted out," Cherie added, feeling she needed to give some sort of explanation for rushing off.

"So, where is the tour starting?" Gus asked – interested.

"Oh, it begins in Birmingham tomorrow night for two nights. And then I return to London on Saturday night after the show, and we start all over again next Friday in Manchester for two nights and so on."

"Can I come to watch?" Gus asked smiling.

"Well, we'll be playing in London at the end of June," Cherie informed him.

"I may wish to attend one of the out of town performances," Gus said teasingly.

"Well, I'll tell you what, if you give me your e-mail details, I can send you the itinerary – how's that," Cherie said encouragingly.

"Yeah, that sounds great," Gus said, as he went to fetch some writing materials. He returned with a pad and pen and wrote down his e-mail details, handing it to Cherie.

"Thanks – I will definitely be in touch. We need all the support we can get," Cherie said warming to her new friend.

Gus gave her a deep lingering look before confirming, "I'll send Jeff a cheque tomorrow," as he scrutinised the invoice.

"Thank you and I hope your car turns up undamaged," Cherie said, suddenly noticing the sad look that crossed Gus' face. She realised she had "burst his bubble" by reminding him of his troubles. "Don't worry," Cherie said attempting to rectify the damage she had obviously caused, "leave it in God's hands".

"I would, only I don't suppose God would be interested in

someone like me," Gus said and chuckled.

"Oh, you'd be surprised – Jesus is interested in you, no matter how bad you feel you may have been – he gave his life for sinners, you know – how great a love is that?" Cherie said as she looked pointedly at Gus and smiled.

That was not the reply that Gus had expected. He hesitated for a beat – thinking. *"She is a bit full on – I was only joking - I'm a good person – why isn't that obvious to her?* Then he began to wonder why Cherie had made such a statement. Was she some sort of Jesus freak or what?

"Yeah," he replied dismissively as he saw her to the door.

"I hope to see you at one of those concerts then," Cherie said smiling, as she proffered her hand, meaning to shake his.

"You can bet on it," Gus said, uncertainly – he forced a smile and, instead of shaking her outstretched hand, kissed the back of it, as he stared straight into her eyes cheekily. Cherie blushed and turned to walk away. She waved to Gus just before disappearing out of sight as he stood watching her go.

Cherie thought about Gus as she walked back to her office. She wondered whether he had any religious persuasion. It had not escaped her notice that he seemed to dismiss her mention of Jesus – she was concerned about that and made a mental note to explore the question of spirituality with him the next time they met as that was very important to her. In spite of her concerns she found herself wondering when she would see Gus again – he had promised to call her and she felt excited at the prospect. "Only time will tell", Cherie mumbled as she wondered what the future may hold for her and Gus Allen. Then she smiled as she walked briskly, and there was no mistaking the joy she was feeling.

After Cherie left Gus returned to his seat where he sat for a long time, thinking, drinking in the memory of her smile. There was no denying the impact that this woman was having on him. *"If she is for real, I may just have found my ideal woman",* Gus mused *"Only time will tell,"* he verbalising his thoughts. But then he recalled the statement she had made about Jesus – she sounded to him like one of those religious nuts and he certainly didn't need that in his life. If he chose to take the relationship forward he would need to explore the question of religion with her – what she believed and to what degree. It was very important to him. It wasn't that he didn't believe in God – he did – but he didn't like overly religious people – he certainly couldn't have a relationship with such a person.

As he sat thinking, Gus completely forgot that he needed to check his bank account paperwork to see that he had not forgotten to set up any other direct debits on his new account. He noted that the sinister presence appeared to lift while Cherie was around – perhaps because he was preoccupied with her. But now that she had left he began to feel the menace return. He also felt tired – so he headed off to bed and as he drifted off to sleep, Cherie's smile filled his mind.

****

Gus struggled to wake up as the man with the invisible face held him down, paralysing his limbs. He tried to speak but could not utter a sound. He struggled and struggled, trying to scream but could not scream. The hands were so strong as they held him down. But he would not give up – he would not relent - he resolved in his mind, the only part of him not paralysed, that he had to get free. Although the strongman showed no sign of letting go Gus fought on. Then suddenly, he broke free.

Out of breath and in a cold sweat, Gus he gasped for air and coughed. "What a horrible nightmare - it seemed so real", he blubbered, wondering what was happening to him. During the nightmare, he had felt so close to death – like he would never wake up again. He certainly hoped that this would not recur – it was the most horrible experience of his life. Glancing at his watch he saw it was only 12.30 am. In his mind he felt as though he had been sleeping for many hours, but his body felt extremely tired and bruised as if he had just been in a brutal physical fight.

Just then his landline telephone began to ring. Gus wondered who could be ringing him at this hour on a Thursday night. He thought it might be Marcus and rushed to answer it. However, upon viewing the number, and noting that it was a foreign number, he immediately realised that it must be Maureen. "Hello,"

Gus said softly.

"Gus, hi – it's Maureen - how are you honey?" He had been trying to contact Maureen for more than a week now, but had not been able to speak to her because she was always in the middle of something. He could feel that they were drifting further and further apart. He no longer had the urge to fly across the world to be with her and she no longer asked him to. She hadn't been to visit him for months either – 5 months to be exact. His feelings for Maureen had mutated into platonic ones. He was not sure whether the same was true for her.

They "caught up" for a few minutes before Maureen's tone turned more serious. "Gus, I've got something to tell you," she paused then launched on, "I've met someone else, who I've been seeing". "I wanted to tell you before you read about it in the news," Maureen paused for a response.

"Well, we have been growing apart," was the only response from Gus which left Maureen somewhat surprised. She had at least expected him to "kick and scream" a little. But instead he appeared to be letting her slip through his fingers without so much as a tiny struggle. Not that she should care as she was now head over heels in love with her new beau and had in fact accepted his proposal of marriage – after all she wasn't getting any younger, and she wanted to retire and have lots and lots of beautiful babies.

"It was on the cards really, wasn't it?" Gus continued.

"Yeah, I guess it was," Maureen said – why should she care if he obviously didn't, and to think she had been worried about hurting him. "I think I should tell you that I'm getting married soon too – I don't want you to find out from anyone else first," Maureen said thinking *"let's see how you handle that revelation, Mr I couldn't care less"*.

"Married, married – how long have you known this guy, Maureen?" Gus almost shouted.

"Oh I've known Ezra for over two years, but just as a platonic friend". "It was only recently that the nature of our relationship has changed," Maureen lied. In fact, she'd been having an on/off intimate affair with Ezra Kennedy for over two years, and this had turned more serious three months ago after Ezra's wife left him because of his infidelity with a string of beautiful black women. Maureen was not worried that he had been caught out with other women though. As far as she was concerned, they weren't serious then and now they were. Ezra intimated to her that he wanted their relationship to move to a deeper level a few days after his wife left him. They had been married for 10 years, and in that time Ezra was rumoured to have had a different lover for each week that he was married to Fay. But Maureen was not swayed by any of the bad press or gossip, all she knew was that she loved Ezra and was grabbing him with both hands. After all the man was FINE. She realised now that she has always loved him and wanted more from their relationship and now that he had confessed that he felt the same and had proven it by breaking off his other relationships and by proposing to her and giving her the largest yellow diamond rock that money could buy, she could not wait to marry him as soon as his quickie divorce came through. Which woman wouldn't jump at the chance to be with the richest and most handsome white man that Maureen had ever seen – and he was famous too. She was a happy woman and she hoped that Gus would not be bitter. There was no denying that Gus was one of the best looking men Maureen had met, but his status could never compare with that of Ezra Kennedy's, and although she liked Gus, she had never been in love with him. She knew he loved her and hoped she didn't hurt him too much, but it couldn't be helped. She hoped they could remain friends.

"Ezra – unusual name – not many men called Ezra". "It's not Ezra Kennedy the film actor, is it?" Gus asked.

"Yes, it is," Maureen replied after a short pause.

"Well, I wish you the very best – sincerely – I hope you will both be very happy – show biz marriages are a bit risky though," Gus replied almost too quickly, (*he wanted to add that everyone knew Ezra was a bit of a notorious womanizer but bit his tongue.*)

"Yeah, that's true, but I'm going to give up modelling after I'm married". "Ezra and I both feel that that is best in order to provide stability in our relationship". "I would like you to attend the wedding – it would be good if you could come," Maureen said, sounding sincere.

"Yeah, yeah, when is it happening?" Gus asked.

"Hopefully 14th February next year - in Barbados". "We are flying out just a few good friends and family members to share in our special day". "I'll send you an invite and a ticket," Maureen said, hoping to soothe the hurt she imagined Gus must be experiencing.

"Yeah, yeah, that would be good". "I wish you the very best, and Maureen ...."

"Yeah Gus",

"...we can still remain friends, you know". "I can be your baby's godfather or something". "After all, we go back some long way," Gus said.

"Thank you, Gus, that's a sweet thing to say," Maureen said, touched.

In spite of the fact that he no longer had romantic feelings toward Maureen, Gus was initially shocked by the revelation but as his mind returned to normality he began to feel genuinely happy for Maureen.

They talked for a while longer before ending their conversation. When he hung up, Gus realised why he could never have gotten serious with Maureen, let alone consider marrying her. He did not even feel the inclination to mention to her the problems he was experiencing even though they had talked for almost half an hour. Maureen was a lovely lady, but it was all about Maureen – it always had been and it always would be, and Gus was far too bright to remain in anyone's shadow like that.

Gus's thoughts drifted back to Cherie and how easy it was to talk to her even though they had only just met. And he shared with her something he did not even desire to share with Maureen - someone he had known for over 3 years. To Gus that was indicative that Cherie was special – very, very special indeed.

Gus thought about Cherie some more before dropping of to sleep, and this time he slept soundly - until 3 am.

CHAPTER 6

"Look Out"

It's Thursday 27 April 2010 and Tricia is busy doing what she likes best, thinking. Ever since her separation from Gus, Tricia did little else. First she thought hard about the break-up. No-one had ever ditched her before - she was usually the one that called the shots, when she had exhausted her use of a particular man. Those who had tried to take control before soon realised that Tricia never let go until she was good and ready. But Gus Allen, this audacious fellow did not get the message, he thought he could draw a line that Tricia could not cross and she was mad as hell.

So she had thought about pay-back. She hungered to get her own back on Gus, which longing grew and mutated into a bitter sinister craving. Thereafter Tricia had formulated an evil strategy for revenge and implemented it – but had it worked?

And since putting prophet Osiri's instructions into action Tricia was consumed by curiosity, hope and doubt as to whether the curse that she put on Gus' life was working - she thought about little else. So at varying times most days and nights (mostly nights), Tricia could be found disguised in an afro wig and large rimmed glasses sitting in her father's car, parked somewhere along the road where Gus lived, from which look out point she watched his comings and goings. Today she had arrived at 4.15 pm and waited for over an hour with no sight of Gus. Then at 5.30 pm she saw someone getting out of a taxi that had stopped in front of his house. At first she did not realise it was the same handsome, vibrant man she used to date. For one thing she was accustomed to seeing him drive his black MXLX. Luckily she was paying attention or she might not have recognised him. She watched as he entered his house, noting with satisfaction that he was looking very stressed indeed, almost haggard in fact. She could tell from the confused expression on his face and his posture that all was not well. He walked sluggishly with his shoulders slumped, painting a perfect picture of dejection. Tricia wondered what could have happened to alter

Gus' usually confident swagger to this somewhat inconsistent gait. And where was his beloved car – his object of worship – his status symbol? Tricia began to laugh at a very funny joke only she knew about. She decided to hang around for a while longer to check for any further developments. More than three hours later, Tricia was still on the look out.

Dazed by the monotony of gazing ahead, Tricia closed her eyes briefly to relieve eyestrain and promptly nodded off. She began to dream about Gus' total ruin and her triumph when she was awoken by the beeping of a car's horn. Aroused from catnap, she jumped up from what felt like a full night's sleep. However, when she looked at the clock she saw that it was just 8.43 pm – she'd been asleep for just 10 minutes. "Weird," Tricia spoke her thoughts. Stiffness was creeping into her limbs, prompting her to stretch her body, wriggle from side to side and roll her shoulders then her head in a circular motion. Stretching her legs though proved impossible and she was tempted to get out of the car in order to stretch her whole body, but she quickly dismissed that thought – it would be too risky as Gus might see her. So she settled for sitting as upright as she could and stretching her legs the farthest that she could.

A gentleman walking past showed her a little more interest than was warranted and Tricia poked her tongue out at him, prompting him to pull his body upright, lift his nose high and walk briskly by. She smiled and returned to gazing in the direction of Gus' front door. It was then that she noticed the woman standing there. She stared manically at the person, rage building within her. *"Who's that then?"* Tricia verbalised her thoughts. She glared as the woman waited to be let in. Then it dawned on her that she knew the woman from somewhere. Tricia wracked her brain to try and remember where. That figure - that profile - that complexion - that hair - the mannerisms – it all added up. Of course, it was none other than Cherie Johnson. "That snake in the grass," Tricia snarled. "What's she doing here? She continued to murmur, her voice rising as she became enraged with jealousy.

The idea that Cherie might be a relation or platonic friend - even a stranger to Gus did not occur to Tricia. She fumed, "One thing is certain, I will not allow this to continue, no, no, no", Tricia said. "This has to stop right away", she declared.

At 10.10 pm Tricia was still watching as Cherie emerged from Gus' home. A sense of relief washed over her tense body - her worse fear that Tricia would stay the night had not been realised. "Maybe they haven't gotten to the sleeping together stage as yet but I'll have to see that they don't," Tricia said, continuing her monologue, vowing vengefully, "I'll have to stop this before it gets any further".

As Cherie walked away Tricia put the car in motion and followed her slowly, stopping and starting in order to keep a safe distance. She watched menacingly and laughed when Cherie tripped up, "*****, serves you right – you should drop and bruk you neck - I'm going to deal with you – that is just the beginning," Tricia spat. Then she watched as Cherie entered her office building. "The ***** doesn't even know what she is dealing with," Tricia cussed. She watched to see whether any lights went on in the building, but apart from those already on, no other light was switched on. She waited for two hours before nodding off. When she awoke it almost 2.00 am and all the lights in the block were off. Concluding, disgruntledly that Cherie must have left the building while she was asleep Tricia sucked air through her teeth and swore before suddenly realising that she had to get back home fast to carry out the ritual of lighting the candle and chanting as instructed by prophet Osiri. So she started the engine and headed home, driving faster than she had ever driven in her life.

After finishing the ritual, Tricia dropped off to sleep and slept deeply for 5 hours. She awoke with a jolt and sat up in bed, simultaneously grabbing her mobile – it was 10.20 am. Jumping out of bed she pulled on the same jeans and tea-shirt that she worn the previous day. In fact she had worn the same clothes for many days and it was a couple of days since she had showered. In a moment of sanity, it occurred to her that she needed a shower but she soon dismissed that thought – she didn't want a shower. In another moment of lucidity, Tricia contemplated briefly what might be happening to her. She was usually so scrupulously tidy and her personal hygiene impeccable. But lately she was letting herself go.

Tricia made her way to the bathroom where she relieved herself crassly and then proceeded to look at her reflection in the mirror, indifferent to the gaunt image that stared back at her. Then suddenly she loathed herself - she was the one that used to hold her nose when she travelled on the bus or tube, looking down at other people who she perceived lacked her own high standards of hygiene. She was the one that looked disapprovingly at women who did not bother or could not afford to dress immaculately. She was the one who sneered at colleagues whose hair, skin and nails were less than flawless. A tear welled up on the inside of her left eye, which she wiped away and began to make an effort to clean up herself with a damp flannel, but soon lost interest again.

Still unwashed she walked back into the bedroom and sat on the side of her bed. Her father, came up the stairs and called out to her, "Tricia, you alright - you not going to work again today?" "How you feeling – you sick again?" "Tricia, what's wrong with you?" Donald asked kindly, fully prepared for the rejection he would receive.

"What you mean – mind your own **** business – why don't you get a life and keep your nose out of mine?" Tricia said as Donald sighed heavily.

"Tricia, you know if you don't go back to work, you will lose your job." "At least go to the doctor and get him to sign you off for a week or two." "If you explain that you not feeling too good, I'm sure he will understand and maybe give you some treatment." "But you can't just leave it like that and not go to work – you will lose you job, and good jobs are hard to come by these days." Donald chided his beloved daughter in a kindly manner.

"Who says it's a good job, anyway – look just mind your business right". "Why don't you get you self a woman or something," Tricia said as she got up and slammed her bedroom door, bringing the conversation to a firm close.

Her father's concerns were not unfounded because Tricia had not been to work for over three weeks and was not intending to go in today either. She had taken to spending all her time doing nothing.

After a while, Tricia proceeded down to the lounge where she sat in front of the TV, remote control in hand. Scrolling aimlessly up and down through the channels, not really thinking about what she was watching. Her mind was preoccupied with what might be happening with Gus. When she wasn't parked outside his home spying on him, all she did was sit in front of the TV, eat, smoke and think, having apparently lost the urge to do anything else. But today she had added something new to her agenda - she also began to think about Cherie Johnson.

The telephone rang and Tricia ignored it. Donald answered it from upstairs. Mr Morrell, Tricia's boss, had asked his Assistant to call and find out what was wrong with Tricia, as she had not been to work for the eighth day running, and to ask when she might be returning. This was the third time that Mr Morrell had called her this week, but although Donald took and passed on messages, Tricia never returned his calls. This time, however, Tricia decided she would take the call, and picking up the downstairs receiver, she cut rudely into her father's conversation. "Hello, who's that?" she said.

"Hello Tricia – is that you?" Stella, Mr Morrell's Assistant replied.

"I'm not well," Tricia answered abruptly, not sounding at all ill.

"Mr Morrell asked me to call you to find out ….,"

"Goodbye," Tricia said banging down the receiver, before Stella had finished speaking.

When details of this conversation were relayed to Mr Morrell he became extremely angry. He was sorry that he was left with no choice but to dismiss Tricia - she was a "jolly good secretary". But Mr Morrell could not abide staff taking "unauthorised time off", when they were poorly, let alone when there was apparently nothing wrong with them. Tricia's attitude had caused him to wonder whether she was "going loopy". As far as Mr Morrell was concerned, many disadvantaged young women like her would give their right arm for a job like hers in an office like theirs.

As far as Tricia was concerned, she did not care - she had had it up to the eyeballs with "Grumpy Morrells", as she commonly referred to her boss.

Still fuming for no apparent reason, about the conversation with Stella half an hour earlier, Tricia angrily flicked from channel to channel. There was nothing worth watching on TV which infuriated her even more. She looked at the time - 11.35 am. On her agenda today was a visit to prophet Osiri. She wanted to consult him again about the potential new problem that had arisen. But first she wanted to be certain that the woman she had seen entering and leaving Gus' house was in fact Cherie Johnson. So without wasting any more time Tricia jumped to her feet and headed for the door – destination Islington.

Arriving at Cherie's office block at 11.30 am, Tricia sat and waited in the car – watching. An hour went by but no-one fitting the description of the woman she thought was Cherie Johnson either entered or left the building. So she decided to leave the car and take a closer look at the entrance in the hope of gathering clues. An inspection of the two buzzers by the front door revealed that the first buzzer was for a company named "Technical Graphics", and beneath the second buzzer appeared the name "Smooth Management", which did not help much. Tricia pressed the second buzzer for much longer than was necessary. Upon receiving no response, she buzzed the first buzzer. Almost immediately a very sweet voice answered. Tricia asked whether Cherie Johnson worked there. "No, she's with Smooth Management, I think - use the other buzzer," came the very helpful reply. "Result - Oh, so it is her," Tricia said smiling as her left eye twitched repeatedly. Contemplating what a clever ruse she had used in order to smoke out Cherie's identity, Tricia smiled smugly as she left the building.

On returning to the car she found a parking ticket stuck to the windscreen. The Traffic Warden had moved on, but was still nearby. Tricia approached her and asked that she cancel the ticket, stating that she only went to collect something for a couple of minutes. The Warden refused and Tricia proceeded to argue with her. The warden proceeded to ignore her and walked away hastily. Tricia gave her the evil eye as she went - wishing that everything very bad would happen to her. She thought about casting a quick spell on the warden, but decided not to bother – she wasn't going to pay the parking fine any how – her dad was.

The rather dilapidated sign announced that she was entering Foxton Green. Tricia followed signs to the station and found that she could easily remember the direction to prophet Osiri's shop from there. Five minutes later she arrived at the shop but was informed that the prophet was not there - she decided to wait for his return. Forty minutes later, to her surprise prophet Osiri walked in wearing denims and trainers and looking like an ordinary man - she almost did not recognise him. Seeing him in everyday casual attire caused some loss of faith, but Tricia tried not to show it.

When the prophet had changed into his usual apparel, he beckoned Tricia to come into his consultancy room.

"Yes, what can I do for you," said the flustered man behind the desk. Tricia did not reply to his question straight away – she was struggling to regain her faith in this man now that she had seen him in his day-to-day attire. She closed her eyes for a beat and thought about the first time she had visited the prophet, then she opened them and replied. "I... I.... I.... came to see you a couple of weeks ago – I.... I.... came to see you again today because I would like you to do something else for me", she blubbered.

"I do nothing – it is you that will do the work – I merely guide", replied the prophet. His voice resounded commandingly which had the effect of renewing Tricia's trust.

"It's…..it's….. I………, Tricia stuttered.

"Well, speak up, I haven't got all day – what is it?" said the prophet loudly, causing Tricia to feel uncomfortable in the same way that she had on her first visit.

"I….. it's Cherie Johnson, she is a person …. that I used to know a few years ago". "She is trying to steal my boyfriend," said Tricia, fully believing her lie.

"What do you want to do about it?" asked the prophet.

"I would like to stop her and I want him to have nothing to do with her," Tricia said, her stutter suddenly gone.

"How do you want to stop her - do you want her to leave the country, or to be crippled, or do you want her to die?" the prophet said rather matter-of-factly in a booming voice.

Tricia thought for some time, but the prophet became impatient and said, "Well, what do you want to do?" boomingly.

"I…. I….. want her to leave the country," Tricia said uncertainly, then she had second thoughts. If Cherie left the country

Gus would probably go with her. She thought of how much pleasure she would derive from seeing Cherie run mad, then said. "No, I want you to drive her mad," retracting her earlier statement.

The prophet looked intently at Tricia and said, "So you are going to drive her mad?" Then he laughed aloud, the familiar laugh that Tricia recalled. He then set about carrying out her request by reaching into a small cabinet behind his chair and, after some rummaging around he pulled out two small dolls and handed one of them to Tricia. "Say the name of your enemy," he ordered. Tricia stared at him blankly for a couple of beats before her brain sent the correct signal to her lips, "Cherie, Cherie Johnson," she said. The prophet gave Tricia some further instructions which she followed. When she had finished she looked expectantly at the prophet.

"Take this," came the next order. Tricia took a small package.

"Open it, said the prophet. When she had opened the package, Tricia saw a large needle. The prophet gave her further instructions on what to do with the needle which Tricia could not easily commit to memory. She extracted a notepad and pen from her handbag and made a note. Then she stared intently at the prophet who returned her gaze unnervingly. Then without warning he began to speak again, loudly "But I caution you gravely, your enemy is very powerful – be warned there may be consequences to you – be warned," said the prophet, without explaining what he meant.

"What consequences," Cherie enquired.

"Everything one does carries consequences – some good, some bad – your enemy is very powerful – there may be grave consequences to you – be warned," the prophet continued loudly in the Queen's English then laughed bitterly.

Tricia felt uneasy as she sat staring at the prophet. He returned her stare unnervingly, causing her to fidget with her bag. Then he spoke again loudly and without warning, causing Tricia to jump.

"Here, take this, take this", said the prophet impatiently as he handed Tricia the second doll. "This is your boyfriend", the prophet continued.

Tricia took the doll, and the prophet once again proceeded to give her instructions which, fishing for her pad and pen, Tricia made further notes of.

When he had finished speaking, the prophet sniggered as he stared straight into Tricia's eyes, causing her to feel more uneasy than ever before. Then he proceeded to ignore her as he rummaged in his drawers some more, mumbling to himself. After a while, realising the prophet had moved on to other things, Tricia figured the consultation was at an end. "How much do I have to pay for this," she asked.

"Nothing, I have done nothing – you pay only for the materials," said the prophet tersely.

Tricia asked how much the materials cost. The prophet did not reply.

She rummaged in her purse and pulled out a £20 bank note and placed it on the desk behind which prophet Osiri sat.

Osiri looked at the bank note and said, "That's too much".

When he said nothing more, Tricia pressed him gently, "How much do I have to pay you then." The prophet still did not reply. Tricia placed two £5 notes onto the desk. The prophet still made no response. She also placed a £1 coin onto the desk – still no response. She placed two more £1 coins on the desk and the prophet proceeded to pick them up and put them into the desk drawer. Tricia waited for a moment but he said nothing more. She said a questioning "thank you," to which he replied "No need to thank me, I have done nothing," as he continued rummaging, whereupon Tricia made her way out of his "chambers". As she reached the door, she paused and looked back at the prophet. He glanced in her direction briefly, an expression of derision on his face before proceeding to stare into space in the opposite direction, apparently in a world of his own. Tricia closed the door and left.

Back in the car Tricia noted that it was now 2.10 pm. She decided that she would head towards Islington to see whether she could see what was happening with Gus. On arrival she noted that Gus' car was not in its usual parking space and surmised that he was not at home. She decided she would wait to see whether he came home.

While waiting she extracted the dolls from her handbag, put the larger one representing Gus close to her mouth and spoke her command. "You must have nothing to do with Cherie Johnson". Then she took the small doll, recalling the warning that had been given by the prophet. He had warned of consequences which now caused a bitter taste in Tricia's mouth. Her brow creased as she contemplated whether she wanted to take the next step in view of the severe warning, but her desire to have control over the situation outweighed her sense of caution. Anyway, she decided, she would be adequately protected from any adverse consequences by the ring that she had obtained over a year ago from another powerful mystic. She reasoned that nothing had happened to her since she did the ritual on Gus, so why should anything happen to her now. Satisfied, Tricia proceeded to remove the needle from its package while glancing around at all the houses to make sure no-one was watching her, then looking up and down the road to ensure that no-one was coming, she proceeded to follow the prophet's instructions. Then she returned the doll and the needle to her handbag and continued to watch Gus' home. She wanted so much for the spell to work on Cherie, who she considered an old enemy anyway, that she repeated the needle ritual several times with vigour over the next two and a half hours.

The curtains twitched as someone peered at Tricia from the house outside which she was parked. She was still sitting in her car watching Gus' home and had been doing so for the past 2 hours. She was becoming irritable and hungry because the biscuits and snacks she kept in the car had finished. Her muscles were becoming fatigued from sitting in the same position for so long and she was developing a headache. She rubbed her forehead and temples to try and alleviate the pain that was developing. Tricia rarely suffered with headaches, and this one was developing into the worse she had ever had. Narrowing her eyes to try and block out some of the light she squinted but instead of getting any better the headache worsened. She rested her head against the headrest and turned her neck slowly in a circular motion but to no avail - she needed to go and lie down and was just about to leave when she saw Gus get out of a car – another minicab – she could tell as he paid the driver before entering his home. And today he looked much worse than he had yesterday. Today he looked as though he was carrying the whole world on his back. Tricia smiled, in spite of her pounding headache – "It's working – it's working", she said, sniggering. Then she started the car and drove off slowly, not wishing to accentuate the throbbing headache which was now so severe that she felt like she might be going mad.

CHAPTER 7

Hit the Road

Falling to her knees, Cherie thanked God for the favour that she had enjoyed on the first night of the tour. The only downside was that during the evening a severe headache had developed and it seemed to be getting worse by the minute. So Cherie also asked God to heal her. Due to the throbbing in her temples, it hurt when she spoke so she fell silent and continued to pray in her mind and spirit. Her brow tensed and creased as she bit hard on her back teeth, tightening her jaw but this availed little.

As Cherie ended her prayer she whispered an "amen," and immediately felt a release as the pressure in her head began to relent. After that the head pain subsided rapidly and she reclined on her bed, musing over the events of the day. The tour had kicked off with a bang and she was overjoyed with the outcome of the first show. The level of success was beyond anything she could ever have hoped for. With just one show she looked to have covered more than a quarter of the overheads of the whole tour. The local press had advertised the performance well and the turnout for the first night was phenomenal. Never in her wildest dreams had she imagined this sort of turnout would be possible. All the tickets had sold out, even the standing room ones had all gone and many people who came along to queue with the hope of getting a ticket or last-minute cancellation had been turned away. Cherie was so surprised because she was not aware that either Sera Ocel or Ebony Son was so popular. She had sent some courtesy copies of Sera's debut album "Maximum Exposure" and Ebony Son's "Loving Man" to local radio stations in Birmingham and the surrounding suburbs, asking them to play the records and publicise the concerts and the release of the albums that would coincide with the kick off of the tour. Cherie almost pinched herself several times during the evening to see that she wasn't in fact dreaming. Ever cautious and attempting to keep a level head and feet planted firmly on the ground she told herself that this first night could be just a fluke –

beginner's luck. There was a long way to go yet before she would hail the tour as a complete success, but the signs were more than promising.

Both Ebony Son and Sera Ocel had performed like seasoned professional entertainers, much to Cherie's surprise. The whole crew - the backing group, support band and the rest of the entourage, including Cherie (who sang back-up vocals), had put on a fantastic show, and the audience participation was remarkable – they loved and warmed to the new stars as though they had long arisen. Sera demonstrated the most charisma, a fact which was reflected in the subsequent sales of CDs, DVDs and other memorabilia. They sold all the Maximum Exposure CDs - over three hundred, and most of the DVDs. And they could have sold perhaps twice as many CDs if they had not run out of stock.

So altering her original plan not to return to London until Saturday night, Cherie decided she would have to travel back in the morning to collect more CDs, etc, returning in time for tomorrow night's show. Much as she loathed the thought of making the round trip to London and back, her business savvy dictated that it was an opportunity that could not be missed.

The other members of the crew went out to celebrate the success of the first night at a local jazz club, but Cherie did not have the inclination to accompany them, not only because of the headache, but due to the fact that she did not find such environments in any way conducive to her spiritual uplifting. It once more occurred to Cherie that it made no sense for her to continue promoting secular music and artistes. And she, once again, told herself that in a few short months she would change course. For now, she endeavoured to see that the concert venues were drugs free by providing good security and over indulgence of drinking was strongly discouraged.

After a while Cherie realised that the headache had completely disappeared and she smiled to herself as she contemplated God's loving-kindness in answering her prayer.

Crawling into bed, Cherie nestled beneath the luxurious duvet as she breathed in deeply enjoying the smell of freshly laundered and perfumed fabric. A smile played about her lips as her thoughts turned to Gus. A frown replaced the smile as she wondered why he hadn't called. She was convinced that he would telephone her today - she might have bet her life on it if she were a gambling woman. But had she been mistaken as to the signals that he was sending? Reasoning within herself, Cherie shook her head. No, she had not been mistaken – he had come on to her big time and she had made it patently obvious that she was interested in at least a friendship if nothing else. *"But I should have known he was too good to be true,"* Cherie thought aloud. Then she began to beat herself up mentally. What had she been thinking – why had she been taken in by this man whom she barely knew anyway? Shouldn't she have realised by now that her love life would never be that straightforward – that she would not so simply be that lucky in love?

A wave of intense and contrasting emotions washed over Cherie, and suddenly the idea of telephoning Gus occurred to her. She dismissed the idea - for one it was far too late and secondly, her experience with George had taught her never to take the bull by the horns as chances were that she would end up being mauled. So she closed her eyes, and said a silent prayer that God would change her love life and send her an angel. She found herself wishing that that angel could be Gus Allen. A small tear welled up on the inside of Cherie's left eye. She sniffed, willing the urge to cry to retreat - but she failed. The tiny tear turned into two globules – one in each eye - that coursed down her face unabated. After a minute or so, she dried her eyes and tried to pull herself together, but thoughts of Gus continued to churn over and over in her head until she felt extremely tired. As sleep threatened to descend like a thick cloud, Cherie resisted – she did not wish to sleep, she wanted to think some more - about Gus – albeit to wallow in the pain of disappointment. A small voice told her to stop wasting her time - the fact that he had not called her showed his disinterest and she should forget about him and move on. But the sobering thought that perhaps he had a good reason for not calling as promised prevailed. So Cherie continued to think about Gus' smile, to hear his voice echo in the archives of her mind and she smiled back through her tears.

Earlier in the day Cherie had sent Gus an e-mail of the tour schedule as she promised to do and it suddenly occurred to her that a reply may be waiting in her in-box. This thought niggled at the fringes of her mind until curiosity got the better of her and she got out of bed and switched on her laptop. Disappointment was forceful as having searched her in box Cherie did not find a reply from Gus. This added to her frustration. Switching off the lap-top she proceeded to check her 'phone thoroughly for missed calls or messages that may have been missed earlier but there was no contact from Gus.

"But we seemed to be getting on so well yesterday - there was a real connection, I was not mistaken, was I? No I was not, he was coming on to me," Cherie said to herself. There was certainly something there - she could not deny that – at least she felt something. But once again it occurred to her that most probably the feeling was one-sided and she concluded, "Gus Allen probably behaves that way to most women he meets".

Exhausted by the revolving thoughts about Gus, as much as from the physical exertion over past weeks and particularly over the past two days Cherie crawled back into bed. As she fell into deep slumber she was comforted in her dreams by the man who told her he was her father – he hugged her and told her that everything would be alright - that he would look after her – and he wiped away her tears.

Next morning Cherie awoke bright and early. She jumped out of bed and almost shouted "Thank God, I'm alive – all things are working out for my good," before heading straight to the bathroom where she went under a lukewarm shower. Singing as she showered, she luxuriated and the chorus "Shackles off my feet" had never been rendered quite so vigorously. When she had finished she wrapped the large bath towel about her and returned to the bedroom, where she prepared her attire for the day.

Now dressed, Cherie sat on the edge of the bed leafing through her diary until she found the appropriate page – Saturday 29 April 2010. She read through her proposed movements for the day, which included going along to two local radio stations for interviews in order to publicise tonight's concert – on paper she would be free by 1.00 pm. Sera was supposed to accompany her, but had informed her last night that she would be unable to make it as she "needed her beauty sleep", much to Cherie's exasperation. And she now reminded herself of her plan to drop Sera like a hot ton of bricks at the end of the tour which provided her with some consolation. Cherie wondered whether she should take Ebony Son along with her – he would be only too happy to go, but she dismissed that plan, as it would not be fair to spring this on him so suddenly. He was scheduled to attend the radio interviews in Manchester next week and Cherie decided best to stick to that plan.

A much looked forward to shopping spree for the day had to be cancelled because of Cherie's trip back to London – she also anticipated she would miss the sound check. This was not what she wanted - she needed some time out for herself and she did not relish the thought of missing the sound check either, as Miss Ocel needed to be constantly monitored. One thing was certain – she could not be in two places at the same time, George would have to deputise to see Sera toed the line.

George answered his phone straight away and assured Cherie that he was happy to step up. When she finished speaking to George, she telephoned the distribution house to ask them to have 1000 CDs made up of a variety, ready for her to collect at 2.30 pm. No-one answered the telephone - Cherie left a message. Then she glanced at the 'phone – it was only 8.00 am – no wonder no-one would be at work as yet. So she also rang Singer, the owner of the distribution company, on his mobile and left a further message. Singer had earned that nickname because he had tried to make it as a vocal artiste. But everyone agreed that he was a terrible singer with absolutely no hope and after a few knock backs he had taken the hint and gone into distribution instead. He proved to be a talented business man with the rare gift, an uncanny knack of identifying hit artistes from their very first recordings. He had a likeable personality - if a little eccentric, endearing others, including Cherie, to him. They had hit it off from their very first meeting, when introduced by George. Cherie now counted him as a friend and relied on his business instincts and efficiency. It had been Singer's idea to release the track "Heavy Love" as the first single from Sera Ocel's album and so far his instincts had proved on point.

The productive interview at Vibes Radio was over, and Cherie smiled to herself as she drove out of the car park. She couldn't be more pleased with the interest generated so far on the tour. Everyone at Vibes Radio had been so excited about her dropping by, treating her like a big celebrity - much to her surprise. And the listeners who had 'phoned in provided assurance that her artistes were a sure hit. They confirmed their love for the sound of Sera Ocel and Ebony Son, which many said were the right sounds for the time. They appreciated Sera Ocel's material, the reality lyrics which were arranged to an edgy mixture of Jamaican Ragga, R & B, with a ting of rock. The sweet original sound of Ebony Son was also highly acclaimed. And the support artistes Kingdom Praise, with their combination of jazz, soul and reggae inspirational gospel were also well appraised. Kingdom Praise had sold almost as many CDs as Ebony Son, and had, surprisingly, proved equally as popular. Cherie made a mental note to extend their slot by one extra number, nodding her head as she pondered this decision.

Arriving at Sonic Radio's premises Cherie glanced at the time - 12.15 pm – she wondered how time had flown. Her tight schedule meant that she would only be able to spend 45 minutes at Sonic Radio. Hurriedly, she parked her car and headed towards what looked like the reception area of the old dishevelled building. It appeared to be a small outfit, and as she entered the building Cherie was surprised to see that it was so rundown, belying its status as one of the most popular stations in the area. There was no-one at reception and Cherie waited for a while. After a few minutes, when no-one appeared, she began to fidget. She could hear music coming from somewhere in the building - perhaps they thought she wasn't bothering to come, as she was over 30 minutes late. She headed in the direction of the music and called out, "Hello," but no-one answered or came out to meet her. "Hello," she called a little louder as she got closer to the music.

On reaching the door of the room from which the sounds were emanating Cherie virtually shouted, "Hello". "Hello – just a minute," came the response. Cherie fell quiet and waited by the door - she could make out that the owner of the voice was apparently presenting a radio show. He introduced the next track and hurried to open the door to usher her into the small overcrowded room. "Sorry, sorry - you are Cherie, right," he said breathlessly.

"Yeah," Cherie replied.

"Sorry baby," said the radio presenter. "Eric Knight," at your service, come in and make yourself comfortable," he gestured for her to take a seat. "Is Sera Ocel with you?" Eric asked to which Cherie replied, embarrassed, "No, sorry, she couldn't make it this time", and smiled.

The small radio studio was so cramped that Cherie felt uncomfortable. Eric stretched out his hand and Cherie grabbed hold of it.

"Whaa pen – me glad you could mek it," he said excitedly. "Bwoy a was at the concert last night, and man Sera can blow – I was thoroughly entertained, and as for Ebony Son - absolutely phenomenal" Eric said, sounding nothing like he looked. He was a red haired white male, who looked every ounce a full-blooded Englishman who should speak the Queen's English, but rather confusingly he spoke with a broad authentic Jamaica accent that Cherie struggled to understand. Eric twanged further about the concert, going on to mention Kingdom Praise in complimentary terms, although he admitted to Cherie that he was not religious and was not really into Christian music, "Maybe I need to get to know more about the Christian music offerings – Kingdom Praise are fresh, exciting - they really surprised me." Eric enthused. Cherie smiled and replied "Yes, they are certainly on fire for God". Eric fell silent and looked uncomfortable. Cherie was not perturbed by his reaction – she was accustomed to people behaving that way at anything more than a blasé reference to God. She proceeded to hand him some complimentary CDs including a copy of the Kingdom Praise CD which had been on general release for more than a year. Eric promised to pass it on to the Christian DJ. "I will pass it over to Gary, he will definitely give that some air play, definitely", Eric reassured.

Then without prompting he proceeded to talk about himself, telling Cherie proudly about his Jamaican roots and ancestry. He spoke fondly about his life in Kingston and St Elizabeth, where he was born. Cherie found him to be very engaging - someone she would like to keep in touch with. However, after about 15 minutes she began glancing at her 'phone – a victim of time constraints.

Eric noticed her anxiety and then proceeded, without warning, to introduce her live on air. Cherie was taken aback, but decided she'd better try to relax and go with the flow.

"Birmingham massive, we have Cherie Johnson in the studio dis morning – we glad fe 'ave you wid us Cherie," Eric said as he smiled to the listeners.

"It's good to be here as your guest, Eric," Cherie replied, smiling back. Eric went on to give the listeners some brief information about Cherie, stating that she managed Sera Ocel, Ebony Son, Kingdom Praise and other artistes. He then spoke directly to Cherie,

"Yeah man, I was at the launch concert last night, and I must admit that I was surprised. He went on to discuss Sera Ocel, "That lady certainly has a gift – so, where did you discover Sera Ocel, Cherie," asked Eric expertly.

"Well," Cherie began and went on to give a history of how she had discovered Sera when she had attended an audition.

Later they talked about Ebony Son and Eric introduced a competition, the question "What was the name of the new Sera Ocel single", for which the prize was a pair of tickets to tonight's show. First to call in with the answer "Heavy Love", was someone who had attended last night's show which Cherie took as serious validation - she was ecstatic.

Wrapping up the interview Eric played "Heavy Love", and plugged the single big time. Cherie was surprised by how much at ease he made her feel and how much information he managed to solicit from her.

Finally getting away from Sonic at 1.30 pm promptly, Cherie headed straight for the M1 on her way toward London, with thoughts of Gus Allen to keep her company.

CHAPTER 8

My Mentee – My Mentor

Feeling lethargic, Gus forced his body into a standing position. He felt as though he was coming down with the worse sort of virus. However, he tried to focus his thoughts on all he had to accomplish for the day. He had just awoken from another nightmare - the same faceless man had tried to suffocate him - pushing the air out of his lungs – stifling him. He felt drained, sore and he also had a clanging headache. But he was determined to achieve his aims today, 22 May 2010.

He had arranged to meet Martin and Donna today for an extra training session, but first he had to pick up a rental car. He was tired of catching taxis everywhere - it was proving to be very expensive. Ever the thrifty one, Gus hated the very thought of wasting money and each time he entered a taxi, images of starving third world children invaded his thoughts, making it an uncomfortable ride.

After collecting the car he planned to go and inspect the works being carried out to a property that he had purchased 6 months previously in the East End. The ex-Local Authority block contained four flats, which he bought cheaply at auction. A lot of work was needed to bring it up to living standards as the almost derelict block had lain empty for many years - even the more well-to-do squatters had moved on. Prudence saw Gus commission a full structural survey of the block before he purchased, which revealed that the foundations were sound. He had proceeded with the purchase under no delusions as to the challenges (both in financial and other terms) that he would face to restore the building to its former glory. But now he was wondering whether he had bitten off more than he could chew, because the project was proving far more expensive than anticipated. The main reason for the additional costs was that the builders he usually contracted were too busy to take on the project and he had employed others that were far more expensive and less efficient. Much to his inconvenience and annoyance, he found that they needed constant supervision to get anything done. He was accustomed to briefing his usual builders and leaving them to execute the project immaculately, economically and without supervision, within the agreed timescale.

After checking up on the builders Gus had a meeting scheduled for 1 pm, with the letting/managing agents who handled most of his portfolio. He wanted to try and re-negotiate a new deal with them, because they had recently advised that they would be increasing their charges by a whopping 4% - he hoped they would be open to negotiation, because if not, he would reluctantly have to move to pastures new.

Sluggishly, Gus ambled to the bathroom where he splashed cold water over his face. He felt momentarily refreshed as he concentrated on the day's itinerary. After quickly showering he returned to the bedroom, where he dressed casually as appropriate for the training session later, groomed his hair and face and headed to the kitchen to prepare himself coffee and toast.

As he sat eating his breakfast Gus' mind drifted to Cherie Johnson – he thought about her often. Immediately a warm feeling surged through his body – the intensity of which surprised him. True to her word, Cherie had e-mailed him the itinerary for the tour. If he had his car, he might have driven to one of the out of town shows to support her. He wondered how the tour was going – he hoped well. He had been meaning to call her but so far had not been in the right frame of mind to do so - he would call her when the time was right.

Then the thought of Maureen and her unexpected decision to marry someone else came to the forefront of his mind. He was relieved though – she saved him the trauma of ending their dead relationship - he thought about Cherie again and felt a happy surge that he was now free to start dating if he wished. As soon as he sorted himself out he intended to ask Cherie on a date. Gus smiled, his current problems momentarily forgotten as he arose from breakfast and made his way out of the front door.

Having collected the car, Gus made his way to his next port of call. He was running late, having been delayed firstly by public transport problems and then by having been made to wait at the car showroom. When he finally arrived at the block it was 12.15 pm. He had employed the element of surprise, turning up unexpectedly. The builders were taking so long to progress the work which he knew should have been finished by now, that Gus wondered what they did on a daily basis. His worse fears were realised when he found only two workers present, out of the four that should have been on site. And those present were just sitting around, apparently having a tea break. On enquiring as to the whereabouts of the other two, no plausible explanation was put forward for their absence. Gus shook his head in realisation that his suspicions were not unfounded. Suddenly he became noticeably angry - these cowboys were obviously taking him for a ride. The way things were looking, they would not finish for at least another two or three weeks, and this work should have been finished two months ago. The longer they took to complete the work, the longer he would be paying the mortgage without receiving any revenue from the property.

The two skivers soon busied themselves under Gus' watchful gaze. However, they appeared to be lacking instructions, as their supervisors were not present. It also appeared that they did not have the necessary materials to work with. Gus waited for an hour to see whether the foreman would return to the site, but he did not. Due to time constraints he had to leave. As he left, he telephoned Cyrus to ask him if he could supervise the remainder of the work which should take no more than one week to complete. Cyrus was happy to oblige, lifting a weight off Gus' mind.

Although he was very short of time Gus knew he had to stop and grab something to eat before his meeting - he would need energy for the training session with Martin and Donna later on. It was now 1.20 pm as Gus made his way to the managing agents' offices – he was annoyed with himself because he was running late. "Oh well, it couldn't be helped", he mumbled trying to make himself feel better but failing.

The managing agents' Director, with whom he had the meeting, was not pleased when he finally arrived at 1.35 pm. Probably to some degree as a result of that, the meeting was not a success. Gus did not manage to negotiate any acceptable new deal. The agents insisted on increasing their charges by 4%. And he was generally unhappy with the way they were managing the properties in any case. In the past month and a half, more than three quarters of his portfolio had become untenanted – tenants were not renewing their tenancies and new ones had not been found - others were breaching their tenancy agreements by commiting criminal damage and leaving the property in severe disrepair. And of those that remained nearly all of them had begun defaulting on their rent. So Gus made a decision to find a replacement agency to manage his portfolio. "Things better change soon or I will find it impossible to sort out this financial mess", Gus mumbled as he left the agents' offices.

After the unproductive meeting Gus made his way to Wash House where he was to pick up Martin and Donna at 3.00 pm. Arriving at 3.15 and 3.25pm respectively, he apologised for keeping them waiting. It was half-term week and the youngsters were available to attend the training session during the afternoon, as opposed to evenings and weekends only. Martin was eagerly waiting for him when he arrived, and expressed surprise to see the car he was driving. "What happened to your old car the MXLX?" Martin enquired. "Oh - it's a long story," Gus said deciding he did not want to talk about it. "Sorry I'm running a little late", he said effectively changing the subject.

When he collected Donna the apology was repeated. "I hope you're ready for some hard work," Gus said.

"Well, I know I am," said Martin in an enthusiastic boyish manner.

"Yeah, yeah," Donna said, less than enthusiastically.

"What happened to your old car?" she also asked. Deciding he may as well tell them about his misfortunate Gus replied, "It was stolen", whereupon the youngsters each commiserated with him. Gus changed the subject and made small talk, indicating he didn't want to talk about it and the youngsters got the message.

Gus threw himself into training with his two protégés with enthusiasm. For the next 3 hours, he managed to push all other matters from his mind, concentrating on doing something he loved. At the end of the training session he felt satisfied that a great deal had been accomplished. Martin had managed to shave nearly half a second off his personal best time for the 100 metres, and Donna was continuing to develop a more positive mental attitude to training. Gus could tell this because at the end she enquired with delight when the next training session would be.

After the session Gus drove them home – first Donna and then Martin. After he had dropped Donna off, Martin began to tell Gus about how he was getting on in school. Gus had sensed earlier when the subject of school arose that all might not be well and now without prompting Martin talked about the problems he was encountering at school and in his neighbourhood generally. He told Gus of the drastic changes that had taken place in Wash House over recent years, explaining how it was to live there as a teenager in the present day. Gus listened intently, yet unbelievingly as Martin gave him a vivid insight into the way that drugs and gangs operated in the neighbourhood and their negative effects on the lives of the ordinary people on the estate. Apparently those most affected were the younger people. Martin told Gus how he was coming under sustained pressure from gang members to join their set-up and was being victimised because of his refusal to so.

According to Martin, if you did not join one or other gang, you left yourself vulnerable to attack from any of the gangs. Most youngsters joined a gang so that they could have protection on the streets, because if others knew that you were a member of a gang, they respected you - left you alone. It all sounded a little far-fetched to Gus, especially when Martin proceeded to tell him about the various weapons that were readily available and donned by youths in the gangs. Martin said that he knew of several teenagers (some as young as 12) who owned guns and that most of them – even some that attended the training sessions, carried knives. Martin would not tell Gus who, but assured him that he himself did not carry a weapon.

The young protégé proceeded to inform Gus that he had chosen to take what he considered to be the most sensible and intelligent approach to "the madness" as he referred to it. He had chosen to be single minded – to stand alone – without gang or weapons, even in the face of constant threats by others who were unhappy about his stance.

"I just carry my sword everywhere", Martin said as Gus listened thinking that Martin was obviously joking since he could not see that he had any sword upon his person.

"Basically, I just want to do something positive with my life - you understand", Martin continued. "But most of dem man my age, and even younger than me, just want to play bad man, to run with gangs, deal drugs, carry guns and knives and ting", Martin shook his head from side to side as he spoke. Gus watched him, drawn in by his animation. He began to believe that Martin was not joking after all, however far fetched his story sounded.

"And dem always looking for trouble, bruv - always looking for an opportunity to prove – to make a name for themselves". "Because, when dem get a reputation for violence, dem get more respect on the streets, from other gang members and other gangs - it's sheer madness bruv - I can see it's madness, because a whole heap a man lost dem lives to prove seh dem bad", Martin said in his decidedly dodgy Jamaican twang.

"But surely their parents should stop this madness," Gus interjected.

"Parents – dem don't care about parents", Martin replied with renewed vigour. "Most of them have good parents but they don't listen to them – they don't respect their parents - they haven't even got time for dem families – they only have time for the gangs and gang activities", he continued. As Gus listened intently he interjected with short comments - "really", "wha" "man" etc, encouraging the youngster to bare his soul.

"They are caught up in the "live fast, die young" culture – they are not afraid to die – life has lost respect and value to them". "And they will do anything to make money", Martin continued as Gus listened, a picture of hopelessness forming in his mind. But what Martin told him next was the most disturbing. "Many innocent youths end up seriously injured – some of dem affected for the rest of dem lives, and a lot of dem dead – all for what bruv?" Martin sounded incredibly brave and wise to Gus ears. "The drugs are the major problem". "Every time you walk down the street - man offering you drugs", Martin divulged. "Even in school dem dealing drugs." "And hear this, sometimes dem even offer you the drugs for free, but I always refuse - I can see that they just do that to get you hooked - to turn you into an addict, dependant, and then you have to start buying from dem". "Basically, if you refuse, dem try to ridicule you – to mek you tink that you are odd, the only one not doing it – they laugh at you – try to mek you feel ashamed". "Then if that doesn't work, they threaten you to mek you feel afraid for refusing dem, but I know seh I ain't stupid and I do not fear what man can do to me – I only fear God", the conversation became one-sided as Martin spoke and Gus listened. "Nuff man begin to take drugs just through peer pressure". "It's only a few like me who refuse and stand firm". "It's not easy, bruv - it's a constant battle, man – an everyday struggle – it's just a jungle," Martin said sounding like a brave young solder in his peculiar lilt of dubious Jamaican and English. The youngster allowed all that he had inside to flow out as though a dam had burst, often repeating over what he had said previously, demonstrating his frustration.

"But the only ting that keeps me saying no to the gangs – no to the drugs – no to the weapons and the violence, is that I can see that it don't pay in the long run – thank God for showing me that". "What's the use in taking drugs and ending up a junkie – can't help you self, can't help you family". "Then 'nuff of dem man end up dealing drugs to feed dem habit or robbing people for their next hit". "And even if they don't have a habit when they started dealing, they usually end up acquiring one because others with habits inveigle them to", Martin continued. "Basically, when dem selling the drugs, they think that dem going to get rich from it – all they think about is money, dem don't see the downside – the negatives". "They don't think about the shame they bring on dem families or the lives of the addicts that they ruin". "I can see that there is more likelihood that they will end up dead, bruv – dead, and for what". "As far as I'm concerned, I don't need to make money like that". "I would rather not have a penny than to do that". "As far as I am concerned drugs just destroys people – whether it is just a little smoke or harder stuff". "But dem drugs man dem don't respect human life". "They don't see or care about the lives that they ruin", Martin informed.

"And another thing, 'nuff man losing dem life because dem trespass on another gang's turf – knowingly or unknowingly", Martin said opening a new chapter. "Sometimes man all get kill off because dem in the wrong place at the wrong time or the wrong postcode – how crazy is that, Bruv?" Some get gunned down because dem look like another bruvver – it's pure sick madness a gwane – bruv - I can see that," Martin paused before continuing. "Whole heap of my friends that I grew up with have turned into junkies already". "Fourteen, fifteen and they are junkies – just makes me want to cry, bruv, reality". "Dem steal and rob people to feed dem habit". "I don't even hang with most of them no more because I can't trust them and I don't want to get caught up, bruv". "Nuff of dem gaan a yout custody and ting". "Most of their parents don't even know what dem a gwane with on the street". "A good friend of mine got involved with a gang, and last I heard he ended up dead in Wash House canal because he upset a rival gang boss", Martin said becoming reflective. Then he fell silent as he hung his head down in sadness.

At this point Gus reflected on his own brother Marcus, who had become just such a victim, although he did not say anything to Martin. He felt a great sadness engulf him as he thought about his dear brother. Why hadn't he noticed what was happening to his younger brother? And if he had, could he have saved Marcus from what he had now become? How come he himself had never gotten caught up in the same way that Marcus had? All these questions vied for prominence in Gus' mind but he had no answers to them. The next thought made him sadder – he knew that Martin needed guidance as to how he might deal with this problem, but he didn't know what he could say to this young man. How could he even begin to guide him when he had not been able to guide his own brother many years ago before this problem became so prevalent? What could he possibly say to this young man to help him?

When Gus spoke again his voice trembled. He tried to encourage Martin not to succumb to peer pressure – tried to assure him that he was doing the right thing to keep away from gangs and drugs. However, all that Gus was saying to Martin sounded wholly inadequate to his own ears. "If it helps to talk about anything at all, or if there is anything I can do to help, please let me know – don't be afraid to ask," Gus said, thinking how pathetic he must sound to this intelligent young man – it certainly sounded feeble to him. Martin obviously needed more than he was able to offer him. Gus felt helpless – he wanted to do something – to say something to help, but it seemed that this problem was too large – too tricky – had too many components and was too sinister for any one person to even begin to unravel. Gus was certain that there could be no simple answer – he certainly didn't have any himself. And Gus felt a deep respect for Martin, for the way that he had chosen to handle what sounded like an insurmountable problem.

Martin, perceiving Gus' feelings of hopelessness from the look on his face, said, "But, I don't worry too much – I just leave everything in the hands of God". "I know that I can trust Him to look after me – to keep me safe – to guide me." "I rely on my sword", Martin said causing Gus to wonder a second time what he was talking about.

"My Bible – that's my sword – God has all the answers in his words," Martin said answering Gus' obvious curiosity.

Gus looked at Martin as though seeing him for the first time. What the young man had just said sounded like far more of a potential remedy than anything else he could ever recommend. Martin went on at length to elucidate about his faith in God. Gus was astounded that one so young had such a deep consciousness about God, for Gus had been plagued by perplexity about spiritual matters for many years.

Later, as Gus was driving home he pondered deeply the things that Martin had told him, trying to make sense of it all. What Martin had told him seemed, at first hearing, like a very simple philosophy about God and life. But the young man's theory had also raised numerous questions in Gus' mind which he now contemplated.

Martin said that God was in ultimate charge of his life - that he left everything to Him and believed that He would work it out for the best, because he had surrendered his life to Him. According to Martin each person has been given freedom of choice - a free will to do whatever they pleased. And he had chosen to put

God in control of his life, thereby surrendering his free will back to God. And he believed that God now had full charge of his life, and caused everything to work out for the best for him - he apparently reposed full trust and confidence in God. Martin had also read a bible verse to Gus – *all things work together for good for those that love the Lord.*

But what if you did not put God in control – did not surrender your will to Him? Martin's theory was apparently, that if one made a decision by themselves – without God's input - then they would be bound by the consequences of that decision. He said that God would not intervene in one's life if you did not ask or allow Him to. The young man had also pointed out though that even where individuals had made a free will choice with adverse consequences, God could still intervene to work things out for good for that person if they called upon Him for help, but that in order to enjoy God's total and continuing guidance and protection, it was advisable to surrender your life to Him.

Now the question of who was in control of his own life presented itself in Gus' mind. He had never thought about it before. Martin said that one had to surrender or commit their life to God for Him to take full control. But was it possible to commit to God subconsciously. Gus conceded that he had never consciously or expressly surrendered his life to God. However, he had always lived his life by godly principles hadn't he? Surely that was enough. *"I'm a good person,"* Gus reasoned to himself. *"I've always helped others less fortunate than myself". "I'm a good citizen - not a criminal – I don't do bad things". "I work hard and do no harm to others – not even animals,"* he thought. But according to Martin that was not enough.

Gus had to admit that he had always lived as though he was in charge of his own destiny - doing everything by his own efforts. So was the fact that his life had gone so well down to sheer luck? Many people would say that he was blessed and he certainly thanked God for all he had achieved - his success – his talents and everything else that was good in his life. Up until recently he had suffered no adverse consequences as a result of the free will choices that he had made. But what if that was now changing? What if the run of bad luck he had encountered recently continued? If he called on God, would He be willing to help him?

At this point Gus thought long and hard about people he had known who blamed God when things had not worked out for them. But in light of what Martin had told him those individuals had no right to do so because as far as Gus knew, not one of them had surrendered their lives to God's total control.

Martin had said that although things were not always perfect for him, yet he had joy in all circumstances – he had quoted yet another Bible verse to Gus "The joy of the Lord is my strength". He said that if you surrendered to God he would give true peace, happiness, contentment, direction, fulfilment and protection in your life. Gus thought about this long and hard. Was it because he had not surrendered his life to God that he worried so much? And was that why he sometimes experienced such emptiness in his life? For there was no doubt that he did experience many hours of purposelessness – a void that just would not be satisfied - not by what he possessed, ate, drank, or anything else he did – even during problem free times? Gus thought about how he sometimes experienced a hunger deep inside that often became unbearable - but a hunger for what? He could not tell - he only knew that he often experienced a profound feeling of incompleteness. Now he wondered whether it could be a hunger for God. And if he surrendered to God, would that recurring emptiness and void be satisfied? According to Martin's philosophy it should be.

Martin's explanation for the behaviour of his peers was that they did not know God and had not submitted their lives to Him. He seemed to think that belief and surrender to God was the elixir to cure all that was wrong in people and the world. Now although Gus questioned this simplistic viewpoint, he had to admit that it was a far better explanation than he had ever come up with in the hours that he spent wondering why Marcus' life turned out the way it had. Did Marcus need to surrender to God – would that save him? And if so, would he be deserving of God's grace - did any such delinquent, who had made a conscious choice to do bad things deserve forgiveness? Martin had stressed that God was all good and loved and wanted the very best for everyone – he would forgive the vilest of sinner. That regardless of how sinful that person was, if they called upon God, He would forgive them.

The young man had also said that when a life is surrendered to God, the spirit of that person becomes henceforth reborn. Martin explained - and Gus understood - that all were born as sinners because of the original sin of Adam and Eve, and remained sinful unless they repented and asked God to forgive them. That Jesus Christ was crucified – had to die on the cross – that his blood was shed as the supreme sacrifice for the sins of mankind. That when one surrenders to God and asks his forgiveness, God washes their spirits in the spirit blood of Jesus and their slates are wiped clean, and in place of their sinfulness God sees the righteousness of Jesus, who is sinless and blameless. Martin explained that that was what the term "born again" meant. He went on to elucidate that when one is born again, their spirits are reborn and they become more like God - a new creation spiritually speaking. He said that when one is said to be filled with the Holy Spirit, they have God's spirit living inside of them so that they automatically behave right and have a one-to-one relationship with God. He said that God could change the most heinous of thug into a saint. *"That's just what Marcus needs,"* Gus thought. *"But if what Martin had said was true, I myself am also a sinner and needs to be washed"*, Gus spoke his thoughts.

Martin had read another Bible verse: "For all have sinned and fallen short of the glory of God", which meant he (who had lived an almost exemplary life), was in the same boat and also a sinner like Marcus (who had chosen to live his life on the wild side), a thought that Gus found hard to accept.

Thoughts continued to churn over and over in Gus' mind as he recalled the conversation with Martin. He also thought about his conversation with Cherie and about the numerous times that his father had tried to discuss salvation with him. But nothing had had the profound effect on him as today's revelation from one young enough to be his own son.

As Gus drove the thought of how one could surrender to God perplexed him. It could not really be as simply as Martin had said, could it? Far more plausible was what most people thought, that

God was some untouchable, unreachable deity requiring one to undergo some form of ritualistic cleansing or other ceremony in order to obtain absolution?

Then Gus recalled something else that Martin had said - that he talked with God about his problems? Gus recalled that his mother used to say she was talking to God when she prayed. When Gus was younger he would attend church obediently just to please his mother - he was just going through the motions without thinking about what was taking place, even though he always believed that God existed. Gus cast his mind back to those times and recalled that the brethren used to say they were talking to God when they prayed, and he had always wondered whether that was in fact the truth. Then the words of the prayer that his mother taught him as a youngster – the Lord's Prayer - which he still said from time to time, more as a matter of tradition than anything else, without really thinking about what he was saying - came to mind and he spoke the words as he drove. And for the first time he consciously wondered whether God was actually listening to him as he recited the prayer. Was that why he always felt such peace each time he repeated it in the past?

Another curious thing that Martin had said was that God spoke through his words. He had given various scripture references to Gus for him to read for further guidance. Gus was aware that the Bible was supposedly the word of God because his mother used to tell him that. His father had also told him that on many occasions, and had actually bought him a Bible for his 16th birthday. When he had first received it, Gus tried to read it a few times, but not being able to understand it, he had given up trying, blaming the archaic language in which the Kings James Version was written. *"Thee and thou – no-one speaks like that nowadays!"* Gus verbalised his thoughts once again. Then he questioned how Martin, at 14 years old, could understand the Bible yet he couldn't. And Gus decided that he would take another look at the Bible - if Martin really did understand it then perhaps he would also – perhaps he needed to try a little harder. And the recollection that Martin had said that the Bible was available in different, more up to date version, provided Gus with more food for thought.

As soon as he got home Gus went into his bedroom. He knelt down and began to say the Lord's prayer again. This time he thought more deeply about what he was saying, analysing each phrase, seeking to understand the conversation he was having with God. He imagined that God was listening to him as he spoke. At the end of the prayer Gus felt a stronger than usual wave of peace waft over him. And a sense of enlightenment – a liberating feeling as he appreciated that he could now speak to God anytime he liked.

Next Gus had an overwhelming urge to read the Bible. However, he denied the urge, choosing instead to go into the kitchen and fix himself something to eat. As he busied himself cooking, he tried to shift the compulsion that now dominated his thoughts. *"I wouldn't even know where to find the Bible,"* it suddenly occurred to him. But as he continued to fix his meal, the desire to read the Bible gained strength. "Well, God, if you would like me to read the Bible, please lead me to where it is because I certainly wouldn't know where to find it now," Gus said to God, before wondering whether he was losing his mind.

After eating Gus washed up then returned to the lounge where he switched on the TV to watch the news – it was 10 pm and he wondered where the evening had gone. Suddenly he remembered that he had to check some documents which he stored in a fire proof cabinet. He ran upstairs and into the bedroom where the fire proof cabinet was situated. Having checked the documents he replaced them in the filing cabinet. As he did so, he noticed the red leather bound Bible at the back of the cabinet. Yet as often as he went into the cabinet over the past months, Gus had never noticed the Bible was there. Perhaps he had noticed it now because he was thinking about it. Or perhaps, God really wanted him to read it. He slowly picked up the Bible.

Reverently Gus opened the Bible and began to read one of the scriptures Martin had quoted earlier - Chapter 3 of St John's gospel. He read about Nicodemus and what Jesus had said about being "born again," a term which had always puzzled him. Now as he read with the benefit of his earlier conversation, Gus had a clearer understanding than ever before.

He read on and understood that the requirement to be born of the water meant to be baptized. At this point Gus recalled that he and his siblings had all been baptized when they were babies? But following his conversation with Martin he now realised that the baptism of the Bible was something different. So he needed to be baptized. And Gus read that he needed to be born of the Spirit, which must be what Martin was talking about earlier – being washed in the blood of Jesus – cleansed and have God's Spirit living within.

Gus continued reading the scriptures Martin had given him until he came across something that caught and held his full attention:

"For God so loved the world that he gave his only begotten Son, that whosoever believeth in him should not perish, but have everlasting life.

For God sent not his Son into the world to condemn the world; but that the world through him might be saved.

He that believeth on him is not condemned: but he that believeth not is condemned already, because he hath not believed in the name of the only begotten Son of God."

Gus pondered the words as memories of his mother came flooding back – she used to tell him about Jesus - the son of God. He also recalled that in Sunday School they talked about Jesus all the time. He recalled the beautiful story of the baby born at Christmas time – but there was more to Jesus' birth – Gus had been taught so but had never really digested that information, now he wracked his brain to remember, wanting to give it further thought.

Pondering the scripture and making a mental note to read it again later, Gus flicked through the pages. The next scripture Martin had given him provided food for further thought:

"That if thou shalt confess with thy mouth the Lord Jesus and shalt believe in thine heart that God hath raised him from the dead, thou shalt be saved.

For with the heart man believeth unto righteousness; and with the mouth confession is made unto salvation.

Gus closed the Bible. He paced back and forth for some time

thinking about the amazing coincidence that the second scripture seemed to follow on directly from the first. It occurred to him that perhaps God was talking to him through his young protégé. If so, God was trying to tell him that belief in Jesus alone was not enough – that there had to be a confession – that there should be a baptism. But how would one word such a confession? Gus wondered. Suddenly he yawned involuntarily – he was tired. He decided that he needed more guidance about the question of confession – but it would wait - now he just wanted to sleep, so he proceeded to run his bath and when he had finished having his bath, he climbed into bed.

Before falling asleep Gus thought about Cherie - he might give her a call tomorrow to find out how the tour was going. Then he fell asleep and dreamt about her – a beautiful dream in which he was very happy. But suddenly his dream changed into a nightmare - the recurring nightmare that had plagued him for weeks. A man dressed in a cloak, whose face he could not see, tried to kill him by stifling his breath. He could not breathe and his limbs became paralysed. He struggled to break free.

Finally Gus awoke in a cold sweat. He jumped up from the bed and gasped for air. For a while he felt as though he was being pursued and had to get away to safety. Then he realised he was still half asleep. He went into the bathroom where he splashed his face with cold water. Returning to the bedroom he picked up his 'phone and looked at the time – it was 3.10 am. He had only slept for 3 hours. Now, although he felt very tired and weak, as a result of the nightmare he had just had, he was disinclined to go back to sleep. So he went downstairs and switched on the TV.

After two hours, Gus fell into a fitful sleep on the sofa. He was awakened two hours later by the ringing of the telephone. Grabbing the 'phone and answering before becoming fully conscious, he spoke to the caller incoherently. "Yeah, hello….hello … yeah …. yeah ….. hello – yeah," Gus slurred his speech sleepily. "What do you mean burnt down …… where ……when ….. how?" Gus was still not fully awake as he reacted to the news he was receiving. It was the managing agent telling him that the police had informed them that one of the blocks he owned had been destroyed by fire last night. As Gus listened to what the caller had to say, the blood drained from his face, leaving him looking ashen under his dark hue. After a beat he found his voice again, "What are you saying, the whole block has blown up or burned down – what are you saying? There was an explosion – how - explain what you mean – I don't understand – how could the whole block have burned down – two people critically injured – who... how? I'm going down there right now," Gus said jumping up and going in search of his clothes. In a few minutes he was out of the door.

CHAPTER 9

Hard Road

His mind was preoccupied with the recent events and, unable to think of anything else, on Tuesday 30 May 2010 Gus returned to the block that had been destroyed by fire a week earlier. He walked around the building, but was not able to enter as it was still cordoned off by the police, who were treating it as a crime scene and continuing to investigate. Two people were seriously injured in the blast, and the whole building had been devastated by the ensuing flames. The Police suspected that the blast may have been deliberate, but had yet to confirm the presence of an accelerant or any combustible or flammable substance. They were trying to ascertain who might have a motive to burn down the building and whether there were any witnesses to the suspected crime.

In the alternative, the Police believed the blast may have been caused by a defective boiler, as a result of the negligence of the Landlord and Gus had spent hours at the station helping them with their investigation over the past week. He had also spent a fortune on lawyers' fees in in attempt to preserve his liberty.

Needing to clear his head, Gus left the scene and drove around and around, stopping at intervals - still trying to make sense of everything. He had been doing much the same thing for days and it dawned on him that he needed to talk to someone about the recent chain of misfortunes that he had encountered. His first thought was of Cherie, but he was immediately reminded that he hardly knew her, and that he should have called her by now. Gus was dying to talk to Cherie, but he couldn't bring himself to burden her with his problems - all he had to talk about at the moment were problems. He sat observing the tail end of rush hour traffic and people making their way home. His mind was in a whirl. He was thinking about so many things at once – he thought about the recurring nightmares, his stolen car and the blast. He also thought about the mass exodus of tenants leaving his properties and the failure to find new ones to take their places.

Taking a deep breath Gus tried to pull himself together – *worrying never did anyone any good whatsoever,* he recalled his mother used to say.

To add to his worries, Marcus had been in touch to request yet another loan which Gus could ill afford. But Marcus pulled the emotional strings attached to his heart when he told him what would happen if he wasn't able to raise the cash, "You might as well start to plan my funeral, bruv, because I will be a dead man". So Gus had sacrificed some of his mortgage payments to loan his brother £5,000, in addition to the other amounts he had loaned Marcus previously which he would no doubt never get back.

"Dear brother Marcus - my only brother – how could I just ignore your pleas – but I don't know whether I am in fact helping you by giving you money – I know that is not the solution, but what is? What can I possibly do that I have not already done or tried to do for you Marcus", Gus mused, before his thoughts returned to the blast.

On contacting his buildings insurance company today, Gus was informed that the insurance on the block had also lapsed due to non-payment of the premiums. And once again he was beating up himself for being so careless in forgetting to inform the insurance company of his new banking arrangements.

Desperation saw Gus pull over to call his father to find out what he was doing that evening – he needed a listening ear, a word of wisdom, anything. He hoped Cyrus was free – it was long overdue since he had last paid him a visit – maybe he would take him out for a meal or something. Of late Gus had been so taken up with his problems that he had been neglecting his relationship with his father.

Drumming fingers on the sofa, Gus waited for Cyrus to answer his call. This was the third time he had tried to call him. He was just about to hang up when his father's warm tones greeted his ears, "Hello".

"Hello, dad, how are you?" Gus replied warmly in spite of the depression that threatened to overcome him.

"How you doing son," came the affectionate response. Gus smiled as he listened to his father's familiar Caribbean lilt. After they had exchanged pleasantries he asked Cyrus if they could hang out for the evening. "What's wrong son – something wrong?" Cyrus' response did not please Gus.

"No, no, nothing's wrong," Gus said. "Nothing needs to be wrong for me to come and see you". "I hope you don't think that, dad" Gus said worrying that he may have neglected Cyrus far too much.

"It's not that son, but I had a dream last night that you wasn't very happy - that's all," Cyrus reassured.

"I'm okay," Gus lied.

They agreed to meet at a Caribbean restaurant close to Cyrus' home - Gus would pick him up at 8.00 pm. This would be the first time they went for a meal in over two years, Gus realised. He and Cyrus used to hang out together regularly, and now Gus found himself wondering why things had changed. Perhaps it was due to the fact that they were both satisfied with seeing each other at the stadium every Wednesday.

Cyrus did not appear to be his usual agile self as he practically hobbled towards the car. Gus became concerned about the older gentleman's health. It crossed his mind that he should perhaps volunteer his services to pick up and drop off the youngsters on Wednesdays as he could tell that Cyrus was having real difficulties with his movement. He did not know exactly what the problem was but his dad had been complaining about pains and stiffness in his right knee for many months, which problem appeared to be getting worse. He made a mental note to encourage him to have his knee looked at by a doctor.

As they socialised, Cyrus made him laugh and relax in his very own inimitable way. As usual he regaled Gus with varying stories, tales and information in his familiar and endearing Jamaican lilt. It wasn't that his father said anything that was particularly funny in itself - it was just the way in which he said things that amused Gus. Gus could remember when he was younger, Cyrus couldn't complete a single sentence without being asked to interpret some word or phrase to him, but these days it proved less necessary. Still, Cyrus would surprise him sometimes, with a new (or rather old) word or phrase that Gus had never heard before, and he would ask him to provide an interpretation. However, the fact that Gus now understood the words and expressions did not detract from the humour he derived from them.

During dinner Cyrus asked whether Gus had seen or heard from Marcus, and Gus told him that his brother had been in touch with him recently to borrow yet more money. Upon receiving this information Cyrus had shaken his head from side to side in a gesture of hopelessness and tutted - he had proceeded to speak about Marcus. "So weh im livin at de moment – eeeeh Gus?" he had asked Gus. Gus replied that he had no idea, whereupon Cyrus had continued, "Dat bwoy – I don't know how im cum so at all, at all at all". "Ow im cum so, Gus, eeeh. Eeeh Gus?" "De bwoy jus a wase im life aweh so – jus soh soh so". "Lard, I don't know and I can't tell how im cum so at all". "Umm, a no likkle pray me pray fe him inno Gus – a nah likkle talk me talk to him inno". "Im dear madda talk so till she dead before her time, and the bwoy just won't listen". "I jus don know and I can't tell what else gwaan change dat bwoy". "A mus-a only God alone gwaan change im". "Lard hab mercy". "When Alison was alive she use to ask me fe talk to Marcus – every week the same ting - talk to Marcus, talk to Marcus, and after so many years of talking to Marcus, I give up because a cud see it nah mek not a ounce a difference – just a wase me breat – talking to the bwoy". "Bwoy start fe laugh after me and kiss im teet and walk off." Gus had interjected, "really?" This interjection appeared to provide Cyrus with more impetus, and he continued with renewed gusto. "Yes man, bwoy use fe kiss im teet and walk off – nat a likkle manners him don't have". "After the good way how im madda grow im up – bwoy turn rotten, rotten to the core – spoil lakka spoil tomato". "Im pick up bad company and im carousen dem change im up – shame, shame pon im". Gus wanted to stop Cyrus to ask him the meaning of "carousen", but thought better of it and tried to work out the meaning himself. He figured it must refer to Marcus' live fast - die young, drug dealing criminal buddies. Gus thought quickly in order not to miss anything of what Cyrus was saying. "Nat even a likkle job de bwoy caan keep". "But I believe God will change him". "A goin to keep on praying fe im". "Yes – ah goin to keep go dung pon me knee dem a night time fe him," Cyrus said as he patted his knees.

He continued, "Gus, when you hear from Marcus again, tell 'im I want to see 'im, to talk to im. I don't know if 'im will see me or not, but tell im for me, yuh hear". "I gwine talk to im one more time," Cyrus said as he closed the chapter on Marcus.

As Gus listened to his father ranting on fervently about Marcus, he knew that Cyrus was so passionate when he spoke of Marcus because, like himself, he loved him - that it was breaking his heart. Gus too had felt heartbreak at seeing the state in which Marcus had found himself.

The fact that both Denise and Marcus had distanced them-selves from them in recent years, severing the close link they once enjoyed when Alison was alive saddened Gus and his father.

They went on to talk about the upcoming Youth Conference and discussed how Gus intended to address the youngsters. Cyrus was as encouraging as ever and after speaking to him, Gus felt a confidence in his ability that he never had before.

At various intervals during the evening, Gus' mind strayed to the problems he was facing - he had intended to share the burden with his father, but could not bring himself to broach the subject of the financial difficulties that he had because he did not want his dad to feel that he only wanted to be with him when he was in trouble.

"My faith means everything to me – because of it I do not harbour doubt or fear – I am not even afraid of dying because I have a hope that death is not the end" Cyrus announced out of the blue as Gus wondered (not for the first time) whether his father was telepathic. He wanted his dad to expand on his statement but said nothing. Cyrus, as though reading his mind some more, added that he trusted God even in the face of adversity because he believed the Bible to be the truth. He then quoted the same verse that Martin had quoted, *"All things work together for good for those that love the Lord"*, then his smile widened.

It baffled Gus how his father could always tell when he was worrying about something, even though he kept up an impene-trable front. He was amazed by the words of encouragement that Cyrus provided throughout the rest of the evening, seemingly sens-ing instinctively that Gus needed to hear them. Cyrus also spoke of his own past experiences and of the fact that he was grateful to God for what he had given him in life, that although he was not rich, he had everything he needed. Then he went on to count his blessings, mentioning his health, his sanity, his job, his home, his car, and his family, his church and loved ones.

Of course his father never missed a chance to bring up the question of his meeting the perfect woman whom he had previously mentioned to Gus, (having conveniently forgotten that he had promised to leave it for Gus to raise the matter in future). However, Gus did not become annoyed this evening. He simply breathed deeply knowing that his father only had his best interest at heart. And apparently given a free rein, Cyrus just would not let the subject drop.

As the evening drew to a close, Cyrus grasped the opportunity to invite Gus, to church yet again. He gave the usual speech about the beautiful choir and the warm fellowship. Smiling, Gus considered his father's invitation. He promised to let Cyrus know by Saturday whether he could make it on Sunday. He was intrigued and wanted to learn more especially since he had read the Bible the previous week, and recalling all that Martin had said, but he knew he wouldn't take his father up on his invitation as he yielded to the negative voice that told him he wasn't ready.

A little smile was on Gus' face as he drove home following dinner with his father. His mood had lifted significantly during the evening and he felt almost normal again. As he drove he thought about the pleasant evening they had enjoyed. On arrival at home the sense of freedom he had felt during the whole evening remained with him. Tonight Gus was reminded just how much he loved his father – he realised that seeing him at the stadium on Wednesdays or in passing on other days was no substitution for spending quality time together and made a mental note to spend more time with his dad in future.

But less than an hour after he entered his home reality threatened to gatecrash Gus' party as he was reminded of his problems. Soon the worries that had hovered on the boundary of his psyche, returned to occupy his mindspace. He tried to keep them at bay by thinking about his father's testimony of praise, which sort of worked. He encouraged himself to feel privileged that in spite of everything, he still had a choice of beautiful homes to come home to and his health, and the positive words that his father had spoken helped to lift Gus above impending gloom.

Getting up, to stave off the heaviness that threatened to descend upon him, Gus walked around the house and as he did so he thought of those who had no homes to go to – no food to eat – no clothes on their backs, and he appreciated just how fortunate he was. Meeting with his father always had a positive effect on him and, hearing about his unshakeable faith in God tonight, really made Gus wish he had what his father had - the peace, joy and contentment, the connection with God that caused Cyrus to repose total trust and confidence in that omnipotent, omnipresent and omniscient being, knowing that all things would work together for his good. Gus had seen this same contentment in Martin and in Cherie. He marvelled at their confident assurance and conviction, appreciating that the common denominator was that they were Christians. But although he wanted what they had - that special quality – Gus shrugged, he wasn't ready to do what they did to obtain it. And he made a concerted effort to stop thinking about spiritual things, at least for now.

Turning his attention to the TV Gus tried to watch the news. Images of Cherie's face flashed across the screen of his mind and he closed his eyes to visualise her more clearly. He longed to speak with her again and yearned to hear her beautiful voice. Suddenly overwhelmed by the intensity of his feelings for her (a lady whom he hardly even knew), Gus sat up stiffly as though in shock, realising that he had never before in his life felt this way - a longing, that made each second without her smile or hearing her voice, unbearable. So powerful was the moment that he wondered yet again why he had not called her, and how he could possibly have survived without doing so for so long.

Gus reached for his 'phone and began to scan his contacts for Cherie's number. He was just about to hit "dial" when his memory was swiftly transported back to his circumstances. Conversely, the next moment it occurred to him that he was overreacting to these problems – why was he allowing them to dominate all areas of his life? But a more commanding thought intruded, that he wanted Cherie to have him at his best, not at his worse.

Anyway, Gus suddenly recalled that she may be a little too religious for his taste and he was trying to avoid such complication in his life at the moment - he did not wish to get romantically involved with someone like that. *"But she is certainly beautiful, tantalisingly, deliciously beautiful ….. no doubt about that,"* Gus mused. Thoughts of Cherie's loveliness overwhelmed until Gus relented, *"religious or not, I'm going to call her".* However, as he picked up his 'phone a second time, he glanced at the time and saw that it was past midnight - too late to call her now. *"Well that settles it"*, Gus spoke his thoughts, *"I was not meant to call her tonight after all."*

As he drifted off to sleep, Gus promised himself that he would call Cherie first thing in the morning. He dreamt of her – tasted her sweetness and savoured it as he kissed her luscious lips, over and over gently then with intensity. He talked to her, and heard her voice – then suddenly she was gone and the faceless man stood in her place.

The terror was intensifying as the faceless man had mutated into a grotesque creature. Sweating profusely Gus struggled awake – he felt the most severe pains all over his body from the beatings received during the nightmare and he had a splitting headache. He breathed deeply and furiously in and out, as though trying to expel the symptoms from his body. Anger welled up inside of him and mingled with indignation that there appeared to be nothing he could do to stop the nightly attacks. He felt violated, helpless and weak. He was a man in need of help.

Reluctantly and in desperation Gus' thoughts turned to what Martin had told him about talking to God through Jesus Christ – surrendering his will. He wondered whether the recurring nightmare would cease if he surrendered to God. Next moment he dismissed what Martin, Cherie and Cyrus had told him as the negative voice spoke loudly that he was not the religious type.

As he seemed to nod off, Gus imagined he heard a gentle voice that said *"Come to me – for my yoke is easy and my burden is light"*. Next moment he was wide awake again and he wondered whether he had just heard the voice of God speaking in his spirit. But suddenly, like his mind was on a rollercoaster ride, Gus was bombarded with feelings of cynicism. "Jesus – where is he today". He began to ponder whether he actually believed the story of Jesus. Next moment he conceded that he did believe that Jesus had existed at some point in history. Jesus was a cute baby that was laid in a manger by his mother and father many, many years ago - Jesus was a nice story that was told to children at Christmas. But did he really believe that this cute baby, who grew to become a man, a carpenter, was actually the son of God who was born to die for the sins of mankind like Martin said. And if Jesus was supposed to be the saviour of the world, why were there so many things still wrong in the world? Was he ready to believe that the devil and not God was responsible for the wrongs in the world? Then the question if God was all powerful why not stop the devil occurred to him. Gus recalled that Martin had explained that many people suffered because they exercised their free will and allowed the devil a hand in their lives. Martin had also said that if people would turn back to God the world would become a better place. Martin had read a scripture about this: *"If my people ... would humble themselves and pray and seek my face, then will I hear from heaven and will forgive their sins and will heal their land"* which Martin had explained meant that God wanted to help and would help if the world turned back to Him. The main thing that Gus recalled of their conversation was that Martin had stressed that God was all good and all loving, that "there is no unrighteousness in God". Gus conceded that he was ready to believe in the goodness and righteousness of God. He was convinced because of the obvious intelligence of Martin and Cyrus – Gus had to admit that they were both far more astute that he could ever hope to be. And Cherie too had impressed him on their initial meeting as a rational individual. All these highly intellectual individuals had demonstrated such passion about Jesus and they could not all be wrong. He recalled that Martin had said that his experience with Jesus had made him become fervent for Him. "More food for thought", Gus spoke his mind. But was he ready to follow in their footsteps? Gus decided he needed more time.

CHAPTER 10

Sharing the Load

Cyrus invited Gus to church often and had done so yet gain. Gus had been tempted to take him up on the invitation as he was intrigued to learn more about God, mainly because he wondered whether God could help him through the problems he was encountering, but at the last minute he put off going, telling himself "maybe I'll go next week". "I really need to catch up on all the things I could not do in the past week", Gus mumbled as he locked his front door behind him and set off to jog to the nearby park.

After an hour he returned home and made a sumptuous breakfast, which defeated the whole object of the earlier jog. After breakfast he drove to the nearby petrol station to wash his rental car. By 10.30 am he was back home with a stack of newspapers. He waited 15 minutes until 10.45 am before dialling Cyrus' number, allowing the 'phone to ring and ring, knowing full well that his father would not be there to answer it at that time as he would already have left for church. The answering machine clicked on and Gus left a message, apologising that he was unable to make it to church today – he said nothing more – no mention of making another service on another day or anything, not wishing to encourage Cyrus whom he knew would seek to make him come good on even a whiff of a promise. *"I will go to church, but I will go when I am ready"*, Gus spoke his thoughts as he headed upstairs to the bathroom.

Having taken a long shower, Gus returned to the lounge where he set about catching up on the latest news. But he found it impossible to relax as the feeling of unease fell heavily over the room. He moved upstairs to the bedroom but found it was no better there. The thought that he would soon have to get ready to go and meet with Martin and Donna later that afternoon brought some relief – but there was still a couple of hours to kill. Next it occurred to him that he could very well have gone to church with his father but

Gus quickly dismissed that idea. His mind was then directed to think about Cherie. It has been nearly 3 months since he promised to call her. He still intended to do so when he had sorted himself out.

As time passed the temptation to call Cherie was becoming almost unbearable but Gus continued to resist. "I will not burden her with my problems", he spoke his thought. Recalling how easy it was to talk to her, he knew that if he called he would involuntarily blurt out his worries. "Anyway I still don't know if I would wish to get involved with someone who is so religious", Gus continued to speak his thoughts. He told himself that Cherie was obviously a devout Christian, in which case they would have little in common and he didn't want to hurt her, or to get hurt himself. However, a moment later he conceded that none of those excuses could assuage the longing for her or detract from the strong magnetic pull he felt towards her. He further conceded that she may be just the friend he needed. "If only it was as simple as deciding whether we should be platonic friends or not", Gus spoke his thoughts, as he conceded that it would be impossible to be just friends with Cherie as his true feelings demanded that they be more than just buddies.

The Sunday afternoon training sessions with Martin and Donna was now a regular fixture, and today, 9 July 2010, the youngsters once again demonstrated to Gus just how worthwhile his efforts with them was proving to be. This was the seventh week in a row that they had met on a Sunday afternoon and they also met up on a weekday evening twice a month - just the three of them, as well as with the full group sessions on Wednesdays. Gus couldn't have been more proud of the development of his protégés. So confident was he in their abilities now that he was planning to enter them both for the up and coming junior athletics championships.

After the session, he dropped Martin off first, even though it would have been more practical the other way around. He always dropped Martin first since their long meaningful discussion weeks earlier – Gus wished to avoid a repetition of the tête-à-tête. Their talk had left him with too many unanswered questions which he had tried to address, and had gone some way towards doing so, but the religion thing was way too deep – too complicated - and he did not have the time or inclination to pursue it at the present time – but he would certainly want to look into it again with a clear mind when this season of bad luck and problems had passed over.

After Martin bared his soul to Gus, Gus was not unconcerned about the young man's predicament – he wracked his brain but just did not find any real solution. So the fact that he had arranged the Sunday afternoon training sessions in addition to the mid week sessions was Gus' own efforts toward trying to keep the teenager doing something positive, leaving him less time to encounter trouble. He was also giving thought to Martin's future and had ambitious plans to sponsor the young man's education – hopefully moving him and his family away to a safer neighbourhood too – just as soon as he could sort himself out.

Returning home from the day's session Gus entered his bathroom where he took a quick shower, and as the warm water washed over him, he contemplated the direction of his life. He continued to suffer nightly attacks – nightmares - which meant that he was not getting enough sleep. He tried sleeping during the day but it made no difference - he still suffered the attacks. Ever observant, his father had conveyed concern for Gus' health, noting his rapid weight loss and gaunt appearance.

Emerging from the shower Gus caught sight of himself in the full length mirror. For a brief second he did not recognise himself, the lack of sleep was beginning to tell on his features. Stepping closer to the mirror he inspected his face, concerned at the unhealthy ashen appearance of his dark skin. He noted that the worry lines on his forehead were becoming more defined and that the laughter lines that had graced his eyes had given way to huge dark circles. It occurred to him that he needed to see his doctor, something he had been putting off doing for some time. It also occurred to him that he may need to see a psychiatrist or hypnotherapist, or seek some other medical or self-help therapy to try and deal with the nightmares. So far he had put off taking any such steps, hoping that they would have ceased as suddenly as they had begun. It was now almost three months since he experienced the first of the nightmares, and they had now intensified. Lately every morning he awoke feeling as though he had actually been in fisticuffs.

The nightmares seemed to Gus to have been a harbinger for his unprecedented bad luck in business as well as in his personal life and his fortune had deteriorated to the extent where he was looking bankruptcy square on in the face. All this was weighing heavily on his mind and affecting his mental state. For in the past month he had become extremely forgetful and now heard ugly voices that taunted and derided him. But conversely, often when he was just drifting to sleep or just waking up Gus thought he heard a sweet voice in his spirit, calling him. He had heard it again today, saying, *"Come unto me you that are burdened and I will give you rest",* and Gus wondered whether it was the voice of Jesus.

Consciously Gus nurtured hope in his heart for a better tomorrow. But such hope was failing to bear fruit and by 27 July 2010, the eve of Raj's stag do his circumstances had gotten worse. The stag do was on 28 July, which Gus attended, and put on a show that convinced his friends that all was well with him, wishing only for Raj to have a happy and memorable time. However, in spite of the fact that he was the life and soul, all his friends still commented on his weightloss.

When Gus attended the wedding the next day, 29 July 2010, he was also the life and soul of the whole event, making a concerted effort to disguise his sadness. Having dressed to impress for the affair, Gus had taken taxis to and from the venue, not wishing his friends to see that he had been reduced to driving an old dilapidated car. And he sacrificed what little money he had to buy food for a whole month to buy the couple a worthy gift.

So he was only too happy to accept an invitation to dinner on 6 August 2010 from his friend Marshie, who had recently moved into his new flat with his girlfriend. He and Marshie had not met up for nearly 4 months because Marshie was busy with his new love interest, Emma. But they still spoke regularly on the 'phone. They shared a close friendship based on total trust, and although Gus had not told Marshie about his recent problems, he wanted to do so today – he needed to talk to someone or he felt he might go insane.

On arrival Gus pressed the buzzer and was let into the gated community where Marshie and Emma lived. He parked his car in the small visitors' parking area and climbed the stairs to the second floor to find Marshie was waiting for him by the door. "In ere mate," Gus smiled as Marshie's loud cockney voice took him by surprise. Marshie waited for him, holding the door open in a welcoming gesture. "Ow are you mate?" Marshie asked, grabbing him in a manly embrace.

"Yeah, yeah, not too bad man," Gus responded smiling back at his friend. Marshie was wearing a sleeveless sweatshirt and jogging bottoms. He was barefooted – a picture of relaxation. His shocking bright blond hair was worn short and spiky – stylishly rumpled. At 6' 2" in his bare feet Marshie was very well built with the handsome chiselled features of a photographic model. He liked to show off his muscular body which he worked very hard to maintain. Unlike Gus he had not gone on to play for any other club after leaving Walmouth Town but had gone back to studying, later graduating and starting his own computer support business.

Marshie showed Gus into the small living room, which was tastefully decorated in an ultra modern, minimalist style and Gus felt immediately at home. "Emma" Marshie called out to his girlfriend, who came running in from the balcony.

"Oh hiya," she said before being introduced.

"This is my good, good friend, Gussy - Gussy, this is Emma, the love of my life," Marshie said as Emma smiled prettily. Gus liked her immediately, warming to her genuinely friendly and hospitable nature. He was not surprised by the fact that she was a dark black beauty as Marshie had dated all races - never one to discriminate in his women, or friends. Marshie was a "personality" man, who had the rare quality of being able to see past a person's appearance to their inner selves, and Emma was typically his friend's kind of woman, tall, slender and beautiful – warm friendly and engaging.

Emma made Gus feel right at home as she offered him something to drink, which he gratefully accepted as it was a warm evening. After Emma had settled the men, she excused herself and returned to the balcony where she had been sitting for most of the afternoon sunning herself - as if she needed it. This gave the two men a chance to catch up. Marshie talked mainly about Emma, whom he had met only 7 months earlier. They had moved in together after three months, which Gus calculated, was about the time he last saw Marshie, who had stopped calling him on an almost daily basis round about then.

Having apparently exhausted details of his love life, Marshie began to push Gus to divulge details of his own. Gus, his back against the wall, concocted a relationship - with Cherie. He dishonestly stretched the details of their meeting and pretended that he and Cherie were now an item – but in the early stages of a relationship. Marshie bought the tale "hook line and sinker", and that suited Gus just fine - anything to keep Marshie quiet, or he might take it upon himself to try and match Gus up with someone – usually one of his girlfriends' mates.

Gus marvelled at how easy he found it to talk about Cherie, filling in the grey areas with details of his fantasy ideal woman/ relationship. He had to fob Marshie off though, when he expressed an interest in their forming a foursome and going out together the following week. He told Marshie that Cherie would be away on a tour – *"at least this part is true,"* he thought. However, it suddenly occurred to him that he was not aware whether the tour had now ended. He found himself wondering what Cherie might truly be up to at the present time. As he spoke about her he began to feel guilty – then foolish - for never having called her as he promised to do. *"And now it was too late to call her"*, he mused. *"I wouldn't know what to say to her"*, he thought. *"In any case, nothing has changed, I'm still plagued with personal problems – I have nothing to offer her at the moment, not even good conversation - I know I would end up talking about my problems – she was so easy to talk to, so easy to confide in"*, Gus' mind ran away with him.

"You alright mate?" Marshie asked looking perplexed. Gus had fallen silent in mid-sentence as he spoke about his girlfriend. "Stop daydreaming – it must be love", he continued chuckling.

"Sorry, I was just thinking", Gus said, feeling slightly embarrassed.

"Don't apologise, mate, I know how it is – I was the same

when I first met Emma – love gets you like that", Marshie said reassuringly.

Dinner was simple but healthy and satisfying – Gus ate gratefully as it was the first well-balanced meal he had eaten in a week, since that consumed at Raj's lavish wedding.

After dinner the friends talked for a further hour before Gus rose to leave. He intimated to Marshie that he needed to talk to him about something and they arranged to meet up at the Platinum Place in Camden for a drink the next Friday evening.

By Friday night 11 August 2010, Gus was gasping for someone to talk to. The Platinum Rooms was Marshie's favourite place in Camden. He and now also his girlfriend, were regulars there, where they liked to sit out in the small beer garden on the roof terrace. But Emma was not with Marshie this evening - it was strictly a boy's night out.

When Gus arrived a little late, Marshie was already there and greeted him positively beaming. The two men bear hugged as those around them stared on, some inquisitively, others enviously. It was obvious that theirs was a solid friendship - one that most people wished for in their lifetimes but never found. They bought drinks at the bar and retired to a corner of the terrace garden where they sat chatting easily.

For the next hour and a half they chatted, Marshie about Emma and his new found happiness and love, and Gus lied some more about Cherie and updated Marshie on what Benza and Raj were doing with themselves.

Lying did not come easily to Gus but Marshie kept on pressing him for more information about Cherie, leaving him with no choice. Then he slipped up when he said that he was meeting Cherie the next day.

"But I thought she was away on a tour," Marshie observed.

"Yeah, yeah well, the show is going to be in Bracknell and I'm driving up there to see her," Gus lied.

"What time is the show, I'm sure Emma would love to come along – I know I would love to see a live show and Bracknell is only up the road, innit?" Marshie said enthusiastically.

"I don't know, I don't think it would be the right time to meet her – she will be working and she won't like it". "I know she would prefer to meet you both when she isn't working - so let us plan another time," Gus said leaving no room for negotiation. "Yeah, okay," Marshie said uncertainly, failing to find logic in Gus' argument but deciding that he wouldn't press any further.

Then Marshie raised the question that Gus did not seem to be his usual happy self. This was the cue that Gus was waiting for and he gushed to admit to Marshie that he was experiencing serious problems which were apparently beyond his control. He poured his heart out to his friend - like a caged animal that had just been released from captivity. He so needed someone to talk to – just someone to listen, if nothing else. And Marshie was a good listener. Gus told him everything, from the beginning of his troubles to the latest in a line of catastrophes, which was that he had been advised today that his days at the stadium were to be cut from two days down to one, thereby halving his salary. He had also been informed over the past two weeks that five more of his tenants were not renewing their tenancy agreements, and new tenants had not been found to replace the vacating ones. And most of the other properties that he owned had become untenanted over the past two months.

At first Gus had blamed the managing agents for not finding tenants, and placed his own adverts in the property section of several local newspapers, and on a popular letting website, but those initiatives had proved fruitless. Things were not looking good. It was as though he was rapidly losing everything.

Marshie listened to his friend's woes sympathetically. This was the first time that he had been on the listening end while Gus told him his troubles, for it was usually the reverse – he often bended Gus' ear with his problems. Marshie recalled when he came very close to giving up on life altogether, after his ex-wife Margo had cheated on him and left him for another man. How he had talked to Gus - leant on him – depended on him for counsel and advice. Marshie would talk and Gus always listened and consoled him - telling him to look ahead, that the future would be brighter, that he had his whole life ahead of him. It was Gus that checked on him every day, and even when his own family had given up on him, Gus did not. Marshie recalled how Gus had put him up when Margo "took him to the cleaners" when they divorced and he had lost his house and had no money to pay rent. And it was Gus who had helped him back onto his feet.

Unbeknown to Gus he had saved Marshie from committing suicide in those dark days, when hopelessness had almost driven him to the edge - to end his life. Now Marshie listened with empathy and was touched by his friend's own suffering. He wished he could help Gus the way he had helped him, although all Gus asked of him was to listen. He would certainly do that, but if only he could do more. Marshie felt so helpless – his business was struggling, and he and Emma were just managing to make ends meet. The only advice he could give was for Gus (whom he affectionately called Gussy on occasions) to get a loan to tide himself over. "Why don't you get a loan, Gussy?" "I know it's not ideal, but it will help you through this difficult patch," Marshie advised wisely. Gus smiled and nodded and Marshie smiled back satisfied he had at least been of some help. He went on to encourage that things would get better – the bad times would not last forever.

However, Gus had already gotten two loans to help him keep up the mortgages on the untenanted properties and had exhausted the funds borrowed with no means of making any of the repayments.

They parted company at 10.00 pm and Marshie promised to be in touch the next day to see that Gus was okay. On the drive home Gus felt a lot better than he had before meeting up with Marshie – as the old adage goes "a problem shared is a problem halved". Gus was happy to know that he had a friend who would just listen and try to bear the burden with him. He knew he was truly privileged and was aware that Benza and Raj would also give him their ear to just listen if he chose to off-load some of the burden upon them. Gus knew he was lucky to have such people in his corner. However he had chosen to talk to Marshie alone about his problems because he knew Marshie had been through a similar trauma some years before and could empathize with him. Because he had helped Marshie through his own midnight hour, a special bond of confidence existed between them.

Cyrus too was always ready to listen and could provide wise advice, but Gus had ruled out talking to his father about his problems, not wishing to cause him anxiety. He was aware that his father worried far too much about his well being – he had to be a man and face his problems.

As Gus was at his front door he heard his landline and hurriedly opened his front door. The lock appeared loose and he made a mental to inspect it after he had answered the call. Marshie was on the line, ringing to check that he was okay. Immediately after he hung up Cyrus also rang to see that he was okay. They spoke for a few minutes about the training sessions, and Cyrus' impending departure on a one-week holiday to New York the following Thursday. During the conversation Cyrus invited Gus to accompany him to church on Sunday. "Son, I am inviting you to church on Sunday". "There will be a special speaker present and you will enjoy it, son", Cyrus solicited.

"I'll get back to you about that tomorrow if that is okay", Gus' responded.

After ending his conversation with Cyrus, Benza rang "just to say hi". They went on to talk about Cynthia, who was due to give birth in a week and Benza promised to inform Gus as soon as the baby came.

Lastly, Raj rang to thank him for his gift – he encouraged Gus to look after his health. He was off on a delayed honeymoon the next day and promised to invite Gus and Benza around for dinner when he returned from Kenya in September.

Later Gus examined the lock and found that it had been tampered with. However, at first glance it appeared that nothing was missing.

That night Gus fell asleep easily, comforted by the thought that he was surrounded by loving friends and family who cared for and truly loved him. He felt blessed in spite of his circumstances.

In the nightmare, Gus watched himself sleep. He was awake watching himself sleep. He could see the man with the red menacing eyes standing over him as he slept, and begin to hit him with a weapon, although Gus could not make out what the weapon was. Then the man turned into a beast with horns and the beast spoke to Gus. "I AM GOING TO DESTROY, DESTROY YOU. DESTROY, DESTROY YOU – YOU WILL LOSE EVERYTHING," the beast said as he struck him repeatedly - announcing its intent - total destruction. In his mind Gus tried to fight back, clawing, kicking screaming but the mental signals did not transmit to his arms, legs or mouth – he was frozen. He tried to speak to tell the man/beast that he would fight him back - that he could not destroy him, but he could not speak. Gus could feel the life being pressed out of him as he struggled to breathe, to fight back, to breathe, to fight back. Then suddenly he awoke gasping for breath, coughing and spluttering. He breathed deeply to regain composure. Then he began to feel sick. Tears spilt from his eyes – tears of pain and indignation - he had to do something to stop this terror, this infringement of his liberty. What was this all about? Why was this happening to him?

Realising he had left his mobile in the livingroom Gus reached into his bedside cabinet for his watch to check for the time but found that it was missing. His watch was incredible valuable and Gus felt an emotional blow in the pit of his stomach. He proceeded to search for his other valuable items and found that several were also missing. Then realisation dawned on him – he had been burgled.

CHAPTER 11

Battery Recharge

The sun streamed through a chink in the curtain as Cherie yawned and stretched and made her pronouncement – *"Today is the first day of the rest of your life Cherie Johnson – and you must get some rest today"*, Cherie said, feeling exhausted. Nestling between the sheets, she felt safe as she breathed in deeply the fragrance of the freshly laundered bed clothes. A wave of happiness and belonging spread through her being as she savoured the fact that she was in her own bed after two nights spent in a hotel room.

They had returned from Oxford at 3.45 am, after the one and only Sunday night show which had been put on by popular demand. Not one to miss church on a Sunday, Cherie had attended a local church in Oxford that morning, which she had enjoyed immensely. But as though speaking directly to her the sermon had been entitled "Remember to keep the Sabbath Holy". Now, as she stretched her limbs, Cherie was engulfed by an acute awareness that she had violated God's law. She had not appreciated that she would be so affected by her decision to do a Sunday night show and made a conscious decision never to do so again.

Getting out of bed and falling to her knees, Cherie begged for God's clemency, promising that she would never do another Sunday night show, and felt a weight lift from her spirit. Arising from prayer, she reached for her 'phone and saw that it was only 7.45 am. "Ooh", she mumbled, annoyed to have awoken after less than three hours sleep. She certainly had no intention of getting up early or at all today. For today she was taking the day off. If she didn't get some quality rest, her health might start to deteriorate and she would be no good to anyone if she became ill. Due to the punishing schedule of the tour, she was becoming drained and run down – it was necessary for her to recoup some energy as she was nearing burn out. And even though she had a whole lot of work to catch up with, Cherie knew that it was the only sensible thing to do.

"There will never be a nervous breakdown with my name on it", Cherie said, making an uncharacteristic second declaration for the day. It then occurred to her that what she had just said did not really make any sense.

"How could a nervous breakdown have my name on it?" Cherie muttered, feeling stupid. She cast her eyes towards heaven and decided she needed to sleep as she was clearly losing her marbles.

So sleep she did, and deeply, for the next 4 hours, awaking at lunchtime, feeling more tired than ever. She had not appreciated that going on tour could be so taxing on one's body, both mentally as well as physically.

The unwelcome thought of the mountain of paperwork that was generated by the tour – which had been neglected because of the tour, which awaited her attention at the office, presented itself at the forefront of Cherie's mind.

"The paperwork will just have to wait – my health comes first," Cherie mumbled, shooing the thought to the back of her psyche. She looked at her 'phone and saw that Naomi had tried to contact her several times and a feeling of guilt niggled at the fringes of her conscience. She did not like to leave Naomi to cope alone, but it then occurred to her that Naomi was well capable of managing at least one day without her. So Cherie punched out a brief text to Naomi, advising that she would not be at work and did not wish to be disturbed unless there was some urgency. Then she tried to go back to sleep.

After an hour Cherie was still tossing and turning, unable to fall back to sleep – her mind was churning - she was thinking about one thing or the other. The sleep that she so desperately needed would not come - but the thoughts kept coming. "Well if I must think, I will think about something nice – not anything to do with work", Cherie said. So she thought about her mother and made a mental note to give her a call later as she had not seen her or Lester in over two weeks. Although they spoke every day, it was not the same as spending time together and Cherie was missing them terribly. She smiled to herself as she saw her mother's beautiful face in her mind's eye – so vivid – *she must also be thinking about me,* Cherie thought, recalling the old Jamaican adage that when someone's face was so vividly imprinted on one's mind, the other person was thinking of them. Cherie wondered what Jean might be thinking. She tried to guess, and surmised that she would be wishing to see her so they could chat, or go shopping, or just potter around the garden – Jean doing all the pottering and Cherie the watching, as they were accustomed to doing.

The thoughts of Jean and Lester subsided, and Cherie found she was unable to suppress thoughts about the ongoing success of the tour, so she relented, allowing her mind a free reign. Last night had been a runaway success – the best yet, she mused. The on-going success of the tour still continued to amaze her and the rest of the crew. Every night so far tickets were sold out and the venues were filled to capacity – sometimes way beyond capacity. And they had been pressed by demand to book a further two dates at the end of the tour – one in Birmingham and the other in Manchester. But it was the CD and DVD sales that were the most surprising. For as soon as they collected the stock, they sold out. Even the small supply of records (catering for old fashioned DJs) had sold out. Cherie was not aware that so many people still bought records - one or two DJs maybe - but up to 10 records at each gig had come as a complete surprise? A live DVD/video that had been recorded at the last night of the Birmingham shows was selling very well too. It was George's idea to do the recording and to provide a few records for sale along with the CDs and both hunches had proved to be spot on.

Along with the main artistes, Sera Ocel and Ebony Son, the Kingdom Praise album was holding its own, almost eclipsing the stars' sales figures. And most surprisingly, the crowds continued to appreciate the support artistes' performances as much as Sera Ocel's and Ebony Son's. And even the CDs of the other Smooth Management artistes who were not appearing at the shows were selling well.

Cherie tried to limit her thoughts to the success of the tour but found that she was unable to do so - she began to think about business. She made a mental note to contact the distributors and order an extra 300 copies of each album for the coming weekend's shows in Cardiff. Then she gave some thought to putting in place a system whereby orders could be placed online. She then recalled that the Smooth Management website was not fully developed as yet, and needed more work to become fully functional - she would need to attend to that as a priority. Many people had telephoned the office to purchase, CDs etc., and this arrangement was not working, because poor Naomi already had her hands full with other work and couldn't spare the time to deal with orders. They had so much work that Naomi now worked most days and Cherie was considering taking on a second person to assist her and Naomi generally, and to work as an order clerk. Interviews were set up for Wednesday and she needed to give some contemplation as to whether she would take the successful applicant on a casual basis and see whether things worked out, or as a permanent employee. She made a mental note to discuss the issue with George, her wise counsellor.

Quite a few expressions of interest had been received from Europe and even Japan over the past two months and Cherie was thinking of exploiting those markets more fully - perhaps she would arrange a few short tours in those regions when the national tour ended on 26 August. She would need to develop contacts in those provinces as soon as she was able to do so. If the foreign gigs proved to be half as successful as the domestic ones, Cherie knew that she might have to re-structure her business completely as significant expansion would be inevitable. But she was wary of expanding too fast.

One thing was certain, at the end of this tour, Cherie would need to take at least a 2-week holiday – get away from it all and catch some sun on a beach somewhere, because all work and no play was making her a very, very tired and irritable girl indeed.

As her mind continued to buzz with a whirlwind of thoughts and ideas, Cherie accepted she was not likely to get any more sleep today. So she jumped out of bed and headed downstairs the kitchen, to make a hot drink.

The strong cup of coffee had the effect of perking up her senses, giving Cherie a feeling of exhilaration. It reminded her of the way she felt at her last meeting with Gus Allen, and suddenly she found herself bombarded with thoughts of him. She tried to dismiss them, but failed. *"I'm blessed not stressed"* Cherie announced out of the blue, breaking protocol for the second time today. This was partly due to the fact that she was unaccustomed to sleeping until the afternoon and mostly to the fact that she was endeavouring to exorcise thoughts of Gus Allen, but to no avail.

She climbed the stairs vigorously and headed to the bathroom where she splashed cold water over her face. Then she dried her face, while staring at her reflection in the mirror, searching for tell tale signs of lack of sleep. Such evidence presented itself without reasonable doubt in the dark circles beneath her eyes. She brushed her teeth, and headed into the second bedroom where she ran through her usual exercise routine – something she had been neglecting to do since the beginning of the tour.

Following a vigorous 15-minute workout, Cherie knelt by her bed and began to hum as her spirit worshipped. "We bless you Lord Jesus for the great things you have done", Cherie sang as she meditated on the words of the song. "The great things that you have done – we bless you Lord for all that you have done". As she praised and worshipped God for sparing her life to see Monday 14 August, Cherie felt as though she was joined by a host of angels glorifying God. Picking up her Bible she found Proverbs, one of her favourite books and, her eyes resting on Chapter 3 verse 5 - she read out loud, "Trust in the Lord with all your heart and rely not on your own understanding", she paused to digest the words into her spirit before reading on verse 6, "In all your ways acknowledge Him and He shall direct your path". Cherie repeated the words over and over as they sunk into her spirit. Then she sang again, a song of praise, thanking God for his love. "Thank you Lord, I want to thank you Lord for being so good," Cherie sang from her heart, receiving confirmation in her spirit that her worship and praise was pleasing to God. She spoke with Him again for a few more minutes and felt more peaceful than she had in a long time. Then Cherie heard God speak within her spirit, "Gospel". Cherie pondered the Lord's guidance – he had spoken to her before and she knew what he meant – she needed to change her musical direction.

Having mentioned to George that she was thinking of dropping Sera Ocel and Ebony Son, he had expressed shock surprise, stating that Jute Records would be only too happy to snap them up. George had been more helpful than he knew because, knowing that there was a company that would take on Sera Ocel and Ebony Son, left Cherie with a clear conscience. She now contemplated approaching Jute Records herself with a view to striking a deal with them that would leave her free to pursue God's new direction. She would speak to Sera, Ebony, Daton and Maxi as soon as the tour ended, and would waste no time in searching for new Gospel talent to nurture. Cherie would, of course, keep Kingdom Praise for as long as they wished to remain with her, and Daton Reese, may wish to remain with Smooth Management and follow the new direction that Cherie was inclined to take, since he was a professing Christian.

Bubble baths always provided her with the ultimate relaxation and as she luxuriated in the most wonderfully pampering bath, Cherie, abandoned all muscular control of her body, allowing her limbs to lull unrestrained. After half an hour or so she began to feel sleepy again and as the bath was getting cool decided she would return to bed. She dried herself quickly and put on a fresh pair of silk pyjamas, savouring the feel of the fabric against her skin, sprayed herself with her favourite perfume, and breathed in deeply savouring the bouquet.

Awaking refreshed after a further 2 hours' sleep Cherie sat up in bed and dialled Jean's number. "Hi mum", she said fondly.

"Hi sweetie", Jean replied in sugary tones. "I've been thinking about you all day", she continued.

"Really", Cherie replied, continuing, "You know there might be some truth in that Jamaican saying after all, because I saw your face in my mind's eye vividly today", Cherie said easily.

"Really – you know I was just about to call you myself – fancy meeting up", Jean said, taking the words out of Cherie's mouth.

They arranged to meet at 4pm. It was a lovely warm sunny afternoon and they agreed that Cherie would pick Jean up and they would go to a favoured outdoor park café, just a stone's throw from her parents' home.

Jean looked radiant in a casual white linen trouser suit. She had accessorised well, with chunky silver jewellery, and she wore light make-up to complete her trendy look. Cherie complimented her mother, a feeling of pride rising within her heart. "Oh mum, you look so beautiful," she said hugging her tightly, and kissing her softly on her cheek. She marvelled at the softness of her mother's skin, which had always been her most beautiful feature.

Returning her daughter's warm hug, Jean felt like never letting go. She thought of how much she truly loved her daughter and of how proud she had made her. Every time she looked at her baby, Jean marvelled at what an amazingly beautiful woman she had matured into – one so incredibly wise and exquisite.

Cherie drove the short distance to the aptly named, Park Café, and parked in its expansive grounds. They alighted from the car, hugged once more, then they broke apart and stood back to admire each other, smiling, both their countenances radiating with reciprocal love and pride.

As they walked towards the Park Café, Jean glanced sideways at Cherie, contemplating her daughter's resemblance to her father. She was always amazed at the incredible likeness, although she had never told Cherie so – she had the same high cheekbones, cinnamon complexion and beautiful eyes that glistened when she smiled – just like his. In recent years, mostly thanks to Lester, Jean has gotten over her bitterness towards Tyrone and could now admit to herself that her daughter looked like him. And she has been meaning to talk to Cherie about her father, to give her what limited information she had about him. She was sorry for her behaviour towards Cherie in the past when her daughter had naturally expressed curiosity to know more about her father and now accepted that her behaviour was totally unacceptable. Jean was beating herself up mentally for having forbidden her daughter from asking about her own father. And she felt ashamed that because of her intransigence she may have denied her daughter the chance of possibly tracking down her father or maybe of ever developing a relationship with him. Lester was to be credited for causing her to realise that Cherie had a right to know her father. Jean was now ready to admit her gross error to her daughter – she was just waiting for the right time.

"How's Lester doing?" Cherie asked affectionately.

"Aw he's keeping very well – working hard," Jean replied, smiling – an obviously happy and fulfilled woman.

The two women sat over pre-dinner drinks whilst taking in the beauty of the park which was overlooked by the café. A warm breeze caressed them as they conversed, causing Cherie to comment "What a beautiful afternoon". And in truth the haze of the low sun, the swaying of the trees in the light wind and the perfect warmth of the advancing early evening made for a dreamlike ambience that one would wish to preserve in the memory for a lifetime.

Cherie seized the moment and began to take snapshots with her mobile 'phone, firstly of the surrounding nature - concentrated mostly on the nearby pond and its wildlife. Then she began to take snaps of her mother. Jean then fished inside her handbag and came up with her own camera and proceeded to emulate her daughter. Then they both viewed the photos, while giggling like naughty teenage schoolgirls. A gentleman sitting at the next table offered to snap them together and they thanked him furiously before striking various model poses, which rendered superbly artistic results, and elicited further glee.

Later Cherie provided Jean with an update on the tour, excitedly informing her of the success that they were encountering and going on to invite her mother to attend one of the London shows in two weeks' time.

"Yeah mum, you and Lester will have to come to the final show in Hackney – a lot of my friends that you know will be there, as well as Tia and Annette" Cherie enthused. "We'd love to come," Jean replied excitedly, accepting the invitation, but insisting that they be allowed to pay for their own tickets in order to support Cherie.

"I wouldn't hear of it", Cherie almost shouted indignantly.

"Oh, alright then", Jean said, knowing better than to argue, recalling that Cherie's stubbornness was another trait inherited from her father.

Jean was just about to seize the opportunity and say *"Honestly you remind me so much of your father sometimes,"* when Cherie started to tell her about a young man that she had met. Blushing through her tanned hue, the young woman relayed to her mother the way in which they had met and everything she had learned about Gus Allen. Jean listened intently – glad to hear that her daughter had met someone special.

"But mum, I'm just wondering why he hasn't 'phoned me – it's been nearly four months now," Cherie confided.

"Nearly four months, gosh that's a long time - I thought you only just met him," Jean replied surprised.

"No, but when we met – it was so special, mum". "I know he felt the same way about me". "He said he would 'phone and I still believe that he will," Cherie said, for the first time realising that she must sound a little pathetic.

"Well, perhaps he will – he may be busy love dear, or perhaps he's got loose ends to tie up," Jean said wisely. "Sometimes when you first meet someone they hold back getting too deeply involved because perhaps they may have loose ends to tie up before committing to a new relationship". "It could be any number of reasons why he has not been in touch with you as yet". "But I'm glad you haven't written him off as yet – it's wise to give him a little more time". "But try not to think about it too much, love, leave it to God". "And definitely do not take matters into your own hands – don't 'phone him first," Jean was old fashioned and always taught Cherie that the man must make the first move. Cherie appreciated her mother's wise words, but sought further clarification. "Funny you should mention that mum, sometimes I wonder whether I shouldn't just call him myself," Cherie said sounding impatient.

"No, make sure you don't do that," Jean said quickly. "Give him some time, and the very best advice that I can give you is to pray about it," Jean admonished.

"But I have been praying about it mum," Cherie said sounding hopeless.

"Prevail in prayer my dear, keep on praying and leave it with the Lord," Jean took her daughter's hand and squeezed it gently as she spoke. "Just leave it with the Lord and you'll see, he will answer your prayers," she said, sounding incredibly wise.

"Oh mum, you always have a knack of making things sound so simple," Cherie said smiling as she wondered at her mother's ability to make her feel so much better with just a few simple words.

It was the first time that Cherie had ever discussed her love life with her mother and Jean realised that she must be serious about this young man. And she made a commitment in her heart that she would pray for her daughter in earnest.

Then Cherie said something to her mother that she had never spoken to her before. "Mum, you know that God could use you greatly – you are so gifted and so wise, yet you never use the gifts you have in the church". "Do you realise that God needs you?" As Cherie spoke, she felt as though she was listening to herself with little control over what she uttered – she realised that the Holy Spirit must be speaking through her. She had always wondered why, although her mother attended church fairly regularly, she remained on the periphery of church life, never getting truly involved - almost like a bystander. Now she listened, awaiting her mother's reply – there was a long pause before Jean spoke. "You're right, my dear – although I love God, I've always sought to remain aloft due to the experiences I had in the past, but God has been dealing with me too, and I have come to realise that my actions has been purely selfish." "I fully intend to get back to where I was many years ago. I will become more committed to service". "Yes, it's definitely time for me to stop being a church attendee and start doing some work for the Lord", Jean said smiling.

"I am just glad that you have never followed my example – that you have chosen to dedicate time to doing God's work," Jean said and went on to assure Cherie that she would join Lester in the hospitality team at their local church very soon.

"You must come and visit my church one day mum, I'll invite you when there is a special event on, okay," Cherie enthused.

"Okay, I look forward to it," Jean replied.

Jean again thought of broaching the subject of Tyrone but got cold feet and decided to put off doing so until she had prayed about it some more. She would speak to Cherie over the telephone initially, in order to cushion her embarrassment.

They dined and parted at 8.30 pm, having consumed almost a whole cheesecake between them after dinner. "Now that you're winding down the tour, you must drop by one evening after work", Jean invited.

"Yeah mum, but no promises right – I have a lot of work to catch up with", Cherie replied.

"I won't hold my breath then", Jean replied jokingly.

Cherie didn't reassure her mother, as Jean was probably right – she couldn't guarantee that she would be anywhere but in the office, or hunched over her laptop, or on the telephone – at least not until sometime after this tour had ended.

On the way home Cherie resisted the urge to pass by the office, reminding herself that today was strictly her day and she was going to enjoy the rest of it. She planned to pamper herself the rest of the evening by taking a much needed sauna and having a massage at the private health club she attended, which was open until 11.00pm. She also needed to have her hair done and a facial, but for that she would have to fix an appointment for later on in the week.

After her visit to the sauna Cherie felt like a new person as she climbed into her car and started the engine. Cynthia popped into her thoughts and she suddenly realised that her friend was due to give birth very soon. Glancing at the clock she noted that it was 10.55 pm, but unperturbed she dialled Cynthia's number – they were girlfriends who had never placed any curfew on the times they could call each other. And now was as good a time to catch up as any. As the phone began to ring Cherie put her mobile headset in place and as Cynthia picked up she set the car in motion. "Hey girl," Cherie said smiling. There then followed a very loud and excitable exchange between the friends before they calmed down and had what you could term a normal conversation. Cynthia was glad to hear from her friend. She wanted Cherie to come and see her and though Cherie couldn't really spare the time, she wanted to be there for her friend at this important time - so she agreed to drop by the next day. They chatted until Cherie arrived home. Pulling up in front of her home, she continued to chat with her friend for a few minutes before ending their conversation.

Later as Cherie reflected she thought about her lifestyle. She hated that her work schedule prevented her from seeing those dear to her as often as she would like but vowed to herself that she would make it up to them. Just a few more weeks to go and she would be relatively free - at least for a while.

Tonight Cherie wanted no more distractions – she needed to sleep well and proceeded to switch her 'phone off. And retiring to her bedroom, she turned on very soft inspirational gospel music and Kim Burrell amongst others caressed her ears and soothed her to sleep.

Thoughts of Gus Allen suddenly besieged her mind and Cherie recalled what her mother had said – she would pray about the matter some more. Picking up her Bible, she read again the scripture she had read earlier in the day (really yesterday now), *"Trust in the Lord with all your heart and rely not on your own understanding. In all your ways acknowledge Him and He shall direct your paths"*. Cherie mediated. Then she prayed about Gus, asking God to take control of the situation. Later she said a prayer of thanksgiving to God for blessing her, her prayer interspersed with praises to God for His sovereignty and lordship. She prayed for her family and friends. Then Cherie asked God to help her find her father before crawling back into bed.

"Daddy, daddy, don't leave me," Cherie cried. She had regressed to her childhood and saw herself standing vulnerable in the middle of a field. Her father was walking away from her across the field and she was crying after him. She stretched out her hands toward him as far as they would go. But rooted to the spot she found that she was unable to run after her father. Then she began to sob, and as the tears filled her eyes, he disappeared. She sobbed uncontrollably, slumping to the ground. And then he appeared again. He came towards her, reaching out to take her hands and lift her up from the ground. Then she saw his face, clearly, for the first time, he smiled at her and she recognised him – she knew who he was.

Cherie awoke suddenly. She remembered that she had been dreaming but couldn't recall the full details of the dream. She felt that it was a very important dream and she wanted to remember it, but try as she may, she just didn't seem able to. Then she remembered what Gran 'ma used to say when she was a little girl - that if you wanted to remember a dream you had to lay really still and it would all come back to you. So Cherie lay really still allowing her body and mind to relax. As she did so pieces of her dream flitted onto the screen of her mind – the small girl in the field; the tears - her father. And then she remembered his face - she knew who he was. His real name was Donald Syrenson, Tricia Syrenson's father. Cherie gasped – could it really be. She recalled that everyone used to mistake her and Tricia for sisters as they resembled each other so much. She also recalled how much Tricia's father had resembled the man in the faded picture at the back of Gran ma's photo album. And she remembered that Tricia's father spoke about living in America – everything seemed to fall into place. And Cherie had a distant memory that Gran'ma had told her that Tyrone's surname was Syrenson. Her bottom lip drooped as she recalled this important detail and it suddenly dawned on her that this was too much of a coincidence.

"Oh my goodness – I'd better ask mum", Cherie said without fear - she silently resolved to make her mother see sense. And Cherie made a decision – if Jean didn't co-operate she would approach Donald Syrenson herself – she had no choice. Luckily she still remembered where he lived.

CHAPTER 12

Backlash

It was 1.19 pm on Wednesday 23 August – not that Donald was aware of that – the days came as they went - he had lost track. One day rolled into another – time went by – a day became a week and a week a month and it had now been three months since he got laid off from work.

Donald was sitting at the kitchen table where he spent most of his time since being laid off. He had just returned from his daily trip to the Job Centre – another wasted journey. Once again he had failed to find any work – much needed work. Now he sat alone, the picture of despondency, nursing his half drunken cup of coffee and thinking. His beloved laptop had stopped working, severing his lifeline to the world and he did not have the means to get it repaired, so he worried about that. Time was all he had left - a lot of time to think, time to remember the past, a lot of time to worry and a lot to fret about. He worried about the fact that he was almost 55 years old and jobless with no real prospects of ever finding work again in the current recession which looked set to last for many more years. The lay-off was supposed to have been temporary but there was no indication that he would ever be called back to work – and that worried Donald.

Donald used to have some savings – around £2,000 - stashed away beneath his mattress. His savings would have tided him over, but his savings have disappeared and Donald thinks that Tricia has taken it because no one else comes to the house. He believes that Tricia is taking drugs or something – Donald smelt the strange smoke almost every day. But he dare not ask Tricia whether she has in fact taken his savings or whether she is taking drugs - so he just says nothing.

The mortgage was not being paid – has not been paid for the last two months – prior to which no payment was missed in 20 years. Donald did not contact the mortgage provider - he wasn't good at dealing with that sort of thing. Margaret used to take care of such matters – if only she were still alive. All he could do was hope against hope that he would find work to enable him to pay the mortgage because Donald worried a lot about not paying it. All he knew how to do well was work, and pay for what needed to be paid for – it was all he had ever done. But now he had no work and no money and all he could do was worry. He also fretted about the household bills which so far he had managed to pay from savings, but his savings were exhausted, so what would he do now? He was eating as little as possible and the cheapest of foods in order to survive. He could afford to buy just enough to keep Tricia and himself alive – one day at a time and that concerned Donald.

The car has been playing up too and Donald worried about that because he did not have the means to fix it if it broke down completely? He was also concerned about the car insurance, the Mot, the tax – all needed to be renewed at the end of the month. Tricia drove the car a lot and Donald worried that his dear daughter would be deprived of her means of transport if it broke down. He pondered upon all these problems but could find no solution to them. There was no-one to turn to – no family that could loan him money to tide him over, and no friends that he was close enough to, to borrow from. Most of his family were in America and Donald thought about selling the house and emigrating, but he would not know how put into effect such ambitious plans – Margaret would have though! Anyway, what would happen to Tricia?

That was what concerned Donald more than anything else, his one and only daughter who had taken to sitting in her room all day doing nothing. She locked her door and stayed in her room, neglecting even her bodily hygiene. She did not speak to him – did not acknowledge him when he spoke to her now, insulting him at a whim. And at night Donald often heard her chanting over and over again in the wee small hours, but could not make out what she was saying. He was aware that she went out at some time – probably when he was at the job centre during the day – only he never saw her come or go, but she used to leave empty food wrappers and packaging in the dustbin, though he had not seen any for the past week or so. Donald was aware that Tricia left her room at night too, because she would eat the meals that he had prepared, leaving the dirty dishes in the sink.

Tricia no longer went to work. Just before he was laid off she had stopped going in, claiming that she was sick, without providing any certificate. All she did was to inform her workplace that she "wasn't feeling well" – nothing more – no certificate or explanation as to what was wrong with her. After the first week off she didn't bother to call her workplace at all, nor did she take their calls. And they had then written a couple of letters to her – Donald recognised the postmark. But she had just read the letters and then angrily ripped them to shreds. And although she had not told him so, he believes that she must have been dismissed from her job, because her workplace didn't call anymore and no further letters had come from them for over two months now.

"Tricia my beautiful daughter – the one apple of my eye, what happened to you?" Donald questioned aloud as he wondered at the drastic change in his daughter. And he was not even aware of the true extent to which Tricia had in fact changed, because he had not seen her for weeks. For Tricia who was once so glamorous, had now allowed her hair to remain in a nappy, unruly and uncombed state – day after day, until it began to lock into thick smelly unpleasant clumps. She who once loved to look into the mirror now avoided sight of herself. She who loved to dress up now wore the same drab dirty jeans and food stained tea-shirt day in - day out. She who was once so sociable and outgoing had become reclusive, and now avoided people, refusing to answer telephone calls from friends or respond to messages left for her to call them. She who was once so gregarious, now refused to answer the door to personal callers, peering out at them from her bedroom window, being careful not to be noticed. She who was once so intelligent, now found the simplest thought formation mentally challenging.

Those of Tricia's callers who cared a little questioned Donald as to her well-being. But in the main, most of them after leaving one or two messages on receiving no return call, just stopped calling. The fact was that Tricia never had any real friends, just party friends that she went out and had a good time with – fair-weathered friends. There were no true friends that she could confide in, could trust to be there through thick and thin. But then she had never been a real true friend to anyone herself. She had never been the friend that one could confide in, had never given a shoulder for anyone to lean or cry on. Tricia had always been a "good time" type of friend – there when things were going well but nowhere to be found when things got rough. In return she had expected no more than that of her "friends", and she had gotten just what she expected.

For the main part Tricia hardly ventured out of her room during the day. She would only do so when her father went out, being careful to go back into her room and lock the door before his return. At night though, she ventured out when she was certain he was sound asleep – when she could hear him snoring loudly. She would sneak out of her room and down the stairs, confident that she would not wake him. Ever since she was growing up she had learned that her father slept like the proverbial log and that once asleep, waking him was akin to waking the dead. Now she took advantage of that knowledge and did most things at night, sleeping late into the afternoon.

But Tricia was not aware that her chanting into the early hours was so loud as to wake even Donald. Each chanting session would start in a whisper and then rise to a crescendo, a pattern that was repeated over and over. She was not aware that the chanting would become manic, as she wafted away into a trance, and it was then that Donald would be able to hear her. Unbeknown to Tricia her father had tried many times to decipher what she was saying by placing a glass to the wall and listening. But he had so far been unable to make out fully what she was saying, due to the fact that her speech was slurred and uneven, as though she were drunk – another change in her character. The only words he had been able to make out were "lose" and "everything" as they were the ones on which she placed the most emphasis. Her father gathered that she was not praying, or singing or rapping, but definitely chanting - some sort of curse.

Donald couldn't think why his daughter would want to curse anyone and surmised that all was not well with Tricia – not well at all. Tricia needed help – mental, physical – or both. It appeared she may be losing her mind, but he didn't know what to do about her. She never even spoke to him anymore, so he could only guess what the problem might be. Donald felt trapped in a vicious circle of hopelessness and helplessness. He blamed himself for his daughter's condition, for all the problems. For Donald had not always been the good person he was now. He had committed some vile acts in his lifetime and Donald was certain that karma was paying him back for the wrongs he had done so many years ago. Things he had conveniently pushed to the back of his mind - wrongs that he kept secret from others - even from the dearly departed Mags.

Donald often meditated on the verse from the Bible that warned *"The sins of the fathers is visited upon the third and fourth generation"*, and accepted that he deserved everything that was happening to him. But Tricia was caught up in the backlash and she didn't deserve to suffer for his misdemeanours. Donald often cried for Tricia – she did not deserve to suffer for his sins. The thought occurred to him that she needed to be sectioned. And he had given serious thought to that over recent weeks. He used to try knocking at her door and calling to her, asking her whether she was okay, and, apart from shouting "Go away", she would completely ignore him. But one day three weeks ago, when he knocked on her door, she opened it and charged at him with a knife shouting, "If you knock on my door again, I will ****** cut you to pieces". So Donald was not even tempted to knock at Tricia's door any more.

It often occurred to Donald that if Mags were alive she would know exactly what to do. He had asked Mags several times when she visited him, and the last time she spoke to him she told him that she would soon tell him what to do, so Donald was waiting for Mag's answer. Until Mags told him what to do, the best he could do was to make sure that Tricia was eating well by cooking healthy balanced meals and leaving them in the kitchen. He has taken to shopping mostly in the market with the little money that he has And Donald has to hide the little money he gets from the government from Tricia because she will steal it if she sees it – she has done it before, three weeks ago and they had no food to eat for four whole days. That was when Donald discovered that if he went along as the market was closing he could pick up many free items discarded by the stallholders in the bins at the back of the stalls. Some had passed their sell-by date but were still perfectly good to eat, Donald had discovered. This week he had picked up most of the meals from the bins at the back of the stalls. He found that he wasn't the only one and had met some very decent people doing the same thing. Donald knew that Tricia was at least eating well because food that he cooked and left in the kitchen would disappear, and he would find dirty dishes in the sink. He had left a note for Tricia on the kitchen door asking her to wash up after herself three weeks ago, just before the knife incident, but that request had gone unheeded. So now he just washed the dishes dutifully himself and continued cooking enough for two – it was the least that he could do for his obviously troubled offspring.

There was another thing that preoccupied Donald's thoughts. There was always a strange presence in the house – as though his movements were being monitored by someone or something unpleasant. He perceived an ominous, foreboding presence, a spirit that breathed heavily – fire, smoke - a hovering, menacing, soul-piercing, malevolent, intruding, sinister and forceful presence. It did occur to Donald from time to time that it was he that needed help – perhaps he was also going mad. But he reasoned that the fact that he actually considered that he might be going mad, must surely mean that he was not. Donald tried denying what he sensed and told himself that his mind was playing tricks on him, but that did not work. The oppressive spirit remained, intangible yet perceived, unseen yet apparent - unwelcomed, violating, invading and infiltrating his home and personal space.

The thought occurred to Donald that perhaps he was not doing enough – too much time to think, hence the strange feelings, so he had tried playing music softly to no avail. Then he had tried playing loud music which didn't help either. He had tried inviting his two acquaintances over, but found that even while they were there he could still sense the loathsome presence, and clearly they could too as they never stayed for very long before making excuses and leaving. And when they left, it remained hovering, oppressing, invading his home and personal space. Donald wondered whether, even though he thought he might be going mad which proved that he wasn't, he was in fact going mad after all. He thought about going to see the doctor to talk through his fears, but had so far put off doing so – how would he begin to explain them?

A solitary oppressed figure Donald sat in front of the TV with the unwelcome presence for company day after day and night after night. Tonight the heaviness seemed much worse than ever, prompting him to get up and go for a walk, not wishing to stay in with just an unseen malevolent companion. After walking for just 10 minutes he felt inexplicably tired and a headache was developing so he needed to return home and lie down. Donald walked affectedly, dragging his feet as he made his way home, his head down and his shoulders hunched forward – a perfect picture of dejection. As he entered the house he realised that Tricia was in the kitchen. Suddenly, his mood lightened and he became happier. It had been weeks since he last saw his beloved daughter. "Tricia, how you doing?" he said walking towards the kitchen.

Suddenly there was an almighty crash on the kitchen floor and Tricia rushed past him shouting. "What are you doing coming back home already. Why ain't you ******* got any ******* friends anyway?" She continued to shout at her father as she rushed upstairs to her bedroom, her speech peppered with some of the worse swear words Donald had ever heard.

As Tricia slammed her bedroom door shut, still cussing to herself, Donald fell crumpled onto the settee. And depression hit him hard – like a solid brick wall. The headache continued, a thumping painful throb and he clasped his head in both his hands as he was engulfed in total confusion and pain. He wept uncontrollably. Seeing his beloved daughter – what she had become - was all too much for him to bear, and so he wept, not caring that he sobbed aloud. Not caring that great globules of tears were flowing down his cheeks and that his nostrils dripped mucus shamelessly. Not caring that men weren't supposed to cry - let alone weep. Not caring about anything - Donald wept. Then curling himself into a foetal ball he hugged his knees in an effort to find solace, but comfort eluded him and the tears continued to flow unchecked, unabated, and the sadness that he felt sunk deep into his very soul, forming a lethal weapon that pierced his heart.

Donald jumped up from sleep, awoken by Tricia's chanting. The clock on the mantle informed that it was just 3am. He had cried himself to asleep on the settee after nearly two hours. His eyes were swollen and he could barely open them. His mind was a whirl of confusion and paranoia. The chanting was far louder than usual, and he could feel the menacing presence all around him – threatening, overwhelming.

Stopping up his ears with his fingers, Donald attempted to block out the offensive din as he fell to the floor. He got up from the carpet and fumbled his way in the pitch blackness, not bothering to turn on the light. Groping around, he made his way upstairs to his bedroom where he started weeping with renewed vigour. Many thoughts jumbled together in Donald's mind until he lost control. "Why am I suffering like this", he shouted. "Why, why, why – why is my daughter going crazy? Why is everything going wrong? "Why, why, why".

With each moment Donald sunk deeper and deeper into depression until he abandoned his spirit in a state of utter confusion and hopelessness, then absolutely exhausted physically as well as emotionally, he found some peace in a very deep sleep.

Life continued in a downward spiral for Donald and he sunk deeper into depression. On 29 August, 2010 he lay in bed - uncharacteristically, he did not want to get up. Hours passed and still he did not move - he didn't need to get up – he had time – plenty of time, more time. Yes, he had all the time in the world – time to kill before he joined his beloved wife. "Mags", Donald spoke his dearly departed wife's name aloud as he reflected. She came to him. "What shall I do about Tricia, Mags – about this whole unfortunate situation?" "What shall I do to put things right? Donald asked Mags. He had been asking her the same question every day for weeks now and awaiting her reply.

Then he heard her sweet voice, calling to him as she stood next to him - she beckoned him. He looked into her eyes and was mesmerised by her. "You're so wise my darling", Donald said as he smiled at Mags. "I knew you would come through - I knew you would not leave me to cope alone – I knew you would come through for me", he said as he looked into Mags' loving eyes, thinking how wise she was.

Over the next two hours Donald conversed with Mags just as he had done when she was alive, becoming caught up in her charm all over again. "Ha, ha, ha – you are so beautiful, my love, so very beautiful". "I'm coming with you – don't leave me", Donald said. "Just sit down a while, my love", he motioned for Mag's to sit beside him on the bed. Then he hugged her close to him, "You're so beautifully, so soft, so warm, my love – my beautiful Mags". "I'm so happy now, I'm so happy now, I'm so happy now," Donald repeated.

Then suddenly Donald stopped talking and just listened to Mags as she told him what he needed to do to solve the problem. And as she spoke to him in her usual sweet way, he drank in her presence and stared into the depth of her wise eyes. Then he repeated what she had said to him, to show her that he understood. Yes, Donald understood what Mags was telling him to do – he understood perfectly.

Getting up from his bed Donald headed to the shed in the back garden - there it was, just what he was looking for. He removed some of the large objects blocking his path to the item he needed. When he had retrieved it he clutched it close to his chest as he returned into the house with the treasured article – the solution – Mags had said. He did not bother to return the things he had removed from the shed in his quest. Nor did he bother to shut the shed door behind him. He climbed the stairs quickly, eager to complete the task set by Mags - he was ready. At last he knew what he had to do, and he had to do it quickly – no time to waste now.

Mags had told him not to disturb Tricia and Donald obeyed. So he did what he had to do as quietly as possible - there and then Donald did what he had to do, with Mags by his side beckoning him on. He did it expertly and he could see that Mags was pleased which made him ecstatic. He chuckled loudly, happy at last - Mags chuckled too.

CHAPTER 13

Accidental Revelation

She would not usually take particular notice of a headline in the Hackney Chronicle but today, 4 September 2010, Cherie stopped and stared at the picture on the front page of the local newspaper. She had dropped by the store on her way to the office to pick up some milk, sugar and a newspaper, when the headline caught her attention. Now she stood transfixed staring into the eyes of Donald Syrenson, the familiar name captioned beneath the familiar face in the photograph. She was particularly affected because over past weeks she had been having a recurring dream about Tricia Syrenson's father and in her dream he looked exactly as he did in this photo. He was the man who, each night when she fell asleep, announced to her regressed childhood self that he was her father – a fact she had been intending to ask her mother to verify - the man to whom she intended to pay a visit and ask personally whether he was her father if Jean refused to cooperate.

When Cherie had composed her thoughts she read the headline "Man Seriously Injured in House Fire", and gasped involuntarily, her bottom lip dropping down in an expression of awe. She began to hyper-ventilate, breathing in deeply – more than was necessary, until her head spun. Her hands trembled as she gripped the newspaper as though it belonged to her, crumpling its pages and prompting the newsagent to cast a menacing glance, willing her to hurry up and leave his shop. But Cherie was oblivious to his glare as she stared intently at the page - her eyes agog. The story heralded:

"…..Donald T. Syrenson apparently set fire to himself by dousing in paraffin and setting it alight….."

Cherie covered her mouth as she gasped loudly. She devoured the whole tragic story unashamedly, as the shopkeeper continued to cast "daggers" in her direction. She had met Donald Syrenson only once, when she was a teenager, his daughter Tricia having invited her to her home. And as she contemplated his tragic story she recalled the very high opinion she had formed of both he and his wife, who were the complete opposite to their wayward daughter. And Cherie wondered what could have driven this dear soul to such desperate lengths.

The story informed that Mr Syrenson's wife had died 5 years earlier and that his daughter who lived with him had apparently escaped unharmed. There were apparently no other casualties. Cherie sighed with relief on learning that Tricia, who she recalled was an only child, was okay, in spite of the fact that they had never liked one another.

Slowing picking up the paper and the other items she needed, Cherie paid for them at the counter and left the shop. As she drove, she stole glances of Mr Syrenson's picture which she had left open on the passenger seat. She noted with sadness his resemblance to the picture of her father that she had studied as a child and recollections of all she knew of Mr Syrenson rotated in her mind – she thought about his American connection - he had lived in that country. He was about the same age as her mother. And Cherie was certain that Gran ma told her that her father was called Mr Syrenson when she was a small girl. Or did she just imagine that? She also thought about her uncanny resemblance to Tricia Syrenson and how people used to mistake them for sisters. Memories flooded back of how others used to mix them up when they attended dance classes. She became mildly excited at the prospect of meeting a half-sister as she became convinced that the clues could not simply amount to coincidence – she had always wanted a sister?

But suddenly a mixture of emotions bombarded Cherie's mind as she recalled the extent to which she and Tricia had fallen out, and the despicable way in which Tricia had treated her ever since. She struggled with her conscience which wanted to endorse her dislike of Tricia. Then a feeling of sympathy at the sadness Tricia must no doubt be feeling at this time presented itself in her mind. This was followed by momentary repulsion, on recalling Tricia's outrageous antics, as Cherie realised that they were most certainly blood relations. Pushing the negative thought away, Cherie concentrated hard on the fact that she may have at last found her father and if so, that he was an honourable man.

Suddenly Cherie recalled how she came to know that her father's surname was Syrenson – Gran 'ma had not told her after all. She had overheard a conversation between her mother and her Gran 'ma when she was four years old. Her grandmother was debating with her mother as to what surname she should be registered with when she started school. And Cherie recalled that Gran 'ma had said that her surname should be Syrenson because that was her father's name and that was the name on her birth certificate. "There is no way this is just a coincidence", Cherie spoke her thoughts.

And now realising that Donald Syrenson was indeed her father, Cherie knew she had to find out which hospital he was at so she could visit him. She also needed to get hold of a copy of her birth certificate immediately as she recalled that she had never before seen that document. Her mother had applied for her first passport - it was in the name of Cherie Johnson and she had simply renewed it each time it expired. It now all made sense to Cherie why she was having the recent recurring dreams about Donald – they were obviously a premonition, a forewarning of the fact that she would soon discover that he was her father.

As she drove, Cherie wondered why it had never dawned on her before that Mr Syrenson was her father. She questioned why she had never made the correlation between the various pieces of information despite the strong resemblances. And she knew in her heart that speaking to her mother to seek confirmation would be a mere formality.

On arrival at the office Cherie was greeted warmly by Naomi - she reciprocated and headed straight into her office, asking not to be disturbed for any reason for at least the next half an hour. Entering her office, and closing the door behind her she stood with her back against it for a while. Her right hand clutched the door handle behind her, as though she was afraid to let go of it. Slowly she released the object and walked to her desk where she fell to her knees, her head resting on her right hand, which she had placed palm-down. Cherie tried to say a prayer for Tricia and her father, but her efforts were thwarted by an inability to focus.

For 10 minutes' she endeavoured to focus in prayer but her efforts were challenged. Then she received a release. And she prayed that God would help Tricia and her father to be strong and overcome the problems that had led to the tragedy of his attempted suicide. Cherie could not understand why she felt such compassion towards Tricia, or the compulsion with which she was seized to continue praying strongly for her – perhaps it was that she realised now that they were almost certainly sisters. She continued in prayer and was led by the Spirit to pray strongly for Tricia's deliverance from evil. She began to feel a great unease in her spirit as she prayed for Tricia, someone she had not seen or communicated with for many years. She became aware of a great burden being lifted from her Spirit, a load that she had not previously appreciated she was carrying. Relief spread over her as the burden alleviated but she felt a compulsion to continue praying. So obeying the prompting of the Holy Spirit, Cherie prayed on. She rose from her knees and began to pace around her office, gesticulating with her hands as though at war – fighting in prayer. The burden tried to return and a strong evil force began to invade the atmosphere, a vindictive, insolent force that Cherie knew from experience to be demonic. It had an intensity that she had never before encountered.

Sensing that the force she was coming up against was extraordinary, and recalling that her pastor always encouraged brethren to pray together when faced with difficult situations, Cherie decided to call Bishop Fredericks to request special prayers. Then she continued to fight in prayer, crying out to God to protect and deliver her. The force abated but then returned with renewed vigour. This happened over and over again until Cherie was dripping sweat. But although she felt exhausted, she continued in prayer, being prompted by the Holy Spirit to carry on. Finally, the force disappeared and Cherie felt an air of calm come over the atmosphere. Soon she ended her prayers by repeating Psalm 91, from which she always drew strength. Empowered by the word, Cherie knew that God had taken control of the situation - whatever it was.

Her prayer ended, Cherie set about the business of the day. She was happy that Naomi was also a Christian and understood her need to pray on occasions. Suddenly a song arose in her heart, and she began to sing quietly to herself in a worshipful manner. *"I want to come home, I want to come home – been away too long, I want to come home".* Tears filled her eyes as she sang the self-penned hymn. She wondered why the Spirit had brought this song to her mind today. Then a Bible verse sprung to mind, *"Come unto me all who are weary and heavily laden and I will give you rest".* Cherie meditated upon that verse, mulling it over and over in her mind. Suddenly Gus' face appeared vividly in her mind's eye. He had a worried look on his face and his brow was lined - she felt a strong urge to pray for him. So Cherie asked the Holy Spirit to lead her as she prayed for Gus. She prayed for his guidance, direction and deliverance, she continued to pray for his protection and his salvation. As she prayed, tears filled her eyes.

Cherie marvelled at how deep her feelings were for this man she barely knew and why, despite the fact that he had not called her for over four months, Gus still had such an effect on her emotions. She should have dismissed him a long time ago, but each time she thought about him she felt a renewed longing within her soul.

Then Cherie said a personal prayer for herself - that she would receive guidance and direction – that she would have a revelation to know what was happening to her - to know God's will for her and Gus. Having finished praying Cherie remained still, silently waiting, expectant. Then she heard the familiar still small voice speak within her spirit, *"Be patient".*

The Holy Spirit was not finished with her yet apparently and Cherie was led to pray still more – so she obeyed and prayed for her family, friends, church, and acquaintances. Then she was led to pray especially for her mother - but she resisted, putting it off until later - she prayed for her parents everyday in any case and she felt it was time to get to work. So Cherie wound down her prayer time by asking God to bless her day at work, and in the week ahead.

The beginning of week prayer time would usually take up to half an hour - not almost two hours, as she noted it had done today. Cherie busily set to work in an effort to make up the time, while she continued to commune with her creator in her spirit. Then thoughts of Donald Syrenson returned to the forefront of her mind making it difficult to concentrate.

Everything seemed to add up, except that her fathers Christian name was Tyrone, not Donald. But Cherie contended that lots of people changed their names these days and remained hopeful that her mother would confirm her suspicions very soon. Then she recalled that Mr Syrenson's middle name began with a "T", the newspaper story had confirmed that – "But of course, the T must stand for Tyrone", Cherie resigned.

Cherie became sad as she thought about her paternity and the way that she had been denied all knowledge of her father by her mother. And anger arose in her as the question "What if Mr Syrenson had died in the fire", presented itself. For Cherie would never have had the opportunity to know him. And in the unlikely event that Mr Syrenson wasn't her father, it dawned on her that she may yet never get to meet the man who fathered her. Angrily she resolved that she would waste no more time in confronting her mother.

Cherie tempered her emotions by taking deep breaths – she did not want to allow anger to control her. But as righteous indignation rose up inside her, she allowed her mind to accept that she had a right to know about her father - whether her mother liked it or not. She was a grown woman now and could make decisions for herself. It was no longer up to her mother to decide what was in her best interest. "Mum has a new life now and cannot possibly be hurt if I want to know about the man whose genes make up the half of me", Cherie mumbled. Continuing to muse that even if the memories were painful for her mother she now had support from Lester.

One of the main reasons that she had held off broaching the subject for so long was because she respected her mother so much – was eternally grateful to her for the sacrifices she had made in bringing her up alone. But suddenly that did not seem a good enough reason for her to go on "suffering". Cherie was stunned for a moment – by her own thoughts – she was taken aback by the thought that she was actually "suffering". So strong a word, but was it too strong a word? Delving deeper within her soul, she searched, and realised that in all honesty, she was, had been suffering in silence for many years and the bad dreams, nightmares and feelings of dejection and insecurity were all manifestations of her torture.

Energised by the revelation that she was suffering in silence, Cherie reached for the 'phone, but before she could pick up the receiver to dial it rang. Naomi enquired whether she was now taking calls, and receiving an affirmative answer, announced that her mother was on the line. When Jean was put through Cherie greeted her, "Hi mum, you gwaan live long you see," she used the old Jamaica adage. I was just thinking to call you - just about to pick up the 'phone when you rang," she continued.

Jean returned her daughter's greeting, laughing at Cherie's far less than genuine Jamaican accent, "Hello darling, how are you.

"I'm good," Cherie said. "Mum, do you remember Tricia – the girl I met at dance school when I was sixteen?" Cherie asked.

"Oh yes, I could never forget that one", Jean replied with a chuckle.

"Well Tricia's father is in the local paper today – he tried to commit suicide mum, do you believe that", Cherie heralded.

"His name is Donald, Donald Syrenson", Cherie informed her mother and waited for her response.

After a long pause, Jean replied, "I didn't know Tricia's surname was Syrenson", then said nothing else. Then she changed the subject.

"Darling, I need to talk to you about something," Jean said.

"What's that," Cherie asked expectantly. She wanted to ask her mother why she had paused but held back – she would save her questions for later on.

Jean replied after a further significant pause, "Your father dear - I need to talk to you about your father," there she had said it.

As soon as the words left her mouth, Jean felt a weight lift from her shoulders. She felt so much better within herself. She had been meaning to speak to Cherie for many months now but could not pluck up the courage to. For the last couple of years she has been contemplating the way she handled the situation of her daughter's paternity, and she now realised that she had been totally selfish – in seeking to protect herself and her own feelings, she had denied her daughter the chance to know her father, to build a relationship with him. Jean felt ashamed, and had recently begun to feel unworthy of the love that her daughter lavished on her and the trust she reposed in her. Lately she had begun to wonder whether her actions could potentially have affected her daughter more than she had previously realised. She wondered whether anything in Cherie's childhood had led to her singleness and obvious inability to develop a serious relationship because she has never brought home any men or introduced any potential suitor. When questioned about the subject Cherie always said that she was waiting to meet the right man but Jean was beginning to wonder whether there would ever be a "right man" to suit her daughter's fastidious tastes. Jean had also gathered that her daughter wished to marry a Christian man – one who was in the same faith as herself - but surely there were nice young men in her church?

She was somewhat surprised to find out that the Tricia girl had the same surname as Tyrone. And Jean immediately recalled that Tyrone was Cherie's father middle name, not his first name. Jean never found out from Tyrone what his real first name was because he did not like it and kept it a secret. But Jean had said nothing to Cherie – she hoped Cherie was not related to that awful young woman Tricia though. She would wait to see the picture of Donald in the newspaper before making any comment.

Jean was prepared to give her daughter as much help as she needed in an effort to find her father – she was even prepared to bear the costs involved. Maybe that would go someway towards helping to put right the emotional wrongs that she had inflicted upon her daughter. Jean knew one thing - she owed her daughter a big apology.

Cherie was silent for a moment before speaking, "Would you believe that that was the very thing that I wanted to discuss with you, mum?" she confessed.

They arranged to meet that afternoon for lunch. Jean would come and meet Cherie and they would go for lunch at a small restaurant nearby, where they would sit and talk about her father - Cherie couldn't wait. She felt as though she would burst with excitement.

For the remainder of the morning Cherie drifted around the office as though on a very fluffy cloud. She sang as she went through the paperwork – nothing could bring her down. For the first time in her life she realised just how she had suppressed her true feelings about her father. Now she could express those emotions - she felt as free as a bird. She was about to embark on a new adventure, and whatever the outcome, she would be satisfied just to find out just who he really was – who she really was.

By the time the buzzer sounded at 1.30 pm Cherie was behaving like an excited 4 year old at Santa's Grotto. "I'll get that," she shouted to Naomi as she bounded for the door release. She spoke into the intercom without asking who it was, "Come on up", and released the door. Then she returned to her office to fetch her handbag, and organise her work so that she could pick up easily when she returned from lunch. As she returned to the main office she saw two Police officers speaking with Naomi, who beckoned to the officers as Cherie entered the open-planned area. "Here comes Miss Johnson now".

"Miss Cherie Johnson?" the first officer asked in a monotone.

"Yes, yes, I'm Cherie Johnson," Cherie replied, a hint of annoyance in her voice. Whatever they wanted, she did not care - their timing was way off. She was looking forward to enjoying lunch with her mother – a life changing lunch, something she had waited for all her life, and they choose now to show up. Cherie took a deep breath and tried to calm herself with the thought that their visit would probably be a short one – she had no idea what they might want to talk to her about but she was not perturbed. She had no reason to be concerned. Then she remembered that recently there had been a spate of car-jackings in the vicinity. And the thought occurred to her that they must be looking for information or potential witnesses.

"Can this wait until another time officers, I was just getting ready to have lunch with my mother – can I call you later – please say this can wait", Cherie said.

"Is your mother Mrs Jean Jones?" said the second Police officer.

"Yes," Cherie replied quizzically.

"I'm afraid I have some not too good news about your mother

Miss Johnson", the second officer continued.

"What...... what bad news about my mother? Cherie said abruptly, immediately panicking.

"Your mother has had an accident - she has been taken to the Mount Alloisus Hospital." the officer continued.

"Accident, what accident, my mother – no not my mother, is she okay – please tell me she's okay – no not my mother". "I told her she should drive carefully," Cherie said becoming hysterical.

"Would you like a lift to the hospital, Miss Johnson - I would not advise you to drive in your present state of shock," the first officer said kindly.

"Yes, yes I would, thank you," Cherie said as she rushed out of the office, followed closely by both officers.

"Don't worry Cherie," Naomi shouted after her, taking control, "I'll look after everything and make sure that the office is properly locked up later". "I'll call you to see how you and your mother are later on."

At the hospital Cherie was not allowed to see Jean immediately but was made to wait for what seemed like an age, but in real terms was an hour. Lester was there too as the Police had also informed him of the accident. Cherie found him pacing up and down the waiting room, drinking cup after cup of strong black coffee, until he finally sat down stating that he had a headache.

When they were finally allowed to see Jean, she was very weak and could hardly speak. Cherie tried to stay strong and not break down, although it was very hard for her not to. Lester sat by Jean's bedside where he held her hand and whispered to her gently, endearments of love and care. They were not allowed to stay for very long and were later advised to go home and allow her to get some rest. But they both declined to leave, returning to sit in the waiting room.

When they got the chance to speak with the doctor, he assured them that Jean would be okay, and just needed to rest. But still they refused to leave and come back in the morning.

Cherie went outside to make several telephone calls to let her friends and associates know of the latest position. She also telephoned Bishop Fredericks, for the second time today, to ask for prayers for her mother and her family from the members of the prayer ministry team. Bishop Fredericks was very sympathetic and gave many words of encouragement, promising to pass on the news to others at church and to keep Cherie, her mother and family in fervent prayer.

Upon receiving the news Cynthia, who had given birth only two weeks earlier to a beautiful baby girl, and her boyfriend Benza came along to the hospital to lend their support. They had left the baby with Cynthia's mother who was happy to look after her first grandchild at any time. When they were ready to leave they convinced Cherie to go home with them. She succumbed, realising it would be the wise thing to do. The invitation was also extended to Lester but he declined, stating that he would prefer to stay at the hospital. It was 1.00 am when they left the hospital, and 2.00 am when Cherie finally crawled into bed in Cynthia and Benza's spare room. She fell into a fitful sleep, awaking 4 hours later to the very annoying voices of two passers-by having a heated argument in the street. She got up and headed towards the bathroom where she washed and changed her underwear for new ones which Cynthia had provided for her. She also brushed her teeth with her own portable toothbrush which she carried in her handbag at all times. Cherie teased her hair in the mirror, and satisfied that she was presentable left quietly and headed for the nearby cab station.

Wash House was a daunting and bleak estate with unsavoury characters at every turn, but Cherie did not notice, too engrossed in her own personal crisis to care.

Arriving at the hospital at 7.30 am, Cherie headed for the waiting room where she found Lester seated in the same chair that she had left him in, his head leant to one side as he snored gently signalling that he was asleep. She did not wake him but went instead in search of a nurse or doctor if she was so lucky. She wanted to obtain the latest information about her mother's condition.

The nurse informed her that the doctor would begin his round at 8.00 am and that there was little that she could tell her at this time, except that her mother's condition appeared to be quite serious but stable. Cherie felt helpless but decided that she would use the time she had frugally. And the best thing she could think of doing was to read her Bible and to pray for her mother's recovery.

So, returning to the waiting room Cherie sat down and opened her Bible to a favoured page and read. "He that dwells in the secret place of the most High shall abide under the shadow of the Almighty." Closing her Bible and her eyes, Cherie reclined in her chair and meditated on the words, mulling them over and over in her mind. Then she decided to demonstrate her trust in the Lord by beginning to thank and praise him. She went to the ladies room where she checked to see that she was alone and proceeded to raise her hand towards heaven and thank the Lord for sparing the life of her mother, for sparing her own life, for Lester, her faithful step-father. She thanked Him for her good friends and the people at her church whom she knew would be praying fervently for her family. She also thanked God expectantly for leading her to her father. And then, without thinking about what she was saying, Cherie thanked God for sending Gus into her life. She paused to ponder what she had just said, and felt a reassurance and confirmation within her heart that Gus would someday play some positive role in her life. She thanked God for this revelation, then realising that someone else had just entered the ladies room, and was giving her the most peculiar of looks, Cherie exited hurriedly and returned to the waiting room where she continued to read her Bible.

When they had had a chance to speak to the doctor he confirmed that Jean's condition was serious but stable. Apparently she had broken her foot and the doctor suspected that she may have fractured or bruised her ribs and that she had a fractured or broken collar bone and some other internal bruising. They would have to operate later that day to find out the full extent of the internal injuries and to repair any damage if possible, but he would allow them to see her for a short while. The operation was scheduled to take place at 3.00 pm that afternoon.

Jean tried to speak to them but instead coughed weakly, her face contorted in pain. Cherie gestured to her that she should not try to speak. She smiled serenely down at her mother and then stroked her hair reassuringly. Then she bent over and kissed her on the cheek and stood back to allow Lester to draw close to his wife. As Cherie looked at Lester, she could see from the lines in his face how worried he was and how much this incident had affected him. He looked like a shadow of his former robust self and Cherie wondered what she could do to help. She knew she had to be strong for both of them, as evidently (uncharacteristically) Lester was falling to pieces. She would find more strength by drawing closer to God at this time.

The nurse came into the room and asked them to leave as Jean had to take her rest, and they reluctantly obliged. Cherie tried to encourage Lester to go home and get some rest, and at first he resisted, so she had to convince him that it would serve no real purpose for him to remain there if they would not allow him to see Jean anyway. She reminded him that he had to look after himself and be strong in order to offer Jean the support that she would inevitably need in order to reach full recovery. That argument won him over and Lester finally succumbed - they walked out together and hailed a cab.

Cherie could see how much of a state Lester was in and decided that it would be best that he did not go home alone at this time to sit and wallow in grief. So she suggested that he come home with her as she lived closer to the hospital, and he accepted, pleased that she was behaving like a real daughter.

They drove over to her parents' home, where Lester collected a change of clothes, while Cherie looked around. She was reassured that she had done the right thing in convincing Lester to stay by her for a couple of days – her mother's presence was everywhere as though she was in the next room – only she wasn't. When Lester was ready, they left and got back into the waiting taxi which took them to Cherie's place.

On arrival at home Cherie prepared a hearty breakfast for them both while Lester took a bath. He was in the bathroom for so long that Cherie wondered whether he had fallen asleep. When he finally emerged he looked refreshed but appeared a little confused. The past day's events, coupled with little sleep, were obviously telling on him. Cherie beckoned him into the kitchen and made him sit down at the breakfast bar, where she served his breakfast. She also took a seat and they both silently picked at the sumptuous meal that she had prepared. Lester shuffled around restlessly in his chair and hardly ate any of the food, later apologising for his lack of appetite. Cherie likewise had no inclination to eat but forced herself to.

When they had finished Cherie encouraged Lester to call his family and let them know what had happened. He did so but was so choked up that he had to pass the receiver to Cherie to explain what had happened to Jean. Lester's family, who were also very fond of Jean, wanted to visit her in the hospital and Cherie promised to call them back to let them know when they could do so. They also wanted Lester to stay with them and Cherie did not object – they would finalise arrangements to collect him later.

When Cherie hung up the telephone she attempted to make conversation but Lester was not responding and she herself was finding it far too much of an effort, so they passed the next hour in silence, drinking cup after cup of tea and coffee before Lester fell asleep on the sofa. Cherie retired to her bedroom, where she also slept fitfully for an hour. When she awoke, she was pleased to see that Lester was still asleep. Careful not to wake him, she tiptoed around, gathering up her handbag and a light jacket before leaving the house stealthily to go and collect her car - catching taxis everywhere would prove too costly.

Later, she returned to pick Lester up, only to find that he had already left. Upon checking her mobile, she noted that he had sent her a text to say that he was going back to the hospital. She noted the time of the text, realising that he must have woken up very soon after she left.

When she arrived at the hospital, Lester met her outside Jean's room. The doctor was with her mother at the time. When he came out of the room he led them to a small private room where he informed them that Jean would need several operations to fix bones that she had fractured or broken in her shoulder and ankle and collar bone.

He stressed, however, that her injuries were not life-threatening and that she was expected to make a full recovery, though she would need to remain in hospital for some considerable time – at least a month, and she would be unable to return to normal everyday activities for at least 6 months.

As she sat in the waiting area, Cherie contemplated the upheaval that this accident would cause to her usual working routine, as she realised that she would need to be more supportive to her parents over the next few months - she would certainly have to put off arranging any tours for a while, but such sacrifices were small ones - she was grateful to God for sparing the life of her dear mother.

CHAPTER 14

My Mentor - My Mentee

On Friday 8 September Gus dropped by his house in town. Stepping over the pile of mail behind the front door, he struggled to close the door behind him. As his fortunes declined, he spent less time in Islington and more time in Radleigh - there were less reminders that his life was rapidly falling apart there. All alone in the suburbs, Gus spent hours drinking wine and other alcoholic beverages from the once fully stocked wine cellar and bar, which over the months had become depleted. Except for a glass of wine at meal times, he never drank before and used to frown upon Benza's tendancy to overindulge. But over the past months he had begun to drink heavily in an attempt to forget his worries, invariably until he was drunk. It didn't help though because even when he got drunk he still suffered the nightmares and often the beatings were even more severe than when he was sober.

Gus usually passed by the town house each week to collect his mail, but having found no inclination to do so, he had not stopped by for over two weeks. All he expected in the mail were bills anyway – bad news with no solutions. He was becoming resigned to his fate – there seemed to be no way out, and Gus was expecting his financial affairs to blow up in one great big final bang any day. It was a miracle that so far none of his 82 properties had been repossessed. The banks had allowed him every chance to make amends in light of his previous impeccable credit record, but mortgagees on 21 of his properties had now instituted legal proceedings to recover debt, and it was only a matter of time before Judgments was issued against him from the right, the left and the centre. As to his other creditors, it was only a matter of time before they realised he was in irreparable financial difficulties. "I can't even continue borrowing from Peter to pay Paul",Gus mumbled as he stooped to pick up the letters.

As the red letters continued to arrive thick and fast, Gus buried his head deeper in the proverbial sand. Mild depression prevented him from taking positive steps to help his self such as approaching creditors in an effort to agree settlement plans. Having re-mortgaged and mortgaged a variety of his properties, all funds obtained from such ventures had been exhausted. He had tried to mortgage or remortgage some of his other properties but all his applications were refused by the banks and building societies that he approached. This was very strange to Gus as such organisations used literally to throw offers of loans at him in the recent past. He had now given up hope of being able to obtain further loans to enable him to continue paying the mortgages and all his credit cards were at their maximum level. He was not even able to make the minimum payments each month. Now all but one of the properties he owned was empty. And all attempts by managing agents to entice potential tenants had failed, despite huge compromises on rent. Gus was at a loss to understand the incredible run of bad luck. At the beginning of the year his properties were in demand and all tenanted but now no-one seemed to want to live in them.

In desperation Gus had put several of the properties up for sale, but fifteen of them had been on the market now for over two months. Another eighteen had been up for sale for over three months. And as yet no purchasers had indicated any interest in even one of those properties. The estate agents were doing all they could and had informed Gus that they were baffled by the lack of interest since the properties in question were desirable and situated in the most sought after areas.

"If only I could sell just two of my more expensive houses, I could sort myself out", Gus said, feeling like he was living a nightmare. Clutching the huge wad of letters to his chest he headed towards the kitchen, where he deposited them on the table. Then he opened the windows and patio door to allow air to circulate. Returning to the lounge, he also opened the window and fresh air wafted through, causing the curtains to swirl around frantically. Back in the kitchen he drew up a stool and proceeded to go through the post. He scanned through the mail without actually reading – he was aware of the content – the only differences might be in the increased outstanding balances. If he read through each, he would only sink further into despair and he wanted to avoid doing so. Having opened all the letters Gus sat at the kitchen table for a while just looking around him, then, realising that his mind had began to dwell on his on-going misfortunes, and to avoid the heaviness from weighing him down, he jumped up and walked around. Glancing at his watch, he sighed with gratitude, realising that it was almost time for him to collect Cyrus to take him along to the Youth Club.

For the past two weeks Gus had assisted his father at the Youth Club, and it was doing him a world of good, helping him to con-centrate – if only for a few hours at a time – on other things except his personal circumstances. He couldn't deny he loved the feeling of warmth and comradeship that exuded from most of the people he encountered at the church. And each time the club meetings came to an end, he found himself looking forward to the next one – he felt welcomed at the church and, if he had to choose a word that fitted the circumstances he would select "whole" – yes, being among those people made him feel that he was a more complete person – worthwhile and needed, in spite of his current mental state and circumstances. Gus credited the fact that he had not completely cracked up to his visits to the Youth Club. Peace seemed to embrace his spirit when he entered that building – a feeling of wellbeing. However, he felt like an outsider looking in and he couldn't deny his curiosity as to what it might be like to go deeper, really get involved in church life.

In addition to the momentary peace, there was the sense of ful-filment that Gus derived from helping and mentoring the young people that attended the Club. The fact that he had to portray a positive message to the youngsters somehow helped Gus to remain optimistic, if only while he was at the Youth Club. But the bubble soon burst as soon as he was alone again.

The car door creaked as Gus eased behind the wheel. He had purchased the old well-used car 8 weeks ago for £380 from a local dealer - it was cheaper than renting. Although this was seriously cramping his style (as if he had any style left to cramp), it seemed the most sensible thing for him to do as he had spent almost a fortune on rentals and taxis since his car was stolen, and now he looked back with hindsight and wished he had had the good sense to buy a used car from the outset. He could have saved a fortune and could have bought a far better car than the one he now drove. However, in spite of its appearance, the car was very reliable – if a little noisy, and it got him from "A" to "B", for which Gus was thankful.

When he arrived at Cyrus' home, his father was waiting at the door. He was greeted warmly, as usual, "Hello Son, 'ow are you?" Cyrus lilted.

"I'm good – it's good to see you". "Ready?" Gus replied smiling.

"Yeah, I just need to get my light coat". It's getting a little bit chilly now". "The winter is almost upon us again," Cyrus said pessimistically. He had never liked the cold.

Gus helped his father to the car as his bad leg appeared to be getting worse. "Dad, you need to get your leg looked at", Gus said concerned.

"Yes, son I have a hospital appointment for next week" Cyrus replied much to Gus' relief.

As they drove, Cyrus asked Gus to play a gospel CD. The strong soulful undulating voice of the lead vocalist captivated their musical ears and kept them enthralled. Cyrus rocked gently from side to side as he savoured the melody, shaking his head, as though in concurrence. At intervals he joined in the chorus, melodiously harmonising with the other singers. "Wow, dad I forgot how well you could sing," Gus complemented.

"Oh, thank you son," Cyrus chuckled, flattered by Gus' compliment of his singing. He then went on, "I still sing in the church choir – you must come and watch me". "They are singing again next Sunday – and maybe they are going to let me sing lead vocals", Cyrus said, trying to entice. Gus smiled his reply.

When they arrived at the church, some of the boys were already waiting outside. Gus hurried to open up the door for them, as he greeted them, "Al' ight". He then returned to aid Cyrus out of the car, while one of the young men – Desmond – held the door open to assist him.

The group had really warmed to Gus. Some of the young men already knew him because they attended the training sessions at the stadium. All the attendees of the Club seemed to look up to him and Gus could see in their eyes that they regarded him as a good role model. Although he loved the fact that he was doing something positive, Gus sometimes felt a huge weight of responsibility rested on his shoulders. He only hoped that he did not let down or disappoint any of the youngsters in any way in the future. They perceived him as a successful black male, but lately that seemed like one big lie.

Truth was that most of the youngsters did not really believe the hype about Gus' success – if he was so rich, why did he drive an old banger car – surely he could afford something better than that. But even those who had not known him when he drove the MXLX still showed Gus the utmost respect – revering him as a most decent human being – someone to be admired.

The youngsters interacted well on Club nights. They were developing into wonderful young men as Cyrus and now Gus helped to nurture them. Often they also welcomed guest mentors who came to give talks and presentations on varying subjects. Gus managed to secure donations of 4 brand new computers (to add to the one already owned by the club), from various football and business connections of his and the boys enjoyed the very latest technology which they took turns amicably to exploit. They played various games which fostered bonding and mental development, and generally conversed and related.

Later in the evening Martin cornered Gus alone in one of the offices off the big hall and asked him why he never attended any of the church services. Gus was left dumbfounded by this direct inquisition, and recalled why for many months he had avoided one-to-one conversations with Martin. He waffled for a minute, – trying to think up an excuse but could not come up with anything plausible and so promised that he would make Sunday morning service on the next Lord's day.

"Okay, but I'm gonna remind you," Martin said, pointedly, sending Gus a message that he was refusing to let him off the hook.

"Great that's all I need, being bullied by an over-zealous teenager," Gus murmured under his breath, slightly annoyed. He had no intention of being bullied into going to church. Even though he liked Martin a lot, Gus felt that he was becoming a little too pushy and over-stepping some boundaries.

True to his word, Martin did not let up on Gus - he telephoned him at least three times during the next day – Saturday 9 September 2011. On each occasion Gus hesitated to answer Martin's call but then felt a prompting to pick up. Usually he found it easy to ignore calls from people he wished to avoid but he did not know quite what was happening to him now. Each time he ended a call from Martin he resolved not to answer the next one, but when Martin next called he found himself inexplicably picking up the call.

At 9 pm Gus' telephone rang – once again it was Martin. "I'm just calling to remind you about tomorrow – church, remember", Martin reminded as if Gus had forgotten. "Could you please pick me up on the way, please?" Martin asked nicely, backing Gus into yet another corner. He did not wait for a reply, but continued, "Thanks a lot, it's really difficult to get a bus on Sundays". "I know it's only three stops, but I hate walking on street when I'm dressed criss in my Sunday best", Martin paused as though to allow Gus to respond.

"Yeah, yeah, I understand," came the reply.

"Church starts at 10.30 am so, please call for me at 10.00 am, it's not good to be late for church Sunday morning," the youth said pointedly.

Gus found himself nodding and saying "yeah" in agreement although he couldn't recall the last time he had even attended church, let alone been late.

When Martin finished speaking with Gus he immediately got on his knees and prayed, asking God to ensure that Gus did not change his mind about coming to church the next day. He had been praying for weeks for God to save Gus, and since Friday night for God to bring him to church on Sunday. God had been revealing to Martin that his mentor was going through some difficulties which He wanted to help him through. And Martin had acted on the prompting of the Holy Spirit to push Gus to attend church and to draw closer to God.

After he ended his conversation with Martin, Gus sat and

stared at the wall blankly. He had a miserable expression on his face. He was annoyed that Martin was trying to force him against his will to attend church. Suddenly his mind was drawn back to the time when Martin had first told him of his Christian faith. Suddenly Gus recalled what Martin said then - that he had put God in charge of his life - that God provided peace, happiness, direction and guidance to those who placed Him in charge of their lives. Gus immediately felt ashamed for being angry with Martin, realising that the young boy was merely looking out for his interests in the only way he knew how. He realised that Martin thought it best for him to get to know God better and that in trying to force him to attend church he was only demonstrating his love and care. A tear welled up in the corner of Gus' eye as he contemplated the selfless actions of his young protégé. For he now appreciated Martin's endeavours over many months past to invite him to church on numerous occasions, and his perseverance even in the face of his constant rejections.

So Gus decided he would go to church with Martin the next day – if not because he really wanted to, then to please Martin who obviously cared a lot about him. His thoughts also drifted to his father who also loved and cared about him and the untold joy he would bring to Cyrus by attending church. Having made his decision, Gus resolved that he would not be late for church in the morning. He went to his wardrobe and selected the clothes he would wear – an understated grey suit, light blue silk shirt and navy tie. Before he went to sleep, Gus was prompted to read his Bible. He opened it and read "Cast your burdens on to the Lord because he cares for you". And as he fell asleep, Gus mulled the words over and over in his mind until they sunk into his spirit.

Up with the proverbial larks on Sunday morning 10 September 2010, Gus started his day by going for a short jog before returning home to fix porridge for breakfast. As he pottered, he could not deny the mounting excitement he felt that he would shortly be in church. If the testimonies of Cyrus, Martin and Cherie were to be believed, Gus could expect to find succour for his troubled soul if he encountered God in church today. And for the first time in months, Gus nurtured true hope in his heart.

After breakfast Gus showered and dressed, taking pains to look his very best. When he was ready he called Cyrus to say that he was coming to pick him up. Cyrus was overjoyed and thanked God that at last his son was on the right track. He wondered what had brought about this development.

On the way to collect Cyrus, Gus collected Martin. Martin greeted him heartily with a manly hug and handshake, looking smart in a black suit, white shirt and a navy tie. He thanked Gus for coming – something Gus did not expect. Then Gus remembered what he really liked about this young man - he had a special quality and possessed integrity not usually present in one so young these days.

Cyrus was positively beaming as he hobbled towards the car. He had been looking out for Gus' car and made his way outside as soon as he saw him parking. Martin hurried to get out of the car and hold the door for him as Gus rushed to his side to guide him into the passenger seat. "Praise the Lord – it's good to see you son". "Martin - how you doing?" Cyrus said, acknowledging the younger male with a cordial nod of his head.

"I'm okay, good to see you are looking younger every day," Martin said turning on the charm. Gus smiled broadly, enjoying the camaraderie. He played the same CD that Cyrus had left in his car last time, but this time they travelled in silence, savouring the peaceful Sunday morning atmosphere. Gus had always found Sundays very surreal, and he found that his thoughts were more lucid on Sundays than on any other day of the week - as he drove he wondered why.

When they arrived at the church, Gus became apprehensive – was he ready to do this? He smiled nervously as he helped Cyrus out of the car and into the church but inside he was wondering whether he had done the right thing. Then he reasoned within himself – that it was no big deal - people went to church on Sundays all the time. Martin made his excuse - he had to go and help out the musicians - leaving Gus feeling even more vulnerable than before. It occurred to him as they made their way to their seats, that everyone was looking at him. Smiling coyly, he led Cyrus to a seat fairly near the back of the cathedral. However Cyrus coaxed him gently, "Let's sit a bit closer, my ears not as good as they used to be and it's better if I sit a bit closer".

Somewhat reluctantly Gus obliged and as he walked up the aisle his palms began to sweat. He would much rather have sat at the back where he could sneak out if things became too intense for his taste. But now he wouldn't be able to just walk out - he would have to stay until the end of the service. "Great", he mumbled under his breath.

Praise and Worship was a vibrant affair which found Gus abandoning his inhibitions and allowing his self to join the celebration. He clapped hands along with the congregation, even sung along to the catchier tunes, and was amazed that he was actually enjoying himself - he hadn't realised that church could be such fun.

When it was time for the offertory, Gus listened as an appeal was made for a special offering to cover the building restoration. He was surprised as the speaker asked everyone who could, to make a special offering of £50. The speaker added, "If you give willingly, God will bless you and multiply what you have given back to you "a hundredfold"". Gus wondered what that meant. He was reluctant to give any offering at all, reasoning within himself that he did not know what they would really use the money for. On looking around him, he observed the happy faces and noted that no one else appeared to be at all perturbed by the request for offering. And he suddenly had the urge to give, to trust God and see – well he really had nothing to lose. So Gus reached into his pocket for his wallet. He found that all he had left was £30. The realisation hit him that that was the last money he had. He did not know what he would do for food if he gave it all. But Gus wanted to put God to the test - it occurred to him that he had relied on his own efforts so far which had not helped him, so he would try giving his problems over to God. He remembered the words he had read the previous night, "Cast your burdens on to the Lord because he cares for you," and decided that he would do just that. So he gave the last £30 that he had. He did not ask God for anything in return, without prompting he simply resolved to let Him have full control of his life in the future.

The sermon for the day was brought by a young pastor and was entitled "When all else fails – try Jesus". The preacher expounded the word proficiently in a way that Gus fully understood. Gus drank in the points made and by the end of the sermon he had a new outlook on his present circumstances and what he had to do to change them. It seemed that the preacher knew all that he was going through and was speaking directly to him. He learned that he had already begun the journey to change his circumstances by taking the decision to trust God. It all sounded so simple. Now, if what the preacher had taught was correct, his circumstances should begin to change for the better, Gus thought, a degree of scepticism clouding his mind. He quickly pushed away all negative thoughts and concentrated on the lessons being taught.

Gus learned that he needed more than just monetary blessings – he needed something that money could not buy, the pastor had stressed that what he needed most was salvation through Jesus Christ – just as Martin had told him. And having searched his soul, Gus now knew that he wanted to be saved – he wanted the peace and contentment that Cyrus and Martin and the other people around him had, and he was ready to begin his journey today.

It pleased him to be reminded that God was not interested in the fact that he had not acknowledged him in the past. Apparently God was only interested in what he did from today onwards. And Gus knew that from today he would acknowledge Jesus Christ as Lord of his life. But when the pastor called forward those who wanted to give their lives to Jesus Christ he hesitated, too nervous to move. He was pleased when Pastor Jerry led the confession, which he referred to as the "Sinner's Prayer. Gus understood that that was what Martin had tried to explain to him – what he had read about in one of the Bible verses that Martin had given him. And Gus eagerly made the confession meaningfully along with those who had heeded the call and stepped forward:

"I acknowledge that I am a sinner and am not worthy of God's love and grace";

"I believe that the Lord Jesus Christ is the son of the living God";

"I believe that Jesus Christ was made flesh and dwelt among men";

"I believe that Jesus Chris was crucified and died";

"I believe that Jesus Christ's blood flowed as the supreme sacrifice for my sins";

"I believe that Jesus Christ triumphed over death and hell and rose from the dead";

"And I now confess that I accept you Lord Jesus Christ as my Lord and Saviour";

"Please come into my heart by your Holy Spirit and live in me from this moment";

"Dwell in me – change me and use me to do your work, amen".

During the prayer Gus closed his eyes and felt as though waves of light were washing over him – from his head down to his toes. Then he felt as though waves of heat were washing over him too. A light breeze seemed to waft around him and then waves of joy and happiness washed over his soul. This feeling increased and peaked in intense euphoria, then lingered in a sense of exhilaration and untold bliss. At at the end of the prayer he felt light and buoyant. He had never felt that way before. Untold love filled his heart. Hope overwhelmed his mind. He felt liberated, as free as any bird. Gus consciously cast all his burdens upon Jesus and suddenly felt that he could soar like an eagle, above all his circumstances. And he knew he would overcome.

If asked to put his feelings into words Gus would say he felt like a beautiful, rare and exotic butterfly emerging from its cocoon; or like a seed that had been planted in the ground, that had died and which now began to grow - sprouting its first tender shoot, being nurtured by the sun or like dry ground washed by the falling of torrential rain after many months of drought – being refreshed and renewed.

Gus felt brand new - he felt that something life-changing had happened to him, although he did not know what exactly, or how this would impact on his life, but he was ready to find out – he was ready to start learning the ways of God.

When the service ended, many people came over to Cyrus and hugged him, some shook his hands, while others engaged him in enthusiastic conversation - he was obviously very popular and much loved. Cyrus introduced Gus to some of the brethren, "This is my son, Gus", he could be heard loudly and proudly announcing several times over. After a few minutes, Gus smiled amiably and seized an opportunity to whisper to his father that he would meet him back at the car. Cyrus wasn't best pleased about this as he had wanted to show Gus off to others, but nodded reluctantly.

Making his way through the congregation that had now spilt over into the aisles, chatting joyfully, hugging and kissing each other on cheeks, Gus attempted to make his way to the foyer. As he fought his way through the crowd, some wanted to shake his hand. Others embraced him, and upon finding out that it was his first visit, welcomed him. He was touched by their warmth and congeniality and smiled accommodatingly, but kept moving towards the exit, where he spoke with the head preacher.

Bishop Fredericks shook Gus' hand heartily and asked an assistant to take his name and contact details. Then he had a conversation with Gus, interspersed with greetings to other departing brethren. He told Gus that he discerned that he needed to get closer to God and that as he did so, he would see the glory of God in setting him free from the bondage he was presently under. He advised Gus that today was the beginning, but that he had a fight on his hands to become totally free. The Bishop kept repeating that there was a certain person who was at the root of his problems but that he needed only to trust God to be set free. Gus did not ask any questions of the Bishop, although many arose in his mind. Instead, he just listened, taking in all that was said, being particularly intrigued by the mention of a "certain person" - but who? He took the card handed to him by Bishop Fredericks who asked him to call and book and appointment to see him.

When Bishop Fredericks finished speaking with him, Gus made his way out to where he had parked his car. He sat in the car watching the people milling around, greeting one another, walking together, entering cars and driving away - he waited patiently for his father but found enjoyment in the experience. After 15 minutes or so, there was a slight tap on the passenger side window. He leant over and looked up to see Cyrus' smiling face.

Getting out of the car Gus hurried to the passenger side to

help his father into his seat. When he had done so he closed the door and was walking back to the driver's side when he suddenly stopped – he thought he saw someone he knew. As he turned his head back to take a second look, she also turned to face toward him causing Gus' breathing to quicken and his heart to skip a beat.

"Hello there," Gus said involuntarily, almost biting his tongue, as he stared into the beautiful eyes of Cherie Johnson.

"Hello ….. Gus", Cherie said hesitantly after getting over the shock of seeing the man that had dominated her thoughts since their first meeting months earlier. They stared at each other for a beat.

"Hello Sister Cherie", Cyrus said smiling, having wound down the car window to enable him to converse.

"Hello Brother Cyrus", Cherie replied, smiling back. Just then she was approached by a very expensively attired heavy set lady who spoke authoritatively.

"Sister Cherie, I need to talk to you – it's very important", she interjected.

"God bless you Sister Marriott", Cyrus greeted the intruder with a smile. "Hello Brother Cyrus", Sister Marriott replied and smiled back at him absentmindedly obviously preoccupied, before whisking Cherie away without allowing her the chance to say goodbye.

As Gus drove Cyrus home, the elder gentleman tried to broach the subject of Cherie and how they were acquainted but Gus quickly changed the subject. He felt somewhat affronted by Cherie's offhand and cursory greeting, conveniently forgetting that he had not kept his promise made on their first meeting, that he would call her. But he could not deny the chemistry between them. Then a feeling of happiness spread through him as he appreciated that she was obviously a member of the church – he would get to know her better when the time was right.

After dropping Cyrus off Gus made his way over to Marshie's for a prearranged visit. He looked forward to spending the afternoon and evening enjoying a well prepared meal with a glass of fine wine and the good company of Marshie and Emma.

"***** You're early - make yourself at home, mate", Marshie

266

said having prefixed the sentence with a mild swear word as he was accustomed to doing. As he spoke he chuckled, oblivious of the fact that he had ruffled Gus's feathers by reminding him of his reputation for tardiness.

They later enjoyed a beautiful roast dinner and then the two sat chatting, Emma having excused herself to take a 'phone call in the bedroom. Marshie talked about Emma mostly and Gus, not wishing to keep lying about Cherie talked about his work at the youth club. When Marshie asked about Cherie Gus lied that it had not worked out - that they had decided to split up - at least for the time being. But instead of letting him off the hook, Marshie pushed him to find out why they had split – wanting to console his friend. Gus made out that he was pained by the split and didn't want to talk about it and Marshie reluctantly backed off, merely consoling him by commenting that he didn't need to worry as there were plenty more fish in the sea.

"Emma has got this lovely friend – Lacey her name is. You too would get on really well", Marshie suggested and continued, "Maybe we could get together as a foursome next week – we could go to the pictures or something", he said gleefully. Gus smiled but declined, "No, I'm not really ready for anything like that at the moment, Marshie", he said convincingly.

"Oh, I understand – you need some time", Marshie said, causing Gus to sigh with relief as he repented in his heart for the lies he had just fabricated.

Now that he had decided to commit his life to God, Gus had no intention of getting fixed up with anyone for a quick fling. He at least knew that sex outside of marriage was forbidden by God and the church. He would wait for the right person, and as his thoughts drifted back to Cherie, he conceded that it was probably her. He intended to be a devout Christian, in which case she would be exactly what he was looking for in a wife. He only hoped that she would still be available when he had sorted himself out. He would call her but there was no way he was going to do so until he had sorted out his mess of a life. And with that thought Gus promised himself to employ every effort in order to resolve the muddle in which he found himself. For one he would pray more –

and with God on his side he would not be fighting alone.

At 9 pm Gus rose to leave. "Come and say goodbye to Gussy" Marshie called out to Emma who had spent much of the afternoon and evening on the telephone, and ending her girl talk, she dutifully obliged as Marshie disappeared into the bedroom and returned wearing his jacket. "I'm just going to walk outside with Gussy, darling," he said, kissing Emma on the cheek. When they reached the car, Marshie asked Gus to give him a lift to the nearby shop.

On the way to the shop, Marshie asked Gus to stop at a cash point. When he returned to the car Gus enquired, "So, where can I drop you then?"

"Look Gus, I know you must still be going through some real financial challenges at the moment," Marshie paused, taking a deep breath before continuing. "You have never before come to visit me without bringing a bottle of wine or a CD or some other gift", as he spoke he searched his friend's face for eye contact, then without saying anything further Marshie handed a wad of notes to Gus, "Here is £300 to repay you in part for all that money you gave to me when I was down and out," Marshie said.

"I don't remember giving you any money - and you were never down and out," Gus replied laughing uncomfortably.

"You may not remember Gussy, but I remember, you lent me hundreds, and if you take living accommodation into consideration, thousands of pounds when I didn't have any money – oh and I was too down and out". "I was a sad down and out no hoper – giving up – giving in, but you remained my friend – you refused to give up on me when even most of my other friends and family did". "You may not realize what you did for me, Gussy, but you saved my life man," Marshie said touchingly. "Please take this, I can afford it now, I just got a huge contract and the business is picking up fast". "I've got more to give you but this is all I can draw out right now". "If you refuse to take it you will hurt me deeply – I love you man, like a brother – it's real man," Marshie began to squirm uncomfortably as he spoke words of endearment uncharacteristically.

After a small pause, Gus took the money gratefully, "Thank you my brother," he said, simply, a single tear welling up in the corner of one eye.

"No problem," Marshie said, looking pleased with himself. Then he directed Gus to drop him off at a nearby shop. Before exiting the car, he said goodbye to Gus.

"I want to walk it home – I've been stuck indoors all weekend and need to walk off millions of calories that my lovely missus has been feeding me," Marshie said smiling contentedly.

So Gus got out of the car to say goodbye and they exchanged a manly embrace. Then Gus headed towards Islington with a renewed determination to face his problems head on – no more hiding away. He would start by sleeping at the house in town tonight and facing whatever red letters arrived in the morning.

Upon arriving home Gus crashed on the sofa spread-eagled. He did not switch on the TV or any music, but savoured the peacefulness that he felt within himself. Then he contemplated what had taken place over the past few hours - how he had attended church and invited the Lord Jesus into his heart. He thought about the significance of his giving his last £30 and Marshie giving him £300 – was that the hundredfold blessing of which the pastor had spoken? Well a blessing it certainly was, because at least he now knew where his next meal was coming from. Gus smiled to himself - was this God's provision or simply coincidental? "Well, whatever it was I'm just thankful," Gus smiled as he verbalised his thoughts.

In addition to his new-found peace, he felt untold joy bubbling up inside – partly because of the act of kindness that Marshie had demonstrated, but also since making his commitment at church to Jesus Christ. Waves of peace and joy kept washing over him – he was caught up in a rapture of untold estacy. He felt like a new person – was this the practical effect of being born again? He certainly felt as though his spirit had been reborn, or washed clean – he felt brand new. And he knew that he must now be experiencing what Cyrus and Martin felt everyday.

On retiring to bed, Gus read over the scripture upon which the pastor had based his sermon, meditating on the words as he drifted to asleep. He slept well all night, awaking next morning revived and refreshed.

Monday 11 September dawned with renewed peace, joy and hope. Gus marvelled that he had not experienced any nightmares during the night and noted the date specifically, marking it as the turning point in his life – by faith. He knelt down and said "thank you Lord for allowing me to sleep restfully". Then for the first time ever, he said "halleluiah", the word felt odd being uttered from his lips and sounded strange and foreign to his ears. He repeated it to himself, listening to his own voice as though someone else were speaking. "Hallelulah – he knew what the word meant, and kept on repeating it as he consciously gave God the highest praise.

There was a sudden and urgent need within him to learn more about the things of God so Gus decided that he would speak to Cyrus first and then Bishop Fredericks - he couldn't wait to start learning. He also wanted to tell someone about the joy he was feeling or felt he might burst. So, although it was only 8.30 am, he reached for the 'phone, and made arrangements with Cyrus to pay him a visit later in the day.

As Gus vigorously made his way to the bathroom he thought of all that was on the agenda for the day. He felt re-energized by a good night's sleep and believed that now that God was in control all would be well. First on the day's schedule was a meeting with his Bank Manager. After that he had to go and see the property management agents who handled the lettings of his properties to discuss with them further strategies for attracting tenants. He was losing close to £30,000 a week and it would make more sense for him to collect half of that than nothing at all. At least he would be able to pay some of the outstanding mortgages on the properties, if nothing else. If he wasn't able to pay the mortgages on 8 of his properties they would be repossessed soon, and Gus wanted to avoid that. As he busied himself showering, he heard a still small voice speak in his spirit, "I will restore all - fear not - trust Me - be obedient," and Gus knew he had heard the voice of God yet again. Suddenly he was no longer concerned about losing rents and decided that he would not reduce the asking rents but would trust God to provide tenants who would pay fair market rents.

The Bank Manager, refused to see Gus when he arrived over 40 minutes late. Gus pleaded with the receptionist, explaining that he really needed to see Mr Marshall apologising for his tardiness and much to his surprise she agreed to appeal on his behalf. He was glad she had not enquired as to his reason as he would have had a job justifying having run out of petrol making it necessary for him to walk the last mile to the bank. After 10 minutes she returned to say that the Bank Manager would see him briefly. Mr Marshall, who for the past three months had refused to assist Gus in any way, was congenial and agreed to increase his credit facility by £20,000, which meant that Gus could pay some of his pressingly urgent debts, so that at the eight impending possession Court hearings his properties would not be taken away.

As he drove to Cyrus' home, Gus praised God with hallelujahs for the significant breakthrough he had encountered today. He thanked God for allowing the Bank Manager to see him despite his fault in arriving late and promised himself as he had done so many times before, that he would never be late for anything again. He reasoned within himself that he had driven without enough petrol only because he was short of cash the day before. But he failed to make himself feel any better. So he tried to dismiss the point and concentrated instead on God's manifested love.

As always, Cyrus was glad for his son's company. He could not get around as he used to due to the mobility problems with his right knee. So he welcomed any visitor with added verve.

The two men spent the afternoon talking about God and reading various scriptures. Gus eagerly drank in all he was learning from Cyrus and Cyrus was jubilant as he expounded the Word to his son. He was tempted to broach the subject of Cherie Johnson yet again but refrained from doing so, instead he decided he would pray about it, believing that God was working out all things for good. They parted at 9.30 pm, having arranged that Gus would collect Cyrus on Thursday morning in order to drive him for his hospital appointment.

CHAPTER 15

Changing Gears

Gus pulled up in front of Cyrus' home half an hour earlier than he was scheduled to arrive - it was Thursday 14 September and he had come to collect his father to take him to his hospital appointment. Since his commitment to Christ he was filled with a joy that overflowed in his heart which made him hungry to live as full a life as possible.

As soon as Gus arrived Cyrus came hobbling out of the door. As was usual for him he had been ready half an hour in advance. Gus hurried to aid his father, and Cyrus, seeing him approach, smiled brightly through his pain. He was dressed to match his smile in a bright orange shirt and royal blue tie with a light grey overcoat. Gus contemplated the colour-code of his dad's attire and concluded that although they were an odd combination they did in fact go together. He also concluded that Cyrus was a brave man to even attempt wearing that colour-code in the first place, but he was definitely off the hook this time as it had worked for him. "Like the shirt," Gus said pointedly.

"Yeah, nice and lively," Cyrus replied chuckling.

They loaded into Gus' car and set off, Cyrus joyfully humming and Gus silently optimistic that all would work out for his good.

****

Cherie sat in the waiting area of the hospital, willing herself to be patient. She had been waiting to see her mother for more than four hours. Jean had just undergone the second operation in less than two weeks, to repair the fractures and breakages to her collar bone, foot and ribs and had only just come round. The doctor had just informed them that they could see her and Cherie allowed Lester to go in and see his wife alone first – she appreciated that married people needed time alone, whether they were ill or not. As she waited Cherie reflected on how she had found strength in prayer throughout the ordeal of her mother's illness. While reflecting she arose involuntarily and headed toward the ladies' room where she could pray and praise more openly than in the waiting room. As she walked she reflected.

Having ascertained that Donald Syrenson, the man who was almost certainly her father, was in another intensive care department of the same hospital, Cherie had paid him an initial visit during the first week of her mother's admission. He was in a coma and bandaged from head to toe. The nurses advised that Mr Syrenson had suffered third degree burns to parts of his body. She went back to see him several times after that, and though his condition improved, his mental state was such that he did not seem to understand what was taking place around him. His face was unrecognizable – Cherie was greatly saddened by his condition. She learned from the nurses that she was his only visitor which also caused her anguish. She wondered why Tricia did not visit her father and it occurred to her that she should perhaps pay her a visit to find out if she was alright. However, she had not done so because she did not know how Tricia might react to a visit from her. And anyway she had enough on her plate, with the worry about her mother. Cherie did not divulge to the medical staff her suspicions that Donald Syrenson was her father and they viewed her only as a good Samaritan.

But one day last week when Cherie went to visit Mr Syrenson she was informed that he had been moved to another hospital. His primary care nurse was not on duty at the time and she had left a message asking that she contact her to let her know where Mr Syrenson had been transferred to.

Due to the fact that Jean had not yet recovered from her injuries, Cherie did not broach the subject of her fatherhood with her mother, not wishing to distress her. Nothing was as important to Cherie as her mother's health and well being and she decided that finding out for a fact whether Donald Syrenson was her father would have to wait.

****

After parking his car Gus helped Cyrus out and into the common waiting area of the hospital of of where the physiotherapy clinic was situated. They sat together talking easily as they waited for

Cyrus' name to be called out.

"Excuse me, I really must go to the gents", Gus said. He had being putting off doing so before leaving home and now urgently made his way to the WC. As he entered and the door closed behind him, Cherie exited the ladies room - they narrowly missed bumping into each other. She proceeded to walk back to the waiting area, where she was surprised to see one of her church brothers. "Hello Brother Cyrus, how are you – I hope you are well?" Cherie said quizzically, hoping that Brother Cyrus was not ill - he was one of her favourite people.

"Yes, I'm fine except for a pain in my right knee – I don't know what is causing it, so I am here to get some physiotherapy, you know", Cyrus said, putting Cherie's mind relatively at ease.

"I heard about your mother's accident - how is she doing?" Cyrus asked, changing focus.

"Oh, that's why I'm here you know, she has just had another operation". "She had a lot of fractures and broken bones". "I'm just waiting to see her now," Cherie replied as she observed Lester coming towards her.

"Yes - I'm just waiting for my son, you know the one you saw me with at church on Sunday - he just popped round the corner – he'll be back soon," Cyrus said.

Cherie's heart leapt as she realized that Gus had accompanied his father, "Ooh, oh, that's nice ..." she stuttered.

Just then Lester cut in, "I've been looking for you dear, you can go in and see you mother now," Lester said, and then realizing he was interrupting her conversation he apologized.

"That's okay," Cyrus replied

"This is Brother Cyrus, one of my church brothers – Brother Cyrus this is my dad Lester ...," Cherie said.

Lester and Cyrus shook hands as Cherie walked away, "I'll see you later, Brother Cyrus, if you're still here when I come out," she said as she walked off.

"I would come to pay your mother a visit, to pray with you, if I wasn't waiting to be seen myself - and I'm waiting for my son and he would wonder where I've gone". "But never mind maybe another time" Cyrus said waving after her.

When Gus returned to the waiting area, Cyrus introduced him to Lester, who had taken a seat next to him. Gus shook Lester's hand and stood by, next to the two seated older gentlemen. Cyrus continued to converse with Lester, "Yes, Sister Cherie is a lovely young lady – the very best – you must be very proud to be her father," Cyrus said as Lester grinned proudly.

"Yes, yes, she is wonderful – my one and only lovely daughter. She is a pretty young lady and a beautiful person, just like her mother," Lester complimented.

The two men smiled and warmed to each other, and as Gus listened his ears pricked at the mention of the name "Cherie". *"They must be talking about my Cherie",* he thought and then catching himself he scolded within him – how could he think of her as "his Cherie". But then the thought returned – "my Cherie", and lingered tantalizingly in his mind, as Gus pictured Cherie's beautiful face and smiled.

Shaking his head, Gus returned to normality and made himself useful by going over to the receptionist to ask how much longer they would have to wait. "I'm afraid we're running a little late this morning due to staff shortages - Mr Cyrus will have to wait for at least 45 minutes before he is seen – I'm very sorry," was the reply, which mattered not in the least to Gus – he had set aside the whole day to accompany his father to his hospital appointment and was not worried about the time. Returning to Cyrus he relayed the information to him. "Oh, that means I can go and pray with Sister Cherie then," Cyrus said rising from his seat immediately.

Lester arose also, "Yes, I'll take you along," he volunteered.

Following behind Lester, Cyrus gestured to Gus, "Are you coming, son", but Gus declined, "no, I'll wait for you here", he was not yet ready for any close encounter with Cherie Johnson.

"Okay, I'll be back very soon, son, Cyrus said shuffling as quickly as he could.

"Yeah, - Ok, I'll just step outside to make a telephone call," Gus replied.

Lester and Cyrus approached the private ward where Jean was recovering from her operation and Lester knocked on the window before proceeding to enter without waiting to be asked in. Cyrus followed. "Come in Brother Cyrus - you came after all," Cherie said in a welcoming whisper, not wishing to wake her mother who was still groggy from the anaesthetic.

"Yes," Cyrus said as he approached the bedside. He stared at the woman lying down and noted that she must have been in a terrible state following the accident as he now observed her after almost two weeks and she looked awful. He couldn't tell if her face was familiar due to the extensive scarring.

Cherie stretched out both hands – one to Cyrus and the other to Lester. "Let us make a circle of prayer for mother," she said.

"Yes, that is a good idea," Cyrus said, "What is your mother's name Cherie," he asked".

"Jean" she replied.

"Jean …. Jean", he repeated.

After saying a brief prayer, Cyrus made his excuses and left hurriedly, not wishing to miss his appointment. He noticed from the corner of his eye the strange looks exchanged between Cherie and her father as he hobbled quickly out of the ward. Out of breath, the colour had drained noticeably from his face when he returned to the waiting room and Gus, who was back from making his phone call, showed concern, "Are you okay dad?", he enquired.

"Yes, I'm fine," Cyrus replied..

After a few minutes Cherie returned to the waiting area. As she turned the corner, she spotted Cyrus and went over to him to say a proper goodbye – she sat down beside the older gentleman. Gus stood close by but Cherie did not become aware of his presence immediately.

"Brother Cyrus, are you okay - you rushed off," Cherie questioned.

"Yes, I'm alright - I didn't want to miss them calling my name, that's all", Cyrus said. Cherie nodded her head and smiled.

Gus looked on, trying to decide how to handle the situation. *"So it is the same Cherie after all"*, he thought. "Hello Cherie," he said, his voice betraying a slight tremor.

The sound of Gus' voice startled Cherie and her head jerked upwards suddenly, her eyes meeting his. "Oh Gus – ho… how are you?" she stuttered.

Gus nodded his head, "I'm fine, and you?" he said cordially.

"Yeah, I'm fine … yeah," then she was lost for words.

The receptionist called out Cyrus' name, breaking into the awkward silence. Gus moved to assist him but Cyrus shrugged him off. "Its okay son, I can manage," he said giving Gus' hand a firm push away. Gus felt a little embarrassed by his father's rebuff and the humiliation added to his feeling of awkwardness. He stood rooted to the spot, wishing that the ground would swallow him up as Cyrus hobbled off independently. Cherie stood up as Cyrus walked away.

Cyrus now out of the way, the two stood side by side, palms sweating, cheeks burning, knees shaking, adrenalin pumping nervous energy through their veins.

It was Gus that spoke first, "So, how come you're at the hospital?" But, as soon as he had spoken he wished he hadn't said what he had. After all it was none of his business what she was doing at the hospital. Why was he so stupid anyway, fancy asking her what she was doing at the hospital, as if he had any right to know what she was doing there. Then he added quickly, "Sorry I didn't 'phone you – I've meant to but, you know, with one thing and another cropping up, I have not been able to find the time to …. you know what I mean," Gus said, hating himself even more than before. *"Of course she doesn't understand. You haven't called her for more than four months not four days – you moran",* Gus thought.

Cherie did not say anything. Even though she was feeling nervous, she was in full control, allowing Gus to do all the talking deliberately – he would have to have a good reason for not calling her and she wanted to hear it, after all, he had promised to call her nearly five months ago. *"I'm still waiting to hear your plausible explanation,"* Cherie's expression said. She could feel herself becoming mildly angry but smiled sweetly as she listened to Gus dig himself into a huge chasm.

Realising he was rambling foolishly Gus took a deep breath and tried to think before speaking again. Cherie's pressing curiosity rescued him – "So Cyrus is your father – what a small world". "We have attended the same church, for more than 5 years you know," she said.

Gus breathed relatively normally again – thank God a safe subject to talk about. "I attended church for the first time when I saw you there last Sunday, but I will be attending a lot more often in future", he stressed pointedly, seeking to impress Cherie. But the point that he was seeking to make was missed by Cherie as she came under bombardment from all kinds of emotions at his nearness. Having been in fervent prayer about Gus and received a revelation that he was to figure in some way in her future, she was not fully aware of what God's plan was for her and Gus. As he had chosen not to contact her since their last meeting, he had clearly demonstrated a disinterest in her romantically. But if that was the case why then was he looking at her like he was now? Cherie was confused. *"Is he playing with me?"* She mused, a perplexed expression clouding her countenance.

Once again an uncomfortable silence fell over the pair of them as they both applied reins to their true emotions – the silence was soon broken when Curtis walked in.

Curtis had been a tower of strength to Cherie since her mother's tragic accident, encouraging her to talk, to eat healthily even when she did not feel like it, and generally being a true friend to her. And she was glad that the message that they were just friends seemed to be getting through to him at long last.

Spotting Cherie talking to the taller and better looking man Curtis immediately became jealous - he walked over possessively. "Hello darling," he said deliberately planting a kiss on her mouth. Cherie immediately stepped backwards, shocked and embarrassed, as she pulled away. "Curtis this is Gus – Gus this is Curtis, an old friend of mine," Cherie said avoiding Gus' stare and hoping that he had picked up the accent on "friend". Gus smiled warmly and proffered his right hand to Curtis who ignored it. Curtis proceeded to sidle up to Cherie, placing his arm around her waist, as she visibly squirmed to be released from his grasp. Gus observed the parody, drawing the conclusion that there must be something between the two or Curtis would not behave so possessively towards Cherie, and although he was gravely disappointed by this new development, he kept up a front of insouciance.

Curtis cut Gus a sideways glance – he had seen him before – at church on Sunday – he was certain of it. He wondered, but did not ask what Gus was doing at the hospital, but decided it was best to get Cherie away from him as quickly as possible.

"You ready, darling?" Curtis asked, annoying Cherie.

She felt that she had no choice but to say that she was. "I'd better go," Cherie said to Gus then continued "Curtis has kindly come to pick me up and drop me off at work since he figured I would be too tired and stressed to drive," she continued, trying to explain to Gus the reason for Curtis' presence.

Curtis stood by fuming. *"How dare she explain me away to this strange man,"* he thought. It seemed obvious to Curtis that Cherie had some feelings for this man – Gus or whatever his name was. He could tell by the way she looked at him. Oh how he wished she would look at him in that way, but try as he might, he had never been able to influence Cherie to take the least bit of romantic interest in him. But he was not about to give up trying. Cherie was a fine woman, and he would stop at nothing to win her over – even emotional blackmail – he was prepared to use any means necessary. Curtis' mind began to tick over as he contemplated his next move - then it dawned on him that the best way to beat your enemy was to befriend him. So Curtis changed tack.

"I know where I've seen you before – at church on Sunday," Curtis reached out his hand to Gus who shook it, a quizzical look on his face. "You must come along to the men's night next Tuesday – it will be fun," Curtis continued.

Cherie looked on, amazed by the apparent transformation in Curtis' attitude.

"I can meet up with you and we can go along together – if you like," Curtis said expectantly. Gus did not speak, silently trying to analyze the reason for the sudden change in Curtis' attitude towards him.

"We usually watch a movie and then we just chill and fellowship – man to man". "We always have some really meaningful discussions from the male perspective – you'll enjoy it - I can guarantee it," Curtis encouraged.

"Oh - why not?" Gus said finally smiling. He had nothing to lose - after all it wasn't as though he had any plans for next Tuesday evening anyway. "I'll come with Cyrus," he said not wishing to get too pally with Curtis until he could properly figure him out – decide what he was really about.

"Okay, I'll see you there," Curtis said as he grabbed hold of Cherie's hand possessively and led her towards the exit before she could react.

Gus watched reflectively as they walked away and Cherie appeared to pull her hand away from Curtis' grasp. He was still watching them as they faded into the distance.

CHAPTER 16

Revelation

His mind pre-occupied with a multitude of questions Cyrus hardly spoke to Gus on the journey home from the hospital. Gus too was disinclined to maintain conversation, as his mind was also pre-occupied with a multitude of issues. And unbeknown each to the other there was a common object of contemplation – Cherie Johnson.

When Gus dropped Cyrus off at home, he did not stop, needing some time to hisself. They hurriedly finalized arrangements to meet the following day – Youth Club day. They also discussed briefly church on Sunday and the men's evening the following Tuesday, and then Gus headed home.

****

Gus drove home with thoughts of Cherie for company. He just could not shake them off, so he dreamed of the day when he would make her his wife, being careful to remind himself that he was only dreaming.

The following Tuesday evening 19 September at the men's evening Curtis made certain that he sat next to Gus and Martin (Cyrus cancelled at the last minute). He wanted to find out as much as possible about Gus – he needed the information as it might come in handy some day. Gus was cautious. He could see right through Curtis' motives. He found Curtis' behaviour quite humorous to say the least, except that he was not in the right frame of mind to appreciate jokes. Having given further thought to the situation, Gus concluded that Curtis obviously viewed him as a threat for Cherie's affections and was overly stressing or insinuating that there was something intimate between them, because there most probably was not. He believed Cherie that they were just friends – nothing more. And Gus decided that any romantic connection between Curtis and Cherie was strictly a figment of Curtis' imagination. But Gus would not – allow any thought of

Cherie or jealousy of Curtis to dominate his mind and so he dismissed them. He was in no position to embark on any relationship with Cherie Johnson, even suggesting that she wanted a relationship with him. His life was in far too much chaos – he could not – would not even entertain the thought of inviting that beautiful person to share in his recent misfortunes. *"Perhaps if I sort myself out a little,"* Gus thought, then arrested his thoughts just in time before they completely ran away with him. Any such ideas could not be seriously entertained since at present it looked as though it would take several years to get back on his feet again.

****

The shock close encounter with his old acquaintant had left Cyrus' mind in turmoil. And he was dumbstruck to say the least by the realization that the beautiful young lady he had known for over 5 years as Cherie Johnson was almost certainly his own daughter. The daughter he had longed to find - had searched for since his return to London in 1987. But the truth suddenly dawned on Cyrus that he had given up looking for his daughter many years ago.

Upon returning to London, Cyrus had gone back to the old neighbourhood where Jean had lived with her parents, but was surprised to find that things had changed drastically in the few years of his absence. Jean, her parents and his Princess had moved away and enquiries made of the members of Mount Zion Miracle Pentecostal Church had proved virtually fruitless. He had learned that the family moved to Brighton soon after he left for America, but no one was able to provide a forwarding address for them. Cyrus had practically begged Eve to let him have their number but she had refused stating that he had done enough damage. She had promised to pass his number to Jean though but he had never received any contact from Jean, despite the fact that he kept the same number to this day.

Thereafter, Cyrus had travelled to Brighton on numerous occasions, attending many churches and community functions in the hope of bumping into one or other member of the family, knowing that the Johnsons were Christian people who would definitely attend a church. For many months Cyrus undertook this futile exercise, often staying in hotels or guesthouses for several days at a time and attending a variety of churches, hoping that he would one day discover the worship home of the Johnson family, but he had never succeeded in locating the right congregation.

The idea of making further enquiries, perhaps instructing a specialist firm to find his daughter had occurred to him, but at first such ambitious plans were stymied by financial constraints, and later Cyrus kept putting off doing so for one good reason or another. And before he knew it, the years had flown by and it had dawned on him that Cherie would be a teenager by then, and fear that she would want nothing to do with him presented itself as an insurmountable obstacle. Now as he contemplated his position, he had to accept that although he had tried very hard to find his daughter, he could have done far more. How would he explain to her his failure to leave no stone unturned in his quest to locate her? Any answers that he might put forward seemed inadequate to his own mind, and would surely be viewed as grossly insufficient by Cherie. And for the first time Cyrus saw the mountains that for many years had presented themselves as impossible to climb, as flimsy molehills that could easily have been stepped over. And he reasoned that Cherie would never understand the fear of rejection that had gripped him into a state of inertia leading to his giving up actively searching for her. To advance such an excuse would surely strip him bare in her eyes as a coward, a weakling or as simply an uncaring and truly selfish deadbeat – a monster and no less.

Inside his bedroom, Cyrus stared into the mirror, looked himself in the eye and hated his reflection – a stupid, insensible person, disguised as a fine gentleman and good citizen stared back at him causing him to feel nauseous. He loathed his kind eyes, and the benevolent contours of his face which as he gazed were revealed to be in truth those of a self-absorbed fool, a coward of a man who had allowed pride to inhibit his search for his dear innocent Princess because of an irrational fear of being insulted or rejected.

For days Cyrus agonised about the situation, seeking self forgiveness. Yet he could not find it – for he considered he had behaved unforgivably. Suddenly it dawned on him that now that he had found his Princess, it would be an even bigger mistake to go on pretending that he had not done so. And an overwhelming urge to get to know his daughter, a force stronger than pride, led him to make the decision that he would try as much as he possibly could to put right the wrongs of his past. Should Cherie reject him, even if she spat upon him, he would just have to bear it – he would beg her to forgive him even in the face of such harsh rejection. He would not give up - he would do all within his power to win her over – if not her love, then at least her acknowledgment that he is her father. Any small part of her life that she might care to share with him would be gratefully accepted and cherished. It may be late in the day, but he intended to spend the rest of his life giving her as much love as she would allow him to.

Now that he had reached his decision, Cyrus set about deciding the best way forward. He knew that the first step to take was to seek for Jean's forgiveness. He would try and iron out his differences with her before approaching Cherie. So Cyrus decided he would visit Jean in the hospital when she was feeling better. He would allow a week or so to elapse before paying her a visit. He did not wish to cause her too much stress and hoped that the unavoidable shock would not prove too strenuous for her. The thought that he might cause trauma to Jean made Cyrus concerned and he wondered whether he should just forget the whole idea. The thought occurred to him that he could just approach Cherie and reveal to her who he was, but that idea was swiftly dismissed - he had to go and see Jean - it was simply the right thing to do.

Conveniently Cyrus had to attend the hospital for a follow-up appointment on Tuesday 26 September 2010, and he decided to go and see Jean just before his own appointment, so that if he were to run into anyone – say Cherie or Lester – he would have a good excuse for being at the hospital. Having ascertained when the morning visiting hours were, Cyrus was relieved to learn that they began an hour and a half before his appointment.

The days passed slowly and uneasily till Tuesday rolled around. Cyrus was up super early, and dressed an hour before he needed to leave for the hospital. He sat at the dining table, stirring a huge cup of tea while waiting for his eggs to hard boil. As he stirred his tea, he reflected on the events of the previous Sunday when he had seen Cherie at church.

He had skilfully averted direct eye contact with her, admiring her from a distance, amazed at how truly beautiful she was. He already knew what a wonderful young lady she had grown into. Now he studied her bone structure; her height; her complexion and hair; her eyes, as a dedicated fan might do. He also studied her mannerisms – noting the similarities with his own. He stared at Cherie so much on Sunday that a few brethren were prompted to give him some decidedly strange glances whereupon he had reluctantly toned down his inquisition.

After church Sister Monica Clary, a widow who had been attending the church for over two years had offered Cyrus a lift home which he had gratefully accepted. Tall dark and beautiful, Sister Clary still commanded the attention of a woman half her age. Naturally charismatic, she was attractive to both sexes - as a friend. Cyrus found her to be kind and thoughtful and easy to talk to but was blissfully unaware of her deep interest in becoming more than just his friend. When they arrived at his home, they sat in the car talking for a while, mostly about the service and the Word. But unable to resist doing so, Cyrus had brought up the subject of "how lovely Sister Cherie Johnson had looked in church", a comment that Sister Clarey appeared not to appreciate, because unless Cyrus' imagination was playing tricks on him, she had cut their conversation short and promptly left. And as Sister Clary drove away Cyrus breathed a sigh of relief because he had almost divulged to her his true interest in Cherie and the time was not yet right - he needed to talk to Jean first.

Later on Sunday Cyrus' mind had been bombarded with a question which popped into his mind without warning, reverberating over and over. What sort of father had he been? And suddenly the feelings of pride which he had felt on seeing Cherie in church that morning were replaced by feelings of shame, and a depressive cloud of guilt fell over him. He slumped into his favourite seat – a large leather recliner, and there he sat for an indeterminate length of time, having no inclination or appetite to eat the pre-readied sumptuous Sunday meal. Instead he sat staring at the ceiling and walls and wallowing in regret until darkness fell. Later he went to bed hungry as though to punish himself. Loneliness and depression had embraced him and he had slept fitfully.

And now as Cyrus sat eating his boiled eggs he contemplated Sister Clarey's response to his mention of Cherie as they had conversed on Sunday. "Well soon everyone will have to know that Sister Johnson is my daughter – very soon," he said aloud. Having surmounted the depression and guilt, although he still felt undeserving Cyrus felt proud again that he was the father of such an exquisite human being and couldn't wait to tell everyone. He was ready to face anything to perfect the blessing that God had given him, to become reconciled with his long-lost daughter, be it rejection or degradation. He deserved whatever he had coming to him – the only thing he did not deserve was Cherie's love but he was resolute that he would spend the rest of his life working as hard as he could to earn it.

The taxi collected Cyrus at 8.30 am sharp and as they drove through the rush hour traffic he revised what he would say to Jean over and over in his mind, trying to commit it to memory. He had the urge to recite parts of the speech that he had prepared aloud, but resisted, not wishing the driver to think him mad.

Arriving at the hospital at 9.15 am, as anticipated, Cyrus was almost 2 hours early for his appointment at 11.00 am. As he entered the main entrance of the hospital he felt as though his heart would burst open as it pounded loudly within his chest. All attempts to breathe normally were failing and as he approached the room where he had seen Jean the week before his heartbeat began to gallop. Cyrus knocked lightly at the door and was asked to "Come in". But he was perturbed to note, on entering the room, that the person in the bed was not Jean but an elderly white woman. Somewhat shaken by the anticlimax Cyrus apologized and left swiftly. He went in search of a nurse who informed that Jean had been moved to Harwich Ward, and pointed him in the right direction.

Harwich Ward was a recovery ward not far away and soon Cyrus stood at its entrance, peering through the glass panel of the door. Visiting time had not yet begun as it was just before 9.30 am and there did not appear to be any visitors present in the ward. Cyrus could not see Jean's bed from outside the door, and he was hoping against hope that she was alone. He lingered for a full minute by the door before making his next move. Taking a deep breath in, he opened the door and walked into the ward. As he did so he was approached by a ward nurse, "Can I help you sir, have you come to visit someone?" the nurse enquired. Cyrus stood rooted to the spot. He opened his mouth to reply but stuttered uncontrollably, "Yyyyess, I aa aa came to see.....", as he spoke Cyrus looked around him to the bed on the left that was hidden from view outside the door. The bed was occupied by a very small Asian woman, who nestled down in the sheets, almost out of sight. "I aa aa came to see Jean, Jean Johnson," Cyrus said, suddenly realizing that Jean's surname must have changed.

"We don't have anyone in this ward by that name," replied the nurse. "But we do have a Jean Jones," the nurse continued, and she gestured to the bed on the right hand side of the door.

Cyrus turned to look at the woman in the bed, and as he did so he recognized a familiar sound, "Tyrone," Jean said questioningly. "Is that you, Tyrone?" Cyrus was stunned by the sound of Jean's voice, and even more taken aback by the way she addressed him. No-one had called him that for years. Not many people knew him by his real middle Christian name, only his family and oldest friends. But even those who knew him by the name of "Tyrone" had become accustomed to calling him by the name Cyrus – a phonetic short form version of his surname, Syrenson.

As Cyrus walked towards Jean's bed and then stood next to it, he felt the years roll back. Jean stared him straight in the eye, as lowered his eyes to avoid her direct gaze. He felt as though she was stripping his soul bare with her eyes, searching deep into his inner self – looking at a person she had never truly known before. Cyrus mused that he also had not known himself. He knew that he could not begin to apologise to Jean for the hurt and pain he had caused her all those years ago. But he would have to try. He would reassure her that he had made a terrible mistake – an error that he would never have made had he known himself – one for which he himself had paid dearly. And perhaps it would soothe her somewhat if he made her aware of just how much he had been compensated for his wrongs.

Shuffling uncomfortably Cyrus stuttered, "H...h..hello J.. jean". He then tried to launch into his rehearsed spiel, but his memory abandoned him, and he was left with no script. Silently he pleaded for God's mercy, asking for guidance, and the answer came that he should speak from his heart.

And so Cyrus bared his soul to Jean, in hushed tones to avoid eavesdropping, apologizing wholeheartedly to her for the way he had treated her – had cast aside her love – her pure and beautiful love for him. He apologised for breaking up their family and frustrating her hopes of marriage to him. Unashamedly he recounted to her details of his ill-fated first marriage to Evangeline and her unfaithfulness with his own brother to whom she remained married to this day. He stressed that if it was any consolation Evangeline had turned out to be far less of a woman than she was. He confessed that he had wanted to come back to Jean then, but that he had been too ashamed to do so. He went on to tell of his search for happiness in the arms of his second wife, a woman he never loved, but that she too had eaten the fruit of infidelity. Candidly, Cyrus related to Jean his realisation that he needed her back then, but that it was too late by 1987 when he came to his senses and returned to London only to find that they had moved away.

Jean listened and felt compassion towards this man that she had once loved so deeply and had later loathed bitterly for so many years. Then she too felt ashamed. And the remainder of pent-up anger and vengefulness seeped out of her soul. She responded in equally hushed tones, realizing that the man standing before her was a broken soul, one who needed her unconditional forgiveness more than anything in the world. Shame at her behaviour almost overwhelmed and she became choked up with restrained tears. For having denied him all those years, by her actions, the chance to obtain forgiveness (in the process having denied her one and only child the chance to know her father), and have a relationship with the daughter he had always loved. Jean felt that she also needed to be released from the heinous sin that she had committed. And so she asked Cyrus to forgive her for not having forgiven him and for having denied him the chance to share in his daughter's life. She told him that she had not been able to forgive him before, but that she now forgave everything that he had done without reservation. She apologized for the many letters of his that she had destroyed; she apologized for ignoring the many messages she had received from Eve that he was diligently searching for them; she apologized for destroying the contact details Eve had relayed to her; she even apologized that she had broken her contact with Eve simply because she kept relaying information to her about him.

Cyrus felt as though a burden had been lifted off of his shoulders – a burden he had carried for many, many years without realizing the true weight of it. He thanked the Lord in his mind for this development, thanked God for having touched Jean's heart, as he realized that the sins that he had committed against this dear lady were by far greater than any sin she might have committed in retaliation. For any sin that Jean had committed against him, by denying him access to his daughter, by denying her daughter access to him, had been purely as a result of his maltreatment of her in the first place and he had to take full responsibility for the consequences.

Large tears welled up in Cyrus' and Jean's eyes as they whole-heartedly forgave each other their respective wrongs, tears that flowed freely down their faces. Then drying their tears, they smiled at each other for the first time in years – pure smiles, smiles of forgiveness and pardon - smiles of friendship, hope and new beginnings.

Cyrus confirmed that he had met Lester and could tell that he loved Jean dearly, and spoke of his joy in knowing that she had found true love and happiness in her lifetime.

They talked briefly about their families and old friends and what had become of them. Sharing and exchanging details of bereavement, re-settlement in foreign lands, marriages and divorces. And finally they talked about their daughter – Cherie. Cyrus informed Jean that he had known his daughter for many years now without realizing who she was. He confirmed that they attended the same church. And Jean said words that made Cyrus' heart sad - then skip a beat - then dance – "Cherie was always very interested in finding out about you".

Jean informed Cyrus that she needed a little time in order to inform her husband about the situation and to speak to Cherie in order to prepare her for the significant upheaval.

And the two bade each other goodbye, as Cyrus went off to keep his appointment. He promised to return to see her again and they exchanged telephone numbers and Cyrus gave Jean his address.

After Cyrus left Jean sobbed uncontrollably, but she could not say why.

That afternoon when Lester came to see her, Jean told him all about Cyrus' visit that morning. She also told him that Cyrus was Cherie's biological father and that he wanted to get to know his daughter. Lester was amazed, but accepting and encouraging. "But of course – that will explain why he behaved so strangely the other week when he came in to pray with us – he must have recognized you then". "Oh - no wonder," Lester repeated the last two words several times as he nodded his head slowly. He went on to thank Jean for putting him in the picture as her husband, and showing him that degree of respect, adding that he appreciated that she had a life before she met him. "Cherie is an adult so it's her choice what she wants to do, but we must support her in whatever she decides", Lester advised. "In any case I think we should actively encourage her to get to know her father - he seems like really a nice bloke", Lester said, happy that Cyrus was almost family. He had enjoyed conversing with him when they met the other day. "Would you like me to arrange for them to meet up", Lester continued. "No, it's okay dear, I think it's best if I handle the matter myself", Jean replied and smiled.

That evening when Cherie came to visit her mother, Lester made his excuses and left early.

Cherie brought seedless black grapes for her mother – her favourite. She washed the beautiful fruit and placed them in a small bowl by the bed and Jean sat eating them – one grape at a time, thinking of a way to broach the very important matter on her mind's agenda. After a few minutes, she decided not to waste any more time, and simply launched straight in.

"Cherie I must apologise to you for having deprived you of the chance to know her father all her life", Jean said in hushed tones as she averted Cherie's direct gaze. She continued, "I had no right to behave in the way that I did – it was not fair to you – I hope you will forgive me". "I'm sorry darling", Jean said as a single tear welled up in one eye.

Cherie stared at her mother, eyes agog, her surprise and excitement that her mum was at long last willing to discuss her father evident. "Oh mum, I forgive you", Cherie said, hugging her mother, then continued – I know, it's Donald Syrenson, isn't it mum?" Cherie beamed, "mum he was in this same hospital for over a month, but they moved him away two weeks ago", Cherie enthused.

Jean took a while to digest what Cherie was saying before responding, "No dear - it's not Donald Syrenson".

"Isn't it? Cherie asked a look of incredulity on her face.

"No dear – it's a gentleman you know as Brother Cyrus", Jean paused then continued, "he attends your church....", but was unable to end the sentence as Cherie cut in.

"Brother Cyrus?" Cherie whispered loudly, questioningly.

"Yes dear - of course, that's not his real name. His real name is Tyrone Syrenson", Jean continued, unaware of the degree of astonishment her revelation had provoked in her daughter.

"You mean Brother Cyrus – the Brother Cyrus ... is my father", Cherie repeatedly whispered, a wide smile emerging to light up her face.

She had expected her mother to say that her father was Donald Syrenson, or someone else, someone she didn't know, anyone else but Brother Cyrus. But she had said that it was Brother Cyrus. Cherie shook her head from side to side in shock, finding it impossible to digest this information that had hit her like a thunderbolt out of the blue. "Brother Cyrus - no wonder he had behaved so strangely when he came to pray with us last week – he must have recognized you then mum," Cherie said excitedly. "But why didn't he say something?" "No wonder he kept looking at me strangely in church last Sunday," Cherie said. "I thought he was taking an unhealthy interest in me or something, but now I realize why he kept on staring at me and looking away when I caught him,"

Cherie chuckled, not allowing Jean to get a word in edgeways. "Brother Cyrus is my father" Cherie repeated this sentence over and over again, shaking her head from side to side. Then she told her mother, "Mum, I have always loved Brother Cyrus, you – oh, you just don't know how happy I am – Brother Cyrus is my father", Cherie said feeling as though she was floating on a wafting cloud – then she burst into uncontrollable tears.

"Do you have his address or his telephone number", Cherie asked when she had composed herself. She did not wish to waste any more time – she wanted to get to know beloved Bro Cyrus as her father immediately.

"Yes, he left me his number", Jean said handing over Cyrus' note to Cherie.

Leaving the hospital earlier than usual that evening Cherie sat in her car and tried to call the mobile number her mother had given to her. However, it diverted to voicemail. She thought about leaving a message, but at the last minute decided that she would not do so. She tried to call two more times but got no reply. She wondered where her father might be on a Tuesday night then realized it was men's fellowship night at church. Cherie thought of dropping by the church but resisted doing so not only because she would be the only woman in attendance but also because Curtis would be there. When she got home, before she dialled Cyrus' number for the last time at 10 pm, she made a diary note on Tuesday 26 September "The day I found my father" it read. She got no reply but once again she was too nervous to leave a message and hung up - she would call again tomorrow.

For the best part of the night Cherie tossed and turned - unable to sleep. She was thinking about her father. She couldn't wait to start getting to know him. "Dad, dad, dad," Cherie soliloquized over and over as she hugged her pillow to her chest. She was so excited and wanted to share this good news with someone, but thought it best to wait until she had confirmed the facts with Brother Cyrus, not that she thought her mother was wrong - she wanted to assess Brother Cyrus' true reaction first.

Morning dawned and Cherie jumped out of bed at 7.00 am. She performed her daily ritual of reciting a motto for the day,

"Today is the first day of the rest of my life," she said boldly. Then she said a short prayer, asking God's blessing on the day. She showered and dressed in record time, ate muesli with enthusiasm and then sat drinking coffee and clock-watching. It was now only 7.58 am – last time she looked it was 7.55 am, although it seemed to Cherie that an age had passed. It was Wednesday 27 September and Cherie made a diary note, because this was the day on which she hoped she would start getting to know her long-lost father.

After what seemed like two hours had passed, Cherie looked at the time again - it was still only 8.30 am. She drummed her fingers on the sideboard impatiently, and involuntarily, grabbed her mobile. Once again she dialled Cyrus' number and once again she was put straight through to voicemail. Nervously, Cherie left a rambling message, "Hi, it's Cherie – Sister Johnson – from church". "You know my mum, Jean Jones – I mean Johnson – you will know her as Johnson, I believe". "I don't know what mum has said to you, exactly, but I was wondering whether we could meet up later – have a chat". "Please give me a call to arrange it". Then Cherie left her mobile number, her home number and her work number, not wishing to leave anything to chance.

As she drove to work Cherie was bombarded by thoughts of her father. What was he really like – not the Brother Cyrus person that she knew – the real him? Would they get on well? Then suddenly the thought hit her like a ton of bricks – she and Gus were brother and sister. It dawned on Cherie that that was perhaps what God was trying to reveal to her in the numerous dreams she had had and in the revelation that Gus would figure in her future. Cherie felt a pang of sorrow, then telling herself that she should be pleased that she had a brother, she tried to be optimistic. "But why does it have to be Gus", Cherie said with anguish. The fact that she now knew Gus was her brother, did not cause the strong feelings she had for him to disappear. She did not have feelings that a sister has for a brother, but feelings that a woman has for a man. And Cherie struggled to erase what were effectively incestuous thoughts about Gus from her mind.

All day Cherie waited for a return call from Cyrus, but no call came. She thought of calling him again, but decided against doing so. No – she would wait for him to call her back. Thursday, Friday and Saturday passed too without a call back and Cherie had to face the fact that Cyrus was not nearly as interested in getting to know her as she was in getting to know him. Then she became angry, "What could he be up to, I wonder," she asked herself. "Perhaps he's busy," she countered. "Busy, how busy could he be – he shouldn't be too busy to meet me after all these years," she said becoming indignant. "How dare he treat me in this way – what is he playing at anyway?" "I really do not understand what sort of silly game he might be playing". "And he seemed like such a nice gentleman" Cherie shouted angrily. As she spoke she looked at the telephone as though it was an object of grave offence.

Then an attitude of indifference seized her mind. She would not call Bro Cyrus ever again – she would stop chasing after him, whether he was her father or not – and if he wanted to know her, he would have to come after her himself.

****

Cyrus could not understand why the new mobile that he had bought was not ringing. There were several symbols on the display but he didn't understand what they meant. He knew that something was not right because it had not rung for days. He had tried reading the user manual to see if he could diagnose the problem, but it was all mumbo-jumbo to him – he had found it all to be technical jargon. It was far easier just to ask Gus or one of the youngsters at the youth club to explain it to him. He had intended to ask them on Friday but had forgotten.

Sunday 1 October and morning dawned overcast and dreary. Heavy rain was forecasted, and fully fortified against the elements, Cherie made her way to church, arriving just on time. She sat near the back of the church in order to facilitate a quick escape at the end of the service. Looking around surreptitiously in an attempt to ascertain where Brother Cyrus was sitting, she spotted him in the usual pew where he liked to sit, near the front of the congregation. Throughout the service Cherie covertly observed him, noting any resemblance that he might have to her. It was unmistakable that she had taken his colouring and his ears – definitely his ears.

She also noted that her eyes were similar to his – hers were a cross between his and her mother's. Cherie marvelled at how much of herself she could see in Brother Cyrus, and wondered why she had never acknowledged the strong resemblance before. Then she recalled that when she was first introduced to Brother Cyrus over five years ago, she had actually imagined that her father might look something like him. Cherie smiled to herself in amazement at her recollection. Then as she turned her eyes again towards his direction, she noticed that Brother Cyrus had turned around to stare straight back at her. He was smiling at her and at first she ignored him, averting her eyes – still angry that he had not returned her calls. But when she looked at him again he was still smiling at her. And so she involuntarily smiled gently back at him, and felt the warmth of long-denied paternal love flooding through her body.

Cherie enjoyed praise and worship, and she praised and worshipped God from a glad heart. But as the service went on, she found herself wishing it was over so that she could smile, once again, at her father, and hopefully that he would come over and talk with her. Then she asked God to forgive her for wishing that the service would hurry up and finish.

Cyrus praised God from a joyful heart. He felt elated at the developments of the past week. He decided that this must be how it felt to float on air – and it was Cherie, his daughter's smile that had caused such elation – the sweet smile of his long lost Princess. Cyrus found himself wishing that the sermon would not be long today, because he couldn't wait to see her smile at him again. Then he asked God to forgive him for wishing that the sermon would not take long.

As soon as the pastor pronounced the benediction, Cyrus shifted round in his seat to look at his daughter. But to his amazement, she was no longer sitting there. He looked around everywhere, but could not see her anywhere and sadly conceded that she must have left. And so he greeted and fellowshipped in the usual way, before finally making his way outside to find Sister Clarey, who had offered to give him a lift home.

Standing by the front gate of the church, Cyrus thought about Cherie, wondering why she had left church so early, without saying a word to him. He knew from her smile that Jean had spoken to her, but he couldn't imagine what her true reaction might be to what her mother had told her about him. However, he was prepared for her to reject him – he would give her a little space but would definitely not be giving up on his attempt to get to know her.

Suddenly he felt Sister Clarey tap him on his left shoulder, summonsing her presence – she was ready to depart. He turned around to acknowledge her but was amazed to see that it wasn't Sister Clarey after all – it was Cherie, his dear long lost daughter.

Cherie stared into Cyrus' eyes, noting his resemblance to her – a resemblance which must surely have been obvious to everyone but themselves. Then without seeking permission from anyone, she hugged him tightly as tears filled her eyes. "Hello Daddy – I've waited all my life to do this," she said, saying the words that she had waited to speak all her life.

"Hello my dear daughter, I've been waiting for this since you were a little tot," Cyrus said, as tears of joy flowed unabated down his cheeks.

Just then Sister Clarey came out of the church and apparently in shock, she gave them both a distasteful look and made to walk off. But Cyrus spoke quickly to correct the distorted notion, "Sister Clarey - you know Sister Cherie, don't you?" he said all puffed up. He went on, "I thank you for offering to give me a lift, but it seems I won't need to trouble you after all, because my daughter here will be driving me home," he said proudly without asking Cherie – he instinctively knew she would agree.

CHAPTER 17

On the Road to Recovery

Gus was surprised at how much he enjoyed the men's fellowship that first evening. So much so that he had tonight, 3 October 2010, completed his third consecutive weekly visit. And he was particular happy tonight because, having divulged to Brother Jevan that it was his birthday who had shared this information with those gathered, all had warmly wished him the best and celebrated his 31st birthday with him. The only downside was that his father was not in attendance tonight. Gus last spoke to him when he telephoned him on Sunday afternoon. Cyrus had informed him excitedly that he had met his long lost daughter, Princess. Gus was not even aware that his father had any long lost children. As his dad sounded preoccupied, Gus cut their conversation short. And since then his father had not been in touch – not even to wish him 'Happy Birthday' like he was accustomed to doing without fail each birthday.

Now Gus sat thinking, wondering how his father could have forgotten his birthday, and feeling neglected by the one person he loved most in the world. Gus tried to channel his thoughts elsewhere and began to reflect on his visits to the men's fellowship evenings, he thought about the annoying way in which Curtis kept on clinging to him as though they were old buddies, when the fact was that they most certainly were not. In fact after the very first evening, Gus had made a decision that Curtis was the person he would least like to get to know better. But he had so far not been able convey that message to Curtis.

What Gus disliked the most about Curtis was the way that he kept making innuendoes that he and Cherie was a couple – he never missed a chance to stress the point – and Gus became more annoyed each time. He was tempted to ring Cherie and let her know just what Curtis was saying about her, as he was certain that she would be very interested to find out. But so far he has resisted calling her, deciding that it was really none of his business what

Curtis wanted to say about Cherie. After all it wasn't as if he had any personal interest at stake – was it? "Oh she's a lovely girl – no disputing that fact, but I just can't allow myelf to become emotionally involved at this time," Gus repeated aloud for the third time tonight. And tonight, as was usual, he tried to push all thoughts of Cherie aside, deciding that he had far more pressingly urgent matters to worry about.

Each night was a repetition of the next as a variety of thoughts churned over and over in Gus' mind - one worry to next, for which solutions were elusive. Even though the nightmares had stopped, and things had dramatically improved for him over the past month, and notably since committing his life to Jesus Christ, in that he now had nearly half of his properties rented out, and received a payout from the insurance company for his stolen car, Gus was still a long way off getting back on his feet. He was still struggling to keep up the mortgage repayments on the properties, and only just managing to pay the minimum interest on other debts that he had accumulated, without making even a dent in repayment of any capital that was owed. It was a struggle for him to live on the little that was left over and he found that in order to maintain anything like a balanced diet he had to buy the cheapest range in the supermarket. Often his only meal was a tin of beans and he sometimes went to bed without the simplest of meals.

A couple of his properties were still on the market, but as yet no buyers had been found for them – if only he could find buyers, that would solve most of his financial worries and he was praying for that to happen very soon. Of course, if tenants could be found for the remainder of the properties, he would soon be able to sort himself out but this looked unlikely at present as due to a spate of bad tenants who thrashed several of the properties before moving out, a number of them needed essential repairs before they could be let out, which Gus could not afford.

As advised by Bishop Fredericks, who has had several revelations about his life and circumstances, Gus has been praying without ceasing. He has been attending church every single week since his conversion, mostly on Sunday evenings in order to avoid the complications with the Cherie and Curtis affair.

This week Bishop Fredericks told him that he had had a revelation from God that Gus needed to fast as well as pray, and he was thinking about doing that. Bishop Fredericks said that the problems he was facing were very difficult spiritual problems and that he needed to fast in order to get to the root of them.

Nodding off to sleep while reflecting, Gus' mind continued to generate thoughts which manifested in a series of dreams – some good ones, others jumbled and confused. On awakening he recalled something Bishop Fredericks had said in his sermon on Sunday and smiled "a dream comes through a multitude of business." "Or in my case, through a multitude of worries", Gus said, his smile broadening as he contemplated the wisdom contained in the Bible.

It's Wednesday 4 October and Gus is excited. He is excited about the next step he will take in his spiritual awakening. Having decided that he would like to follow Bishop Frederick's advice and embark upon a fast, in order to find out more about fasting he telephones his father for guidance. "Hi dad, how are you?" I didn't see you at men's fellowship last night", Gus said jovially.

"Oh, hello son – I'm fine you know – just very busy that's why I couldn't make it last night", Cyrus replied, sounding preoccupied.

"Okay – I won't keep you too long, I just need some guidance about fasting", Gus said.

Without more Cyrus began to expound the various rules associated with fasting. He quoted relevant scriptures and gave Gus some prayer strategies and prayer points to incorporate into his fast.

Gus deliberately did not remind Cyrus about his birthday to see if he would mention it and felt even more let down when he didn't. All his father did was talk about his long lost daughter.

"Son, I'm so happy to have met my Princess again after all this time". "We have been spending a lot of time together, getting to know each other better". You must come over and get to know her too", Cyrus enthused.

"Yeah, I'll have to do that", Gus said, feigning excitement.

"Oh, God is so wonderful, I have been praying for this to

happen for many many years", Cyrus gushed, a smile evident in his voice.

"I am really happy for you, dad, but I never knew you had another daughter somewhere", Gus said sounding a little injured.

"Oh it's a long story son – I will have to sit you down and tell you all about it sometime", Cyrus replied not having noticed the edge in Gus' voice.

"Okay dad", Gus said.

When he had ended his conversation with Cyrus, Gus came to terms with the way he was truly feeling about his father's revelation. He felt hurt that his father had kept something so important from him – he thought he knew everything about his father. And although he was glad that he had found a long last sister (or rather a sister he never knew was long last), instead he was feeling hurt and dejected. And the fact that his father had apparently forgotten about him, not even having remembered his birthday left Gus feeling neglected.

Just then the telephone rang – it was Cyrus to ask Gus if he would allow him a couple of weeks off from the the Club to allow him to rest a little and get to spend more quality time with his Princess. He repeated his invitation for Gus to come over and meet his sister and suggested Sunday afternoon. Cyrus also informed Gus that Princess was taking very good care of him, which caused Gus to feel more unwanted than before. "Yes dad, you need a break anyway – rest your knee a little – I will let you know if I can make it on Sunday", Gus said. "You can ask Brother Jevan to help out while I am away", Cyrus said. "Okay", Gus replied.

For the rest of the week Gus found he was unable to shake off the feelings of dejection brought about by Cyrus' revelation. So instead of honouring the invitation to dinner on Sunday afternoon he decided to give it a miss – "I'll allow the old man to get better acquainted with his long last daughter", Gus spoke his thought. So he telephoned Cyrus to tell him that. He was not nursing any bitterness, he just felt sad that he would be losing a part of his dad to a newly found long last sister. And although he was happy that he now apparently had another sister, he couldn't help feeling forlorn.

Gus felt even worse for not attending dinner at his father's on

Sunday afternoon. By Friday 13 October, having heard nothing from Cyrus, the feelings of dejection and self pity increased. Gus imagined that Cyrus was having such a good time with his newly found long last daughter that he no longer had any time at all for him. He tried to pull himself together but couldn't so he kept up the sulk.

On Saturday 14 October Cyrus telephoned to invite Gus to a special dinner party that he was organizing to celebrate the reunion with Princess. After asking after his wellbeing, and receiving the usual "I'm okay, dad", he asked how Gus was getting along with the training sessions and at the Youth Club.

"Everything is fine, dad - no problems at all", Gus replied.

"Brother Jevans is not only helping to drive the church van and helping out at the training sessions he is also assisting me at the club on Fridays". "It's wonderful that he has started helping because we needed more help anyway". "And it takes the pressure off of you as you have been struggling with your knee for some time", Gus stated. "Now you can rest the knee and allow it to reach full recovery", he continued.

"Yes, it's great to have Brother Jevan on board", Cyrus concurred.

Following a general chat about fasting and the like, Cyrus gave Gus full details about the dinner party he was organizing in three weeks' time to celebrate his reunion with Princess. Apparently there were eleven confirmed attendees, and Cyrus asked Gus to confirm that he would also be coming, adding, "Make sure you make it son, Princess can't wait to get to know you". "In fact it would be good if you could drop by before that", Cyrus added.

Gus confirmed there and then that he would make the dinner party. It was a long time since anyone invited him to a social event and it would certainly beat sitting alone in any one of his palatial homes, with just the walls and his thoughts for company.

CHAPTER 18

The Journey Continues

A – Catching Up

Since the reunion with her father Cherie wafted on a cloud of extreme joy and spent much of her spare time with Cyrus, who she has taken to calling "Daddy". And when she was not with him, she telephoned him at least 3 times a day – just to check that he was okay, in the same way that she has always done with her mother.

Her father on the other hand was doing all he humanly could to try and make up for the lost years. In spite of his bad knee, he had redecorated the spare bedroom in his house and designated it Princess's room, where she often stayed when they had conversed into the wee small hours.

For the first two weeks after getting together, they were insepa-rable. Cherie had taken time out from her gruelling work schedule. Her father also had taken time out from the Youth Club, not only so he could spend time with his newly found long lost daugh-ter, but because his doctor advised that he rest his knee. And the doctor also signed him off work at the stadium due to his knee problems, so he had lots of time to spend with his Princess.

The hours flew by as Cherie listened to her father talk about his life, from the time he had left for America when she was just a year old until they had made the discovery that they were father and daughter. He bared his soul about the loss he had suffered when he was denied access to her as a toddler; recounted the longing he had endured during the years apart. He conveyed his despondency at not being able to find Jean and Cherie upon returning to London in 1987 and related the sadness that he had carried in his heart all those years. He told Cherie of his regret on realizing the pain he had caused Jean. The best part for Cherie was when he spoke of his family in America. And she listened avidly to him, drinking in much longed for information that she had been denied all her life.

Surprisingly her father hardly spoke about his son Gus, except to state the obvious, that he was her brother and that she would meet him soon. He invited her brother for dinner the first Sunday after their reunion but he had cancelled at the last minute, which made her father a little sad. But he had reassured Cherie that Gus would pass by in the next week or so as he was accustomed to doing. Cherie gathered her dad was holding back talking about her brother – perhaps because he did not wish to upset her by constantly reminding her that he had been a father to Gus all those years while she did not have the love of a father. For her part, she was glad that he did not speak much about her brother and she in fact actively discouraged him from doing so by steering him to a different subject as best she could to avoid significant discourse about Gus. The reason being that Cherie still had not been able to quench the fire that burned in her heart for the man she now knew to be her brother and she was afraid that she might betray her true emotions to her father during such dialogue.

Despite her unruly emotions Cherie longed to get to know Gus as a brother and was praying fervently that the amorous feelings would subside and die – that she would begin to love him just as family and no more.

Cyrus also mentioned Marcus and Denise, Gus' brother and sister and Cherie was excited to learn that she had a sister as well as another brother. "Wow, I'm so excited, I've always wanted a sister of my own," she had said chirpily. Her father had explained that Marcus and Denise were not as close as he would like them to be but that she would meet them at the celebratory dinner party that he was organizing. And Cherie had quipped, "Ohh – I just can't wait".

Cyrus was aware that Cherie behaved strangely at each mention of Gus' name. He put it down to the fact that she was perhaps jealous that Gus had such a close and special relationship with him. As he wished to assure her that she too had his heart he avoided bringing Gus up as best he could, although he found it difficult not to talk about his son.

The detailed and colourful picture that Cherie painted with her words as she conveyed details of her childhood to her father, were strong and vivid in Cyrus' imagination. As he listened avidly to many a recounted tale, Cyrus' mind placed him in Cherie's childhood days as he dreamed that he was a part of her upbringing, that he was there to support her through the difficult times and to bring her joy and happiness. Cherie talked about her infancy, her early memories; about her teenage years and her maturity into adulthood. She shared imprints from the pages of her mind, of experiences undergone while growing up without a father at school; revealing how she had pretended that her grandfather was her father in order to prevent wagging tongues and bullying. She spoke of her career and her artistic gifts and they sang together, both agreeing that there was a distinct similarity in their voices and vocal ranges.

But Cherie never spoke to her father about her love life or about romance – or the lack of it in her life - that was too personal. She also reserved details of her secret dreams of meeting and marrying the right man for future divulgence, when they got to know each other better, when she had gotten over her "crush" on her brother and when her mind had ceased to automatically recall images of the contour of Gus' face, of his voice, of his eyes, each time she thought of love or romance.

Wishing to spend more time with her father Cherie asked George to help out at the office. He was only too happy to oblige as he usually was when Cherie required his help. She was totally at ease as she trusted George implicitly. He reported to her on a daily basis so she was fully aware of what was going on, and her mind was free to enjoy getting to know her father. George had to bring documents for her to sign and that was how he came to meet Cyrus, since Cherie now practically lived at her father's home.

****

B – The Message
The first time that Cyrus met George, he received a revelation that George was very ill. It was the Wednesday after the reunion and George had stopped by with some documents that required Cherie's signature. When Cherie left the room to prepare refreshments, Cyrus was prompted to share the revelation with George. George was speechless for a minute, then he spoke, "No one knows about that – how did you know?" He stared at Cyrus in amazement as he

awaited a reply.

"The Holy Spirit revealed it to me, sir", Cyrus replied in his usual humble manner.

George was confused – he knew nothing about that spiritual mumbo jumbo, but there must be something in it after all – how did Cherie's father find out about his illness. He was diagnosed with the disease over, 12 years ago and had never told anyone, not even his parents knew about it. HIV was his life sentence – the cross he had carried alone for so long, knowing how society viewed that incurable disease. Only his doctors knew of his condition. It was the only way he could avoid being stigmatized. "Please - explain .... Sir ..... please explain", was all that George could bring himself to say.

It was obvious to Cyrus that he had alarmed George – something he wished to avoid. However, the Holy Spirit had given him a revelation that he had to share. He did not have time to explain to George as Cherie was due to return from the kitchen at any minute – so receiving further instruction from the Holy Spirit Cyrus said, "I'm inviting you to attend the Healing and Deliverance meeting at my church next Saturday. At the mention of healing, George nodded – speechless – he was willing to trust this great power – for too long he had lived a less than complete life, denying himself of female companionship, being unable to get too close to anyone for fear of his secret getting out or, God forbid, of infecting someone else. So he obediently took the church address from Mr Cyrus, determined to do whatever necessary to try and get free from the scourge of HIV.

As George attended the Healing and Deliverance meeting that Saturday evening, he did not know what to expect. But he discovered that although Mr Cyrus was not present, it was as though he had informed Pastor Kelly that George would be coming and instructed him as to the reason why. For as soon as George entered the sanctuary, Pastor Kelly fixed his eyes upon him and observed him throughout the service, and when the alter call was made and Pastor Kelly called forward those suffering from incurable complaints, he stared intently at George, willing him to step forward.

As George listened to Pastor Kelly calling forward those who were suffering from incurable diseases, he was bombarded by a variety of negative thoughts: that he should leave the sanctuary; that he should forget the thought of ever being healed; that there was no hope for him; that he was stupid for even thinking he could be made whole. But recalling Mr Cyrus' kind eyes and his explanation that the Holy Spirit had spoken to him, George stepped forward. And as he did so, Pastor Kelly, began to praise God.

Pastor Kelly laid hands upon George's head and as he did so, George felt a wave of heat shoot through the whole body, from his head right down to the tips of his toes. Suddenly he felt his knees turn to jelly and he fell backwards – he was caught by the alter workers who anticipated that he would fall. Unbeknown to George, for more than 30 minutes he laid flat upon his back. He was conscious of various light waves and heat waves passing through and over his body and washing over his spirit. When he rose up, he tingled all over and felt like a new man both spiritually as well as physically. He knew something great had taken place because the sensation of vertigo with which he had suffered for many years had disappeared. George felt washed clean – completely healthy and totally at one in his spirit.

Pastor Kelly advised that those who had received their healing should go to their doctors and obtain confirmation. Next day George's was the first telephone call that his doctor's receptionist answered.

****

C: The Fix Up

Recently Sister Clarey has become a regular caller at Brother Cyrus' home, paying visits to Cherie, whom she has taken to treating like her own daughter. Cherie was aware that Sister Clarey was carrying a flaming torch for her father, but did not dissuade her and actively encouraged her visits. It was apparent to her that her father was in need of companionship after so many years alone and she was of the view that the love of his children was not enough - he needed that special someone too and she could hope for no-one better than Sister Clarey for her beloved father.

A knock-out fifty-two year old, Sister Clary looked 10 years younger. She came wrapped up in a package labelled "super cook" and "super businesswoman". For the past two Sundays, Sister Clary has been a working guest at the Syrenson home, presiding over Cherie's preparation of Sunday lunch. She did not have to assist with preparing lunch, but did so of her own free will and enjoyed doing it. The mature businesswoman had done incredibly well for herself, albeit with the combined effort of her late husband, who passed away five years ago. Her business was that of a hair-dressing, beauty and lifestyle salon, with a thriving hair and skincare, cosmetics and toiletries store adjoining. Her son had taken over the everyday manoeuvres and she sat in the back seat, leaving her time to amuse and pamper herself. Sister Clarey advised her with shrewd business savvy and Cherie liked to discuss commercial matters with her, benefiting from her many years of experience. But by far the best thing about Sister Clarey was that she wasn't a stick in the mud like some of the other sisters who attended the church – she was a bit of fun and liked to have a laugh, although mature and spiritually sensitive enough to know when to be serious. Cherie liked her a lot, and did not miss a chance to stir up her father's interest.

****

D: The Invitation to Dine

Cyrus had never been happier in his entire life. He could not believe that it was possible for one event to bring about such total transformation. Where previously he always had time on his hands to spare for other people, he now found it difficult to accommodate them. Most of his time was spent getting to know his daughter, and even when they were apart, he was either thinking about her or preparing in some way for when they were together again.

To celebrate his new found joy Cyrus was arranging a dinner party to be attended by his nearest and dearest. All those that he had invited so far had confirmed that they could make it and Cyrus couldn't wait.

Cherie had inveigled her father to invite Sister Clarey to the dinner by stating that she liked talking to her. Upon receiving the invitation, Sister Clarey had immediately accepted and later telephoned Cherie excitedly to suggest that they should both go to the salon on the day in order to get their hair and make-up done professionally for the big occasion – Cherie didn't need to be persuaded. So Sister Clarey booked the appointment for her - also arranging manicures and pedicures, a full beauty makeover - on the house.

George was also invited (at Cherie's behest), as well as Naomi and her boyfriend. Cherie needed George to be there as she did not want to risk vulnerability in Gus' presence. All of a sudden George had started showing her what she interpreted as romantic interest, a fact Cherie found confusing. A few years ago she would have been overjoyed at this development but now, although there was no doubt that she loved George, she loved him as a friend or brother – no more. But recalling the depth of feelings that she had previous nursed for George, Cherie was hopeful that the flames would reignite. If so, it would be just what she needed to forget her romantic inclinations towards Gus.

On 4 November 2010, the day of the dinner party, ten minutes to her 11 am appointment, Cherie stood in the reception area of the large, well-equipped salon, waiting to be attended to. She couldn't wait to be pampered, and tingled with anticipation at the thought of a complete beauty makeover. Soon she was ushered into the main part of the salon by the receptionist, to find that Sister Clarey was already seated under the dryer. The elder lady greeted her warmly as she was led into the treatment area, "Hi Princess, dear," she said in an artificially high pitched voice, referring to Cherie by the same pet name her father called her.

"Hello, Sister Clarey – how are you today," Cherie smiled broadly and bent to kiss the older lady on the left cheek as she thought "Aaah, she's so sweet".

"I'm fine darling," Sister Clarey replied as she beckoned to one of the employees to come and see to Cherie. The girl came scurrying over and stood to attention, waiting for her employer to finish conversing with the client.

"Okay? the girl asked Cherie, the somewhat harsh tone of this greeting being tempered by her big warm smile. Cherie responded by nodding and smiling nervously, indicating that she was not at all at ease, whereupon the perceptive coiffeur attended to settling her client and putting her at ease.

Treating Cherie like a very special customer, the hairdresser accommodated her right away, going over the top with her treatment of her as royalty or a fragile egg. Her facial was done first, followed by her hair, and manicure and pedicure at the same time, leaving only her make up to be applied as a final touch. When her "treatment" was finished Cherie went over to thank Sister Clarey, kissing her on the cheek and apologizing that she was unable to collect her for dinner but would ask her father to do so. She explained that she had to stop by the office to carry out some essential paperwork that required her personal attention today, and would meet the elder lady at the restaurant later. "Okay darling," Sister Clarey replied sweetly.

As she walked towards the exit Cherie glanced at herself in the row of full length mirrors along the walls of the salon. And she was not disappointed with what she saw – she looked amazing. From head to toe she radiated beauty – if she thought so herself. Her hair was in corkscrew curls and shone healthily, and her make-up, though minimal, was immaculate. To her own eyes, she resembled a top fashion model, and as she exited the salon and walked back to her car she obtained validation.

Quickening her steps, Cherie hurried, as she was pestered by several amorous males, who attempted to woo her with wolf whistles and cat calls, which she proficiently ignored. Although she was used to receiving such attention, she had never before encountered it on such a scale. But, however annoying she found it to be, it nonetheless boosted her ego, and she felt like a million dollar movie superstar as she climbed behind the wheel of her car and drove to her office.

On arrival at the office Cherie immediately set to work on the accounts that needed to be brought up to date. The paperwork could have waited until Monday but she decided to come into the office and attend to them this afternoon. Cherie's intention was to "kill two birds with one stone", for she was making it possible for her father and Sister Clarey to have quality time together on their journey to the restaurant, which she anticipated should take them at least 45 minutes in early Saturday evening traffic.

As Gus contemplated the dinner party, he thought of the loving and close relationship that he and Cyrus' had always enjoyed. And he found himself wishing and hoping, rather selfishly, that things between them would not change too significantly now that Princess was on the scene. He loved his father so much and could not imagine someone coming into the mix. He had forgiven him for not having told him about Princess and was now ready to put that lapse behind him. However, he was still a little hurt that his father had still not remembered that his birthday was recent. In spite of everything Gus was eager to meet his newly found long lost sister.

After showering and dressing casually but smartly Gus set off to the Pumpkin Soup Bowl restaurant in Leeside, the new Caribbean restaurant that was carrying the swing these days. He was feeling relaxed as he drove easily through the late Saturday afternoon traffic. It was mild for the first week in November so Gus had the window slightly ajar, drinking in the sounds and atmosphere of late Saturday bustle. Deliberately, he took the route past the Wash House Market. He could hear the familiar voices of hagglers trying to wrangle last minute deals, and smiled as memories of his mother rolled back the years. He thought of stopping for a hot pattie at Miss Valda's takeaway, but decided against it – you couldn't eat just one of Miss Valda's patties – and Gus wanted to preserve his appetite for dinner later.

Arriving at the restaurant far earlier than anticipated, Gus felt a positive sense of achievement on noting that he was over three quarters of an hour early. The table was booked for 7.30 pm and it was now only 6.40 pm, so he sat in the car checking his texts and voicemail. That done, he decided to telephone Cyrus to let him know he was already there, after all there was no use being early if no-one knew about it.

Cyrus did not answer his mobile for a long while and Gus was just about to hang up when he heard the familiar, friendly voice, "Hello, who is that?" Cyrus asked hesitantly, as though he was afraid of speaking. Gus knew that Cyrus was somewhat apprehensive of his state of the art mobile telephone and smiled to himself. Although he had purchased the gadget over six months ago, he still had not gotten used to its technology. "It's Gus, how are you?"

"Oh, I'm fine – how are you son," Cyrus said far too loudly. "Good, I'm at the restaurant already", Gus stated pointedly, then continued "...what time is the booking for?". "I booked for 7.30 pm but as you are there you can go in and have a pre-dinner drink if you like – they won't mind". "I'm glad you called actually because I'm running late, so make sure you go in and claim the table for me". "They get very busy in the Pumpkin Soup Bowl on Saturday nights, and if you are even 10 minutes late they give the table away, so please go in and keep the table so they don't think that no-one is coming," Cyrus instructed. "I asked Princess to go early already, but it would be good if more than one person turns up on time." "I should be there in about 40 minutes or so, I hope," he continued.

"Okay, I'll see you soon dad," Gus said as he glanced at his watch noting that it was now 7.00 pm – he smiled broadly to himself, pleased as punch to be early – for once.

As Cherie prepared to set off for the restaurant, she had received a call from Cyrus to say that they were running late. Apparently their taxi had arrived late and they were caught up in a monster traffic jam.

"Please go on to the restaurant and make sure they keep the table – they get very busy on Saturdays, and if we are late by even 10 minutes they might re-allocate the tables," Cyrus said, panicking.

Cherie was aware that the Pumpkin Soup Bowl was usually over-patronised on Saturday evenings – she had heard the reports of table re-allocations. And so she hurriedly dressed, retouched her make up and set out for the restaurant as quickly as possible. On arrival at 7.00 pm she entered the restaurant and, with a sense of pride, asked to be seated at the table booked in the name of Mr Syrenson. She was shown to a large table for 20 in a discrete section of the restaurant, by a large window overlooking the canal.

It was apparent that she was the first of their party to arrive. There were 18 others joining her and her father tonight - she had invited George plus a friend, Jean and Lester, her best friend Cynthia and her boyfriend Benza and Naomi and her boyfriend, who had all confirmed they would be coming. She had also invited Sister Clarey. Cherie had been tempted to invite Curtis but had decided against doing so, deciding that it would only give him the wrong impression.

Cyrus had invited his good friend Berisford and his wife Ann, Gus, Denise and her husband, Roger. He had also tried to get a message to Marcus and invited him and a friend or partner. However, Marcus had not confirmed whether he would be coming or not. And as a surprise to Jean, Cyrus had contacted Eve, who was happy to accept his invitation – she confirmed she would be coming with her husband. Wanting to surprise Jean, Cyrus had not told Cherie or anyone else that Eve would be coming.

Standing in the foyer, Cherie was approached by a handsome waiter who smiled flirtatiously at her before proceeding to pull out a chair for her to sit down on. "Another gentleman with your party is already here too," the waiter informed. "Oh really?" Cherie said looking around the half-empty restaurant for a familiar face, but could not see anyone she knew. Then the waiter gestured towards the small terrace overlooking the canal before walking away. And Cherie looked outside to see a recognizable figure standing with his back towards her – it was Gus.

Seeing Gus again, Cherie's heart skipped a beat, as her emotions leapt into turmoil. The feelings she had experienced on their earlier meetings came flooding back more intense than ever before. She took a deep breath and tried to think straight – what should she do? Should she go to him and greet him, or just remain in her seat until he returned to the table? She decided to take the latter option.

The waiter soon returned with the menus and handed a pair to Cherie, leaving her to study the available fare. Yet another waiter came over after a few minutes to check whether she wanted a drink - she ordered herself a tropical fruit cocktail. "And does the gentleman want anything to drink?" the waiter asked efficiently.

"Ahh, I … ahh … I'm not sure," Cherie stuttered, "it might be an idea to ask him yourself," she added overly abruptly.

"Ok, I'll do that," the waiter replied obediently, backing away and almost bowing in subservience. He went out to the terrace to ask Gus whether he wished to order a drink, "The young lady is having something to drink and she said I should ask you whether you would like one", said the waiter, sounding quite confusing to Gus who wondered what young lady he was talking about.

"Young lady?" Gus questioned. And as he spoke, he turned around to look in the direction of the table. His eyes rested on Cherie and his heart missed several beats - the old attraction made its presence felt and it was more intense than ever before. "Yea.... ye... yes thank you, I'll have one of your renowned tropical fruit cocktails," Gus said still staring straight at Cherie.

The waiter scurried off as Gus took a deep breath and tried to focus his mind - wondering what he should do next. But even as he wondered, he found himself walking back to the table, as though being instinctively drawn towards Cherie. He entered the restaurant, approached and spoke to Cherie, causing her to jump slightly, "Hi, I didn't know you would be here tonight," Gus said. He wanted to add what he was thinking - that it was wonderful to see her again, but managed to hold himself back – just. "Oh, hello" Cherie replied, struggling to keep her voice under control. "Oh, oh didn't you know I'd be here?" she said clumsily. The thought occurred to her that the natural reaction to seeing a long lost brother that one had only just discovered existed would be to embrace him, but Cherie couldn't bring herself to act normally towards Gus. Because the thoughts that she was having towards him were decidedly unnatural – they were brother and sister, and yet the way she felt towards him was not what a sister should feel towards her brother – no way.

Gus sat down slowly in the chair next to Cherie. He had intended to sit across the table from her – to put some safe distance between them, but as though magnetically drawn, he found himself gravitating towards her. And now as he sat down next to her, he became fully aware of her nearness – aware of her breathing, ever so delicately. And he wanted to get even closer still – wanted to hold her so close that their bodies, minds and spirits, their very souls would fuse together as one – as man and wife. He drank in her presence like an addict hungry for yet more. Her face was aglow - her skin flawless. Her hair was a vision of loveliness in natural corkscrew curls that hung just above her shoulders. She was wearing a beautiful Kente designed gown, with a fitted strapless bodice and a beautiful shawl covered her shoulders, and even though she was seated, Gus could appreciate the elegance of her form. He struggled to make his heart listen that he should keep his body under subjection.

As Gus stared at Cherie he felt as though his eyes could be popping out of his head and he could tell that he was putting her on edge by the way he was reacting towards her but he just could not help himself.

Cherie glanced briefly into Gus's face, noting his eyes which were as wide as they could go – she felt somewhat perturbed as it occurred to her that he may have lost his mind.

Gus swallowed heavily as his mouth began to water. He also began to sweat profusely and in a few seconds his body was damp with perspiration. His palms were also wet. As he stared intently at Cherie, she avoided his gaze. And then, quite involuntarily, Gus listened to his own voice as though listening to someone else speak. "You're so beautiful – I'm stunned by your beauty tonight," he said, feeling as though he was having an out of body experience.

Cherie was speechless, surprised by Gus' forthrightness, and shocked by the fact that he was obviously coming on to her – his own sister. But what she found even more shocking was her own bodily reactions, for she began to sweat profusely, and in a moment her body was damp with perspiration. Her palms were also wet. And she wanted Gus to continue wooing her – never to stop his forthright mating call. She wanted to allow her heart to join his in this amorous escapade. Cherie wanted to open up and allow Gus free access to her inner self – but she resisted, drawing strength from her moral code - refusing to give in to her will to commit this incestuous adulterous act as she recalled that just a mere look, a mere thought could amount to sin. But why did it feel so right – *"How can something so wrong feel so right"*, Cherie questioned in her mind. Unable to cope with the intensity of the moment, she began to feel caged - a need to escape – to run away, to the ladies room perhaps or out to the terrace or the car park even - anywhere, but she found that she was rigidly rooted to her seat.

Gus, seeming to have lost the ability to control what he was saying, involuntarily blubbered, "I'm sorry I didn't call you when I said I would, but you know, I've been going through some stuff ….. and I didn't – couldn't deal with what I was going through. I can't really explain – I know you won't be able to understand, but I had good reasons for not calling you like I promised", he said pausing before continuing, "I would like a chance to make up for that – will you please give me that chance, Cherie?" Gus asked sincerely as though his life depended on it. "I would like the chance to pick up where we left off, Cherie, I would like the chance to get to know you better," he babbled on.

So long had he suppressed his true feelings that they now came bursting forth with uncontainable force from his soul, and out of his mouth. Seeing Cherie again tonight had aroused his heart from apathy and his eyes were now wide opened. He became conscious of the fact that Cherie already owned his heart – no matter how he had tried to deny it. And so he just surrendered - instinctively knowing that it was the right thing, the only thing to do – no matter what was happening in his life, he knew that he could and would overcome every obstacle just to be with Cherie. For Gus knew at that very moment that he was only half the man that he could be, if he were with Cherie, for she was the one that he had searched for, for many years - the arrow to his bow, the words to his tune – his eve.

Cherie looked towards the entrance of the restaurant, willing someone to enter and join them, but no one appeared. Just then the waiter arrived bearing their drinks - a welcome respite - but only too soon he was gone, leaving them alone again.

"I would really love to get to know you better," Gus repeated. He just did not seem able to control his mind or his tongue. He wanted to add that he had never felt like this before – never been in love like this, but before he could make a complete fool of himself Cherie gained the will to speak.

"Gus, I really don't think that you should be propositioning me in this way". "I know you must be aware that we are brother and sister?" There - she had said it.

Gus paused to digest the meaning of what Cherie had said before replying, "Yes, we are brother and sister – in the Lord - but please believe me that my intentions towards you are totally honourable," he said sincerely.

Cherie was a little bemused by this reply. "Did your father tell you who I am?" she asked.

"My father?" Gus replied. "Oh – you mean Cyrus?" Gus said casually. "Yes, of course I know who you are - you're Cherie and I know you are the one he has been trying to set me up with forever." Gus added and smiled.

"I am Princess – that is the pet name that my father calls me," Cherie clarified.

"So you are Princess?" Gus asked incredulously.

"Yes, which makes us brother and sister," Cherie said resting her point.

"You mean you are Princess?" Gus repeated.

"That's right – didn't you know?" Cherie asked incredulously.

"No, I wasn't aware – so you are my sister", Gus said and smiled, "Oh, that's what you mean", he continued. "Well you see, you are my sister, but you're not," he added winking mysteriously.

"Uhh," Cherie murmured

"Although I am Cyrus' son, I am not your brother – not your blood brother," Gus said, his smile broadening. He was feeling totally relaxed for the first time in months.

"You're not?" Cherie said smiling, timidly at first, but then wider and wider as the full realization of what Gus had just said dawned on her.

"That's right – I will tell you all about it later", Gus said, his smile fixed.

And smiling widely Cherie slowly relaxed and prepared to enjoy the rest of the evening without further reservation.

Smiling broadly, now realizing that Cyrus' newly found long lost daughter was Cherie, Gus was no longer concerned or jealous of losing his father's love, for he did not mind sharing with Cherie – he would share anything with her – he was even ready to share his life.

Gus had known Cyrus since his birth – he was his Godfather. After the death of his father Darcus, when Gus was just 8, Cyrus had come to live within 3 miles of their home, and had made good on his promise to their father on his death bed, to look after Alison, their mother and the children. "Uncle Cyrus," was what Gus had called him back then. But Cyrus had earned an upgrade to the title of "Dad" due to his diligence and the love and care with which he had assisted their mother to raise Gus and his siblings.

George was the next to arrive at the restaurant at 7.25pm – he was alone as his friend had cancelled at the last minute. His eyes latched onto Cherie – she was looking more beautiful than ever. He rushed over to greet her, kissing her on both cheeks as he was accustomed to doing. Now that things had changed in his life, George was able to contemplate romance, and he hoped that this beautiful lady would give him a second chance. However, as he sat down and observed the interaction between Cherie and the handsome man he came to know as Gus, George realized that there would be no second chance.

All but two of the other party members arrived between 7.30 pm and 7.40 pm. On seeing Benza and Cynthia, Gus could not contain his excitement. And he was also overjoyed to see his sister Denise and her husband Roger, whom he had not seen for over a year.

By far the most excitement was generated by the arrival of Eve and her husband – a surprise that Cyrus had organised for Jean, who was on the mend but still on crutches because of her broken leg. The two women had not seen one another for over 20 years and hugged and cried demonstrating deep and heartfelt love before sitting next to each other, and throughout the evening they could be heard giggling like naughty schoolgirls as they reminisced.

The seating arrangements were as follows - Benza sat opposite to Gus while Cynthia sat opposite to Cherie. The two young men shared manly banter throughout the evening while Cherie and Cynthia giggled and whispered excitedly about young womanly things. Next down the table, George and Naomi chatted happily - Naomi having come unexcorted as her boyfriend could not make it, which worked out well for both her and George. Further down the long table, the four mature couples conversed contentedly, commenting on the fare and ambience. They spoke of old times and of common interests, their countenances revealing their delight. After greeting Gus and Cyrus with warm embraces, Denise and Roger sat together holding hands. They smiled contentedly soaking in the atmosphere, obviously enjoying themselves. All joined in laughing at common jokes shared amongst them, and oohed and aahed at issues of interest discussed.

Seeing the two empty seats at the end of the table, Gus enquired of Cyrus as to who else was coming. Cyrus confirmed that he had invited Marcus and a friend. Gus experienced a mix of emotions at this revelation – on the one hand he was looking forward to seeing his brother, whom he loved in spite of everything, and on the other hand, he was hoping that Marcus would be on his best behaviour tonight as he was dreading the embarrassment should Marcus not be at his best.

Cyrus formally introduced Cherie to all in attendance and gave a brief speech about his joy in finally finding his long lost daughter. Cherie also made a similar speech, causing untold joy to fill Cyrus' heart.

By 8.15 pm Marcus had still not arrived and the waiters were pressing for orders to be taken. So left with no choice, the party placed their orders. The food arrived by 8.45 pm and everyone tucked into the sumptuous fare. Silence was broken only by the clink of cutlery against crockery and brief comments on how delicious the food was.

Mid way through eating, Marcus arrived and Gus was pleasantly surprised to see that he was not badly turned out. He was accompanied by a female friend who appeared to be dressed for a way feistier soiree, in a mini dress that threatened to strangle her curves and teetering on killer 5" heels. Her dyed red (extended) hairstyle was as big as it was long and bright, and her face evidenced that hours had been spent on the application of face paint. Marcus and his woman friend conversed amongst themselves, and it became evident to those in earshot that they were not best pleased that everyone had started to eat without waiting for them. In case there was any doubt that they were disgruntled, Marcus soon voiced his opinion to the whole table, "So wait, why didn't you wait for us?" he asked. Cyrus began to explain gently, knowing Marcus' temperament and wishing to avoid any scene developing, but Marcus was not appeased, "What kind of thing is this anyway?" he asked loudly and hissed air through his teeth. Overheard by most people sitting close by – some began to look over. Gus left his meal and his seat and walked to the end of the table where Marcus was seated.

"Hi bruv, you okay", he greeted.

"Yeah, not too bad – this is Mitzy", Marcus responded without a smile.

"Hi Mitzy, pleased to meet you", Gus said and Marcus' waif-like girlfriend reciprocated.

Gus could smell more than a whiff of marijuana and something else as he got close to Marcus and his friend, betraying the fact he was probably high and not entirely in control of his senses. He perused the menus with them both and encouraged them gently to make their selection quickly, suggesting that the lamb, which had been his selection, was very good.

"I want fish but I don't like salmon and that is all they have on the menu", Marcus said. "I'll have the lamb", Mitzy chirped, much to Gus' relief – one down just one to go. Marcus leafed through the menu over and over for some good time, making derogatory comments about the dishes on offer. Finally he decided to have the salmon.

Attempting to settle them before returning to his own seat and meal Gus asked Marcus and his guest if they wanted red or white wine to drink. "I'll have the red, please", Mitzy replied, and Gus proceeded to pour her a glass. But Gus cast his eyes upwards as Marcus replied, "Wine? I don't drink wine you kno", he paused before continuing. "I don't drink wine – red or white or pink - wine is a sissy drink". "I'll have a white rum – a double on the rocks", reminding Gus why he loathed inviting Marcus to social events.

There was no way Gus would allow Marcus to drink pure white rum, which would no doubt compound his inebriation. He informed Marcus that he would go and get his drink and headed off in search of the waiter. Gus whispered to the waiter that he should bring a glass of white rum well mixed with spring water and a lot of ice and the waiter headed off. Now Gus only hoped that Marcus would accept the watered down drink without a fuss. "But wait – what kinda weak so so so rum this?" Marcus said, too loud. "This place is rubbish, man". "I would never come here again", he continued, oblivious to the fact that most eyes in the next section of the restaurant were now on him.

Luckily once his meal arrived in record time, Marcus ate quietly and caused no more commotion and all in all the evening rounded off as a great success. The dinner party ran on until after midnight when, the guests made their excuses and left a few at a time. Denise and Roger were the first to go at 12.05, followed by Cyrus and Sister Clarey five minutes later, stating that they had to attend church in the morning. Cyrus was successful in offering Marcus and Mitzy a lift in their taxi and Jean, Lester, Eve and Stephen her husband, left ten minutes after that, followed by Berisford and Ann at 12.30 am.

Gus, Cherie, Cynthia, Benza, George and Naomi stayed for a further half an hour. They retired to the terrace with drinks where they sat talking about this and that. Cynthia and Benza had left their baby with Cynthia's mother and so did not have to rush off home. When the restaurant closed at 1.00 am the six of them left. After sharing hugs and kisses, they each went their separate ways, feeling that they had not had such an enjoyable time in years.

Before they parted Gus made plans to meet Cherie for church in the morning so that they could attend together and joy filled his heart at the prospect. And as he slept that night he dreamt of a bright future.

CHAPTER 19

Washed

Never before had Gus ever felt so thoroughly rested, although he had slept for only 6 hours. He was up bright and early on Sunday morning 5 November 2010. So excited was he to see Cherie again, that he was showered and dressed immaculately in half an hour, and by 8 45 am he had telephoned her to say that he would collect her for church. Cherie informed Gus that as she had stayed at her own home in Leighton Green, it would be best if they met at church but he insisted he did not mind driving over to collect her. "It will give us time to talk – I have something important to say", he said determinedly. So Cherie gave him her address.

By 9.30 am Gus was parked in front of Cherie's home. As he waited patiently he telephoned Cyrus to say that he would collect him for church. Then at 9.55 am he called Cherie to say that he had arrived and was waiting for her outside.

Looking radiant Cherie promptly emerged from her front door. Gus jumped out of his seat and ran to take her hand and guide her into the passenger seat of his vehicle. "Sorry about the car", he said, feeling embarrassed about his less than desirable mode of transport. But smiling sweetly, Cherie only had eyes for him and it was not apparent that she had even noticed the rickety carriage of her new beau.

Finding comfort in Cherie's presence Gus talked as he drove. Unable to hold back, he began to outline the problems that he had been encountering. And being put at ease by her amenable nature, he opened up more and more until he was baring his soul with ease. Feeling no vulnerability in doing so, he talked and talked, reposing total trust in the woman he now knew would share the rest of his life. Cherie listened and felt led to speak about the subject of fasting. Gus was happy that his new found love obviously had a discerning spirit, as she spoke wisely about strategic fasting and prayer.

Delving into the Word, Cherie wisely instructed Gus. She

spoke out the scriptures that she had internalized and Gus opened his heart to the Word and the Holy Spirit touched him deep inside. Then she proceeded to pray for him as he drove, that God would deliver him totally from all evil.

When they arrived at Cyrus' home he was waiting at the gate, resplendent in a cream dress suit, black shirt and cream tie. The sight of his father made Gus feel decidedly under-dressed although he was wearing an immaculately tailored Oswald Silver cut.

They arrived early for church which made Gus feel proud of himself. Cyrus encouraged them to sit together with him near the front of the cathedral where he always sat. Gus declined and went to sit alone in order to preserve decency – it wouldn't do for all who observed them to surmise that they had become an item – not just yet. However Curtis had seen them arrive and enraged he had stormed out of the church, slamming the swing doors behind him noisily - disrespectfully. Everyone shook their heads in disbelief and disapproval.

Gus was not affected by Curtis' behaviour. He just shook his head like everyone else. He had come to worship God and would not allow anything, or anyone to spoil his reverent state of mind. He had so much to thank God for that today in church he sang louder than anyone else, for the first time realizing that he had a voice. And when Bishop Fredericks made the alter call for those who wanted prayer for deliverance, Gus was the first to go forward. During the prayer, he felt the remaining weight which had beset him lift from his spirit, and when Bishop Frederick laid his hands upon his forehead, Gus involuntarily fell under the anointing of the Holy Spirit. He was aware that he had fallen, and of the waves of light and heat, then peace and pure love that washed over his spirit and soul as he lay there. He tried to move but could not and received revelation in his spirit that God was delivering him and was not finished yet. As he lay there, Gus heard a still small voice in his spirit say, "Total Restoration". When he could move his limbs again he got up and floods of pure love joy and peace washed over his soul. He felt as light as air and brand new, a feeling that could not be described in words, and as he returned to his seat Gus could not stop praising God for the new thing that He had done.

Sister Clarey worshipped with joy in her heart – she was happier than she had ever been since the passing of her husband and she gave all the credit to God – he had answered all her prayers.

Today in church Cyrus was the happiest of men, because all his prayers had been answered too. And when he testified of God's love and greatness, he spread his joy all around and everyone rejoiced with him.

Today in church no-one smiled brighter than Sister Cherie. Today she worshiped deeper than ever before from the very depth of the most thankful of hearts - all her prayers had been answered too.

CHAPTER 20

Washed in Love

Never before had Gus experienced such completeness. In a few short months he had gone from an unhappy, helpless and perplexed individual to one most full of joy in the universe. He firmly ascribed his joy and good fortune to the fact that he had accepted the Lord Jesus into his life and He had made all things new just like the Bible says. Now Gus experienced total security and perfect peace of mind. And as if that wasn't enough, he had also met the woman of his dreams, something he had almost given up hope of doing. And this veritable angel professed her undying love for him too. They were now dating and everyone around them couldn't be happier for them. Cyrus for one was ecstatic that he had gotten what he had always wanted - his adoptive son had found a virtuous woman. And in the bargain he had gotten the most incredible bonus, for it had turned out that his own daughter was that graceful woman of virtue.

Cyrus confessed to Gus and Cherie that he had been trying to introduce them for months, which Cherie found unbelievable but a fact of which Gus was fully aware, for he recalled the many times that Cyrus had annoyed him by trying to set up a rendezvous and he now kicked himself because had he listened to his father, he would have met his wonderful angel almost a year earlier.

Unbelievably, Cynthia and Benza also confessed to trying to fix them up for ages. Apparently they had realized that Gus and Cherie were a perfect match for each other. They all laughed at the unique quirk of fate, and both Gus and Cherie marvelled at how well their friends and father knew them.

A significant change had been taking place in Gus' financial circumstances in the past few months, which he put down to nothing short of miraculous. The problems that he had previously experienced disappeared as suddenly as they had appeared. The menacing spectre that had invaded his environment and which had caused him to have nightmares had now left him and his homes completely. It was as though the problems and the unwanted presence were inextricably linked. The change had begun on his accepting Jesus Christ as his Lord, but had noticeable accelerated when Gus had embarked on a 7-day fast having received a word from God through Bishop Frederick to do so. Bishop Fredericks had also joined in the fasting and prayer strategy along with Cherie and Cyrus.

After the very first day of fasting and prayer, Gus heard from the company who managed his properties that new tenants had been found for nearly all of the vacant properties – all except those that needed serious repairs or the ones damaged in the fire.

After the second day of fasting and prayer, he received a telephone call from the Athletics Association asking him to attend the next day for an interview. When he attended the interview, they had offered him a job – 3 days a week, but full time when necessary in order to prepare the athletes for special events. And the salary on offer was more then three times what he was earning before he was put on short time. He had of course accepted the job straight away.

Following the third day of fasting and prayer, to his complete surprise, he heard from the insurance company confirming that they would cover the loss suffered as a result of the blast which had caused the severe fire damage to the block of flats he owned in the East End. Further it was confirmed that he had been fully exonerated of all blame in relation to the blast which they were now apparently prepared to accept had been the work of an arsonist.

And immediately upon ending the fast, Gus had learned from his Agent that he had been head-hunted to be a guest commentator on a number of football and sport TV programmes, the expected remuneration for such appearances being way above what Gus could ever have asked God for, or contemplated. He also sold the Council block in the East End which he had bought less than a year earlier for over £300,000 more than he had paid for it, which allowed him to wipe out all his debts

Due to his good fortune, Gus was able to replace his old car with a brand new one. He was tempted to get another MXLX sports, but commonsense had prevailed and he purchased a bigger car instead – he no longer had just himself to think about after all and he also had to plan ahead.

And Gus' joy knew no bounds as he planned to ask Cherie to become his wife. They had been dating for three months – not very long – but Gus felt as though he had known her all his life. And receiving revelation from God, he knew she was his wife. Cherie was a lot like her father, and Gus instinctively knew that he could trust her with his life. He knew that the time was right to take the big plunge and set about planning a romantic and unusual proposal to Cherie. He had solicited help from Cherie's mother and on learning from Jean that Budapest was one of Cherie's favourite cities, had arranged a surprise long weekend away to Hungary. Further help from Naomi and Cyrus had been drafted in to ensure that Cherie would be available on Valentine's Day weekend from Friday to Monday and all involved were sworn to secrecy not to divulge any details of the planned trip to Cherie. It was arranged that Jean and Lester would chaperone the couple on the weekend break.

On Friday 11 February 2011, the day of departure Jean went over to Cherie's home and packed her a large weekend bag, having first checked with Naomi that Cherie was at work and the coast was clear. As far as Cherie was aware she was going out for a meal with Gus that evening – all he told her was that he would be taking her to somewhere special, not any of their usual eating places. Gus had arranged to meet Jean and Lester at the airport. He would collect Cherie at 6 pm and make the one-hour drive to the airport.

"Wow, I can't wait", Cherie had gushed excitedly. "I love surprises – it's just like Christmas", she'd continued, sounding like a small child, endearing Gus to her even more.

"You're so funny, Cherie – I love you", Gus chuckled with a slight shake of his head. "I want you to promise you won't ask any questions for at least the next ....aah one hour", Gus said.

"Why not – why don't you want me to ask any questions, Gus", Cherie quizzed smiling widely.

"It's a surprise – promise, no questions", Gus continued to tease.

"Okay, no questions", Cherie said feigning reluctance.

"Good girl", Gus said giving her a sideways glance and a wink.

He smiled contentedly as he drove, contemplating his good fortune and their future together.

They drove for 30 minutes, conversing generally. Cherie was tempted several times to ask Gus where they were going but resisted. After 45 minutes of motoring curiosity got the better of her and she said, "It looks as though we are going to the airport", as she stared pointedly at Gus.

"Oh", was the only reply Gus gave.

"Well", Cherie continued to dig.

"Well what?" Gus replied.

"Well, are we going to the Airport", Cherie said smiling.

"You promised, no questions, remember", Gus said chuckling.

"Oh, but I've changed my mind, I do want to ask a question", she teased.

"No, you can't change your mind now – it's too late", was all he said. "All will be revealed soon", he continued. And Cherie guessed then that they were on their way to the airport and smiled to herself – *"What a wonderful surprise"*, she thought as she went on to contemplate what a wonderful human being she had found in Gus Allen.

Cherie was so happy to see her mother and Lester was travelling with them – she was on a natural high. She was even more ecstatic when she realized the destination was Hungary. On arrival in Budapest, she was overjoyed to find that Gus had booked them all into the 5-star plus Hotel Deniare, a luxurious spa hotel on the banks of the Danube river. She shared a room with her mother while Gus and Lester shared adjoining single rooms.

Gus' joy overflowed when Cherie told him excitedly that she found this surprise very romantic – he was pleased he had planned appropriately.

On Saturday morning 12 February 2011 Cherie and Jean rose up with the larks as they couldn't wait to sample the hotel's spa facilities. Lester and Gus had a lay in, and then went to the hotel restaurant where they ate full rich English breakfasts. Then they went for a walk to discover the beautiful city, being careful to return to the hotel to meet up with the ladies to go on a pre-arranged sightseeing tour of the twin cities of Buda and Pest.

As they were transported around the city by private tour car, Cherie could be heard by Jean and Lester excitedly telling Gus just how much she was enjoying her birthday trip. They looked at each other smiling knowingly – thinking how blissfully unaware she was that the biggest surprise was yet to come, for Gus had found out her ring size from Jean without her knowledge and had bought her the most beautiful platinum diamond ring ever.

It had taken him two whole weeks to plan the perfect surprise and Jean, Lester and Cyrus had sanctioned his plan, giving him their blessings. They were almost as excited as he was, and guarded his secret faithfully, careful not to reveal his plans to Cherie. And they were all pleased that they had succeeded as it was not the easiest thing to keep anything secret from Cherie for long.

Just after the hour of 12 midnight on Monday morning 14 February 2011 Gus proposed to Cherie. It was past closing time as the restaurant usually shut up shop at 12 midnight, but Gus had requested that they remain open as he wanted to propose to Cherie first thing on Valentine's Day. Having enjoyed a romantic meal on Sunday, they were sitting after dinner being serenaded with romantic ballads by a group of performers that had been specially booked through the Hotel. Unbeknown to Cherie, they were commissioned by Gus. And as Sunday night turned into Monday morning, a young lady walked among the tables selling stem roses, Gus bought a single red rose and handed it to Cherie, getting down on one knee as he did so. "Cherie – Princess Johnson – Jones - Syrenson," Gus chuckled, then pausing he became more serious and continued, "Would you please do me the honour of becoming Mrs Cherie Princess Johnson Jones Syrenson Allen?"

Cherie accepted the rose and replied without hesitation. "Oh yes, yes Gus I would love to become Mrs Allen", she said totally surprised and totally happy. She was beaming from ear to ear as Gus rose to his feet and moved towards her. Taking her hand he guided her to her feet, and then they sealed their agreement with a light kiss on the cheek. Gus reserved his presence of mind and broke off the embrace before they could get carried away, realizing that as Christians they had to do things God's way. And suddenly Gus and Cherie became aware that they had an audience. Surprisingly, the restaurant had remained almost full even though it was past usual closing time, as patrons had remained to listen to the beautiful live music. All the staff from the kitchen and the waiting staff had gathered together to watch too and all eyes were trained on them. The congregants beamed as they watched the demonstrative love of the newly engaged couple – all shared their joy.

Returning to his seat Gus sat down observing Cherie for a beat as she smiled sweetly. Their eyes met and they spoke to each other without words – sending messages of undying love. Then Gus realized that Cherie had not even discovered the ring and his love increased, as he received assurance that Cherie just wanted him, and not only was she indifferent concerning his wealth, she was perhaps even wealthier than he was - she simply loved him. The band began to serenade them once more, as the other patrons returned their attention to conversations amongst their individual parties. Gus waited for Cherie to mention the ring, but she did not – she proceeded to make verbal plans for the coming big day. And so Gus had to take the initiative. "Isn't there something missing? he said knowingly.

"You forgot the ring?" Cherie questioned.

"Did I?" Gus replied mysteriously – perhaps I didn't," he continued teasingly. The band played more quietly as the flower lady stood by unashamedly watching developments.

"You bought me a ring – have you bought me a ring - where is it? Cherie asked excitedly.

"That would be telling," Gus replied, then added mysteriously, "Seek and ye shall find".

"Honestly you have taken Bishop Frederick's admonitions to internalize the Word way too literally, Gus", Cherie said jokingly before she proceeded to check inside her glass – then inside Gus' glass for the ring. She checked inside his pockets – then she checked inside her small handbag – then she checked the table and under the table, but there was no sign of the ring. She even made Gus remove his shoes before exclaiming, "Where is it Gus", playfully. She continued, "What have you done with the ring?"

"Seek and ye shall find," Gus replied, once more, still smiling mischievously.

Cherie looked towards the musicians who were all smiling knowingly, but giving nothing away. Then she looked towards the flower lady, who had the biggest smile of all, and Cherie was certain that she had the answer. "The rose – it must be in the rose," Cherie said grabbing the rose. Then she gently prised open its petals to reveal the most exquisite solitaire diamond ring ever. Standing up Gus took her by the hand and gently lifted her from her seat. Then he took the flower from her and removing the ring placed it upon her finger. Cherie looked up into his eyes and seeing his evident love for her she burst into tears.

Every eye in the restaurant was once again trained on them as Gus drew Cherie to him and placed her head upon his shoulder. After a beat, he lifted her head again and looked deep into her eyes. Then after a further pause, he asked, "May I call you my fiancée now?"

"Yes, you may – oh yes," Cherie blubbered to joyous applaud from their captivated audience. And then Cherie stopped crying and smiled the brightest smile you ever saw. Then she confessed to her husband-to-be that it was the best birthday present she could have hoped for and that exactly one year to the day she had challenged God to lead her to meet the right man within a year. And they both praised their Heavenly Father for bringing them together.

Then they sat back down together and straight away set about planning the most beautiful wedding ever at the Born Again Church of God, to take place in three months' time – on 15 May 2011.

CHAPTER 21

A Glorious Celebration

Propped up in bed Gus relived the events of the previous night in his mind – his stag night. It had been a hot night in every sense of the word. He had hired the Star Apple, and invited one hundred good friends and acquaintances, and their guests, with only one criteria - all were men. A lavish meal had been followed by good clean entertainment by Kingdom Praise, the soul and rap gospel band, and the sweet smooth sounds of Ebony Son, both artistes managed by Smooth Management, and later dancing to the very best specially selected music. For this purpose Gus had hired one of the best Christian DJs. There was no superfluity or naughtiness, and no sauciness – no naked women popping out of cakes or gyrating strippers or the like. This was strictly a Christian affair.

The night turned out to be somewhat of a practice run for the wedding reception, as one after the other friends and associates had taken the floor to give speech after speech peppered with hilarity but no vulgarity.

And later those adventurous enough had taken to the mike for karaoke. It was a night that would remain in his memory for ever – his last night as a bachelor. And even though Gus had enjoyed himself, he was glad when the night came to an end and the guests departed, for it meant that he was drawing nearer to the moment when he would say "I do" to Cherie, and they would begin married life together.

****

Propped up in bed Cherie sat reliving the events of the previous night – her hen night. It had been a good night. A far smaller affair than her husband-to-be's stag night, it had begun when as many as 40 friends, all women, had crammed into her home, which, although fairly large, appeared to be very small, for a bridal shower.

The bridal shower started at 3 pm, where everything in the way of lingerie, and romantic accessories – candles – scents – music –

poetry, were given as gifts. Food was buffet style, catered to the highest standard and served by two attendants supplied by the catering company.

After three and a half hours, all the ladies boarded a coach that had been hired to take them to the Barn House Theatre. Some ladies who had either not been able to make it to the shower, or had not been invited to it, had gone directly to the theatre, where the hen party took up more than half of the venue. The advertisement flyer for the comedy production by a Jamaican cast had promised humour without nastiness, and had not disappointed, providing good clean entertainment - and mirth was evidently in abundant supply at the Barn House Theatre last night. Cherie had arranged for the hen night to come to an end by the latest at 11 pm because she wanted to get a good night's sleep so that she would be fresh for the big day. She was satisfied that her chief bridesmaid, Cynthia, who had arranged the hen party, had made the right choice of a venue and Cherie and all in attendance had thoroughly enjoyed themselves, although she was glad that it was over now as she was that much closer to becoming Mrs Allen.

Bringing contemplation of the previous nights events to a close, Cherie directed her mind to the agenda for the day ahead. In just a few short hours, she would walk down the aisle of the Born Again Church of God to join Gus at the altar, and Cherie couldn't wait to turn all her daydreams into reality.

Luxuriating in a bath with bubbles up to her chin she continued to reflect. Making little splashes with her hands, she swirled them around in the water. After a while, she just lay still, enjoying the feel of the warm water and bath condiments soaking into her skin – and she relaxed her mind and her body.

Everything was set for the big event – they were confident that nothing would go wrong, because professional wedding planners had been engaged and many prayers had gone up for God's ultimate supervision. All they had to do was get dressed up in their wedding attire and get to the church on time.

Jean had wanted to help her daughter get dressed but Cherie had banned her mother from her home this morning, stating that she was way too emotional and would no doubt keep bursting into tears, causing her to do the same. Cherie wanted to reserve her tears for after the ceremony. And so it had been agreed that Cynthia would be helping Cherie to get dressed, and as she glanced at her mobile on the side next to the bath, she noted that it was already 10.30 - her friend was expected any minute. Quickly Cherie forced herself to get out of the bath, anticipating Cynthia's knock imminently. However, having dried and robed herself and waited 20 minutes Cynthia had still not arrived. Cherie noted that the hairdresser was also due to arrive at any minute and as though confirming her thoughts, the door bell chimed. It was the coiffeur, who proceeded to talk incessantly as she washed and set Cherie's hair. All the talking proved a little too much for Cherie who started to have a slight headache. And she was becoming anxious and glanced at her mobile every minute, noting that Cynthia was nearly an hour and a quarter later than she had promised to arrive. Worry intensified as did the slight headache and Cherie decided to telephone Cynthia. Her call went straight to voicemail, and knowing her friend very well, Cherie gathered that that was a sure sign that Cynthia was running late without a plausible excuse. She left a message, reminding Cynthia to bring the baby blue eye-shadow that she had promised to lend to her – which would double as something borrowed and something blue all in one. Something old would be the small 18-carat gold diamond cross that her mother had given her for her 21st birthday – and something new would take care of itself – not that she was superstitious, she just wanted to savour the usual wedding traditions.

Cynthia arrived 10 minutes later just in time to have her hair washed and set. Her excuse for being late was that she had forgotten to bring the baby blue eye-shadow to lend Cherie, and had to go back home and get it. *"A likely story"*, Cherie thought as she cast her eyes up towards heaven, indicating exasperation and disbelief. Cynthia observed her friend's gesture but said nothing more, glad to have gotten off lightly - she was here now and set about making up for lost time.

After her hair was set in rollers, Cynthia went straight to the bathroom to have a quick bath, while the hairdresser started to style Cherie's hair. Meanwhile the beautician arrived to do their make-up and Cherie thought it best to do that first and leave her hair until later. Making-up took 30 minutes. Having finished the bride's make-up the beautician waited for Cynthia to come out of the bath, but after waiting for 20 minutes stated that she had to rush off to do another bride.

The hairdresser helped Cherie into her dress, before touching up her hairstyle - a flurry of ringlet curls all over the crown, with the back of her hair being scooped up to embellish the look. She had grown her hair especially for this style but had also embellished with hair extensions, with magnificent results. Her hair was completed by the adornment of a tiara and veil. The veil being pulled back until required. Her look completed, everyone agreed that Cherie looked sensationally beautiful. The hairdresser then rushed off to her next appointment, not having had time to complete Cynthia's style. Cynthia was fuming.

"Well, I hope you have learnt a lesson, Cynthia – if you hadn't been late, the hairdresser and make-up artist would have been able to finish your hair and make-up," Cherie said pointedly. Cynthia did not say anything – she knew she had no-one to blame but herself, but wished Cherie wouldn't rub it in.

Just then the door bell chimed again – it was Sera Ocel who had stopped by to see whether Cherie needed any assistance. She was already dressed in wedding attire, a purple velvet midcalf dress with a silk bodice and criss cross back detail. Sera had changed so much in a few short months, from a totally self-serving individual to a loving and considerate sister.

When the first Smooth Management tour ended, Cherie had discussed with Sera the call that she received from God to deal only with Gospel music. Quite unexpectedly Sera had confessed that she was in fact a backslider who had been contemplating returning to the fold. She had taken Cherie's revelation as God's unequivocal last word and having started to attend Sunday services at Born Again, had rededicated her life to Christ and was now a transformed character. And following much prayer and soul-searching Cherie had decided to keep Sera on with Smooth Management, receiving validation in her spirit of the star's contrition, evidenced in the dramatic change in demeanour. And before long, Sera had produced a huge repertoire of inspirational soul-stirring praise and worship and message songs, all written from a Christian perspective.

Cynthia ushered Sera into the upstairs master bedroom where both ladies were getting ready. In desperation, she asked "Can you style hair Sera?" It turned out that Sera was multi talented and to their surprise turned out to be an exceptional stylist, causing Cherie to comment, "You are certainly gifted Ms Sera Ocel – I didn't realize," before asking her to put some flourishes to her own style, which when she had finished, they all agreed was even better than before.

Cherie looked at her reflection in the full length mirror and smiled – she was very happy. "You look absolutely beautiful, Cherie," Cynthia said. Sera agreed, "Oh you take my breath away – you go girl." "I'm gonna write a song about the way you look today", Sera complimented. Cherie's dress was beautifully cut and fitted, with a bustier bodice encrusted with jewelled embroidery. The dress was tastefully beaded throughout, with a fish-tail skirt which was cut four inches above the ground to the front - revealing her ankles and, white silk kitten heeled shoes with matching beading effect. The dress graduated downwards at the back into a small train. The sleeves of the dress were made of exquisitely delicate lace, off the shoulder and straight, with a peak from the wrist down the back of each hand to the fingers. Cherie's nails were French manicured, and she wore tasteful jewellery. Her veil was mid-length and made of sheer taffeta.

It was nearly 2.30 pm and the car was due to have arrived now, Cherie suddenly realised. On cue, there was a knock at the door. Sera engaged Cherie to pose so that she could snap a photograph, while Cynthia went to get the door. It was one of the bridesmaids who had brought Cherie's bouquet, a beautiful ensemble made up of baby blue orchids, white lilies, and pale yellow roses. The bouquet provided the finishing touch that set Cherie apart as one of the most beautiful brides ever – the kind of bride that graced the covers of the world's most famous and stylish wedding magazines.

As Cherie came out of her home she was surprised to see that a large crowd of neighbours and passers-bys had gathered outside and were congregating around the Limousine in which the bridesmaids were. They greeted her appearance with choruses of "oohs", "ahhs" and "doesn't she look beautifuls".

Then Cherie saw them, standing by the horse-drawn carriage that was waiting to take her to the church – to her destiny. She walked slowly toward the carriage, the train of her dress being held aloft by Cynthia and her other bridesmaids, Naomi, Melissa and Tia. Then, when she was almost there, they came and took hold of her, one by the left hand and the other by her right hand. She looked firstly to her right and then to her left and smiled at her two dads, as they beamed proudly at their daughter. And soon they set off - one seated on her left, and the other on her right - for the church where they would give her away.

At the church Gus waited patiently for his bride to arrive. He was attired in an off white suit that had been specially cut for him by one of his favourite designers, Oswald Silver and he looked gallant and princely as he awaited his destiny. His groomsmen Benza, Raj and Marshie and best man Martin wore dark royal blue perfectly cut suits, and stood to attention, the perfect entourage for the princely groom. They had arrived 30 minutes early as Gus didn't want to be late – he wanted to ensure that nothing went wrong on this special day. And as the organist began to play he smiled to himself – a nervous yet confident smile. He turned to catch a glimpse of his bride walking up the aisle towards him and knew that he had never beheld a more beautiful sight in his entire life, and one tiny tear of pure joy trickled from the corner of an eye.

Cherie was evocative of an angel that had floated down from heaven as she walked nervously down the aisle towards her destiny, all the time saying a prayer of thanksgiving to God. Cynthia, her maid of honour was attired in the palest yellow, a dress almost mimicking her own. And the bridesmaids wore the most delicate baby blue, the dresses cut in similar fashion to that of the maid of honour's. They resembled cherubs as they attended and preened the bride.

****

Kingdom Praise sounded heavenly as they sung angelically and there was the feeling in the air that royal celestial dignitaries were in attendance at Gus and Cherie's marriage. Strains of ethereal voices could be perceived by those with spiritually discerning ears as tears of joy flowed throughout the sanctuary.

The joyful sounds of children could be heard throughout the sanctuary but not such as to detract from the formalities.

The vows were heartfelt and had been personally composed, and many of the guests cried as never before at a wedding.

And when Bishop Fredericks jollily pronounced them as man and wife, Gus moved in to kiss his bride, a long lingering satisfying kiss without condemnation. And as they came up for air, the guests cheered loudly.

****

The sun shone brightly that afternoon as the bridal party and guests gathered in the gardens of the church for photographs to be taken. Many passers-by stopped to observe, drinking in the splendour and opulence of the affair.

The reception was a held at the 5* Bourne Hotel – a lavish affair for 500 guests. The hall was resplendent – a sea of baby and royal blues, pale yellow and white, picking up on the attire of the bride, groom and bridal party. Flowers adorned each table, and balloons and ribbons were tastefully arranged. And the cake did not disappoint – it was a work of art, causing one guest to comment that it was a shame to have to cut it.

The speeches were curtailed due to time constraints, but those giving speeches were notably, Martin, and everyone agreed that this young man's speech was crafted as that of someone much older and wiser. Cynthia also gave a speech as did Cyrus, Lester, Jean. Benza, Raj and Marshie. The verbal tributes were delivered with wit, provoking laughter which rang throughout the reception hall.

Later the couple danced to CeCe Winan's "Joy fills my heart", before being joined by well-wishing couples who thronged the dancefloor.

The couple had flights to catch, as they were jetting off to their honeymoon in Ocho Rios, Jamaica. But before they left, they observed the old traditions with variations – the groom of his buttonhole, and the tossing of the bride's bouquet. First Cherie threw her bouquet, which was not caught by anyone, but which landed on Sister Clarey's lap right where she was sitting.

And then Gus had to throw his buttonhole coronation, which landed right at Cyrus' feet. Cyrus picked it up with a chuckle, "Well, I think I get the message," he said as he stared straight into Sister Clarey's eyes, and she giggled like a teenage schoolgirl and began to blush under her dark hue.

CHAPTER 22

Winning the Race

It has been nine glorious months since Cherie and Gus entered the bond of holy matrimony and they could not be happier.

Each day Gus thanked God for Martin, who through his demonstrative love helped to change his life. He was eternally grateful to the youngster and had shown his gratitude by arranging for Martin and his mother to move into one of his properties in a better neighbourhood, where they now lived rent-free. He also enrolled Martin at the Wilson Academy, a fee paying boy's school that was top of the league tables for achievement. It has now been five months since Martin began to study there and he was doing even better than Gus had known he would. And initial reports from his teachers suggested that if Martin continued to work hard, he would definitely realise his ambition of becoming a Surgeon.

Mr and Mrs Allen have been immensely blessed and have enlarged their portfolio of properties significantly to well over 100. Five months ago they appointed a full time Management Executive to look after their portfolio because it was much more cost effective than using managing agents, who had taken too large a cut out of their profits and in return had not provided a good service. The Management Executive had set up an efficient framework for management of the portfolio, employing freelance staff as and when necessary. The couple thought it prudent to employ Cyrus on a part-time basis, to work alongside the Executive, not only to learn the ropes but also to keep a watchful eye. And the saving they were making more than covered his salary. This proved to be a very wise thing to do as the Management Executive resigned suddenly recently, having been offered more lucrative work elsewhere. So Cyrus had to take over his role, and hit the ground running. Cherie often calls on Sister Clarey to assist her father on a consultancy basis and the business benefits from her shrewdness and business savvy. This has resulted in Cyrus and Sister Clarey getting to know each other better.

339

Cyrus still had time enough to devote to the Wednesday evening training sessions at the stadium but acted mostly in the capacity of a mentor to the youngsters, as opposed to training them. He now left it up to the younger men who have come on board to do most of the strenuous training. He still helps out at the Youth Club on Fridays too when necessary.

Gus' assignments on TV have become more lucrative and he has curtailed his day job in training, limiting such work to the run-up to major events. He continues to devote time as a priority to the Youth Club and to training the youth from Young and Strong at the stadium. Both ventures have expanded over recent months and Gus now shares overall responsibility with Brother Jevan, a faithful hardworking man of purpose.

Benza and Raj have also started to help out at the Friday evening Youth Club. They were impressed to do so because they have seen the positive difference that it was making in the Wash House neighbourhood.

To everyone's amazement Gus is no longer dogged by persistent lateness, and is fast acquiring a reputation for being consistently way earlier than expected.

Cherie has handed over much of the responsibility for running Smooth Management to her new Business Partners, Naomi and George, who are now an item and planning to get married. They have also engaged a new assistant and things are working out swimmingly. Now Cherie spends much of her time working to nurture and develop new and talented Gospel artistes. Recent signings to Smooth Management include Melissa Miles, who is rapidly developing into a gospel superstar. Cherie now devouts time in helping her father to train the church choir.

Some of Cherie's valuable time she also spends helping Cynthia and Sister Clarey, both of whom are planning their weddings within a month of each other this Summer, 2012.

Together Mr and Mrs Allen have also joined the street evangelism team, which visits run down, drugs and crime-ridden areas of the capital to tell others, including the down-trodden about the love of God and his son Jesus Christ. The team goes out every Monday evening for a couple of hours or so. Two months ago one Monday evening Cherie was surprised to see Tricia Syrenson soliciting in the red light district in which they were seeking to spread the Word to the lost. This saddened Cherie greatly not only because she knew Tricia, but because she had recently learned from her father that she and Tricia were in fact second cousins.

****

When they were first reunited, Cherie informed her father that before finding out that he was her father she had thought a gentleman named Donald Syrenson to almost certainly be her father. Cyrus had become excited at that revelation, and informed her that he thought that Donald Syrenson was a long lost cousin of his. They had track Donald down and Cyrus' suspicions had been confirmed. So having become re-acquainted, Cyrus and Cherie had visited Donald in hospital during his long stay there, where he had undergone several reconstructive surgeries to rebuild his features.

When Donald left hospital, Cyrus had moved his cousin into his own home and nurtured him back to physical, mental and emotion health, and continued to care for and support Donald. However, Cyrus had informed her that Donald was not aware of his daughter Tricia's whereabouts.

****

Cherie was amazed to find out that Gus had also known Tricia – he had admitted it to her later on the evening of the sighting during a discussion.

"My goodness, I was so surprised to see Tricia – did you see her, the girl that got out of that blue car as we were standing on the corner of Truro Road – you remember, with the shorter than short mini skirt that looked as though she was high on something", Cherie asked Gus, continuing, "I know her – we used to go to dancing lessons together when I was a teenager," "And …. I…I recently found out that she is my second cousin", Cherie intimated. She was reluctant to divulge that she was related to such a person of ill repute, but on the other hand she did not want to hide anything from her husband.

"Yes, I know the one you are talking about," Gus paused before

continuing. "I must confess love that I used to know her too, bu...
but it was before she became .... she started to sell her body....,"
Gus stuttered his confession.

"You knew Tricia – how did you know her?" Cherie asked, surprised.

Gus hesitated a little too long. "Don't tell me you used to date
her," Cherie asked aghast. Gus looked at his wife sheepishly before
stuttering, "I ..it wwa was before I met you, Cherie - sweetie".

Cherie looked at her husband for a beat before commenting. "I
don't know why I'm surprised – after all you are just her type – she
always liked men that she perceived as having lots of money – and
let me guess, she did all the chasing - right". Gus did not reply,
and Cherie added, "You don't need to answer that, but knowing
Tricia as I do, I think I'm right". And from then on she allowed the
matter to rest, but she continued however, to comment for many
days after, "Tricia – a prostitute, I can't believe it," or "Tricia, my
goodness, her poor father .... I wish I could help her".

And Cherie began to contemplate what could have driven
Tricia to such desperate lengths. She wondered whether it had
anything to do with the horrifying incident of Donald's attempted suicide. So troubled was she by Tricia's condition that she even
began to soliloquise about helping a sister when she is down and
the like. And she could not forget how awful her cousin had
looked.

Cherie told her father and uncle about Tricia's sighting and the
two men decided to go in search of her.

One week after the sighting, Cherie's continued concern for
Tricia's wellbeing prompted her to comment out of the blue to her
husband, "It must have been her father's attempted suicide that
drove her over the edge like that or maybe her mother's death".

"Who are you talking about?" Gus replied.

"Tricia - her father – remember he tried to commit suicide – it
must have been that that drove her to the streets," Tricia said. "I
really want to do something to try and help Tricia", she continued.

Gus wanted to ask his wife to drop the subject, but he could
tell that that would not be the wise thing to do. Cherie had gotten
a bee in her bonnet about trying to do something to help Tricia,

and if he wanted to keep his honey sweet, he knew he had better co-operate. So, when Cherie suggested that they also go in search of Tricia, Gus obediently accompanied his wife back to the street where they had encountered Tricia the previous week - this time without the rest of the evangelism team. When they saw her, Cherie nudged Gus and asked him to pull over, "Pull over, pull over, there she is – let's go and talk to her while she is alone," she said in a loud whisper, although no one could possibly hear them as they were alone in the car with the windows shut.

Obediently, Gus did as his wife asked, with continued trepidation. They alighted from the car and approached Tricia. As Tricia saw the pair of them coming toward her she started to laugh manically.

"Well if it isn't Miss Prim and Proper and Mr Sexual Pervert," she said loudly then guffawed insanely.

"What's the matter Gus – what are you doing out here". "Isn't she giving you enough?" "Is that why you've come looking for me?" Gus did not say anything, but looked across at Cherie embarrassed.

"Tricia, please don't be so disrespectful, Gus is my husband now, and whatsoever you two had in the past is just that – past". "The reason why we are here is because I found out recently that your father is related to mine – they are cousins, which also makes us cousins". "Tricia, we want to help you – you don't have to live like this". But before Cherie could continue, Tricia broke in, "You, you - help me, help me – you self-righteous little piece of ****". "You haven't changed, have you," Tricia sneered in a brashly ambitious Jamaican accent.

Cherie retorted, "Well, okay, so you don't want our help, but I would still like to introduce you to the love of Jesus," Cherie said proffering a track to Tricia. In a vicious stroke, Tricia stepped forward and knocked the track from Cherie's hand, causing Gus to instinctively place his arms about his wife's shoulders to steady her.

"I don't need anything from you, how dare you stand there and insult me – how dare you". "Don't you know I can destroy you – just like that?" Tricia said clicking her fingers for emphasis. Then she continued, "So don't mess with me, right" she said, her voice deepening. Then, in a deep rasping voice and as though in a trance, she added "Or I will make you lose everything, everything," then she walked off, staggering as though she had been drinking. And anyone observing Tricia's behaviour would had to surmise that she had gone mad.

"Come on darling, let's go she doesn't want our help – let's go," Gus said guiding his wife back to the car.

Later he shared with his wife the fact that he thought that Tricia was the one responsible for the misfortunes that he had suffered months earlier. "It was something that Bishop Fredericks said and something that I remember Tricia saying this evening", Gus said and repeated, "I will make you lose everything". "Well that was what the beast used to say in my nightmares when I started to lose everything". "Bishop Frederick told me that a certain person was behind my misfortunes and sufferings".

Cherie contemplated what her husband had just told her then replied. "It sounds strange to me Gus, but I know that there are peculiar things happening in the world these days". "But thanks be to God, we are the righteousness of God and don't have to worry about such things affecting us at all". "As for Tricia, I feel sorry for her". "She is hopelessly caught up in a cycle of darkness, and in spite of any evil she may have done, we shouldn't just give up on her, she needs deliverance – we must keep on praying for her," Cherie said sympathetically. And Gus agreed – "yes we must keep on praying for Tricia", he said with some effort as he pondered God's commandment to show love to those that hate you.

So over past weeks they have been doing just that - praying and fasting for Tricia's liberation. Cherie was happy to learn from her father that they had found Tricia who was now also living at Cyrus' house, and that although she was not fully back to her old self, she was improving every day. So they continued to fast and pray for Tricia, knowing that it was just a matter of time before her condition would change for good.

On a lighter note, in three months' time it will be Gus and Cherie's one year wedding anniversary and they will have reason for a double celebration because they are also expecting their first child, scheduled to arrive on the very date of their wedding. And today, 14 February 2012, as they celebrate the anniversary of their engagement over a Caribbean meal at the Star Apple, which they now owned, having purchased it a month ago and turned it into a Christian venue, Gus draws near to his wife and takes hold of her hand. As he gazes deeply into her eyes, he smiles and his smile widens as he contemplates his good fortune, realising that all the wealth in the world could never buy what he has – the love, the inexplicable peace, the joy unspeakable, the confidence, the spiritual connection, the knowledge that he is safe and protected, the assurance of God's love and total care – and much much more. And as Gus passes his hand over the protruding bump of his beautiful wife, he chuckles with happiness, as one who has discovered the elixir of life, knowing that there is no substitute for being washed.

End of this road.

INTERPRETATIONS:

tink	think
oman	woman
jus	just
dem	them
'im	him
edicated	educated
wid	with
A	I
sey or seh	that
neva	never
wat	what
gwine	going
yard	home
fe	for
buck up	meet up
weh or wey	where
dat	that
bwoy	boy
cum	come
aweh	away
likkle	little
inno	you know
dung	down